A LIFE FULL OF DAYS

A MEMOIR

BY

CHALMERS DALE

ISBN: 1-4107-2606-1 (e-book)
ISBN: 1-4107-2607-X (Paperback)
ISBN: 1-4107-2608-8 (Dust Jacket)

Library of Congress Control Number: 2003091312

This book is printed on acid free paper.

Printed in the United States of America
Bloomington, IN

1stBooks – rev. 09/09/03

To

GEORGE DALE

My Grandson

July 10, 1992 - October 27, 2001

CONTENTS

"LIFE CAN ONLY BE UNDERSTOOD

BACKWARDS:

BUT IT MUST BE LIVED

FORWARDS."

Soren Kierkegaard

PREFACE

Probably because of fear of the unknown, and spending considerable time expounding on how unnecessary it was to have a computer in order to maintain one's existence, in January of 1998, I abruptly changed my tune. Summoning as much courage as I could muster, I purchased one, a Macintosh laptop, and then promptly spilled a cup of hot coffee into the keyboard. It is a long and painful story of what resulted, but I'm happy to report that I am writing this discourse on that slightly bruised awesome piece of engineering with a telltale coffee stain on the CD ROM module; a stark reminder of my carelessness.

Of greater importance, among the many new challenges offered me, I became interested in chatting with people from every corner of the globe, and I particularly latched on to someone with the same name as mine. In one of the more intimate and mysterious chatrooms populated by people from the Far East, the name Dale appeared. It turned out to be someone whose real name was Ashley (it is common to use a pseudonym in chatrooms), and who, after several delightful conversations, asked me to briefly detail my life story in a daily email to him.

He is from a small town in Luzon, in the Philippines, had studied American history at the University of Manila, and was anxious to come to the United States when and if he could ever raise enough money, and obtain a precious visa. He thought, as a result of reading about my background and experiences through the last three-quarters of the twentieth century, he would be more knowledgeable about everyday life here in the country of his dreams.

Thus, more than two years later, using those emails to Ashley as an outline, *A Life Full Of Days* has evolved, and I must give him credit for his persistence in expecting a chapter every day, without interruption. I have yet to meet this determined young man, and may never do so. Even though my children had expressed an interest in my documenting some of my travels, my full life story, warts and all, probably would not have been put to paper if it hadn't been for Ashley's steady encouragement. I truly hope he makes it to this country someday soon and we can have a real visit together, and not just a litany of experiences sent into cyberspace.

But also, and perhaps an even more motivating factor for this chronicle is my desire, resulting from my own varied experiences, to try and lead young people to a better understanding of their anxieties, to ease some of the pain they feel during adolescence, with sexual confusion nagging at them, along with all the teenage, and post teenage angst that comes with growing into maturity. Perhaps they will be able to relate to my troubled times through the early part of my life, and take some encouragement from how things sorted themselves out.

And hopefully their parents will take note of some of the struggles I endured with my own family, and try not to make similar mistakes with their children. I don't pretend to be a guidance counselor or social worker, but I do think it is helpful to people when they are troubled to become aware that there is usually a light, however dim it might be, at the end of the tunnel. For those readers who can't associate directly with my life's journey, but who may have experienced some of the same sentiments, I hope you will read this for pure enjoyment and it will satisfy your desires for an intimate look at someone else's long and winding road to fulfillment—in my case, at CBS.

This has been a true memoir in that I have not resorted to any research materials, recalling everything (with one or two minor exceptions) from deep in my memory bank. I'm sure there will be readers who will find little discrepancies here and there, but I hope, if they exist, I will be forgiven and the errors will not spoil the overall purpose—to tell, as simply as possible, my story of a life as I remembered it. Of course, I could blame any mistakes on my treasured laptop and say that perhaps there was a little brain damage from the coffee spill after all. But then this temperamental, almost human piece of technology might decide to up and erase all my laborious two-fingered typing and determine that all of my memories should end up in the trash can. What a ghastly thought!

PART ONE

A BOY NAMED CHUMMY

CHALMERS DALE

CHAPTER ONE

The somewhat cluttered one room apartment was only about nine by fifteen, with a small entrance hall, a bathroom, a Pullman kitchen with a counter, and a sizable fenced-in garden, shared by a similar apartment next door. There were two single beds, head to head along one wall, that served as a couch. A bureau, a leather sling chair, and a long, narrow coffee table completed the furnishings. On one wall was a large oil painting named "Boys In Boxes," and over the beds were hanging two small Sargent etchings, in oversized black frames. I had never seen pictures framed like this, and I assumed that in New York City artistic circles this was the unusual and dramatic way they did things. In fact, I had never seen a leather sling chair before, or a Pullman kitchen for that matter. The clutter was kind of interesting clutter, with decorative boxes, peculiar shaped ashtrays, and many throw pillows of all sizes and shapes. And there were lots of books, piled here and there, with a few plants occupying what little space remained. And there was a dog named Tiffy.

This was to be my home for the next year and a half. It was Arnie Walton's first floor apartment, a block from the East River and around the corner from the United Nations, in a four story building next to a Catholic church and across the street from a school playground. This particular block of East 47th Street was practically a boulevard, with a row of trees dividing the lanes. It was soon to be named United Nations Plaza, as it should have been years before. For some reason, this small, four story apartment building had a bright red front door, and sat kind of snuggled between much larger structures, almost gasping for air as it sheltered an assortment of New York City theatrical types, like Arnie, who were very contented with the low rents, in a high rent neighborhood.

I hated the apartment, and I hated Arnie. I hated Amy, and I hated myself. I hated the world, and wanted to die. And I cried and cried every time I thought of Tony and Harry. Did I deserve to be deserted by my wife and children? The answer was yes. Had the time come for me to just plain make up my mind which path I was to follow? Amy had made up my mind for me, and rightly so, when she ordered me out of our house in Lawrenceville. Was it time to stop kidding myself and recognize that I was a homosexual? The answer was definitely yes. And so, towards the end of September in 1958, ten years after my marriage to Amy, I was about to be single again, and very unhappy about it, even though the answers to all my questions were yes. I never wanted to see Amy, or my children, or my family and friends ever again. I wanted to disappear, and start all over. Except for my burgeoning career at CBS. Thank God there was that one bit of continuity left in my life.

But when I was listening to Tommy Edwards sing his number one hit song, "…the future's looking dim, but it's all in the game," I was resting my head on the shoulder of someone who wanted and needed me, excess baggage and all. Arnie assured me there was a bright future and, as far as he could see, the game was going to be an exciting one for both of us together. And he would be patient while I slowly got rid of all my hostility, even when it was directed at him. I knew, somehow, that this was where I wanted to be. I had found the right place.

So I put away my things, washed my face, and began to settle into a new relationship of enduring strength, one that has transcended all the idle gossip and raised eyebrows from my old friends on the Philadelphia Main Line and the masses of people who find an alternative lifestyle unacceptable. What a forty years it has been— and still counting! How many plain old married couples can say that they've been together that long? Too few, I'm sorry to say, and those who have didn't have to live with society's albatross hanging around their neck, trying to wrench them apart. It was a lot easier for them. I should know. I've experienced both.

CHAPTER TWO

The early days of my life seem like only yesterday and that momentous evening in 1958, a definitive turning point in my young existence along with many other varied experiences are, with few exceptions, clearly etched in my mind. I've often heard that as one gets older one seems to remember people and places and things that happened long ago much more clearly than the person you might have recently met or the book you just finished only last week. I have certainly found this to be true in my case and recalling the past has brought forth both laughter and tears.

I was told by my father, when I was young, that my mother came very close to dying during my birth. I don't exactly know why, but I'm sure birthing procedures were a lot less sophisticated than they are now. It was four days after Christmas on December 29, 1925, and maybe all of the holiday stress and anxiety was the cause of her difficulties. What had been expected to be a wondrous Christmas gift delivered by God, or man, or Santa very nearly turned out to be calamitous. But, after serious difficulty, we both lived. Was this a precursor of a life filled with complexities, a life filled with extraordinary moments? Perhaps.

I was the second of three boys to be born to Edwin Lyon Dale and Janet Taylor Lord. They had been married at "Broadreach," the Lord family estate overlooking the Hudson River in Tarrytown, New York in what the New York Herald Tribune called the "society event of the season." Their first home, a small, two storied shingled dwelling, was on Hathaway Lane in the town of Wynnewood, Pennsylvania—a wedding gift from my Grandfather and Grandmother Lord, and along with those of many other young couples, it was appropriately located on the Philadelphia Main Line. Named after the main line of the Pennsylvania railroad that headed north and west from Philadelphia, this was a series of suburban towns inhabited, for the most part, by affluent young marrieds and wealthy entrepreneurs like them. The people on the Main Line were considered "nouveau riche" by the old and socially prominent Philadelphians who lived on the other side of the Schuylkill River, in the Germantown and Chestnut Hill area north and east of the city.

Whatever troubles I might have had while growing up started when I was named Chalmers, with the nickname Chummy. My father's stepfather was named Chalmers, with the same nickname, but my parents didn't seem to like him very much, particularly after my father's mother died. He lived with one hundred cats in a glorified log cabin in Cold Spring, New York on the shores of the Hudson River. They thought he was rather eccentric, and I was only allowed to see him once or twice. I just can't imagine why they named me after someone they considered so strange. To this day, if there was just one thing that I could do over, it would be to change my given name and that ridiculous nickname.

I have nothing against my Grandfather Dale, and I love cats. It's just that name that has been so hard to deal with through the years. As time passed, it was shortened to Chum, but still people who didn't know me thought I was Chinese or that they had misunderstood and that my name was really John, or even Chalm. When you're having enough trouble just growing up, to have to explain your name is definitely an added burden.

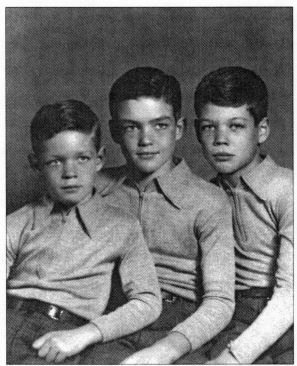

Jackie, Teddy, Chummy

Hillandale

When I was two and a half we moved from Hathaway Lane, to a beautiful brand new eight bedroom tudor-style house on one acre of land high on a hill. It was at the end of a private road off Rose Lane, in Haverford, another Philadelphia Main Line suburban town a few miles north of Wynnewood.

The other member of our family, our dog, Dolph, was a sleek and graceful Doberman Pinscher, and my best friend when I was little. He had been brought over from Germany by the Tyson's, who lived at the foot of the hill. They had no children, and young Dolph wanted to play, as he watched us through a window, scampering around on the hillside above. One day, he crashed through that window and came running to us, bloody, but unbowed. Mrs. Tyson called to thank mother for treating his wounds, and asked if we would like to have him, considering his unhappiness in their house at the bottom of the hill. It didn't take long for a decision to be made, and Dolph came to live at "Hillandale," the name of our new home.

His bed was in my room, and he used to cry when there was thunder and lightning. I would take him in my arms and hug him, and calm his fears. And when I was scared at night and saw strange little bright eyes looking at me from beneath my closet door, Dolph would come under my blanket with me and protect me from those alien creatures. I would have gone to my mother's bed, but my father wouldn't hear of it. It just wasn't manly. Dolph and I grew up together, and I loved him even though he once killed a neighbor's chickens, and bit my neighbor Lily Cresswell on the behind because he didn't like her pushing our car, along with the rest of us, when the battery was dead. She cried a lot and I know Dolph felt badly about it and was quite sheepish. Lil's mother was unmoved and my mother had a lot of explaining to do. Although Lil and I were very close friends, Mother and Lil's mother never were. I'm sure Dolph had something to do with it.

Dolph

CHAPTER THREE

Grandma and Grandpa Lord had asked all of their nine children to raise the grandchildren as Catholics until such time as they could decide for themselves which "heavenly" path to follow. I'm not too sure if all my aunts and uncles abided by that dictum, but my mother did. Even though my father was an Episcopalian, Mother did her duty as a Lord and I was made to attend Catholic Church with her every Sunday, while my father lounged around in his pajamas reading the Sunday papers. I hated everything about it, and perhaps the one saving grace was that I didn't go to Catholic Parochial school. That, of course, was out of the question given that it was attended primarily by what my family considered a lower class of people. My brothers and I all went to The Episcopal Academy, a private day school for boys, which was acceptable in Grandma's eyes, as long as we had after school classes to learn our catechism and prepare for confirmation and holy communion.

The classes were held at "Brookwood," the magnificent estate of my uncle Bill Galey, who was the son of Grandpa's partner in the textile business, and who married Mary, my grandfather's daughter from his first marriage. She was known as Aunt Polly and I loved her but hated the dark and sinister little private chapel, located next to her dressing room. It had crucifixes everywhere, some dripping imaginary blood. I was terrified of the place, and of the irritable nun who was recruited to do the teaching there. The only pleasurable moments were when my cousin "Chick" Galey would let me drive his battery powered "redbug" down to their lake and through their woods after my lessons were over. How I loved that little "car;" I think maneuvering it around the woodsy paths gave me my first lessons in how to be a careful and alert driver, which I still am.

Saturdays I was made to go to confession, to cleanse my soul in order to receive holy communion. I seldom had anything much to confess, so I made up things, and then was ordered by the priest to say three "Hail Marys" and five "Our Fathers" while on my knees facing a huge depiction of a suffering Christ. I was asking Jesus, the son of God, for forgiveness, and I received my penance for sins I had not committed. The church had actually taught me to lie!

Then there was the service on Sunday at Our Mother Of Good Counsel church. It was mostly in Latin, with an ancient priest hurrying through his liturgical mumbo jumbo, delivering a sermon designed to scare the congregation into thinking the wrath of God would descend on them, and they would burn in hell if they didn't "get their act together."

Sometimes I took communion even on those rare occasions when I was able to skip confession, and for that I was certain that I would be struck down before ever leaving the sanctuary. The few other children in attendance were the sons and daughters of the Irish or

Polish household servants, who sat in the shadows in the back while the heads of the households, with their children, occupied the front pews. It seemed the purpose of all of this was to put the fear of God into everyone's mind and to keep the flock as faithful as possible, while keeping the coffers full. It worked in reverse for me. I avoided anything to do with the church when I grew into my late teens, and for many years thereafter.

The Episcopal Academy was located in Overbrook, the Main Line town closest to Philadelphia, and I spent the first nine years of my schooling there. It was quite near where my Aunt Polly and Uncle Bill Galey lived, and was the school of choice for my brothers and me because of the Galey's influence. They were pillars of Main Line society, and patrons of the arts and as my mother's older sister, Aunt Polly served as her guiding spirit. The Galeys knew what was best. At Episcopal we did have a brief chapel service every day and I liked singing the hymns, many of which I can remember to this day.

My father, when he was a boy, had attended an Episcopal church in Brooklyn and sung in the choir. It didn't seem to have influenced his desire though, to get out of his easy chair, to get dressed and attend a Sunday service with his family once in a while. After all, the Episcopal ritual wasn't that different from a Catholic mass and I think I might have taken a greater interest and been a bit more reverent towards God if my father was sitting next to me in the pew and saying the Lord's Prayer in unison with me. Unfortunately, he was more concerned with checking the baseball box score of the Philadelphia Phillies game the day before, and the sportswriter's reports on batting averages were more important to him than the teachings of Jesus and his disciples.

CHAPTER FOUR

From the time I can remember, I was always considered an average student and a fairly good athlete, although there was a period when some of my classmates accused me of being a sissy. I'm still not quite sure why, but apparently they detected something about me, at that time in my life, that seemed a little effeminate to them. How cruel kids can be to each other! And it's not very easy to forget and disregard the taunts and the hurt of kid's teasing. What a lasting effect it can have!

I was forever being told by both my parents and teachers that I could do better with my studies, that I could be more like my brother Ted if only I would apply myself. It was probably true. My older brother had been named after my father, Edwin Lyon Dale, which was customary for first sons in those days. Nicknamed Ted, he was the apple of my father's eye, and I suppose deservedly so, because he was very bright, a good athlete, inquisitive and, his crowning achievement, he ate everything on his plate. He excelled in school, and never seemed to get into trouble, except at home, where he was a tyrant in our neighborhood, expecting everyone to be as energetic and gifted as he was.

Ted and me -- troubles ahead

One time he almost killed me with a baseball bat because I had quit one of his highly organized touch football games which included some members of the Connett family who lived halfway down the hill. I had started to go next door to play with another neighbor, Lily Cresswell, who had quit earlier. It was more fun dressing up her little Scottie in her doll clothes than being brow-beaten by my brother for failing to catch a five yard pass during a simple maneuver known as the "Lil" play, which had both a forward and a lateral pass. It had been appropriately named by Ted, because my friend Lily was usually

17

able to execute such an easy assignment, and when I, a boy, and the brother of Ted Dale, failed to do so, he went berserk. In spite of the Connetts' attempt to restrain him, he chased me into the house, up the stairs and threw open the bathroom door where I had hoped to find a safe haven. While helplessly sitting on the toilet, he hit me with the bat on the front part of my head causing a large gash. For many years after that I had a white thatch of hair where the roots had been deadened. A very attractive addition, I was told by future lady friends, and an aggravation to my angry older brother.

My father generally agreed with everything that Ted did and expected me to follow his example. But life just doesn't always work that way, and my early years were often unhappy ones. I tried hard to keep up with him but we were very different people in almost every way, differences that my parents didn't seem to recognize at all.

When I was ten years old, instead of idolizing an older brother (as good younger ones are expected to do), I worshipped some of the older boys in school and even got up the nerve, after days of procrastinating, to call one of them, who was thirteen, on the telephone at home. It was the most daring thing I had ever done. Of course I didn't know what to say to him, let alone express my love, and so I kissed the phone and hung up the minute I heard his voice.

When I was about twelve, I was awkward and gawky, had continual headaches, began hating life, was sexually confused, and was being beaten down at home by Ted and my constantly nagging father. How miserable he would make me feel when he would sarcastically pick on me for not eating, and compare me, in a derogatory way, with Ted. How many times did I hear, "Why don't you finish your dinner like Ted does?"

Dad was employed as a sales representative by my Grandfather Lord in the family textile business, and if he wasn't yelling at me he was shouting about how the Jews were cheating him out of his commissions, or the country was falling apart because of our hated president, Franklin D. Roosevelt. I would leave the table crying, and go to my room with my closest friend, our dog, Dolph. All this because of a few extra cocktails before dinner.

I turned to my mother for support, and she gave it as best she could. She would come to watch me play in sporting events against other schools, and tried, when time allowed, to take an interest in my academic pursuits. But my father was always too busy with work, as well as his and Mother's active social life, following the Galeys into the country club and dinner party scene. They also maintained close friendships with their old neighbors from Hathaway Lane, who had all moved on, like my mother and father, to bigger homes and a more extravagant lifestyle.

So I took refuge, not only with my neighbors, but with a few Episcopal Academy friends, particularly Ernie Ransome, whom I loved dearly. He was an outstanding athlete, who went on to become one of Princeton's greatest football stars. And because he was my friend, I was pretty much left alone, and wasn't picked on in his presence. Ernie and I did everything together, and because he lived quite far away, in New Jersey, I would spend as many weekends with him there as possible.

"You are the angel glow

that lights a star,

the dearest things I know

are what you are."

One time we skipped school and went to the Fox Theater in Philadelphia to see Artie Shaw's band, and hear "Begin The Beguine," and the band's vocalist, Helen Forrest, sing "All The Things You Are." It might have been one of the first times that beautiful Jerome Kern ballad had ever been performed by the orchestra and it became a top big band classic. It was one of the great moments of my early life, and the song will always be among my all time favorites. It still brings back happy memories of my friend Ernie, who seemed to understand me, and who returned my love, even though it was, at least for him, only adolescent child's play…just boys growing up.

CHAPTER FIVE

I guess some would say I was born with a silver spoon in my mouth, just because I had a nanny and cook and butler to wait on me when I was young. But everyone I associated with on the Philadelphia Main Line was living in more or less the same way, and so I didn't really know anything about people being poor or living a life different and more difficult than mine...or my friends. I was driven to private school every day by Joe, the butler, who changed his jacket, and put on a chauffeur's cap right after breakfast. And Mother would pick me up in the afternoon at five o'clock, after having spent the day in Philadelphia shopping, doing a little charity work at the hospital, and sometimes going to an afternoon movie. Animals seem to be able to tell time, and Dolph was always waiting for me at the bottom of the hill, with a ball in his mouth, when I got home, and I couldn't wait until *Little Orphan Annie* or *Dick Tracy* came on the radio in the late afternoon. I went to dancing class at the Merion Cricket Club on Friday nights, dressed in a tuxedo, with winged collar and stiff shirt, and mother of pearl studs and cuff links.

And thanks to Mrs. Prizer, the indomitable dancing mistress, I met and waltzed around with many girls who became life-long friends. In fact one of the waltzing young ladies became my first "date." How well I remember that day! It was with Happy Fitler, who became Mrs. Nelson Rockefeller in later years. Mother drove us to the movies to see *Little Miss Broadway* with Shirley Temple and I don't recall anything very provocative happening on this first sojourn with the opposite sex. At best, It was a fleeting association, but I remember loving the movie.

If you don't count my father's tirades and my brother's intolerance which led to so much unhappiness, my little world was fairly rosy and uncomplicated, and I had no idea that life was anything more than roast beef dinners, and a new car every year.

Our little neighborhood on Rose Lane had a great deal of influence on me in those early days of my life. In addition to Lily Cresswell, who was almost like a sister, there was the big Connett family. I really think I spent more time in their house than in my own, because I loved their less than formal lifestyle and constant good humor. Unlike the relationships in my house, all five of the Connett siblings, along with their mother and father, truly enjoyed each other's company, and there was hardly ever any unpleasantness or antagonism amongst them. They laughed and played games together, went to the movies and sporting events together, and were all so seemingly fond of each other, that I often wondered if Lil and I were their only real friends.

My favorite time with them was playing charades, with Mr. Connett heading one team, and Mrs. Connett the other. We all dressed up in costumes created from the clothes we discovered in the closets throughout the house, and used their living room as the stage. We spent so much time laughing at each other that often the charade went undiscovered. I loved being there so much that I never wanted to go home to Ted's overbearing dominance, and Dad's alcohol induced diatribes.

It was a profoundly tragic day when they learned that Harold, the eldest child, and a US Navy pilot, had been killed in the early days of World War II. But it seemed to bring them even closer together and I became more involved with them than ever; so much so that I spent many weekends, a few years later, chaperoning Theo, the strikingly beautiful blonde, and only girl among the children, on her sojourns to Yale University, and weekend trysts with her beloved football star, Steve Stack. When they were married I think Lil and I were the only guests outside of the family. I was so close to her younger brother Hugh that, when we were a little older, he was the one person that I ever confided in regarding my confusing sexual inclinations. The first time I told him, as I recall, he sloughed it off as the mumblings of someone who had too many beers, which, in fact, we both had.

CHAPTER SIX

During those prosperous years early in the 20th century, when his nine children were quite young, my Grandfather Lord built an enormous summer home in Beach Haven, a sleepy resort town on Long Beach Island in New Jersey. It was right on the beach and had ten family bedrooms, three maids' rooms, two porches, and one tennis court. For fear of hurricanes, it was built on bedrock brought from the mainland by boat, sunken into the dunes, and probably was the soundest structure, next to the Engleside Hotel, on the island. There was an abundance of hydrangea bushes surrounding the house, and a small, colorful tent set into the dunes for those who wanted to escape the sun.

Beach Haven house

Grandma Lord

Grandpa Lord

Now another generation was enjoying its hospitality, with the sea and sand right outside the front door. As a child I loved it there; being away from home, and along with my seventeen cousins, some of whom were about the same age, I had some memorable summer vacations, just having fun. We would play Skee Ball at the arcade on the boardwalk and buy things at, what was then known as the "Jap" Shop, filled to the rafters with curios from mysterious far-away lands, and the smell of incense to enrapture the mind. Grandma took us to the movies on Saturday night, with the whole front row reserved for her entourage. If this didn't attract attention then the fact that all the male contingent, wearing the ties and jackets we had worn for dinner, made us stand out in the crowd like visiting dignitaries.

When I was about eleven or twelve, my grandfather used to take me fishing in a rented boat owned by crusty old Captain Sprague and, while Grandpa sat upright in his canvas chair dressed in his stiff collar, jacket, and Panama hat, with his long fishing rod dangling over the side, I would try to keep from getting seasick. We didn't talk much, but I knew he liked me being with him. He would insist on going to the inlet where the Atlantic Ocean met Barnegat Bay because, he said, there was a bigger variety of fish there. But it also was where the heaving waves continually rocked the boat, and as he caught one fish after another, Captain Sprague would cut off their heads and throw them to the screeching gulls, and I would become even more nauseous.

One night at dinner, while we were eating his catch of the day, he turned to me, and with fourteen of my aunts and uncles and cousins as an audience, he proceeded to recite:

"I am a boy named Chummy, and Susie's the girl for me.

We love to dine at the Engleside, and I take her out to tea.

She has such red, red hair, and freckles on her nose,

She's not all there, but I don't care, 'cause she wears such stunning clothes."

Everyone laughed, but I didn't care, because I was sure my grandfather thought I was pretty special for him to have created a poem about me. Of course, I never dined at the Engleside Hotel, but I did go to the children's parties there on Saturday afternoon. I loved to listen to Ben Bernie's dance band and hob nob, on the wide verandah, with other summer vacationers, who I used to see year after year, and who I sailed against in our little sneakboxes during the races at the Barnegat Yacht Club. On rainy days I would lie in bed and fantasize about my sailing buddies and wish I could take them home with me. Best of all, I was usually on my own when I was in Beach Haven, away from Ted and often even my parents, as Grandma found me to be quite capable of taking care of myself and following her "house rules" to the letter.

CHAPTER SEVEN

I was not a particularly gifted athlete in my early years, but with the constant prodding of my father and brother Ted, I became a respectable player in football, basketball and baseball at school. I actually grew to love it, almost too much, as I not only played in games against other schools from the age of nine, but became absorbed in following professional teams and studying statistics in the daily papers. Less and less time and attention was being spent on my school work.

But family life became much more tolerable when I could finally talk about my own athletic accomplishments, rather than have to hear how outstanding Ted was in everything he did. My brother Jack, although four years younger than me, was already showing promise of possibly being the best athlete in the family.

Even Mother was involved, not only being a loyal spectator at her sons' games against rival schools, but taught us all how to play golf, a game she played with considerable joy and a fair amount of ability, making outstanding contributions to the Philadelphia Country Club's many championships. In fact, it was the only game that we all played together and had fun with, except maybe for the occasional attempt at a round robin tennis match in Beach Haven, or a board game, usually dominated by Ted's constant interpretation and reinterpretation of the rules, and his relentless desire to win.

Baseball had been in my blood since birth, I think. Maybe it was due to the fact that my father, a left-handed pitcher, had been signed to play Major League baseball by the famous owner and manager of the American League's Philadelphia Athletics, Connie Mack. World War I interrupted his career, and when he returned from overseas, he decided to marry my mother, and go into the family textile business, considered a much more respectable occupation.

Baseball was the center of the few happy moments I had with my father and Ted as I was growing up, and we collectively lived and died with every move of the Philadelphia Phillies, the city's National League entry. They were invariably in last place, and I think our joint commiserating was the strongest bond we had. Ted and I often went to games together, all the way to Baker Bowl in northeast Philadelphia, by train and subway. On double header Sundays, the entire expedition took as many as ten or eleven hours. But I loved being in the care of my older brother, and was fascinated with his intensity and knowledge of the game. Most important, even though I was a captive audience, he seemed to really like me. When the Phils lost both ends of the double header, which was often the case, we were in mourning together.

On one very memorable occasion, my father took me all the way to the Polo Grounds, in New York City, to see the Phillies play the New York Giants. The Phils lost as usual, but it was still a great day, because after the game, we went to the Cafe Rouge, in the Hotel Pennsylvania to have dinner and listen to the Glenn Miller Orchestra with Tex Beneke, Ray Eberle and the Modernaires. My father and me together for one whole day. Baseball and band music. What could be better!

CHAPTER EIGHT

In private school circles, The Episcopal Academy was well known for its Hobby Show, an annual event that brought student and parent together in a creative endeavor. For an entire week the gymnasium was given over to the exhibits to which even the general public was invited. One year my father agreed to help me construct a barometer and it was entered in the show. He was very interested in the weather, and how it affected his daily life. I, like most children, wasn't particularly interested in weather patterns, except when it meant I wouldn't have to go to school because of the snow. Living on top of a hill, with a long driveway, meant we were stranded quite often. A barometer might help with my father's nightly predictions and his decisions about whether or not to put the chains on the car wheels for traction…a major event with much discussion and planning.

So we busily set about constructing a three foot tall barometer, complete with a tube of mercury, mounted on a beautifully beveled, and stained piece of wood. It won a prize in the Hobby Show, and even though Dad had done most of the work, I had been next to him every minute and was proud of it and proud of him. I watched him study it every morning and evening as it hung, for years, in our library at home in Haverford. It was one of the few times we ever did anything together, except shovel snow, burn leaves, go to ball games once in a while and on the servants' day off, cook scrambled eggs together for supper. He just didn't have much time for me. I don't think it was because he didn't care, but more that he just didn't know how to get close to a young boy who needed a father's attention and love so very much.

One time he did confide in me. Alone in the car with him on a drive home from Grandma and Grandpa's house in Beach Haven one summer evening, he told me he was tired of being treated as second fiddle to his brothers-in-law, who were in the Galey and Lord headquarters with my grandfather, in New York. He said he would start his own textile sales representative business, and work out of an office at home. In addition to cotton yarns, it was to be his first venture into synthetics and he would be the middleman between the Dupont Co., the supplier, and several spinning mills in the south. It was so unusual for him to discuss his work with me and I didn't fully understand what he was talking about. But the whole idea sounded great, with his office to be in the room right next to mine. But in the next breath he told me that I was being sent, as a boarder, to his alma mater, The Hill School, following my brother, Ted, who had gone two years before.

Teenager

At about the same time I learned that my friend, Ernie, was going off to Phillips Exeter Academy in New Hampshire so I wasn't too upset, and carrying on the tradition at Hill seemed so important to Dad. But, as it turned out, it wasn't a very good decision, and only caused my troubled mind additional worry and torment. To begin with, following Ted and his outstanding record was hard enough. But being with my peers at night as well as during the day just complicated my life, and led to some questionable behavior and a lot of unhappiness. It started the very day I arrived.

34

CHAPTER NINE

The Hill School was only about thirty miles from our home in Haverford, but it seemed a million miles away. It was located on a hill, high above Pottstown, Pennsylvania, a small industrial town, not known for its beauty or charm. I had been much farther away from home at summer camp for several years, and the thought of living and sleeping in a strange place didn't bother me that much. But the fact that I was taking practically everything I owned and moving to a rather threatening, medieval looking institution of learning somehow wasn't very appealing. The ivy on the walls didn't make it any less foreboding, and the long, dark passageways and cell-like rooms made me feel that I was in some sort of a monastery. If there was one thing I had enjoyed at home it was freedom, freedom to come and go as I pleased, to run with Dolph, to play games with the Connetts, and to just listen to phonograph records and smoke cigarettes in my room. Now, I would be in a "house of discipline," with practically every waking moment programmed to deliver fine, upstanding young men ready to go to an Ivy League college and the promise of a life of leadership and prosperity.

Things got off to a bad start on the very first day, when I decided I didn't like the looks of my roommate from Portland, Maine. He wore glasses and had a large red birthmark on one side of his face that was very unsettling. I immediately arranged a switch, without anyone knowing, making it look as if it was the school's mistake, and roomed for a few weeks with a terror from the midwest, who was summarily expelled for breaking just about every rule. I quickly learned from his "transgressions" just what I could and couldn't get away with.

I subsequently was invited to move from my new boy status, to one of the old boy floors high up in the turret atop the tenth grade dormitory. This was quite an honor as it was a choice place to live and I loved it there, and made some good, and lasting friends. The old boys had ways of smuggling in "girlie" magazines, which we all pored over, and I liked them just as much as they did. Or maybe it was just the camaraderie, and sharing something secretive, that I liked. And late at night, hanging on to the gutters, I was able to climb out my window, over the severely pitched slate roofs, to a friend whose bed was waiting for me, and who had cigarettes hidden under his mattress. I'm sure his roommate wondered what we were doing under the blankets, but said nothing.

When I think back on these hair-raising escapades it's a wonder I'm alive to tell about them. Was a quick sexual fling and a few puffs on a Camel cigarette really worth risking my life? It seemed so at the time.

One Sunday, in the late afternoon, I was listening to a forbidden portable radio which I kept hidden under my pillow. It was December 7, 1941, and I heard that Pearl Harbor had been bombed by the Japanese. Only a wise old seer could have told me that I would be there in less than three years.

Somehow I managed to barely pass my final exams and move on to my junior year, this time rooming with the one person I cared most about, Harry Forbes. He was from Rockford, Illinois, a great athlete, a class leader, blond, and very handsome, and we had mutually agreed to the rooming arrangements. However, it turned out, to my dismay, that he wasn't the least bit interested in "playing around," and sharing my affection. I was so upset that I used to sneak out of my room, walk down to a little bar in town, and illegally drink beer with an old but kindly hooker named Irene, who befriended me. She listened intently to all of my heartfelt problems and let me put my head on her voluptuous breasts and cry, which she said would make me feel better. She was right, and she seemed to really understand my dilemma, never asking me to go any further with her or give her any money. She even paid for the beer and cigarettes. On Sundays the Catholic boys walked into town to go to mass, and Irene would be there, sitting in a pew near the back. She would never let on that she knew me. What a good friend. Up to that time, she knew more about my sexual confusion than anyone, and I suspect it is still a secret, buried deep in her great big heart.

It came as quite a surprise to me when I was selected to be on the dance committee representing the junior class for the fall prom, and with this honor my date was given a special reward, a room in the headmaster's house for the big weekend. I invited Peggy Wright, a girl I had met at the Friday evening dancing classes back home, and someone who lived near me in Haverford. We had made puppy love quite often on Sunday afternoons in front of her big stone fireplace while a pair of dachshunds watched, and her alcoholic mother and father argued upstairs. I liked her a lot and next to Lil was the hometown girl I felt closest to. Knowing her so well, I thought nothing of bounding up the stairs to her room in the headmaster's house to escort her to the dance. She was fully dressed and putting on her shoes when the chambermaid passed by the open door and saw me sitting on the bed. She reported me to the school's Dean of Students, and it wasn't until the next day that I was expelled from school. But that night I wasn't aware of what was to happen, and we had a wonderful time at the gala affair. Peggy was the most beautiful girl I had ever seen (she was to become a high fashion model), even lovelier than the renowned socialite beauty Toni Drexel, who made a grand entrance on the arms of two rather prominent young men—the son of United States Army General George Patton, and the son of

Harry Hopkins, President Franklin Roosevelt's chief advisor. But Peggy's dance card was just as full as Toni's, and deservedly so.

Dad was understandably furious at the Dean for expelling me, and mother stayed in her room and cried. I think he was as mad at the school as he was at me, and he told them so. How could the third generation and fourth member of the Dale family to attend the school be dismissed for such a trivial act! Of course my grades had been poor, and I had many demerits for bad behavior, but still the reason for dismissal was ridiculous. Ted was away at Yale and I must say I was glad to be home, away from a place that had been nothing but trouble and heartache. Tradition be damned. The Hill School just wasn't for me, and I didn't care how well Ted, my father, and my grandfather had performed there. I just wished that my mother and father would have realized that I was different. Different from Ted and, in significant ways, different from my peers. But all they cared about right then was what to do with me. Their answer was a cram school in Philadelphia that turned out to be an even bigger waste of time and money. I was going through about the worst time in my life thus far, and there didn't seem to be any end to the troubles in sight. And nobody seemed to care.

CHAPTER TEN

I had been collecting phonograph records of the big jazz bands for as long as I can remember. And right at this time, in the late thirties and early forties, were the years when the big bands, with their wonderfully talented vocalists, were the most popular. We all were jitterbugging to Peggy Lee singing "Why Don't You Do Right?," and swooning over Frank Sinatra's "This Love Of Mine." And I was in my room at home, with my portable record player, listening to these records which I loved, while everybody else was at school. But I didn't consider myself a bit lucky. In fact I was miserable, and the more I listened, the more unhappy I became. My father had to interrupt his newly formed business to find me a place to go to school, and he certainly let me know what an inconvenience it was. With his office at home, I don't think he wanted me hanging around for very long playing my records and disturbing his important telephone calls. So it didn't take much time to find a place, any place, that would take me, and I was to start as quickly as possible.

Theo Connett had graduated from school and was waiting for her beloved All-American football player, Steve Stack, to complete his studies at Yale. To ease her anxieties, and to give herself something to do, she was attending a secretarial school in Philadelphia in case of the unlikely event that she might have to work after they were married. It was my good fortune that when she drove into town each day she could give me a ride to my new school, which was only a few blocks from hers. Its name, Atlas Preparatory School, should have given my father some insight as to what the school might be like. But I don't think he really cared, as long as it was going to keep me occupied and hopefully prepare me for my senior year at some other school.

It turned out to be a complete waste of time. The classes were jammed full of kids sitting on broken-down furniture in long, narrow, dirty classrooms, chatting away while the teachers droned on monotonously, barely audible above the racket. When the students were not attending a class, which was often, they sat on the front stoop of the old converted attached house and smoked cigarettes and drank cokes. Nobody seemed to care…not the students and not the teachers. The whole thing was like something out of a Dickens novel, so unpleasant that, from the very first day, I would sign in in the morning, make an appearance in a classroom, then walk the nine blocks to the Earle Theater, where the first stage show started at ten o'clock.

The Earle was the home of the big bands when they came to Philadelphia, and during that winter and spring of 1943 I saw every one of them, some two or three times. They ranged from the great ones like Charlie Barnett, Woodie Herman, and Harry James, to Guy Lombardo, Alvino Ray and the King Sisters, and the great swinging black bands of Basie and Ellington. On the bill there were usually two or three acts, with such headline stars as Henny Youngman, The Mills Brothers, and Peg Leg Bates.

At least for those moments, I was in heaven as I sat there alone day after day escaping from the world around me, a world that didn't seem to want me very much. I hated lying to my parents about my day's activities, but I honestly think that sitting there by myself in the Earle Theater, listening to the beautiful melodies of the great composers like Jerome Kern, George Gershwin, and Harold Arlen and the lyric poetry of Johnny Mercer, Lorenz Hart, and Cole Porter was more beneficial than trying to learn anything at that pitifully inadequate attempt at schooling named Atlas.

At the end of the year I received a certificate that said I had passed. Passed what I don't know, and how useful a document it might be was questionable. But the advertisement for the school in the yellow pages guaranteed success, so there it was, printed on parchment, with a pretty satin bow tied around it. At Episcopal Academy they had never heard of Atlas and it was suggested that I attend summer school. Episcopal didn't have one, and so Mother urged me to go and visit The Haverford School, which was located only about a mile from our house.

Haverford was an arch rival of Episcopal and the two schools, plus Penn Charter and Germantown Academy, made up the Interacademic League; they were the schools I had played against in football, basketball, and baseball ever since fourth grade. Because of the intense rivalry, even on the junior level, the thought of going to Haverford was a troubling idea, but the least I could do for Mother, after causing her so much aggravation and tears, was to arrange an interview.

The meeting at Haverford was one of the defining moments of my young life. The Dean, George Black, warmly greeted me and proceeded to work out a summer schedule of study that would prepare me for entrance into the Haverford senior class in the fall. He made me feel as though I was a very important young man and that I would be a great asset to the school. I loved the whole atmosphere of the place, and even though it was very similar in educational standards and student makeup to Episcopal, there was something very different and special about it. Mr. Black seemed to push all the right buttons, and the whole interview was so genuine, so accommodating, so encouraging that I couldn't wait to get started on this new experience at a new school and a year that turned out to be one of the happiest of my life.

CHAPTER ELEVEN

In 1935, when I was ten years old, was the first of four vacations away at four different summer camps, and I always enjoyed the friendships and the less structured life of camp more than I did school. The reason for shifting from camp to camp was because different teachers that I liked at Episcopal Academy seemed to want me to come to their particular camp, and I liked being wanted. It was good being away from home, and Ted's intensity, and I really kind of blossomed each summer like a freshly watered rose. I did well in sports, was a good camper on canoe or mountain climbing trips, participated in the camp "Follies," and received points for my well made bed, good hygiene, and general demeanor.

At one camp I spent all summer making leather moccasins for myself and my father; at another I had a pet falcon; and at a third, Camp Gunston, on Maryland's Eastern Shore, some older boys who went to the Boy's Latin prep school in Baltimore taught me how to play lacrosse. One very happy remembrance of that camp is Blackie, a fat and feisty little pony I was put in charge of, who was only happy when I would sleep with him in his straw bed. I won some blue ribbons in the annual horse show, even one for jumping. Of course, there was always my grandparent's house in Beach Haven where I whiled away the hot summer days.

But the summer when I was seventeen was to be an entirely different one. Getting good grades at summer school wouldn't be rewarded with blue ribbons, or any prizes for that matter, but it would mean entrance into the Haverford School senior class in the fall of 1943. And I was ready, and truly anxious, to face the concentrated study plan worked out with Dean Black, which involved two months of grinding out the necessary work needed to obtain the credits to join that class. Why my sudden change in attitude? Why such a "gung ho" approach? I wish I knew. The only rationale I can think of was an unexplainable good feeling that I had about the Haverford School, its closeness to home and my immediate surroundings. But probably most important was the school's desire to take me on and try to make me into somebody, no questions asked. And, boy, did I respond!

Other than stopping at Nancy Bookmyer's house after school, it was all work. Nancy was an old pal from dancing class days, and she and her close friends would wait anxiously for a few of us to stop by and dance, on her front porch, to the latest records. Mrs. Bookmyer didn't seem to mind that there were fifteen or twenty kids "whooping it up" from four to five every afternoon. I'm sure her Coke bill must have been excessive and I have no idea, with all that noise, how she dealt with the neighbors. But for us it was a great release after a tough day in the hot classrooms and a full evening of study ahead.

Mother and Dad barely spoke to me all summer, they were so afraid of interrupting my concentration, and even Grandma, down on the Jersey shore, was aware of my new academic endeavors and gave me an open invitation to come any chance I had to break away. My grandfather had died recently and as much as I loved Beach Haven and wanted to spend time with my grandmother, I didn't go once that summer. I completed the assignments, getting all A's, and I was excited and ready to enter Haverford for my senior year—an extraordinary turn of events, one that even my father acknowledged as being quite an achievement. He told me that at long last he was sure that I would continue to pursue my obligations conscientiously and not go through life trying to get by on my "charming personality and good looks."

Towards the end of August "Doc" Wallace, the football coach at Haverford, told me he had heard about my athletic accomplishments at Episcopal and Hill. I don't know whether he was teasing me, or not, but he did invite me to try out for the varsity football team and to come to practice before school started. This was a huge break for me, as I didn't really know anyone in the class except for Holstein DeHaven Fox, Jr., a neighbor and the student manager and deluxe water boy for the squad. (Mr. Connett used to refer to him as Holstein DeHaven DeFox, DeJunior). But a few of my new classmates seemed to know me from parties or from hanging out at the Haverford Pharmacy, famous on the Main Line for its milk shakes and ice cream sodas. Or maybe I just had a reputation. What ever it was, they took me into their tight little circle and the many friends I made during those hot, grueling football practices, are friends that I consider to be some of the really special people I've ever known, and who, even now, are with me always, at least in spirit.

The football euphoria carried over into the start of the school year. It appeared that I had crossed that long, imaginary bridge and was on my way to becoming the "outstanding young man" that had been expected of me, but seemed impossible to achieve during all those grim years of puberty and adolescence. But unfortunately I didn't stay focused on my studies, and make it to the other end of that bridge. My senior year at Haverford was everything I could ask for and then some, but I couldn't quite handle such a bounty of riches and balance successfully all that this extraordinary year was to bring.

CHAPTER TWELVE

It seemed deafening to me. I didn't know whether to laugh or cry when I heard a chorus of loud boos as I ran out onto the field. It was the annual Haverford-Episcopal varsity football game, and this year, 1943, it was at Episcopal. I had been good friends with a lot of the boys I would be playing against, and I was sure I would get some rough treatment from some of them. But I didn't expect the kids, along with their parents, sitting in the grandstands to greet me with various expressions of contempt. After all, didn't I have the right to change schools if I wanted to? I guess it was because I was playing for Episcopal's arch rival, Haverford, and that didn't sit very well with them.

The team

48

Things had been going just fine, and I never thought the day would come when I could say I loved going to school. But I did, and one of the reasons was that I was the starting halfback on the team, playing in the game that would probably decide who would win the Interacademic League football championship. Penn Charter and Germantown Academy, the other two teams in the league were pretty much out of it, and it had come down to the Haverford-Episcopal game, as it had so many times in the illustrious history of the two schools. It would not only determine who was to receive the coveted trophy, but it would guarantee that aura of friendly superiority among our friends and associates at the other Interacademic League Schools. We had been preparing for this game all season, and the moment of truth had arrived. In spite of the booing, and my nine year affiliation with Episcopal Academy, I was Haverford School all the way, and I would try to trounce my old friends and teammates from junior football any way that I could.

We lost 7-6. Actually, it turned out to be a battle between Artie Littleton, our captain and fullback, and Newbold Smith, their captain and fullback. They were both big and strong and went on to become All American players in college—Artie at Penn and Newbold at Navy. I knew, first hand, why Artie's nickname was "giant" because I tackled him once in the open field during practice, and my body ached for days. Our coach, "Doc" Wallace, told me years later that it was that tackle of someone fifty pounds heavier than me, running at full speed, that clinched my winning the position of starting halfback on the team.

In those days we played both offense and defense and during the game I tackled Newbold Smith a couple of times, with the same painful result. Offensively, I was able to complete a long pass to the tight end, Sam Baird, which led to our only score. I wasn't the one who failed to execute the kick for the extra point, but I did hold the ball for the kicker, and felt partially responsible for the near miss.

The loss was a great disappointment, particularly to me, and after the game, at the tea party in the headmaster's house, given by the Episcopal players' mothers, I was greeted warmly and offered condolences by my old friends, a few of whom I remembered as having called me a sissy years before. I often wondered whether they would have spoken to me at all if we had been the victors.

My season ended in the hospital, having been kicked in the kidney while trying to throw a block, during a punt return, on the great halfback "Reds" Bagnell of Germantown Academy, a future All American at the University of Pennsylvania. We won the game, and I foolishly played almost the whole time with what was to be diagnosed as a ruptured kidney. I think missing three weeks of school as a result of the injury was at least partially responsible for a series of poor report cards, and for the rest of the year I was right on the edge of failing every subject. I liked the teachers, and the subject matter wasn't all that difficult for me, but I just had trouble concentrating and staying focused on it.

There was no end to the distractions. In addition to sports, and being somewhat of a "big deal" in the eyes of the Haverford student body, my life was filled with boy and girl relationships which were pretty intense and confusing and difficult to sort out. They verged on sexual activity, and possessed my mind a good part of the day and night. Instead of doing my homework, I spent hours on the telephone, even talking to friends whom I had just left a few minutes before. Again, it was that need for peer recognition and approval, particularly from the members of my class. All of these boys, and the girls I knew, meant so much to me. Too much, actually. And they responded. I don't know why, but it was really the first time in my life that I seemed to be liked and wanted by almost everybody, and I guess I just wasn't able to handle being looked upon as one of the "big boys."

Then there were all the social activities. Forgetting for a moment the weekend fun with my new friends, there was the steady round of debutante parties being given by the parents of girls I had known since I was thirteen. As a result of the Friday evening dancing class, I was on the "preferred list," and was invited to most of them. Each tried to outdo the other, with elaborate balls at the best of the Philadelphia hotels. There were tea dances in the late afternoon and dinner dances in the evening, most of them at the parents' homes, but if they were not large enough, at their country clubs. Mother was like my social secretary, answering invitations and keeping my suits and tuxedo properly cleaned and pressed. She loved hearing all the gossip

51

which I enjoyed reporting, as well as my detailed descriptions of the beautiful dresses the girls were wearing. I guess the thinking was that, because so many of us would be going off to fight in World War II after graduation, these parties were grander than ever since the debutantes might be seeing their handsome male suitors for the last time for quite a while.

Without a doubt, one of the most extravagant and unusual of those "coming-out parties" was the one for Ella Widener, niece of the renowned horse owner and breeder, George D. Widener. Known as "Tootie," she received her guests in a real igloo, made of blocks of dry ice. The Bellevue Stratford Hotel ballroom was a beautifully decorated winter scene, with glistening icicles hanging from the chandeliers and simulated snow falling from the starry heavens, accompanied by Meyer Davis's thirty piece orchestra. "Tootie", looking a bit heavier than usual, had thousands of sparkling bugle beads hanging from her ice blue gown, and resembled a melting iceberg. As I came through the receiving line and entered the igloo, she was shivering, and asked me to take her to her hotel suite to "warm up." I respectfully declined and I've always wondered why she didn't have one of her fur coats on hand if she was going to hold court in an igloo.

The one person who dominated my life throughout that school year was the daughter of Dr. Leslie Severinghaus, Haverford's headmaster. Libby Severinghaus was vivacious, sexy, and quite beautiful, and had been the steady girlfriend of Artie Littleton, one of the most outstanding members of the class, and certainly one of the biggest. But, without hardly any effort on my part she left him abruptly and we became an inseparable pair, so romantically attached that in the class year book I was unanimously elected by my peers to be the first to get married!

CHAPTER THIRTEEN

"Money, we really don't need that
we'll make out all right,
lettin' the other guy feed that
jukebox Saturday night."

Tex Beneke and the Modernaires with the great Glenn Miller Band. Big band music was everywhere. In the car, in the record shops, at home, and wherever we went to dance. Libby Severinghaus and I spent a year completely surrounded by the sounds of Jimmy and Tommy Dorsey, Harry James, Artie Shaw and Benny Goodman. We sang and danced our way through the school year of 1943-44, barely stopping to catch a breath. We were able to sing every word of every song and hum all the intricate arrangements. And when we were dancing, we were hugging and kissing and could hardly let go of each other. Even though Libby was two years younger than me, she was a dominant force...never to be denied. When she wanted something, she got it. And that something was me.

Libby and me

During the school week she was not allowed to see me at night, and during the day, after school, there was very little time. We tried to get a glimpse of each other, either at her close friend Varney Twaddell's house, which was located a few steps from Haverford School, or at her own home, the headmaster's house, right down the street. But we never were really apart, talking for hours on the telephone during the week, and of course on the weekends, always together. We usually double or triple-dated, held each other's hands, touched legs, and nibbled on Ju-jus at the movies.

We especially loved the musicals like *Holiday Inn, Stormy Weather*, and *Stage Door Canteen*. The one that I think was our special favorite was *Meet Me In St. Louis*. Somehow Judy Garland's romance with Tom Drake, the mysterious stranger who moves next door to her, struck a chord with us and we went back to see it several times. The after the movies ritual was always cheeseburgers and cokes and dancing 'till midnight at the Last Straw, a little "road house" with a swinging jukebox, run by some Haverford College boys. We must have jitterbugged hundreds of times that year to Glenn Miller's "In The Mood", and Harry James's "Two O'clock Jump." The evening wasn't complete until we did some heavy petting sitting in my father's car parked high on a cliff overlooking the spewing blast furnaces in the neighboring industrial town of Conshohocken.

On one occasion, just to be devilish, at a Haverford School dance in the gymnasium we prompted my classmate and good friend, Tommy Ligget, to announce from the bandstand, very seriously, that Libby Severinghaus and Chum Dale were being married in the locker room downstairs. Everyone rushed down to see the two of us, amidst the smelly sweat socks and jockstraps, going through the motions of a mock wedding, complete with rings, and a "minister" reading from scripture and pronouncing the vows. The Headmaster and Mrs. Severinghaus and their guests, Libby's aunt and uncle, Henry and Claire Booth Luce, were the chaperones for the evening and were decidedly not amused. Or at least they pretended not to be, and called an immediate halt to the proceedings before the rings were exchanged. I suspect Dr. and Mrs. Severinghaus, at that moment, hoped and prayed that their daughter, when the time came for the real thing, would choose some one who was a little less of a "cut-up" and a bit more mature in his thinking.

But for me, my love for Libby was left on the Severinghaus doorstep—at least until the next day—after we hugged, and fondled, and kissed good night. I'm sure when she went to bed she thought a lot about me and I wished I could say the same about her. But I had other things on my mind. I seemed to be the driver on most occasions, and after dutifully returning all the girls home, there were usually my two best friends, Tommy Ligget, and "Spider" Shaw, to drive to their houses. We would sit in the car for a while and review the night's activities, listening to the Dawn Patrol on the car radio and laugh at "Spider's" imitation of Billy Eckstine singing "I Apologize." Tommy's favorite was Frank Sinatra's "Nancy With The Laughing Face." I don't know how or why, but somehow he knew that his future bride would be named Nancy and that she would have a lovely, laughing face.

I remember these songs so well because the times alone with Tommy and "Spider" had even a greater meaning to me than all of the lovemaking with Libby, even though I expressed my love for her with every ounce of sincerity that I could muster. With my friends, I was hardly able to communicate how I felt about them. It was all tied up inside of me, screaming, begging to come out. Again, like my days at Episcopal, where my thoughts were of Ernie Ransome, and at Hill School where I fantasized about Harry Forbes, I was leading a double life. One of those lives was very lonely.

In spite of all the confusing thoughts in my head, I had the very best of years at Haverford, one that I'll never forget. I couldn't play varsity basketball because of the lingering effects of the kidney injury, but everyone said I would have easily made the squad. I went with the team everywhere, and cheered myself hoarse for "Spider" and Sam, consuming a whole box of Ludens cough drops at each game. And I was the hero in two of our varsity baseball games, one as a result of my "squeezing" in the winning run against The Lawrenceville School, and the other, a two base hit down the left field line, driving in the deciding run, in extra innings, against Friends Central. Remembering those moments gives me a special thrill.

There were no highlights in the classroom, however, and when all of the results of the final exams were in, I had failed. I didn't graduate with my class. It wasn't because I didn't care. I really did. But not enough, I guess. I suppose I thought that I could get by just being "Chum." I'm sure I deserved such a severe comeuppance. I'm also sure that it was a difficult decision for Dr. Severinghaus not to present me with my diploma, particularly when he suspected that Libby and I considered ourselves unofficially engaged. I was totally despondent, knowing that I had let down so many people who expected so much from me. And I had let down the Haverford School, this extraordinary place that I loved so much and which had given me every opportunity. I was not able to recognize my priorities and was just plain irresponsible. I'm certain the constant turmoil in my brain trying to sort out my sexual confusion had a great deal to do with my failure.

But there was one very bright note that eased the pain, the disappointment and disgrace. Everyone of my friends treated me as if I were one of the graduates. I was still very much a part of their lives, and Libby was more in love with me than ever. With this love, friendship and support, being drafted into the Navy that June of 1944 didn't seem like a very big deal. But, boy, was I proven wrong!

CHAPTER FOURTEEN

Not long ago, at a dinner party at my home, a bunch of World War II veterans were telling, with considerable relish, their "war stories" about the adventures they experienced during various European campaigns and how much they loved serving our country as a member of our armed forces. They were rather taken aback when I somberly stated that I hated every minute of my tour of duty in the United States Navy and how difficult it was for me to recall most of that two year period. I'm sure I am just as patriotic as they are but it is, with a few startling exceptions, a time I have relegated to a dark corner of my memory bank.

Mother and I went to the movies in Philadelphia the day I was to leave for Navy Boot Camp in Bainbridge, Maryland. We saw *Murder, My Sweet*, with Dick Powell and Claire Trevor, and, in spite of this special, and rather sad occasion, I still remember it as one of my favorite movies of all time. Going to a picture show was always something I enjoyed doing with Mother, but lately I hadn't seen many with her because of my weekend activities with Libby. I didn't even have much time, like I used to, to read the latest movie magazines she brought home from the hairdresser. Right now Dad's business periodicals, *The Underwear and Hosiery Review* and *Women's Wear Daily*, were much more interesting to me, and my friends, with all of those semi-nude women lounging around in their skimpy underwear. I liked seeing sensual women without much on, and I even was turned-on by strippers Ann Corio and Diane Rowland at Philadelphia's only Burlesque house, the Troc, in seedy Chinatown.

Mother liked my friends a lot and they enjoyed her as well, but "Spider" Shaw silently worried that she had something wrong with her legs. He only saw her in the evening when she had just taken her bath and put on her long velvet hostess gown for cocktails and dinner. She was always sitting in her favorite place in the corner of the big couch in front of the fireplace and seldom, if ever, got up from there...at least until dinner was served. "Spider" never realized that she didn't have to go into the kitchen; that we had servants to prepare and serve dinner...something his family didn't have. He told me much later, after seeing her in a regular dress at the A&P, that he was glad her leg was better. He had been sure that her long gown had been hiding some terrible infirmity, like a withered leg.

I guess you could say I was a little bit of a mama's boy, but it was somewhat understandable, considering that I had no place to turn but to her since Dad and Ted never let up with their badgering and criticism for all those years. So it was a very natural thing for just the two of us to be going to the movies on my last day of freedom. Mother seemed much more concerned about my going off to war than

I was and, even though she had been upset about my not graduating from Haverford School, the thought and fear of losing a son in battle was of much greater import at the moment. With my brother Ted already in the Navy and her second son about to join him, she had World War II very much on her mind.

Tommy Ligget, and another good friend, Jimmy Roberts, were going to Bainbridge a week later, but we had said our good-byes, not expecting to see each other for a few years. And we didn't. My Haverford School classmates were scattered everywhere, some to the army overseas in Europe, others to the Pacific Theater, and still others, more lucky and probably smarter, to ROTC programs at various colleges. Thankfully, all of our class survived the war, except for one, a Haverford boarding student from England named Mike Dowling. I didn't know him very well but, like Artie Littleton, I recall he was an outstanding member of the Haverford swimming team.

That summer of 1944 must have been the hottest on record. At Bainbridge, each day started with miles and miles of running before breakfast around a dusty quadrangle. Then we drilled and drilled, marching with a rifle on our shoulders in the hot sun, hour after hour. Several of the draftees dropped, and were carted off to the infirmary. Another man near me had an epileptic fit, which was horrible to see. Someone put a dirty stick in his mouth to hold it open so that he wouldn't swallow his tongue. It saved his life. I don't know what all this had to do with being on board a ship at sea, but I guess the purpose of boot camp was to toughen up everybody, to teach us how to take orders, and to be known only by a number, which was stamped into the dog tags hanging around our necks. The Chief Petty Officers in charge of "training" us were mean spirited, humorless, and were critical of everything we said or did. I guess this was the way to make "fighting men." It was not the most friendly environment. I did make one friend, Maynard Strong, a tall and handsome boy from northern Maine, who, in his down-home way, was most appealing and helped ease the stress of those difficult days.

After six weeks of this intensive training I for one was completely brainwashed, ready to do anything anybody asked of me. We did learn a little bit about the Navy, and certain procedures, but the whole experience was pretty unpleasant, and is not easy to recall. As a matter of fact, the whole two years I spent in the Navy I would just as soon forget forever. But I just can't, completely, because there are a few moments, some unpleasant, that are so much a part of me that I occasionally recall them as clearly and precisely as though they happened only yesterday.

The American people were just beginning to become aware of some of Nazi Germany's persecution of the Jews and others, not acceptable to Adolph Hitler and the Third Reich. Much of this information came to us from Libby's uncle Henry Luce's *Life* and *Time* magazines, which my family had subscribed to from their inception.   The tragic pictures we all saw after the war in Europe ended and the stories of poor, innocent people being herded into boxcars and transported to concentration camps remind me now of a similar type railroad car that I rode in as we traveled across the country, huddled together, sitting on hard wooden benches six abreast.   Of course, there was really no comparison, as we had windows, which were wide open on those hot summer days...a questionable comfort what with the engine soot and stirred-up dirt and dust filling our lungs.   But all was not discomfort; there were sandwiches and coffee and other assorted goodies given to us by the kind people in the little towns along the way.   Their cheering voices and good wishes helped to ease, what was otherwise a miserable five days of very little sleep, and painful rear ends.

But the Navy must have decided that the five-day cattle car trip was enough, so some of us were transferred to a magnificent streamliner, complete with observation domes, for the trip from Stockton, California to Seattle, Washington.   This ride through the Cascade Mountains was an exciting and wondrous experience compared to the boring and unspectacular scenery of the nation's heartland.   I still had no idea just where I was going to end up, but when they told me, after arriving in Seattle, that I was to be sent to the Bremerton Navy Yard on an island in Puget Sound, I felt sure I was getting close to my final destination.   What I didn't know was that my home for the next year was to be the gigantic gray ship that I could see in the distance, anchored right across the bay, with the number BB

40 painted on its prow. It was the Queen of the 7th Fleet, the battleship New Mexico.

Apprentice Seaman

The New Mexico

CHAPTER FIFTEEN

Bill Graham lived somewhere in Northeast Philadelphia, and not very near me, but at least he knew about the Philadelphia Main Line, and Haverford in particular. He had gone to a Catholic school that I had never heard of and he wasn't at all familiar with debutante parties, or summer weekends at the beach. The only thing we really had in common was that we had seen the same strippers at the burlesque. But it didn't matter, because we were all part of one big common denominator on our battleship, the USS New Mexico, and many of the two thousand members of the crew were ordinary seamen just like us.

I met Bill when we were stringing our hammocks among the heating and water pipes in the bowels of the ship, and as lowly deck hands we had to rig our moveable beds every night and take them down in the morning. No matter how hard we tried to pull them tight they always hung just low enough so that anyone over 5'9" walking underneath, in the dark at night, would scrape the top of their head on the heavy canvas, scream in pain, cursing loudly, and whack our bottoms as we lay there trying to sleep. But with all the abuse and the heavy work on deck, Bill and I tried hard to laugh together, and having him as my only real friend made our voyage to nowhere somewhat palatable.

I say nowhere because the day before we left the shipyard in Bremerton, Washington, we were issued a full complement of heavy foul weather gear: fur lined parkas and boots, gloves and knitted caps. Most of the guys had a range of ideas as to where we were going, but the consensus was that we were heading north to the Aleutian Islands in the Bering Sea, off the coast of Alaska. All the pretty pictures of swaying palms and bare breasted native dancers were dashed from our minds. Somehow, Eskimo girls cooking fish in an igloo and covered head to toe in animal skins didn't conjure up the same sensual thoughts.

Actually, we did head north for about half a day, and then abruptly turned south in the direction of the Hawaiian Islands, and the South Pacific. We figured that it must have been a ploy to throw off the Japanese spies who were probably lurking in every dark corner of the Naval Base, and maybe even on our ship. But if they were really there, and had been able to see what was happening on the second day we were at sea, they would have seen me, along with many others, following orders and tossing all that expensive winter gear into the sea as we steamed for warmer climes. What a waste! I guess in wartime one will do anything to fool the enemy.

To make sure that we didn't tell the people at home what we knew, or thought we knew, about our whereabouts and destinations, there was a very strict censorship of all of our mail. Libby and I had worked out a code so that I would be able to tell her in my letters our location. I figured that most people were doing the same thing so I wasn't really concerned about sabotaging the war effort. The code wasn't terribly intricate, but was good enough to get past the censors. She, in turn, would notify my family and anyone else who was interested.

I wrote to her often, but she wrote to me nearly everyday for the entire year I was at sea. And they weren't just little notes. Just as Libby loved to talk, so it was that she loved to write. Pages and pages in her precise hand would arrive, sometimes in bundles of ten or twelve at a time, complete with pictures, or articles from the newspapers. It was unbelievable how much she had to tell me about her daily activities at home. It was almost like a diary she was sharing with me. And I remember the letters smelled so good, and my being amazed that her delicate fragrance would last all the way to the Pacific.

My first coded message identified Hawaii, which I guess everyone kind of expected. But the second one, which pinpointed the island of Yap, a fuel stop, was a mystery that only her father, my old headmaster, was able to solve after considerable research at the Haverford School library.

Although I remember very little about our stop in Hawaii, I do know that it was the last time I set foot on dry land for almost a year. The steel gray walls and decks of the battleship New Mexico were the parameters of my home, and I'm sure it would have been almost unbearable if I hadn't had the good fortune to be chosen, from among all those sailors, to join the Signal Division. I haven't the remotest idea why this happened, but somebody "upstairs" liked me, and that upstairs, in this case, was the signal bridge near the top of the main superstructure of the ship. I don't think they were looking for someone with a lot of Philadelphia Main Line sophistication, but it is possible that some of the good education that I had managed to retain was evident in whatever criteria they used in finding and selecting me. Anyway, it was a piece of good fortune to be joining that rather exclusive club.

The twenty-eight signalmen had one of the few air-conditioned quarters, with real bunks, and were treated as somewhat special sailors because of their 24-hour, 7-day-a-week rigorous schedule, and the fact that they had to man two different signal bridges, one for blinker lights and semaphore and the other for signal flags. I was sorry to be leaving my only friend, Bill Graham, and promised I would wave to him from the bridge while he was swabbing the decks down below.

I was on one of these bridges, to which I had been assigned by Chief Signalman Tony Carter after intensive schooling, when I noticed what appeared to be a single plane falling from the sky. It headed straight down, like a diving bird, and silently landed in the sea, barely missing our ship. It was a strange sight; a plane nosediving into the sea and exploding. I learned soon afterwards that this was our first sighting of a Japanese Kamikaze plane, a plane carrying a huge bomb, guided by a human being with only a day or two of flight training, on a one-way suicide mission to destroy. It wasn't long after, in Leyte Gulf in the Philippines, that I saw a lot more than one, and this time we weren't so lucky.

One of the most memorable and tragic moments of my year at sea, and a lasting image that will be with me always, didn't even involve the New Mexico. And yet everyone who witnessed it, from all the ships in our convoy heading to the waters off the Philippine Islands, must have, as I did, shed a small tear, or at least shuddered with emotion, if they had any soul at all.

We were part of an armada—at least fifty ships in the 7th Fleet, from aircraft carriers to cruisers large and small, to destroyers, all racing at top speed in order to rendezvous with the 5th Fleet for what went down in history as the battle of Leyte Gulf. A carrier near us, and one of the lead ships, began to discharge its aircraft one after the other from its flight deck. It was a beautiful sight to see, as they slowly climbed and seemed to hover in the sky as they formed into a squadron high above us.

I don't know whether their mission was to protect us or to attack the enemy, but whatever it was, there was one plane and its pilot who was unable to accomplish its assignment. As it took off, just like the others, its tail began to slowly dip towards the sea. It struggled to gain altitude and at one point almost seemed to make it. But then it slowly drifted down and plunged into the water, tail first. I could see the pilot waving his arms frantically and struggling to get out of the plane as it began to sink. And we all just kept going, every ship in the fleet passing it as if it were just a piece of debris. Not one ship veered off course to pick up the frantic pilot. My last sight of him, from my vantage point high up on the signal bridge, was a tiny speck, floating alone in the wake of the last ship.

If I didn't know it already, this was a five-minute lesson in just how expendable human life is during wartime. But witnessing this and trying to understand it didn't make it any easier to swallow and I brooded over it for quite sometime, wondering if my fellow signalmen, the rest of my shipmates, and all the men on the other ships who had watched this tragic event take place had been as affected as I was. I never would dare to let on that I cried, but I did that night, and I wondered if Bill Graham, way down in the bottom of the ship, at the other end, lying in his hammock, had seen what I saw and was crying, too.

I was on watch on the main Signal Bridge again, barely twenty-four hours after that lone kamikaze barely missed us and plunged into the water, when we were suddenly attacked by what seemed to be hundreds of huge mosquitoes. They were Kamikaze planes on their suicide mission to hit as many ships as they could, and blow them up. The unskilled pilots were buzzing around, looking for an opening between anti-aircraft shells, shot from our gun mounts along both sides of the ship. Some were hit, and their bombs exploded, others missed their targets and plunged harmlessly into the sea.

But one of them managed to hit its mark, crashing into the navigation bridge right above me. I was knocked to the deck, and a bucket that had been between my legs was completely shattered by shrapnel; yet I only had bruises from the impact and the fall. Our Captain, R. W. Fleming and a *Time-Life* correspondent, Bill Chickering, were both killed instantly, as were twenty-seven others in our crew, as the plane fell to the main deck and exploded. Eighty-seven were seriously injured. Fortunately, my Philadelphia friend, Bill Graham was below decks and survived. A number of the other ships were also hit and I learned later that the total number of casualties numbered nearly one thousand. As I thought about it then, and as I do now, it seems absolutely incredible that these Japanese pilots, totally brainwashed, flying planes without a landing gear or enough fuel to return to home base, would willingly become human bombs and sacrifice their lives for their country. And they knew that if they missed their target, they died in shame.

What had happened was devastating! The New Mexico had suffered extensive damage but we were able to limp to a small atoll that had been set up as a repair depot. The dead had been blessed by our chaplain and buried at sea, while the ship's makeshift band played a mournful funeral anthem. We all stood at attention, the way we had learned in boot camp, and when the burial was completed and the band had finished its sad lament I was told by the Chief to go and get some sleep and try to prepare for another day. I felt so alone as I lay in my bunk that night. Not that I had lost any particularly close friends, but the New Mexico was home and all those aboard were family. My home had been violated and I just needed someone to hold onto, someone with whom I could share the horrors and the fear that had invaded my being in the past twenty-four hours.

But God must have been listening as I fitfully slept that night, because the first of two amazing miracles occurred early the next morning. As I came up on deck, I heard my name being shouted from a small ship docked right next to us. It was a familiar voice, a voice I had known all my life. It shouted, with much enthusiasm, "Good morning, Chum. Gee, I'm glad you're alive." It was the voice of my brother Ted.

CHAPTER SIXTEEN

Thinking back to my days at Episcopal Academy and Hill School, when I was forever being compared to my brother, I knew then that I would never be able to match Ted's achievements. He was extremely smart, a good athlete, reasonably pleasant socially, and very well liked and respected by almost everybody, his peers and his elders. Ted had an insatiable curiosity about everything, always probing, always questioning. The intense way in which he attacked even the smallest challenge, was really quite extraordinary. Perhaps his only real drawback was his lack of patience and understanding of people who he felt didn't measure up to his standards and who didn't completely agree with his opinions, for whatever reason.

I had learned this very fast and early as I was growing up in the same house with him, and he managed to make my life miserable for many years, hardly realizing he was doing it. Our brother Jack was six years younger than Ted and was treated as a baby, having nothing particularly in common with him. With my father constantly expressing his admiration for everything he did, Ted "zipped" through adolescence as if the pains of growing up were just another little hurdle, a slight bump in the road on his way to achieve perfection.

And so it was not surprising that he should graduate with honors from The Hill School and go on to Yale and the ROTC program. His studies were interrupted after his sophomore year by a call to active duty, and he gained the rank of Lieutenant, becoming the Communications Officer on a minesweeper in the Pacific Theater.

That morning, when I looked down from the deck of the crippled battleship New Mexico, to see Lieutenant Edwin L. Dale, Jr. staring up at me from his little minesweeper, I was overcome with emotion and joy. Just his presence gave me a much needed feeling of comfort and security and I was no longer afraid. Being only a lowly Signal man 3rd class, I didn't dare climb down to him, and so we just yelled to each other for a few minutes, and then in his familiar abrupt way, he said his ship was leaving immediately and that he had to go below.

Ted

He did tell me that by being the Communications Officer he had heard on his radio that the New Mexico had been hit by a Kamikaze plane, and that there had been considerable loss of life. He said he was terribly worried that I might have been killed, and how relieved he was that I was alive and well. And with those reassuring words he was gone, and I never even touched him. Not that we would have hugged, but at least we could have shaken hands. But I felt much better having just been with him for a few minutes, and I wondered if maybe he had somehow arranged that our two ships would be tied up side by side. To me, Ted could do anything.

It didn't take long for us to get back into the thick of battle. With the steely eyed Admiral Raymond Spruance, hero of the battle of Midway, directing the attack on the island of Okinawa from our signal bridge, we became the flagship, the headquarters, of the 7th Fleet. It didn't take very long before the Japanese discovered this, and we were the main target of a new attack. We were hit a second time by a Kamikaze plane, this one cleverly and precisely directed down the main stack of the ship, and exploding in the interior. Fifty-four men were killed, with one hundred and nineteen injured. It happened as we were firing our big guns at the island in support of the marine landings, and some of our heavy ammunition exploded, along with the suicide plane's bomb. It was said that the lower half of a woman's body was found in the wreckage, suggesting that Japanese man power had been severely depleted and that the women of Japan had become expendable.

Kamikaze hits USS New Mexico off Okinawa, 12 May 1945

Kamikaze hits New Mexico

The devastation from this latest assault was enormous, but the ship remained afloat and under control. This time, I was below decks when the attack occurred, asleep in our quarters in the aft part of the ship. We were plunged into darkness, but with dim emergency lights I found my way to the carnage and for what seemed like hours and hours helped carry the maimed bodies and body parts up onto the main deck. I was hardly able to see what I was doing and kept slipping in the pools of blood. It was grisly business, and almost

77

beyond description. I've tried very hard over the years to get this horror out of my mind, but my own two hands will never let me forget.

It was not long after this, and two devastating atomic explosions, that the Japanese surrendered and the war in the Pacific ended. With its many battle scars, the New Mexico led the Seventh Fleet on the short trip to Tokyo Bay for the final ceremony aboard the battleship Missouri. On the signal bridge, Admiral Spruance handed me a little brown piece of paper, torn from an old paper bag, and told me to send this message to the other ships: "Proceed to Tokyo Bay. Be on guard against treachery." It was the most important message I had ever sent, and I guess one of the most important moments in my life. I carried that little piece of brown paper in my wallet for many years, only realizing the historical significance of it when the wallet was stolen fifteen years later. How foolish of me to only consider it a personal memento!

Just after sunrise, September 2nd, 1945, the day of the official surrender, I was standing my watch on the bridge of the New Mexico, when I saw a flashing signal light off in the distance, spelling out our number, BB 40. I answered, was asked to identify myself, and was greeted with the words: "Hi, welcome to Tokyo Bay. I knew you'd make it."

The second of the amazing miracles had happened. It was Ted signaling me from his minesweeper, having just cleared the channel into the bay so that the big ships could arrive safely. What a thrill to have my brother near me at this momentous occasion! No one would believe that, in the vastness of the South Pacific Ocean, with thousands of ships scattered over thousands of miles of water, brothers would meet on two different occasions, in two different places. But it happened, and even though we never shook hands or patted each other on the back, or maybe even hugged, we were closer then than we ever had been or would ever be again.

CHAPTER SEVENTEEN

The fog was so thick that I could hardly see my hand in front of my face. It was a little after midnight, and I had just started my four hour watch on the signal bridge of my home for the past year, the battleship New Mexico. We were on our way back to the States, having left Tokyo Bay immediately after the ceremony, a ceremony that I had been able to see with binoculars, as General Douglas McArthur, in his resplendent army uniform, accepted the documents of surrender from the Japanese government officials, dressed in formal attire. What a thrilling moment, one that I felt privileged to have shared not only with my brother on his minesweeper, but with the thousands of Naval personnel who had gathered aboard hundreds of ships for this historic and auspicious occasion.

After all of the day's excitement, standing there alone in the fog filled darkness, looking at absolutely nothing, and my mind a complete blank, was a kind of a surreal experience, and a little bit scary. I could hear the lapping of the angry sea against the steel hull of this mighty ship, the rise and fall of the bow as it rode the waves. Occasionally, in the distance, there was the moaning of a lonely fog horn, but I couldn't see anything. Suddenly, from out of nowhere I sensed a body behind me and felt two strong arms reach around me and hug me. To put it mildly, I was so startled that it was only the pipe railing that prevented me from falling off the bridge. The arms held me tight as he pressed his head close to my ear, whispering that I should meet him, at the end of my watch, in the flag bag. He then kissed me on my neck, and disappeared into the fog.

The flag bag was on a bridge in the aft part of the ship—the storage place for all the signal flags—and was only used during daylight hours when the flags were hoisted to send messages to a large number of ships at one time. It was like a deep trough and I knew it well. Part of my duties were to know the alphabet represented by each flag, to know how to pull them out of the "bag," and, with dispatch, clip them to the halyards and hoist them up the mast. I was good at it and loved doing it as I watched the colorful flags unfurling and snapping in the breeze.

But I had never thought of the flag bag as being anything but just that, a place to store flags, and I was totally confused as to what to do about the surprise invitation to this makeshift love nest. I had had only fleeting desires of this kind for a long while, and yet I was captivated by the possibilities of what might happen with this mysterious admirer. Why had he chosen me? Why had he taken such a risk without being sure of my inclinations? Was it a trap? What if I wasn't attracted to him? All of these questions raced through my mind, as my four-hour watch dragged on and on.

Promptly, at 4 AM, Joe Merriman, from Kansas City, Missouri, was lying in the flag bag waiting for me. I couldn't see him, but I suddenly recognized his voice as a fellow signalman and someone who I had always noticed wore unusually tight dungarees. He had blond hair and a round face and was always very cheerful. I liked him, but didn't really know him very well. The flag bag was damp and musty, but I climbed in anyway, and for the first time in many, many months, I experienced something that was totally unrelated to war and hatred and fear and death. It was peaceful and loving, and there was a mutual understanding between two people who were loyal and trusted sailors, dedicated to their duty, but who held a secret passion in their hearts.

I saw Joe often after our little tryst, but we never talked about it and I had no desire to repeat it. All that mattered was that I was heading for home, and Libby, and all of my Haverford School friends. It had been some time since we had received any mail, but I knew she would be there, looking so pretty in her sweater and skirt and bobby socks. And a pearl necklace resting on those beautiful breasts. We would dance with joy to all our old favorite songs, and Tommy with his "giggly" laugh, Spider with that "beeky" nose, Sam's shuffle, and Jimmy's happy face, would all be with me, telling stories of their own exploits, and discussing plans for their college days at Yale and Princeton. Artie, too, would be there, bigger than life, looming over us. And yes, Haverford summer school would be there waiting for me to make up those credits needed to graduate. I wasn't worried, and aside from being very underweight, I was reasonably healthy, and ready for any challenge ahead of me. If I could survive that ugly war, and those deadly Kamikazes, I could handle anything!

To be sure the thought of at last being home was great, but the getting there wasn't all that easy. I think we left so soon after the surrender, that taking on food and supplies was not on too many minds. At least it seemed that way, because, what was commonly known in the Navy as "shit on a shingle," was served every day. It was supposed to be chipped beef, but was gray in color, and served in a watery sauce. I hated it, and lived on chocolate bars and evaporated milk, feeling kind of dizzy and depressed most of the time. And apparently we were badly in need of fuel also, because a huge tanker pulled along side, and while we were racing along at 20 knots, in very rough seas, enormous hoses were strung between the ships, and oil was pumped through them into our tanks. A fascinating logistical feat to watch, and I thanked God I was not the quartermaster at the helm or the officer in charge of keeping the two ships on a perfectly straight course and the hose connections secure.

But the highlight of the trip home was my first shore leave in nearly a year. Panama wasn't the most glamorous country to be visiting, but after being confined to a warship for all those days and weeks and months, just about any place would have looked beautiful, even the slums of Colon, the city at the northern end of the Panama Canal, leading into the Caribbean Sea. It was here in this decadence that I faced, for the first time, a decision which should have been an indication of just where my libido was ultimately headed.

CHAPTER EIGHTEEN

The Americans at home were so anxious and excited to see their naval heroes and those magnificent warships they had been attached to when they returned from the South Pacific that it was decided that each of the major ships, battleships and aircraft carriers, would put into port cities up and down both the east and west coasts. Huge celebrations were planned in each city, and even though the war had been over for a while, the families and loved ones waiting at home hadn't forgotten. The New Mexico had the farthest to go as Boston was our destination, and we were due there in the early part of October, about a month after the Japanese surrender. It was expected that we would stay through the winter and into the spring, when I was due to be discharged. Of course, Philadelphia or even New York would have been preferable, but at least we were going to be on the east coast and it was a big plus that it was a city that had a major league baseball team.

I had always been a National League fan because of the Philadelphia Phillies, but the Boston Red Sox had the splendid splinter, Ted Williams, and the great double play combination of Johnny Pesky and Bobby Doerr. And I had heard that Fenway park, with its green monster left field wall, was a great place to watch a ball game. I knew there were a couple of good dance halls in Boston because I had heard on the radio some of the great dance bands playing from there. I'd forgotten their names, but knew they were on Commonwealth Avenue and I surely would be able to find them. Aboard ship there had been a lot of talk and raucous laughter about Boston's Sculley Square and a stripper there who had tassels tied to her nipples, and who was able to spin them in opposite directions.

I had missed so many things while I'd been away and I was thinking about them as the New Mexico moved slowly through the great locks of the Panama Canal. I remembered my grandfather telling me one time, when we were fishing at Beach Haven, that he and Grandma had taken six of their nine children, including my mother when she was fifteen, on a long trip, partially by stage coach, across the United States to San Francisco and the California Exposition. From there they went by boat down the California coast and made one of the earliest trips, in 1915, through this canal on their way home to New York. It was in Panama City that my Uncle Jack, five years younger than Mother, was bitten by a mosquito and contracted encephalitis, or "sleeping sickness," and many years later, while visiting us in Haverford, he died from it. Passing through this remarkable engineering feat reminded me of one more bit of family history. It was during the building of the canal in the early 1900s that my other grandfather, Major Chalmers Dale, my namesake, serving in the US. Army, was stationed there to protect the American engineers and workers against foreign intervention.

While I day-dreamed about my family connections to the canal, my fellow sailors were spending most of their time talking about girls and the conquests they were about to make the minute they set foot on shore in the small city of Colon. For most, it would be the first time after many months of forced celibacy. As in so many cities the port was in the poorest section of the town, and even before the gangplank was lowered we could hear the screeching calls of the prostitutes peddling their wares from the doorway of their crumbling shacks. Several of my fellow signalmen asked me to accompany them and I had no choice but to say yes, even though I was somewhat frightened and unsure of myself. I wondered just what I would do, and if I would be able to perform when the time came for "making out." After all, unlike all those bragging and experienced "studs," never shy about telling and retelling the details of their assorted affairs, I was a virgin and not at all sure just where my biological urges would take me. But I had to play the game and let them think that I was as excited as they were about this trip to eroticism.

I didn't have to wait very long because the lines moved fast, each prostitute giving about five minutes of her time for $2.00 per visit. When it was my turn I walked, with all the confidence I could muster, through the beaded curtain and found an older and very voluptuous woman in a pink slip sprawled out on a straw mattress, surrounded by garish religious symbols of the Virgin Mary and the baby Jesus. Hanging on one wall were several dreary paintings on flattened tin cans depicting various saints experiencing the pain and pleasure of stigmata. There was incense burning in a dish beside her, and an emaciated old dog lying in the corner of the tiny room. I immediately gave her the two dollars, and one to spare, and put my finger to my lips with a hushing sound. She seemed to know immediately that I didn't want to lie down next to her, and for what seemed like an endless five minutes we just held hands and stared at each other. I will always remember the feel of her gnarled fingers and her calm and rather bittersweet expression, as if this was just another moment in time, easily forgotten. When the time was up, I gently patted the dog, she smiled and kissed me on the cheek, and I left, showing signs of complete ecstasy to those anxiously waiting their turn outside.

This unforgettable and certainly decisive moment should have spoken volumes to me, and if I had any questions about where my sexual desires lay, this was just one more clue to the solutions I was searching for. But answers to life's questions just don't come that easily, particularly the kind that tormented me, and especially in those days back in the '40s. Even though my recollections of the flag bag incident with Joe Merriman were exciting, stimulating and decidedly positive, as compared to my rejection of the kindly whore in her dismal hovel, I still felt I had to conform to what society called normal. Even with all the questioning and confusion, I was certain that once I was married everything would straighten itself out, and those strange and unusual desires would disappear.

The last time I had heard our band play was during the burials at sea. But this was a much happier occasion as we sailed into Boston Harbor, being greeted by fire boats spraying water in all directions and thousands of people waving and cheering along the shore. It was as if we had just won the World Series! We were dressed in our immaculate "whites," standing "at ease" on all quarters of the ship. I guess we looked like the recruiting poster, but there were a lot of scars behind our fixed expressions. I'm sure it was a wondrous sight to all those friendly faces along the shore, just as it was a beautiful and moving experience to all of us aboard the gallant New Mexico. And on this glorious October day we had trouble holding back our tears of joy. We were safely home and back with our loved ones. But I was deeply disappointed when I received a message that Mother and Dad had chosen not to join the crowds, but would remain in the Copley Plaza Hotel, and that I should meet them there. I guess it was a minor thing, but seeing my friends in the arms of their loving families as we came down the gangplank left me with a moment of loneliness and despair on this otherwise festive occasion.

CHAPTER NINETEEN

Each month that I served in the Navy I was paid a small salary (I can't even remember what it was), and like all those in the armed forces, I was also given a $10,000 free life insurance policy, which was fortunately never collected on and which I still have. The money I earned was stashed away, and very little of it was spent because there was nothing to spend it on except chocolate bars and ice cream. The ice cream had run out long ago, but fortunately there were plenty of chocolate bars for me to live on during the long trip home. And I was glad I had some money because I wanted to buy some nice gifts for Mother and Dad and, of course, Libby. How faithful they had been, along with Grandma, in writing to me regularly, even though they were never quite sure where I was, and whether I was alive or dead. Grandma had one child and seven grandchildren in the service and overseas, and must have been writing letters to someone almost every day.

After my expedition to the Colon slums, and being astounded by what people would do for the almighty Yankee dollar, I was talked into making a quick visit to an exhibition, at the cost of a mere fifty cents a head, to see a young girl and a donkey having sex together. The crowd around the small stage was three deep, with some of the men cheering wildly while others had startled looks on their intense faces. I was totally repulsed and even a bit sick in my stomach, and left hurriedly to do my shopping. I found a very nice small department store and, after some looking around, bought a leather lined alligator purse for Mother, a fancy silver cigarette lighter for Dad, and an onyx heart shaped pendant, with a small diamond in the center, for my dear Libby. The clerks probably saw me coming and over-charged for everything, but I didn't care because I was going home and would have brought everyone the moon and stars if they weren't so far away.

It was late in the afternoon of the day we arrived in Boston when my father actually touched me for the first time in memory. When I entered his suite at the Copley Plaza Hotel he embraced me and gave me a kind of awkward but affectionate hug and pat on the back, while tears of joy rolled down Mother's face. She was hardly able to speak, nor was I, as we just mumbled a lot of "How are yous," and "I'm fines." But it was a joyous moment and one that I will always remember as being very special, for at that moment I was quite possibly closer, both physically and emotionally, to my mother and father than I ever had been before. I had caused them so much grief and heartache, but I knew at that moment they sincerely loved me and were trying very hard to show it even though it was awkward for them.   And all my misbehaving had been forgotten while they worried, and even prayed, for my safe return.

As for the gifts, Dad didn't use his lighter very often, but I recall Mother carrying her purse until the lining was in shreds. I had shore leave for the rest of that first evening and Dad thought, as a welcome home gift to me, and considering how thin I was, that I would enjoy a good steak dinner and an evening of entertainment at the nightclub downstairs in the hotel.

The Incomparable Hildegarde (as she was known) was performing and she was at the peak of her illustrious career, wearing her long white gloves as she played the piano and serenaded the international social set with her signature ballad, "Darling, Je vous aime beaucoup, je ne sais pas, what to do…" I had heard her on the radio, promoting Raleigh cigarettes and the coupons that came with each pack. I didn't want to be unappreciative of Mother and Dad's plans, but Hildegarde didn't particularly excite me the way Billie Holiday or Anita O'Day would have, and I wasn't so sure about how I would handle a big, three course dinner. But the prospect of an evening "on the town" sure was better than what I had been used to.

The management must have known there would be a returning sailor in the audience that night because we were ushered to a table right next to the little platform where Hildagarde would be performing at her grand piano. I picked my way through dinner just as I had so many times when I was growing up, only this time my father, instead of nagging me, just glared and said nothing. I just wasn't used to all that rich food and had trouble getting it down. I weighed only 129 pounds, or about 25 pounds less than when I had left home, and my father was determined to fatten me up as quickly as possible.

When Hildagarde asked me to sit beside her on the piano bench, in a blinding spotlight and in front of what seemed like hundreds of people, I must have looked like a pathetic figure in my ill-fitting navy blues. With her long, delicate fingers stroking me, she sang love songs in my ear, hugged my skinny body, kissed me on the cheek, and tried to coax some of my war experiences out of me. I tried hard to go along with her, and help her with her routine, but I'm sure I was a complete dud, mumbling about the hard life aboard ship and the terror of Kamikaze attacks. She probably hurried through her performance just to get rid of me. Near the end, I heard a girl's voice in the back of the glittering three tiered dining room call out in a loud voice, "Why that's Chummy Dale!" Oh, that name again! Because of the bright lights, it took a moment to locate where the voice was coming from, but when I saw an arm waving I could see it was an old friend from dancing class, Ann Ewing, who was studying at Radcliffe College in Boston at the time. I was mortified and didn't mean to be rude, but I barely waved back.

I got a lot of applause that night, but it was one of the worst and most embarrassing experiences I have ever had and one that I just wasn't able to cope with at that particular time. I guess it was because of what I learned shortly thereafter; that I was severely undernourished and suffering from complete exhaustion. Yes, I was back in the states in one piece, but I wasn't ready to resume the life that I had been looking forward to for so long. But I was sure that a trip to Haverford the following weekend, to see Libby and all my friends, would be the perfect cure. It wasn't.

CHAPTER TWENTY

He was just lying there on his side looking at me, when I came into my room. He had gotten much grayer around his snout and his nose was very dry. The minute I had entered the house I had run up the stairs to see him. Dad had warned me that he was very weak and that he had to carry him down to the kitchen to eat, and outside to do his duty. My dear dog, Dolph, could barely stand up, but when he realized who it was when he heard my voice, he tried. I hugged and kissed him, and he started to nuzzle me like he always did after we finished playing together. I slowly patted him and told him how much I missed him, and loved him, and then he fell off to sleep. The next day, my oldest and dearest friend died. We had been together since I was three, and he was the only one of all my friends, both boy and girl, who gave me unconditional love, without any questions. Dad said he refused to die until he saw me and knew I was safely home. We buried him, with his favorite tennis ball, in a dog cemetery that had only a few graves left for big dogs like Doberman Pinchers. It was a nice spot, under an oak tree.

That happened on my first trip back home to Haverford, and it is the clearest memory I have of all the excitement that weekend. Actually, it was the first day of a one week leave from the New

Mexico, and it wasn't soon enough. I really needed a change, from that huge gray steel floating home, to the warm comfort of our house on Rose Lane, and some rest, hot food and a thorough medical check-up by Doctor Boles, our family doctor. With a big smile, he said I would "live," if I would only start being sensible and think about taking care of myself. But he said it was going to take a while and warned me that it might be difficult at times. And he was right. On several occasions in the coming days I just broke down and cried for no reason at all. One night, at the Zanzibar night club in New York City, where Dad and Mother had come to meet me half-way between Boston and Philadelphia for a big night on the town, I silently sobbed while Maurice Rocco was playing the piano and the Ink Spots were singing. Maybe the song, "Into Each Life a Little Rain Must Fall" was too much for me to deal with at that particular moment.

As I pulled into the driveway, Libby ran across the lawn with her arms wide apart and her face beaming with joy and happiness. She hugged and kissed me and held me tight. I froze, arms at my side, and mumbled something about her being so lecherous, and pushed her away. What was I doing? What in the world had come over me? I can't imagine why such ugly words came out of my mouth after all the months of looking forward to seeing her and holding her in my arms. Was I embarrassed by the attention? Was I so stressed out that I just couldn't handle her exuberant display of affection? Or was I simply turned off by her? I guess I'll never know and it might have been a combination of all those things. She was instantly startled, but then seemed to recognize that I was not the same person that she had loved so passionately and who had been in her dreams for those seemingly endless days and nights that I had been away. I gave her the gift I had brought her but things just weren't the same after that moment, and we slowly drifted apart.

I was different and Libby could sense it, and what was somewhat surprising to me is that I didn't miss not being with her every minute, nor did I miss her complete domination of my life. I was almost glad that she was dating other boys and I was perfectly happy, at least until all my friends had returned from the service, just being with my neighbors the Connetts, and good old Lily Cresswell, my dear friend from childhood. She was already at Bennington College by then, and on one of her visits home I told her about the incidents in Panama. She was so intrigued and horrified that she had to write all about "Chum's Adventures" in the college newspaper.

Each Sunday night, on those weekends when I was home on leave, it would end at 30th Street Station in Philadelphia where I would catch the midnight train back to Boston which arrived, with luck, at 8 AM, just in time for me to report back aboard ship. Even though there were compartments and sleeping cars for those who could afford it, my meager Navy stipend could buy me no more than a plain old coach seat. So I would sleep in the overhead baggage rack, and the passengers and the conductor, being kind to the world weary sailor, would often cover me with their coats to make sure that I was comfortable and warm.

It seemed there was nothing to do aboard ship except to chip paint. And that is all we did all day long, hanging over the side of the hull on precarious platforms. It was tedious, boring work and during the winter months, bitterly cold. But on most of the nights I was free to have fun in Boston, and with a good friend, Jack Hough, from Wheeling, West Virginia, we went to the dance palaces, drank a lot of beer, picked up girls, and danced to the music of Bobby Sherwood's band. I was quite a picture in my new, tight fitting sailor suit, with severe bellbottoms. But the times when Jack went home with a girl, I said I was tired, and returned to the ship. It was always in my thoughts that I would have gladly changed places with her, but I know Jack didn't see it quite that way.

He did love baseball though, like I did, and in the spring we formed a ship's softball team that played in a league against other ships and Navy Yard personnel. There was one very special time together when we went to Fenway Park and saw a preseason game between the Red Sox and my beloved Philadelphia Phillies. We had great seats, right behind home plate, and saw, closeup, the Phils star rookie, Del Ennis, hit two home runs over the green monster. What a day! But the Phils lost, as usual.

One weekend Jack came home to Haverford with me to see a Phillies-Pittsburgh Pirates game and to attend, as my guest, the coming-out party of one of Libby's close friends, Hennie Lazar. The Pirates were Jack's team but unfortunately the game was rained out. Not so the party, however, and Jack, with his good looks and simple hillbilly innocence and charm brought more excitement to the affair than the Main Line debutante scene had experienced in a long time. Even Libby, amidst her whirl of new boyfriends, was totally smitten. I knew exactly how she felt!

I was discharged in May, 1946 in Boston after spending seven months aboard the New Mexico in dry dock. Chief Signalman Tony Carter, the man who had made life almost bearable when he chose me to be one of his flag wavers, wrote a very nice letter of commendation about me, saying how dedicated and conscientious I was. He thought it might help in gaining future employment.

When I saluted the colors, asked the officer of the day for permission to leave the ship, and walked down the gangplank for the last time, I wasn't sorry to bid farewell to the New Mexico. But I must say I was saddened when I read, a few years later, that she was being scrapped in the Brooklyn Navy Yard. It wasn't because I chipped all that paint just so she would look presentable for her burial, but that my "home" for nearly two years was being demolished. I gave a silent cheer when I learned that two of the loyal sailors on board the ship, while it was being towed from Boston to New York, cut the tow lines, and it was adrift for several hours in the Atlantic. A final fling for that majestic Queen of the Fleet. God speed, old girl!

CHAPTER TWENTY-ONE

The whole time I was at sea on the New Mexico, I never heard, not even once, the infamous Tokyo Rose. I never listened to the recordings of the big bands and the pop singers she broadcast over her own radio band. Nor was I ever mesmerized by her supposedly sultry voice delivering propaganda messages against the United States war effort. The word around from all those who had heard her was that the litany of invidious musings were pretty ludicrous, but that the music was just fine. If the purpose was to make the servicemen and women a little bit homesick, and to want to quit fighting, it surely didn't work. There was never any lack of courage or a lessening of commitment to defend our country and win the war against the Japanese.

And I never saw one USO show up close, although while we were anchored a few hundred yards from land, following the battle of Leyte Gulf, I was able to watch (with the extra powerful binoculars that were always available on the signal bridge) Louis Jordan and the Tympani Five giving a concert on the beach. How I longed to be among the men and women on shore to see him play and sing "G. I. Jive" or "Is You Is Or Is You Ain't Ma Baby," but from where I was I could just barely hear the band above the noise of the screeching gulls circling the ship looking for our garbage to be thrown overboard into the bay.

The record collection in my room when I returned home was just where I had left it, neatly catalogued by band name or singer, with Louis Jordan among them. I don't know how many I had, but I'd been collecting them ever since I was about thirteen. Libby, and everybody else, said that I was a good dancer; maybe it was because I had practiced so much in front of the mirror listening to my records, with Dolph watching me with a curious eye. The kind of dancing I liked I didn't really do at the Friday evening dancing classes, but I guess the basics, like the waltz and the fox-trot had to be learned, and I certainly did meet a lot of girls there who flattered me when they expressed their love for dancing with that "tall, dark and handsome boy." The "lovelies" I had picked up at the dance palaces in Boston were, at best, mediocre partners, and now being home there were lots of parties to attend, in the company of my returning friends, where I could brush up on my dancing skills. Of course, when Libby was my partner I was at my best, but more and more I began to see a few other girls and, even though they didn't measure up to Libby, it was kind of nice being with a group and not tied down to one person as I had been while a student at Haverford. Of course, the lingering thoughts of same sex relationships were always present in the inner corridors of my psyche, but "playing the field" kept those playful hormones active in a more traditional way.

One night Tommy Ligget and I took Hennie Lazar to the movies, and we ended the evening with some heavy petting in my father's car during the "goodnights" in front of her house. The next morning at the breakfast table Dad, with one of his sterner looks, presented me with a "falsie" in front of my mother and my brothers and Joe, the butler. He had found it on the front seat and held it out between his thumb and forefinger as if it were alive and about to bite him. It had obviously escaped from Hennie's brassiere during our love making, and come to think of it, she needed all the help she could get. I did return it to her, and her embarrassment couldn't possibly equal what I experienced while eating my Wheaties that morning.

My first summer at home after discharge from the Navy was mainly dedicated to Summer School studies so that I would officially be a Haverford School graduate. But fortunately I didn't have to attend classes. I think that the teachers were anxious for me to get my diploma, and they let me do my work at my own pace in my own home and just trusted me to prepare for the exams that I would take before the regular school started. And this time I didn't let anyone down, not my mother and father or my friends or the Haverford School. At a special ceremony in front of the whole upper school, I and a few others whose studies had been interrupted by the war, finally graduated. Mother was there for the occasion, but not surprisingly, Dad was too busy to attend.

Even though I was graduating in the fall of 1946, I was still considered to be in the class of 1944, and that meant a great deal to me. One of the senior members of the faculty told me, years later, that in the opinion of many, the class of '44, the smallest class in the school's recent history, was also its most distinguished. And to this day, I am very proud to be a member of such an extraordinary group of outstanding men.

CHAPTER TWENTY-TWO

When all my Haverford friends went off to college that fall, I was at loose ends again. My next door neighbor, Hugh Connett, was in the same boat, and we began to think about making a tour of some colleges, with a plan to enter the following January. But to be honest, our hearts weren't really in it, at least mine wasn't, and even though we did visit several we were told, in a less than encouraging tone, that there was a waiting list for people with mediocre academic records like ours.

While we became more and more restless trying to determine just what the next move should be, we would go out and have a few beers at night, mostly at Billy Krechimer's little jazz joint in a narrow alley off Market Street in Philadelphia. Billy played the clarinet like Artie Shaw, and often had visiting musicians sitting in with him during his jam sessions. And once we saw Frank Sinatra performing at the Click, an overly ornate night club with mirrors everywhere and boasting the longest bar in the world. Sinatra was at a low point in his singing career and had not yet received the Oscar for best supporting actor in *From Here To Eternity*. There was only a handful of people in the club, but even with a bad throat, and sipping his honey tea, he gave his all and sounded great to us. We sat just a few feet from him and felt the presence of greatness.

Another time we drove for an hour and a half, all the way to a dingy little club in Wildwood, New Jersey to see Ella Fitzgerald. She was in her "scat" singing phase, which I didn't really like. The night we were there she was so disgusted with the attendance and the audience response, she cursed and walked off the stage after singing only three songs. Again, being almost a private audience to one of popular music's brightest stars is a moment to be cherished.

It was on one of those nights, after many beers, while we sat in my car in front of his driveway, halfway up the long hill to my house, that I told Hugh my dark secret for the second time. I told him, to put it bluntly, that I enjoyed engaging in sexual activities with men, that it hadn't happened very many times, but recalling each incident over and over gave me great pleasure. I told him these desires kept resurfacing and that I had been living with them ever since I was a young boy. This time he didn't slough it off as alcohol induced palaver. He stared at me coldly, then shrugged his shoulders, and without a word got out of the car and walked through the courtyard to his front door. I don't know what I had expected nor did I know what I wanted. Was it sympathy and a friend's understanding, and even acceptance? Or was it that I wanted him? I was stunned by his silent departure and was left to struggle with my apparent "queerness."

I shed a lot of tears that night and didn't see much of Hugh in the days following. I went back to living alone with my demons and my fantasies, wondering what this strange double life meant and where it would lead me. Wouldn't marriage and having sex on a regular basis with a woman be the answer? I'd always been sure that it would. How could I possibly desire other men when my wife would be the most important person in my life?

But instead of continually brooding, I slowly began to realize that I must do something positive with my days instead of thinking about myself all the time, and worrying and wondering about something I really did not understand and had no control over. Getting busy and involved was essential to relieving some of the burden I was carrying. And that fortuitous change came almost immediately.

One time when Hugh and I were muddling over our future plans, he had suggested that perhaps I could use my athletic skills assisting in coaching football at the Montgomery Country Day School. It was the school he had attended as a child before going off to boarding school. Now, with nothing in particular to do and the fact that I was not terribly interested in going to college, at least not right away, the idea of a coaching job seemed like a perfect interim solution to my anxious and troubled mind.

Miss Louise Ratledge, the co-headmistress of the school, was one of the most unusual and special characters I ever met. She, along with Miss Ann Almy, a fellow teacher, had saved a failing school by making it smaller, only grades K through 8, and co-educational. This was something unheard of in private school education in the 1940's, except for a few Friends schools, which were quite specialized and very small. The Interacademic League schools, of which The Montgomery School had been a long-time member, along with Episcopal and Haverford, were all boys, and were the socially and academically acceptable schools for those of us whose parents chose private school education for their children, and who lived in that beautiful northwestern section of suburban Philadelphia—the Main Line.

I remember playing against Montgomery in junior sports when I was at Episcopal Academy, and always liked the boys I had met from there, some of whom having had attended the same dancing class at the Merion Cricket Club. But apparently the school had suffered through some poor administration and was about to close when Miss Almy and Miss Ratledge, stepped in and saved at least a part of it, renaming it the Montgomery Country Day School. It featured small classes with individual attention, had no dress code and didn't require the purchase of a school sweater as did the others. There was a broad range of students with varying scholastic aptitudes and it was freewheeling and quite progressive, at least compared to the schools I had attended.

From my very first day there I knew this was a place where I would be welcomed. I loved the ambiance and the lack of pressure. Miss Ratledge said she didn't know anything about football but that she was sure I would be a great help on the athletic field and that there were lots of other odd jobs that she knew I could handle. I was asked to start immediately, but without pay, at least for the time being. And so the first small steps were taken in pursuing a career as an educator, something that was about as far from anything I would have expected, considering my dismal academic history.

My first contact with young children started with assisting Alfie Hare, the athletic director, with the sports activities each afternoon. With only about 125 kindergarten through eighth grade students and about half of them under nine years old, there wasn't much of an athletic program, at least not like the ones I had been familiar with, but we did have a six man football team that played games against the Church Farm School for Orphaned Boys and The Pennsylvania School For The Deaf, along with several other small schools in the area.

I loved this wide open innovation to the traditional eleven man team, which I had been a part of all through school. And Alfie was a marvelous teacher and coach of the young boys, with just the right mix of skilled instruction, along with compassion and understanding for the various degrees of enthusiasm and ability. As a result of my father and brother Ted's constant pressure, I had grown up believing that winning was all important, and it was not easy for me to learn from him that games should be fun, and only just that, a game. Sportsmanship and team play were far more important than the outcome of the contest.

Miss Ratledge had a small farm in Delaware, and used to bring calves and goats and chickens to the school for the youngest children to study and play with. She transported them back and forth in an old "woodie" Ford Station Wagon, with lots of hay in the back. When they arrived at the school they lived in a miniature stable which she had built herself, attached to the kindergarten building. One of my jobs, in addition to coaching, was to drive that station wagon each morning and evening to pick up and deliver children who lived in outlying areas and who needed transportation.

Those early morning journeys were sometimes a little hard to manage, what with a bit of a hangover on those nights when I was out cavorting with friends, and the ever present animal odors from the back of the wagon. But I loved the kids, and as long as they didn't mind the smell, I could live with it.

In addition to her animal kingdom and agricultural interests, Miss Ratledge was a brilliant mathematician and kept an elaborate set of accounting ledgers that only she could understand. She hurried around the halls of this oak paneled converted mansion with her slip always hanging below the hem of her less than stylish dress, trying to conduct two mathematics classes at once and tend to the school's finances at the same time. And Miss Almy, the more dignified and gracious of the two, quietly taught fifth grade, and presented a more appealing personality to the parents and those benefactors who would hopefully contribute to the school's support. It was difficult for them to turn any prospective students away, not only because they needed the tuition money in order to survive, but because they genuinely wanted to educate children from all backgrounds and ethnic roots. It was a very special place and I was delighted to be a part of it.

CHAPTER TWENTY-THREE

It was the winter of 1946 when things really began to change. Mary Snider, the fourth grade teacher became seriously ill and I was asked to help out in the classroom, teaching, of all things, Greek Mythology. This was an extraordinary turn of events, considering that I had barely graduated from high school and could never be considered, by any stretch of the imagination, a scholarly individual. Actually, the teaching amounted to reading stories and having class discussions of the exploits of heroic Greek characters like Hercules, and the never-ending battles of the courageous Helen of Troy. I loved teaching, and loved the children. They seemed to feel the same about me and it wasn't long before I was given additional responsibilities arranging extracurricular activities, such as school parties and the annual school fair, and my first venture into the world of creativity, directing the school plays.

But sports were really my specialty, and if I was to become a regular coach and teacher I needed at least to be working towards a college degree. Alfie Hare, a graduate of the University Of Pennsylvania, helped me to get accepted into the School of Education and I immediately started taking classes at night. Libby had gone off to Cornell and most of my other friends were attending Yale and

Princeton. And here I was going to an Ivy League college as well! What a piece of good fortune.

Aside from a few weekend visits, I didn't keep in as close touch with my friends as I would have liked, and was fairly oblivious to most of what was going on with their lives at the various colleges. Knowing about their pursuits became less and less important to me, as I was busy doing my job at Montgomery, taking classes at night, and being totally captivated by Amy Bell, the school secretary and jack-of-all-trades. She had come there at the suggestion of one of the teachers, Bessie Crispin, who was a distant cousin and wanted to help her, with special tutoring, to gain a high school diploma while working in the office. Amy was unlike anybody I had ever known, and so very appealing to me.

Almost from the first day of my coaching duties, I had noticed this petite beauty, with her long black hair, deep brown eyes and captivating smile, sitting in the school office typing away. Neither the children, nor their parents, or the teachers who constantly interrupted her work with their problems and requests seemed to faze her. She handled it all with such ease, and never appeared to get the least bit flustered. I would hang out around her desk whenever I could and she didn't seem to mind, particularly when I helped her with the cumbersome, hand driven duplicating machine.

Often, we would meet in the school kitchen where our dear friends Dorothy, the cook, and her husband Napoleon, the handyman, presided, and smoke a cigarette and laugh with them at the many hilarious events that filled every school day. One of my best friends was their dog Rex who not only guarded them and their kitchen, but was there to watch over the whole school as well. The fact is that these little meetings were the beginning of my dating Amy, but because her home was so far from mine, and not on the Main Line, we were together only on weekends, usually spending most of our time in the Philadelphia suburb of Chestnut Hill, where she lived.

Our growing up years had been so different, even though we were about the same age, and discovered, or so Amy did, that we were fifth cousins on both our mothers' side, a fact Amy proudly announced to me one day shortly after we first had met at one of Miss Almy's after school faculty tea parties. She even referred to my grandmother as Cousin Lucie.

Amy was one of six Bell children in a gentle and loving family and I could tell from almost our very first meeting that she was quite content and comfortable with herself, with seemingly very few worries. Unlike me, she seemed to have grown up with a minimum of real problems, but then, she wasn't prone to talk much about herself. Her father had retired from the business world when he was quite young, and the family had lived pretty much on what he had inherited, which included a very large stone house dating back several generations. There was hardly enough income to raise such a large family in the style befitting their affluent neighborhood on Evergreen

Avenue in Chestnut Hill, so Amy had gone to public schools and had to do part time work to contribute to the family's resources. I slowly learned that her values were very different, and more meaningful, than mine. She cared about important things; not the frivolous pursuits of my rather elitist private school upbringing.

The Bells, who were avid pacifists, were a caring family, about each other and about all people. After the bombing of Pearl Harbor, when most people hated and feared the Japanese, they gave shelter to several Japanese Americans who otherwise might have been sent, with many thousands of others, to detention camps. Her father, unlike mine, was more dedicated to his family and to his ideals than being possessed with a need to make a lot of money. And he was always there for his daughter, Amy.

I loved spending time with her family. There was always music on the radio, and with libretto in hand, we listened attentively to the Saturday afternoon Metropolitan Opera broadcasts with Milton Cross, the commentator, "proclaiming" the entire story of each opera, the characters in it and the singers portraying them. He loved pronouncing the names of the European singers with a linguistic flourish, and even gave some of the American performers' names an international twist.

Amy and I spent a lot of time together in the large kitchen, where her mother presided, with two huge cats watching her every move. How different everything was compared to my home in Haverford. There, the kitchen was not a friendly place and when I was growing up I was told not to bother the cook, to select a coke and cookies and then leave as quickly as possible. But at the Bells it was warm and inviting, a gathering place where we sat around the kitchen table, nibbling and chatting, and occasionally commenting about the cooking.

Amy's five brothers and sisters all seemed to care about each other and about the concerns of people everywhere. The conversation was usually about something significant, generally somewhat liberal in nature. I remember clearly them deploring the use of an atomic bomb to end the war in Japan, but otherwise respecting our president, Harry Truman. They even embraced some of the philosophy of Norman Thomas, an avowed Socialist. In addition to all of this, the food was delicious and I can't remember not finishing everything on my plate. There wasn't really much reason for us to go out.

One of these days at the Bells was particularly special. Amy, along with her father, accepted my proposal of marriage, and I gave her a small diamond engagement ring, a Dale family heirloom that had been left to my father by his grandmother. Mother and Dad thought I was too young and unsettled to get married, but they liked Amy and were delighted that she came from an old and respected Philadelphia family. Reluctantly they offered their support. The few times when both sets of parents were together any social or political discussions were studiously avoided and the meetings were decidedly non confrontational.

Now that I was attending the University Of Pennsylvania (albeit at night), my old football captain and good friend at Haverford School, Artie Littleton, invited me to join the St. Elmo fraternity. Even though I'm sure he never completely forgave me for stealing his steady girlfriend, Libby Severinghaus, away from him, we remained good, close friends, and he was someone I greatly admired. Working all day at Montgomery and going to classes at night didn't leave much time for fraternity life, even though I went through the whole ridiculous process of fraternity initiation. I thought it was a pretty big deal at the time, and Amy and I did go to a few fraternity parties after the football games. I think I enjoyed them a lot more than she did, whooping it up with the boys. But she was a good sport and made the best of these boisterous, and often drunken celebrations, whether Penn won or lost.

I was constantly reminded, in my own mind, as well as by others, that I had to be working towards a college degree in order to continue teaching, but sometimes I was so tired at the end of the day, and night, that I wanted to give it all up. My responsibilities at the school had greatly increased from just coaching and that initial introduction to teaching in the fourth grade classroom reading the stories of the Greek Gods and Goddesses. From there I had moved on to becoming the home room teacher for the sixth grade, and had classes in English,

Geography, and Science. I worked studiously at staying a few jumps ahead of the kids and just loved the interaction with them. Being only about ten or eleven years older, there was a rapport and an easy and comfortable sense of community that perhaps an older teacher might not have had. I loved my work so much that I pushed myself as hard as I could to try and complete my studies at Penn in as short a time as possible.

One nice change of pace from this daily grind was when Amy took me to see my first opera, *Tosca*, at the Philadelphia Academy of Music. We sat way up in the peanut gallery where the "clacks" led the applause and where the real opera buffs held court during the intermissions. Amy's mother had been a "spear carrier" when she was young, during several seasons at the Metropolitan Opera in New York City, and she and Amy were so pleased that I enjoyed my first experience at the opera and that I had become aware that there was something more than just the voices of Peggy Lee and Dick Haymes and the progressive sounds of Stan Kenton.

Music was an important part of my early years and I had spent what I considered a few very special evenings listening to music on the radio with my father. He used to love to pretend he was the conductor of the orchestra, waving his arms in time with the music. But the closest thing to trained operatic voices were the featured soloists on the *Manhattan Merry-Go-Round* or *The Bell Telephone Hour*. Giuseppe Verdi and Giacomo Puccini might just as well have been two of Grandma's Italian gardeners for all I knew about the great opera composers. But I was learning, and realizing more and more how limited my knowledge was of the more lasting and worthwhile things in life. I couldn't figure out why I appealed to Amy, but I wasn't about to raise any doubts.

The many pieces of my puzzling past seemed to be fitting together, and I was sure that our pending marriage, dedication to my work at Montgomery, and my studies at night school would finally drive away the strange and bewildering demons that had succeeded in intruding on, and affecting, my daily existence for so long.

CHAPTER TWENTY-FOUR

How could I ever forget the unanimous decision that the Lobster Newberg, served over toast points, was delicious! It certainly should have been considering it was prepared, at great expense, by the senior chef at the Warwick Hotel in Philadelphia. It was one of my father's favorite dishes and he often took visiting business associates for lunch there just so they could sample it. Now, as a result of his being such a good and generous patron, large kettles of it were transported to Haverford for the rehearsal dinner for Amy and me, family members, and those who would be participating in our wedding the next afternoon. There were about thirty guests gathered at Hillandale, out on our spacious terrace high on the hill above Rose Lane, enjoying the pre-wedding celebration featuring Dad's imported gourmet delight.

My friends always enjoyed my father's sense of humor, and he was a gracious host, but I knew in my heart that this was a "send-off" party for me. I'm sure he was not a bit sorry to see me leave the nest and clear out that noisy, smoke filled bedroom next to his office.

And now our big day was at hand, the day of commitment. The day of consummating Amy's and my love for each other. The day that would hopefully end all the turmoil that had existed in my mind for so long. And the day that those moments of pleasure fantasizing

119

about male intimacy, and the pain of worrying about my seemingly abnormal tendencies, would be gone forever and always. This was surely the most important day of my life.

Our wedding was held at the Unitarian Church in Germantown, with the reception at the Bell's home in Chestnut Hill. Poor Mr. and Mrs. Bell not only had to prepare for our wedding in August of 1948, but Amy's sister, Sylvia, had been married in June of that same year at a nearby Quaker Meeting House. Our wedding was a bit more elaborate than hers, with about one hundred and fifty guests at the garden party reception. It was a particularly hot August day, with the temperature reaching one hundred degrees, and my father's brand new tan linen suit was completely soaked in perspiration before the ceremony even began.

I wore a white linen suit and my eight ushers were very nattily dressed in white ducks and blue blazers, with white buck shoes. They were all my closest Haverford friends...Tommy and Spider, Sam and Jimmy. As the years passed, I was an usher in their weddings as well, but they were more formal and elaborate affairs with the appropriate dress being a cutaway or a tuxedo.

My beautiful bride, and her bridesmaids, were stunning in their flowing gowns, in spite of the heat, and even Grandma Lord, dressed all in ice blue from flowered hat to matching satin shoes, didn't seem to wilt as she held court under an oak tree in the Bell's small terrace and garden.

Our wedding day

(LtoR) Ben, Spider, Artie, Jimmy,
Sam, Tommy, Bro. Jack, Homer

The champagne flowed and the watercress tea sandwiches were in abundance; I was sure the wedding was quite a financial burden for Amy and her parents. But to me it seemed just perfect, and I was most grateful for all that they had done. Being very distant relatives, the Bells were anxious to make all of my family members comfortable, and they did it beautifully and with apparent ease and grace. A special welcoming touch on that hot August afternoon was a glass of iced tea, served in frosted glasses to the guests as they waited to pass through the receiving line. Although Amy had gotten to know many of my friends, and liked most of them, I wanted so much for them to see that things were just as idyllic on the other side of the Schuylkill River in Chestnut Hill as they were on the Main Line.

My brother Ted, who was still single and a senior at Yale, was my best man. Whether I considered him my "best man" was really not important. It was the thing to do. His only major function, aside from handing me the wedding ring during the ceremony at the church, was to reserve a hotel room at the Plaza Hotel in New York City for our wedding night, before our honeymoon flight to Bermuda the next morning. I think there were only a few non-airconditioned rooms in the hotel, and much to our chagrin he managed to reserve one of them! I know it wasn't on purpose but perhaps he should have inquired. Air conditioning just couldn't be taken for granted in those days.

Amy and I spent most of our time sitting by the window trying to breathe, and after the hot, dirty train ride from Philadelphia—devoted mostly to wiping off the sticky confetti that "Spider" had thrown through the train window—we were pretty dragged out, even after a short carriage ride in Central Park. We were not exactly in the proper disposition to make love, but we did, although somewhat awkwardly, and married life began as it was supposed to. After worrying so much about not being able to perform properly on my virgin experience, I was amazed at even my limited dexterity, and was secretly elated as well; the huge burden on my shoulders having been lifted, at least for the moment.

CHAPTER TWENTY-FIVE

When we had announced that we were getting married, Miss Almy and Miss Ratledge, our guiding spirits, were beside themselves with joy, and all but told the world that Amy and Chum were made for each other. To show their delight, they offered us, as a wedding present, the charming little cottage on the Montgomery Country Day School grounds to live in, rent free, for one year. It had been, at one time, the gardener's cottage on the large estate which now belonged to the school.

The Bells had arranged for all of our many, and much appreciated, wedding presents to be delivered there, and mother had put in food and other necessities so that on our return from Bermuda we were ready to set up housekeeping, and go to work. We didn't have much furniture, and on the first Sunday morning in our new home Artie Littleton and his bride, Polly, joined us for waffles, made on our new waffle maker, a wedding gift they had given us. We all sat on the bare living room floor using our new china and silver. I had been picked to be the first in the class of '44 to be married, but Artie beat me to it by a few months and silently gloated over it as he devoured yet another waffle.

The one thing we didn't anticipate in our new home was that we were going to be responsible for a border. Montgomery had a few Monday through Friday boarding students living on the third floor of the main school building under Miss Ratledge's care, but Claudette, a thirteen year old, was in need of special attention, being somewhat slow, and it was thought best that she live with us. While I was attending night school, poor Amy had to deal with all of Claudette's early teenage angst, along with her painful shyness; not an easy task considering she was trying to make the cottage a comfortable home for the two of us. On weekends Claudette would be picked up by a giant limousine and delivered to her father, a mysterious gangster type who wore dark glasses and black silk suits. At the end of the year, thanks to Amy's careful nurturing, Claudette had shown a vast improvement, at least in her social graces, and to show his appreciation her father gave a large contribution to the school.

And so our married life began, but not without some difficulties. There was a lack of privacy, and when we were alone in our big double bed we were less than compatible, probably due, at least in part, to just plain fatigue. In addition, we had practically no money to do much entertaining or even go to the movies on the weekends. Our salaries were very small, mine alone being only $100 a month. I was so absorbed and involved with the kids in my sixth grade class that I spent many weekend days at birthday parties or short camping trips.

They seemed to want me to be with them as often as possible, and I enjoyed that. I felt very close to them, always wondering and hoping that my presence and friendly guidance was adding to their overall development. It was almost like being a big brother. Miss Almy had said to me once that seventy-five percent of being a good teacher is to have the respect and admiration of the children you are working with. Fortunately I did have that.

I also got to know many of the parents, and on one occasion two appreciative fathers asked if Amy and I would take their sons, all expenses paid, to Florida during the 1949 spring vacation, and visit the Philadelphia Phillies Spring Training Camp in Clearwater. I didn't need much persuading, and even though it turned out to be a bit of a bore for Amy sitting alone at the beach all day, I was in baseball heaven, watching up close and getting to know the team that I had loved all my life and who, unbeknownst to me at the time, was soon to win their first national league pennant since 1915. The two starry-eyed twelve year olds reminded me so much of myself at that age, watching and idolizing the players. Actually, my feelings weren't that different from theirs, enjoying every minute of the experience. But I was the same age as some members of the team and couldn't help myself from looking at the likes of the handsome Robin Roberts and the appealing Richie Ashburn from a slightly different, and more intimate and private perspective. A disturbing thought.

After our first year of marriage, and living in our three bedroom rent free cottage at the Montgomery Country Day School, Miss Almy and Miss Ratledge decided it was too big for us if we couldn't take on several additional boarding students. We had tried to tell them as nicely as we could that having borders was a little unsettling to a newly married couple trying to establish a happy home and a loving relationship. We didn't say that we were having enough troubles without the added distractions of young children running in and out of our bedroom.

So, we moved to an apartment over the garage, right next door to Dorothy and Napoleon, the oversized and jolly black couple whom we both adored. My mother and father's questioning of this cohabitation of the garage building with the service people at the school fell on deaf ears.

They didn't seem to understand that I was entering the "real" world and slowly emerging from the sheltered cocoon of Philadelphia suburbia that so many of us at Episcopal and Haverford grew up in. The mostly large, substantial homes that made up what was known as the Main Line extended from the town of Overbrook to Paoli, along a thirty mile stretch of Pennsylvania Railroad track. Aptly named the Paoli Local, there was a little electrically powered commuter train, originating in Philadelphia, that followed a nearly round the clock schedule, stopping at each of the fourteen towns which were only a few miles apart from each other. As if the passengers didn't know where they were going, at every stop the conductor rattled off the names of each of the succeeding towns like a laundry list; Overbrook … Merion … Narberth … Wynnewood … Ardmore Haverford … Bryn Mawr … Rosemont … Villanova … Radner … Wayne … Devon … Stratford … and Paoli. The return trip was the same, only in reverse. All of the towns were, for the most part, populated by wealthy upper class families who led somewhat sheltered lives in this Republican stronghold of conservatism and racial and ethnic intolerance.

The fathers rode the Paoli Local through the beautiful, rolling countryside to their banks or brokerage houses in Philadelphia, while the mothers, usually assisted by assorted household servants, tended to their immaculately kept homes in exclusive neighborhoods, and transported their children back and forth to the various private schools, dancing classes, and restricted country clubs.

This was the world that my friends and I knew, and deep-seated prejudices are not easily shaken. But since my relationship with Amy, and being a part of the Montgomery Country Day School family, most of whom were atypical, parents and teachers alike, my eyes were opening to a world of quite different values, values which I was becoming very attracted to.

But Amy and I, when time and finances allowed, did enjoy being with my friends and their new wives or current love interests, and it made me very proud that, almost to a person, they thought that Amy was delightfully different, and extremely amusing. The person I had selected to be my wife became just as close to them as I was. Some of their thoughts and beliefs might have been quite different from hers, but we all joked and giggled and didn't take life too seriously when we were together. Happy feelings and a lot of laughter can often be the best way to understand and accept diversity. What fun we had carousing at weekend house parties at classmate Ben Deacon's summer beach home in Seaside Heights, New Jersey! And we made a very special visit, along with Tommy Ligget and his new bride, Nancy, to Jimmy and Carol Roberts' family summer place. They always called it a "lodge," and it was truly that, nestled among the majestic pines along the rocky coast line of Southwest Harbor, Maine. Then there was Northeast Harbor across the bay, where we mingled with the likes of future president John F. Kennedy, and assorted Rockefellers, at the lavish dinner dance held at the historic and elegant Asticou Inn. It was here that my old friend "Tootie" Widener, the igloo girl from the debutante party days, fell into the pool in her evening dress when I told her I was married. She quite possibly had had a bit too much to drink.

Amy and I had decided, even before our marriage, not to try to have children for a while, and it was just as well because our love making, much of the time, was far from satisfactory right from the day of our wedding. I just wasn't very good at it, demons or no, and I guess one might say I was a bit of a "cold fish." We struggled with it, and grew increasingly unhappy when we were lying in bed side by side. Sometimes, when I was particularly uncomfortable, she would sense it and give me something I learned to dread, the silent treatment.

But life moves along at such a rapid pace that we hardly had time to dwell on this troublesome situation. I loved Amy so much, but just wasn't able to physically express that love very often. I started to become irritable and depressed, and thought a change of scenery from our home, our friends, and school life at Montgomery might help. Maybe spending the upcoming summer in the mountains on a lake, working at a boys camp might ease the situation. I had loved camp as a child and had always yearned to be a camp counselor. Or was it that I was just trying to run away, away from that other self?

Through a business contact of my father's, I was offered a job, at what I considered quite a substantial salary, to head the intermediate group at the rather exclusive Adirondack Camp For Boys, on Lake George in upstate New York. In addition to my group head responsibilities, I would be doing whatever tutoring was necessary of boys who needed some special help. This added assignment was something I was very comfortable with as I recalled those important days at Haverford summer school not that long ago. Amy was to be the camp secretary and would have her own private little cabin by the lake. It all seemed just perfect and we accepted the offer with much excited anticipation. But sadly, as it turned out, I was so busy with my daily activities that we were hardly ever alone together, and the arrangement was not at all conducive to improving our intimate relations, as we had hoped.

CHAPTER TWENTY-SIX

As I have been remembering all those years going back to my early childhood, I think it is important to mention two events that took place at Adirondack Camp that summer. At the time, I had no idea that in about ten years I would be entering into a relationship, one in which my partner would be a young man, and he would be Jewish. But in thinking back, perhaps what happened at the camp was a small but significant sign that I was heading in what turned out to be the right direction.

Early in the morning of the second day of camp, one of the junior counselors came running to tell me that he had been sexually fondled by his immediate superior, a recent high school graduate, the night before. There was no question that, as the senior staff man, it was my duty to report this unfortunate incident to the camp director, and the counselor was reprimanded and sent home immediately. I certainly didn't approve of what he had done but somewhere, deep in my heart, I somehow understood what had happened and I felt compassion for this likable young man, and I told him so. Except for the flag bag episode at the end of World War II when I was at sea on the New Mexico, it was the first time that I was able to relate to someone who I knew was dealing with similar kinds of demons as my own. Even though I didn't come right out and tell him, I think he might have gained just a little bit of comfort, hearing from someone older than him, that he wasn't a hateful person and was not alone in his troubled, and seemingly perverted world. I wanted to hug him before sending him on his way, but I didn't dare.

And the second event that is still with me happened near the end of camp. As is customary at most camps, there comes that time to give out the awards, and my choice for best camper in the intermediate group was Gerald Steinberg, a very personable young man who excelled in every facet of camp life. I was completely surprised when the director of the camp told me he could not give such a prestigious award "to a Jew;" that it would not be in the best interests of such a distinguished camp with the likes of actor Errol Flynn's son, Sean, as well as members of the socially prominent, and ultra-conservative, Knickerbocker Grays in attendance. I was at first dumbfounded, and then furious, and assured him I would not be returning the following summer. At that moment I recalled some of the distasteful remarks my father used to make at the dinner table, and I particularly remembered the time, while driving me to a friend's house when I was about thirteen, he asked why, of all the boys I knew, I had to associate with someone who was Jewish. I told him I didn't know my friend, Don Goodman, was Jewish, nor did I really care. Was my father teaching me to hate? If he was, I wasn't buying it.

In May of 1950, after much soul searching, I decided that teaching 6th Grade and coaching football, basketball and baseball at the Montgomery Country Day School, as well as going to night school at Penn in pursuit of a degree in education was more than I could handle. Even though Amy and I lived right at the school, the days were long and exhausting and by seven o'clock, when the evening sessions started, I was so tired that I began missing classes and knew then that my short teaching career, with only a high school diploma, was coming to an end. We loved it at Montgomery and these busy times were mostly very happy ones, as we both enjoyed the school life, working and living together, and dedicating all of our energies to a place that was so very appealing to both of us.

Between the unorthodox philosophy of the school, and my becoming aware, through Amy, of a whole new set of ideas and ideals, these were defining days that had a tremendous influence on my life and started me on a brand new and much more enlightened way of thinking and being. Miss Almy and Miss Ratledge said that I was a "born" teacher, even at age twenty-four, with the gift of patience and understanding and the ability to impart information with the greatest of ease. They said the children and their parents loved and respected me and it would be a shame if I were to give it up. And they surely would miss Amy, too, with her exceptional ability to run the school office and put off the bill collectors, as well as smooth the sometimes ruffled feathers of the rather eccentric teaching staff. But our stay was coming to an end.

Except for the ever present wayward fantasies that I kept forcing into a dark closet in my mind, my sexual urges were next to what society might consider to be the norm, at least for now, but I knew a change was needed and needed fast in order to preserve our marriage. We seemed to be slowly drifting apart and I was certain that it was my fault. What to do? Where to go?

We lived at the school for one more year as Amy continued in her job there while I made quite a bit of money working, for a short time, at a Hot Shoppe restaurant as a waiter delivering trays of food to people's cars and taking a lot of abuse from the customers. I hated it. Only Amy knew I was doing this and I was constantly afraid that some of my friends might drive in and see me there in my ridiculous carhop outfit. I knew this wasn't getting me anywhere. Then I sold life insurance for Prudential for six months and hated that too, taking advantage of the parents I knew from Montgomery. Even though I was quite good at it, I think the company was only using me for my contacts and I felt ashamed in a way, when I actually wasn't doing anything wrong. After I had exhausted this source of revenue and had to depend on searching for new clients, I quit. Once, I even sold my blood for the large sum of twenty-five dollars. I hope it helped who ever was the recipient to lead a happier and more constructive life than I was experiencing!

As the school year was coming to a close and Amy's job would be ending in a month or so, we would have no place to live. I was without a job and I certainly would not ask my father for financial help and he never offered any. I was not only responsible for myself, but for my wife as well, as she became increasingly anxious about our future. Some decisions, very important decisions, had to made, and made right away!

PART TWO

CBS, AMY AND ME

CHALMERS DALE

CHAPTER TWENTY-SEVEN

They had names like Photoplay and Silver Screen, with Janet Gaynor or Norma Sheerer on the cover. They were the movie magazines my mother either bought or brought home from the hairdresser. And I loved them, even when I was five years old and just starting to read. I hadn't seen any movies yet, but knew about them from those magazines. Twenty years later, when I saw Yul Brynner and Marlene Dietrich the first hour of the first day that I started to work for CBS, I knew I was in the right place.

While I was desperately trying to decide what to do with my life and figure out a way to support my wife Amy, and find a place for us to live now that our days at Montgomery Country Day School were about over, I remembered my first love, those movie magazines, and thought perhaps I should give show business a try. We had bought a television, even with our meager, combined income, and I laughed a lot watching *The Texaco Star Theater* with Milton Berle and hummed along as best I could with the lovely music on *The Firestone Hour*. And the more I watched, the more I dreamed of being a part of that wondrous world. And it was actually going to happen.

William Paley, the founder and CEO of CBS, had lived three doors away from us on Hathaway Lane in Wynnewood, but I didn't really know him because I was only two years old. However, my Aunt Helene Lord, who also lived there, knew him, and his friend and business associate Larry Loman, and when I called her and asked if she would arrange an appointment for me, she happily obliged. She had served with Mr. Loman in the Red Cross during World War II, in Paris, and knew he was a senior executive at CBS. She thought talking to him, rather than to Mr. Paley, would make more sense considering that the newspapers were constantly telling us how busy Mr. Paley was signing Hollywood stars to CBS contracts. He might not think I was important enough to see, even though we had something in common; we both once lived on Hathaway Lane.

I knew it would mean moving to New York City, away from our families and friends, but when the job was offered to me on that eventful day in May of 1951 I took it without even discussing it with Amy. There was no time for procrastination with television growing the way it was, and I was sure Amy would understand. Of course she did, but actually she didn't have much choice considering our desperate financial situation. The personnel man Mr. Loman sent me to had proclaimed rather forcefully, "Most new people don't make it here at CBS because they stare at the stars, and don't do their work. Don't be one of those star gazers, or you won't last six months." So when Yul Brynner and Marlene Dietrich walked by me while I was wrapping some film cans for shipment, I didn't look up, but I knew it was them.

And I knew I had made the right choice, a choice to enter into a business near its very beginning, a business which was to become one of the most significant in the world of communication in the 20th Century. I will be forever grateful to my Aunt Helene for changing the course of my life and helping make it possible for me to start on a new career, with Amy by my side, a career in an industry that grew to unimaginable heights. And I was there to grow along with it for forty unforgettable years.

I suppose everyone remembers their first day on a new job, and that first day at CBS was no exception, not because of the stars, but because of my anxiety about not being late. I had taken a room at the YMCA on West 63rd Street while I looked for an apartment. Amy would join me at the end of the school year at Montgomery Country Day School, and hopefully find a job herself. On that rainy Monday morning, not being sure how far I had to walk or how long it would take, I arrived at the CBS building a half hour early and couldn't get in. It was not the main building, the one where I had been interviewed, but a small, warehouse like structure on West 54th Street in the middle of what was known as Hell's Kitchen. I sat on the stoop in the rain, and when the others arrived I was drenched and looked like a lost waif. Nobody could believe that this droopy little lost soul was a new employee until my boss arrived and I was ushered to the shipping room, which was next to the screening room, which is why Yul Brynner and Marlene Dietrich were there.

In those days most of the network TV programs we saw were live, at least those of us within a 90 mile radius of New York City, and as they were broadcast they were filmed right off a TV set, and 16mm copies were sent to the stations around the country. My job was to wrap and label those kinescope recordings, or "kinnes" as they were called, and send them on their way. I was thrilled just to be handling the film containers, with names like *Toast Of The Town*, and *The Perry Como Show* written on the label. And one day after work, on my way back to the "Y", I wandered past the studio where *The Perry Como Show* originated. The stage manager, "Snooks" O'Brien recognized me as a CBS employee and invited me to come in and watch the telecast. I stood in the wings, right next to Bob Hope, barely able to breathe. He was the featured guest on the show that day, and he said hello to me. Little did I know that thirty years later we would meet again and this time he would say a little more than just a friendly greeting.

CHAPTER TWENTY-EIGHT

Having so little money and a fear of being swallowed up by this gigantic and seemingly impersonal city, my restaurant of choice for breakfast and supper was the YMCA cafeteria. And during that first month, I spent most nights in my little cubicle, reading the show business bible, *Variety*, page by page. There was a lot of news about things other than television, but it all seemed to interest me, and I was totally absorbed. I learned about box office receipts, station clearances, record sales, and who was where, and why.

Maybe it wasn't the least bit important to know that Errol Flynn was in New York for public appearances, but that particular bit of information caught my attention because I had known his son Sean at the summer camp where I had been a counselor two years before. I wondered if Sean was still a camper there, and if his father would go to see him while he was on the east coast. He was divorced from Sean's mother, Lily Damita, who used to spend the summer in a rented cottage across the lake from the camp to make sure, with her pair of powerful binoculars, that her son was being properly taken care of at camp. I do remember very clearly that Sean was as handsome as his father, but rather unhappy and confused. I had spent many hours with him trying to involve him in camp activities, but unlike his father's screen image, I remember him being awkward and shy.

But most of my reading didn't relate to anything I had ever experienced, and some of *Variety*'s "inside" language was like a foreign tongue. But I learned, and learned fast, because it was about the business I was in, and there was nothing at the "Y" to distract me. After a tiring day of lifting cartons and packing and unpacking, I longed to take a shower more regularly in the communal bathroom at the end of the hall. But the problem was that I was afraid of that fat, ugly man who sat behind his partially open door, almost naked, and who's eyes always seemed to focus on my crotch every time I walked past. What if he followed me into the shower room!

Although it intrigued me and I had not been able to completely suppress thoughts of male encounters since my early teens, I had only had a few, mostly juvenile, homosexual experiences and was not very knowledgeable about what I perceived as deviant behavior. I had been taught by the church it was a perversion, and completely unacceptable in society. I was horrified when one day I saw him coming down the hall at CBS. He smiled and winked, and nodded hello. I wasn't rude, but hung my head and pretended not to see him. It was always on my mind, and I couldn't stop thinking that it wouldn't be long before I'd be with my dear Amy, if I could only find an apartment we could afford and I could move out of the "Y" and away from those searching eyes.

I really didn't have time during my lunch break to do much of anything, let alone hunt for an apartment, and so I'd spend the few minutes I did have playing stickball in front of my building with the neighborhood kids on West 54th Street, munching on a tuna or egg salad sandwich as I ran the bases. I not only learned this street version of baseball, but a new language as well, the language of the street.

These scraggly, uncomplicated kids from Hell's Kitchen were unlike any I had ever known, and so very different from the people living on the Philadelphia Main Line, and yet I felt surprisingly comfortable with them. Maybe everything that I had been learning from Amy about making an effort to understand and appreciate people who were different from me was being realized. Whatever it was, it felt good and I knew that I would be perfectly happy living some place other than in the fancy Manhattan neighborhoods, with their doormen and lofty rents, which I certainly could not afford.

One day a fellow I worked with at CBS, who was also looking for a place to live, invited me to go to the borough of Queens with him to look at newly built apartments in the Rego Park section. I couldn't have been more surprised when we climbed up to the street from the subway tunnel and I saw grass and trees and little houses with porches, and laundry hanging out back. It was still a part of New York City, but as different as night and day from that familiar territory around CBS and the "Y." The four story red brick building was by far the tallest in the area, and had a big sign hanging from it saying, "three room apartments, $80 a month, utilities extra." I was making $37.50 a week, plus some overtime, and with Amy working, I was sure we would somehow be able to afford it. The rental agent thought so too, and quickly signed me up for a three year lease, even before I had a chance to call Amy. I knew she would accept it, and wouldn't question my decision, even though this was the second time I had taken such an important step without consulting her. But I had done the best I could by myself.

Since our happy August wedding nearly three years before, our marriage had had its ups and downs with most of the stress in the all important area of sexual compatibility. But now our lives together would begin anew, and we would be sharing a new home, with new jobs, and maybe even some thoughts of something really new, a baby. What ever difficulties we were having would hopefully disappear, and the love I had for Amy, emotionally, would finally be fully consummated. I prayed for that to happen and with this complete change in our lifestyle—a new beginning in a "new" world—we would need each other more and be closer to each other than ever before. I was sure of it.

Our little department on West 54th Street was the life's blood of the television stations across the country. We were called the Traffic Department and every day seemed more hectic than the day before. Between the Deluxe and Pathe Film Laboratory deliveries and the

Emory shipping expediters, there were trucks and vans and cars coming and going all day long. It was a madhouse of labeling and packaging and storing hundreds of "kinnes" and having to make shipping deadlines. It would be some time before all the television stations would be connected by telephone lines, or satellites, to the New York originated "feeds," but until that happened, some years later, many millions of people had to settle for rather grainy looking 16mm images transmitted to their TV sets from their local CBS affiliated station. Along with the "kinnes" poor quality, they saw a program as many as twenty-one days after its initial live telecast. Because it was too costly to provide a "kinne" for each TV station—of which there were more and more each day—we were responsible for arranging the "bicycling," or re-shipping, schedule from one station to another. Even the few shows that were filmed on the west coast, like *The Gene Autry Show* and *Burns and Allen*, were flown across country to us, then scheduled and shipped to the stations from New York.

This was the early '50s and television was the big new discovery. It was certainly on everyone's mind and huge box like TV sets, with tiny screens showing black and white pictures, were selling out, at more than a $300 a piece—a lot of money in those days. Many people felt they had to have a TV even more than the latest conveniences of a modern kitchen or a new lump free mattress to replace the sagging pre-war model. Others considered it a status symbol, with an evening's activities planned around the starting time of a show. Now they would be able to really see all those characters and personalities that they had learned to love only by their radio voices. It was getting to know an old friend in a very different way; this time with a real face, and real hair, and wearing stylish clothes or comedic costumes. Best of all, it was happening right in our own living rooms. We could lean back in our comfortable easy chairs and be entertained, getting up only to change the channel or get another beer. What an invention, one that would change our lives forever.

Amy and I were so poor in those days that it was an important moment when, on one occasion, we turned off the TV and went into Manhattan's Times Square on Sunday to see *Quo Vadis* with Robert Taylor and Deborah Kerr at the Roxy Theater, and then had a hot dog lunch at Nedicks. Or the time we took the seemingly endless subway ride all the way to Brooklyn, to Ebbets Field, to see the Dodgers play the Philadelphia Phillies, winners of the National League pennant the year before, in a night baseball game. Baseball played at night. What a treat! The Phillies were "my" team, and I had grown up loving their every move, usually in a losing cause. But as much as I loved them, it was even a greater thrill to see Jackie Robinson, the first black player to play Major League baseball. We cheered him, along with the demonstrative and frenzied Brooklyn fans, and marveled at how he was changing the whole face of baseball...my game. He had broken the color barrier in America's pastime. And just being in Ebbets

Field, instead of only hearing about Duke Snider and Pee Wee Reese from play-by-play announcers Red Barber and Connie Desmond on the radio, made this evening a memorable one, at least for me.

But the occasional movie or baseball game were rare occurrences with so little in our coffers to do much of anything except buy food and pay the rent. My father, instead of following his usual practice of trading in one of his two cars every few years for a new one, had given us his three year old Mercury as a wedding present. A much appreciated gift, but he told me then, rather firmly, that I was on my own, and that I shouldn't expect any financial help from him in the future. And I was determined not to ask for any even though I had come awfully close during those final, desperate days at Montgomery. We had to sell the Mercury to pay for the move to New York, and our one luxury purchase was a blue pullout couch, which we bought on credit, so that guests would have some place to sleep. We were sure our friends would come for a visit, considering it was New York and I was in such an exciting and glamourous business.

Not surprisingly, Amy quickly found a part-time job down on Wall Street working for the Topping family, famous for their race horses and ownership of the New York Yankees baseball team. Like me, I'm sure Mr. Topping found her hard to resist, what with that simple and quiet elegance and disarming personality. Her commute on the crowded subway was over an hour, often standing all the way. She was quite small, being only five feet tall and she was almost buried in the mass of people. I remember her telling me one day that she overheard another woman, close beside her, mutter to no one in particular, "This is sheer murder," and Amy could only look up and silently nod in agreement.

Amy made $25 a week and received $15 a month from my mother, as a little gift, to pay for a cleaning woman. We didn't tell her that a cleaning woman was hardly necessary and that the money was going for the bare necessities, and those rare splurges...a trip to Manhattan to see *Quo Vadis* or to Brooklyn to see Jackie Robinson. Most of the time we sat on the new blue pullout couch and watched *I Love Lucy*, *Philco Playhouse*, and *Douglas Edwards and the News* on our old Motorola TV that had a screen the size of a window pane.

And we made love. I thanked God for clouding over those many demonic reveries that had been affecting my libido for so long. In those days it was proper, at least in the world that I knew, for both men and women to remain a virgin until marriage, and I had always been certain that, by having regular sex with a woman, it would suppress all those seemingly abnormal thoughts that I wrestled with so often, and that worried me terribly. Now, after some very difficult times making love during the first three years of our marriage, it was finally happening. Amy, having no idea what was going on in my mind, had been anxious and frustrated, but forever patient, and I loved her for it.

CHAPTER TWENTY-NINE

After six months of "hard labor," packing and unpacking an ever increasing number of "kinnes" and Hollywood produced film programs, I got a $7.50 a week raise and a promotion. Several copies of each show, after being "bicycled" around to the stations, were saved in a vast library, with row after row of steel racks for shelves. I became the assistant librarian to Frank Smith, a pompous and stuffy son of an advertising executive. He was only in our department for a short time to learn a little about our contribution to the television network, and made sure we knew that he was going on to bigger and better things very soon. And he did, becoming a top sales executive…at CBS.

He apparently didn't have to worry about money, as he would put his weekly paychecks in his bottom desk drawer, week after week, and never bother to cash them. When he left, I found two of them stuck in the back of his desk and I sent them to him. But typical of Frank, he never bothered to thank me. He obviously came from a family of some means, and probably had many advantages, including a private school education. But so had I, and I never thought of myself as being better than anyone else. Maybe my father did have the right idea when he said I had to make it on my own when I got married and left home. Times were tough, as they were for all of us low grade employees, but at least I wasn't a snob like Frank Smith.

In all fairness I must say Frank did teach me about the library procedures, an important part of which was scheduling screenings of the shows for the producers, directors, writers, and talent, as well as for the entertainment executives and their clients from the advertising agencies. When he left I became the librarian, and now I was really "rubbing elbows" with the celebrities, as they were continually asking for favors and trying to get priority time for their screenings.

One time, the wonderfully talented Steve Allen spent the night in the screening room. He said he needed to get an early start the next day, and then in his whimsical way, he asked me if I might have a spare blanket. I couldn't supply one, but I did arrange for one of my stickball friends to bring him a fried egg sandwich and coffee early the next morning. With these responsibilities, there was no more looking away and pretending not to notice the stars. I was so proud when the likes of Gary Moore and Arthur Godfrey even called me by name.

But the librarian job was not all stars and screenings. It had its downside, too. Grant Theis, my boss, was told by Mr. Paley that he needed a whole year's worth of "kinnes" of the fifteen minute *Stork Club Show* to be delivered as a Christmas present to Sherman Billingsley, the host and proprietor of the club, at 6:00 PM on Christmas Eve. Mr. Paley would be there at that time. The show was on several times a week, and was broadcast "live" from that famous watering hole, frequented by everyone who was anyone. This meant labeling and wrapping dozens of boxes of film cans in appropriate holiday paper and ribbon, and then delivering them to the club many blocks away, in a brownstone on East 53rd Street right off 5th Avenue.

When I bundled out of the taxi, almost knocking down the debonaire Cary Grant, the doorman ordered me around to the service entrance, but I insisted that the packages had to be delivered personally to Mr. Billingsley. I wasn't sure how I was going to carry them all, but when I got there he was waiting, along with Mr. Paley, champagne glasses in hand, to receive his voluminous gift. I was kindly offered a glass of the "bubbly," and received an acknowledging wink and a smile from Mr. Paley. I'll always wonder if he knew that I was his old neighbor from Hathaway Lane. I somehow doubt it, but it's possible because CBS Television didn't have very many employees in those days, and after all, he did send me a Christmas card.

The librarian

The commercial coordinator

In my new position at CBS I discovered there was more to the Film Department, as we were called, than just handling the "kinne" operation and library activities…and delivering Christmas presents to the Stork Club. There were commercials that had to be inserted into almost every show. Though there were a few that were "live," most were on film and were trafficked through us and prepared for broadcast by our film technicians. The volume had increased so much that a third commercial coordinator was needed. Much to my surprise, and even though there had been people in the department much longer, I was chosen. I joined Harry Hess, a wisecracking "operator," who had been in the film business for a few years, and Jerry McNally, a frustrated actor/dancer, awaiting his big break. They were both older, and wiser, and had seniority and, being the new guy, they saw to it that I had the most difficult accounts to service.

The job entailed working closely with the advertising agencies, storing and cataloging their commercials, and scheduling them each day. Some shows, like the soap operas *Search For Tomorrow* and *The Secret Storm*, had as many as ten commercial spots in each daily episode. All might have been Procter & Gamble products, but each brand had a different agency, and a different set of commercials. The agency personnel had their own set of difficulties with their clients and those problems were passed on to us, with late deliveries and never-ending last minute changes. To make matters worse, the reels of commercials were transmitted from a labyrinth of projection machinery, called Telecine, which was located in rooms high above

Grand Central Station many blocks away from our office. The late changes often necessitated a film technician racing, by taxi, to Telecine, and making a frantic switch a minute or two before air time.

By wizardry, the projected images were sent to the antenna on top of the Empire State Building, and from there to many thousands of homes and to the consumers who, in a roundabout way, were paying my salary by buying the products. Millions of dollars were at stake and there was no room for any errors in scheduling on our part. This frantic activity, with the three of us jammed into a little office, screaming above each other's voices on the constantly ringing telephones, could easily have driven a person to drink—and it did, in some cases, including me.

CHAPTER THIRTY

Harry Hess, "operating" as always, sold me an old 1941 black Ford sedan. It had 125,000 miles on it, a little bit of rust, and a tired feel about it, and even though it was probably worth only about $25, I bought it for $50, and was thrilled. It meant that Amy and I could escape from our apartment on weekends and drive to Rockaway Beach and the ocean which we loved, or to Grandma Lord's, about 30 miles away in Tarrytown, and some real country.

We were both very fond of my grandmother, who was Cousin Lucie to Amy and her family, and she often called to invite us to "Broadreach" for Sunday luncheon. Grandpa had died about ten years earlier and now all of her nine children and twenty grandchildren were very much the focus of her life. Yet, I always had the feeling she seemed to find us kind of special and loved our occasional visits. We hadn't gone as often as we would have liked because the trip was so expensive, what with the subway, train, and taxi ride…and it did take almost two hours. But now, with the car, we could go more regularly.

On one occasion she asked us to pick up Grandpa's brother, my great-uncle Kenneth, a widower, at his Park Avenue apartment, and bring him with us for Thanksgiving dinner. The doorman was startled

157

as we drove up in our smelly old relic and he gingerly opened the rickety door for Uncle Kenneth, who was a picture of nattiness in his blue suit, starched high collar and cuffs. He insisted on sitting in the back and allowed he didn't mind the worn out seat with the stuffing coming out. When, on the Saw Mill River Parkway, I had to pull over on the grass and rip off a piece of the bumper, which had been dragging, and toss it into the bushes, he just looked the other way without saying a word. Amy and I were mortified, but Uncle Kenneth was unfazed, and, at the end of the day, thanked us for sparing him the expense of a hired car.

Grandma was such a kind and loving soul. Every Sunday and any holidays when she was at home, she invited Grandpa's two maiden sisters to come for Sunday dinner. They were Aunt Edie and Aunt Mabel to me, but they were known by certain members of the family as "the incredibles." They lived together with a very large dog in a very little house provided by Grandpa down on the main street in Tarrytown. They would literally be pulled up the steep hill to "Broadreach" by the dog, and would arrive red-faced with hair flying, noses dripping and babbling a constant stream of idle chatter about what was happening down the hill on Broadway...in Tarrytown. Grandma greeted them as if they were royalty, listened to all their gossip, and fully expected any member of the family who happened to be there at the time to act as graciously as she did. It wasn't easy.

Broadreach

There are many stories about life at "Broadreach" when Grandma and Grandpa were raising their nine children, and Amy and I loved to listen to them on those Sunday visits. But there was one which Uncle Kenneth told us that Thanksgiving day which, to me, best describes the enormity of the rambling old house and a glimpse of how the family lived.

It seems that one of the upstairs chambermaids, a young, unmarried girl, became pregnant, and as she grew larger and larger she was given lighter duties by my compassionate grandmother and ones that would make certain she never would be seen by my grandfather. He surely would not have allowed anyone to remain in his employ if they were carrying a child, especially out of wedlock.

And after nine months of semi-seclusion she gave birth to her baby, with Grandma's assistance, high up in her attic room, and still

159

unbeknownst to Grandpa. When the new mother was able, Grandma quietly whisked her and her infant child out of the house, and paid, with her household allowance, to have them taken care of in a home for unwed mothers near where Aunt Edie and Aunt Mabel lived, down the hill on Broadway. I don't really know whether they, or my mother and her brothers and sisters, ever knew what was going on, but if they did my grandmother must have pledged them to a lifetime of secrecy, as I had never heard the story before that Thanksgiving Day.

As time went on, I got to know some of the advertising agency people better, and as I continued to knock myself out on their behalf, there were many invitations for those infamous three martini lunches at some of New York City's finest restaurants. Even though I found that martinis could be lethal, I managed to get my work done following these two-hour feasts, and seldom made a mistake as far as I know. The agency people were only trying to show their appreciation, and didn't realize that accurate scheduling of their "expensive, and skillfully produced" commercials might be in jeopardy. Of course, it didn't happen every day, and when there were no plans for a sumptuous "liquid" lunch at Au Galois or Frankie and Johnnie's Steak House, I could still play stickball, and have just as good a time with my neighborhood street friends, eating a simple ham and cheese sandwich on rye. When Christmas time came, Harry and

Jerry and I were overwhelmed with not only luncheon invitations but were showered with costly thank you gifts, ranging from rare French and Italian wines to engraved cigarette boxes from Tiffany. One year I was so appreciated—or at least my work was—that I had to bring the old black Ford into the city to carry everything home.

I was only making about $100 a week, but with all this responsibility and the attention I was getting you would think I was a top executive. A few of the agency men seemed to take a particular liking to me, as did my immediate superior, Gordon Chadwick, and very often one of them would ask me to have drinks after work. Something told me not to, and I'd say no thanks and use the excuse that Amy was waiting for me at home. If I suggested she come into the city to join us, they would beg off and say maybe some other time. They seemed to want me, and me alone, and I was beginning to wonder about it. But life went on, with cocktails at lunch being quite enough, and although strangely tempted, I was determined not to get involved in any extra curricular after work liaisons.

I loved Amy and wanted to be with her. Our marriage was at its best and I hoped to keep it that way. I had struggled with those demons and the dark and lonely room they occupied long enough, and I didn't want anything to come between us. One very special night, while we sat on the blue pullout couch, Amy told me she was pregnant. I hugged her and kissed her, and cried and cried with joy. There was no question that it was the happiest moment of my life, at least until that time. I had been part of the creation of a life, a child of my own, something that I had thought might never happen. I wasn't the "queer" that I sometimes imagined I was, and I was sure I could do anything anybody else could do, and maybe even better.

CHAPTER THIRTY-ONE

Adding to all the excitement and anticipation at home, it was announced that we were moving our offices from West 54th to West 57th Street. CBS corporate headquarters was located at 485 Madison Avenue, and was always known as just "485." It was close to the advertising world, and was where Mr. Paley and his high powered staff of programming, sales and station relations executives did their wheeling and dealing. And it was at "485" where the entertainment and informational programs, which had such a major influence on the country's population, were determined.

But there was a need, for financial and logistical reasons, to consolidate the studios and production operations under one roof. Thus was born the CBS Production Center, a big, ugly, red brick, three-story building, which was converted from an old Sheffield Farms Milk distribution depot, and occupied nearly an entire block between 10th and 11th Avenues. It was there that management somehow found room in that monolith for our little maverick operation. We were housed near the rehearsal halls, and adjacent to the freight elevators and loading dock, so necessary for our daily trafficking activity. The talent, rehearsing down the hall, could attend screenings during their breaks, and eventually the commercials and filmed programs would originate from a new Telecine right beneath us, and much closer to home than Grand Central Station. For now there was still the lingering odor of cow manure and the brown tile walls of the old milking station. In fact, the last cow was leaving as we loaded all of our "kinnes" into their new racks and the commercials into their designated bins.

With this change in location I was finally going to have my own office, with a door that closed and a window with curtains. We even were given some choice of fabrics and colors, and a modest selection of office furniture. It was hard to believe that in a little over a year I had moved from a shy, naive shipping clerk with a locker to a hard drinking junior executive with my own telephone extension and a decorated office. Of course, the salary wasn't great, but there were the many perks from my agency friends, and fringe benefits offered and paid for by CBS. One of these was hospital and medical coverage for both Amy and me which would help pay for the delivery of our new addition, due in a few months.

Still another benefit, which I eventually came to appreciate and realize was of paramount importance, was the CBS funding of my retirement package. Because it was so many years down the line, I didn't think much about it, but it just grew and grew. Based on salary, without any contribution on my part, it was truly a gift from CBS for all the hardworking, underpaid, proud and dedicated workers who made the company into a special, unified, and very talented family. It's no wonder it was becoming the finest source of news and entertainment in the world. Without that pension I probably wouldn't be living the fine life I enjoy today, nor would I be recalling my 40 years at CBS with such reverence and gusto.

Amy and I were happy that we were finally climbing out of our deep financial hole, and what a comfort it was that she could put a little of our earnings into a savings account to help pay for the many things needed for a new baby. We planned carefully, and at the same time we were trying to decide on a name for our expected child. One thing we knew for sure was that he, if it was a he, would not be named after me. Maybe Chalmers could be a middle name, but certainly not the name he would be called.

To settle the question, I told her about the time when my father came home waving a copy of the *Philadelphia Evening Bulletin* and shouting for everyone to gather 'round. There, on the front page, was a large picture of me playing junior football in a school game, with the caption underneath reading, "Here comes Chummy around the end." What must the readers have thought? Who was this "foreigner" with the strange name, unrecognizable because he was wearing a helmet, and chewing on his chin strap. I guess Dad bought up all the copies of the paper he could get his hands on because he sent the picture and headline to all of our many relatives. It was as if he wanted to tell the world, "Look what my boy, Chummy, can do if he just applies himself," or "Look! He's as good an athlete as his brother Ted." I didn't know whether to feel happy or to cry and it didn't take long for my relationships with my father and my older brother to resume their unpleasantness. Amy and I made up our minds right then and there that, if it was to be a boy, he should never be embarrassed or humiliated by his name and that Anthony Chalmers Dale, with the nickname, Tony, would be just fine and never cause him any unnecessary problems. And so it was.

Just as the name Chalmers became Chummy or Chum, the International Brotherhood of Electrical Workers was always known as the IBEW. By looking at their full name you would think that this union, affiliated with CBS, was made up of thousands of wiring experts and people responsible for studio lighting and office lamps. It was, but in addition it somehow included not only the forty film technicians working in our department but the hundreds of skilled personnel handling the camera and sound equipment in the studios. They were the people, the technicians, who made television work, and with their training and expertise and invaluable contributions they managed to carry a very large stick when it came to a voice in the daily operation at the Production Center. In numbers alone there were many more of them than us white collar types, who thought we were so important and irreplaceable. Actually, we worked very closely with them, and when their union ordered a strike that summer, not long after we had settled into our new air-conditioned offices, the company required us to quickly learn to operate and even maintain all the technical equipment.

This was not an easy time for any of us at CBS, with our friends on the picket line, and shouting union slogans outside, while we tried to do double duty inside. As far as any impressions I may have had about unions, they all were learned from my father, and they were, to say the least, all negative. He felt strongly that the so-called working class was beneath him, and should remain that way, in both income and working conditions, and that collective bargaining was a liberal idea to be opposed at all costs. He felt that workers should be beholden to their employer without ever being allowed to question authority. He had experienced several walkouts in the textile mills he was associated with, and cursed the workers for jeopardizing his source of income. He had little interest in any of their demands that might lead to improved working and living conditions, which, incidentally, were deplorable in the mill towns of the south.

The strike at CBS lasted only a few days but for me it seemed like an eternity. It meant being with Amy for just a few hours each night and not being able to get home until after midnight, and then right back to work at the crack of dawn the next morning. I worried about her way out in Rego Park in our sweltering apartment waiting anxiously for the big day to come. On one of those late nights I was delivering the reels of commercials to Telecine (which was still in Grand Central Station), and because it was a job normally performed by a union member, some goon who had been hired by the union hit me on the head and knocked me to the marble floor just inside the station door. I had crossed a picket line! This was something that I hadn't really thought much about before, but I learned in a hurry that this was serious business for union members. It was about their livelihood, about their families, and the contractual differences with the company had a direct bearing on their children's future. I wasn't hurt, and I knew I wasn't singled out, but still it bothered me that my fellow workers, my family, would go to such lengths to resolve their grievances.

Shortly after the contract was settled and the strike ended, I had the opportunity to stand up for a union member, who happened to be black, in a dispute over some missing equipment. I knew him pretty well and was sure he was honest and being treated as a scapegoat because of his race. It was my first real opportunity to defend something and somebody that I believed in, and to actually be able to put into practice a concern for others that I had tried for so long to learn and understand from Amy and her family.

The long subway ride to work became too difficult and tiring for Amy after a few months of her pregnancy, and her days in the apartment were long and lonely. She did have one friend, Nancy, who had a little girl, and who lived down the hall. She was married to an exterminator who traveled a lot, selling his elaborate equipment which he kept stored in their apartment. His last name was Bliss, and who would have guessed that this name would become one of the most recognizable in the exterminating business. Nancy had helped

Amy find an obstetrician not far away in Jackson Heights. But unfortunately she found Dr. Silverman rather brusk and surly and came home after her regular visits almost in tears, with more questions than answers. During the early stages of her pregnancy she was unable to swallow her own saliva without getting sick to her stomach. It was not pleasant having to spit into her tissue filled purse while trying to be nonchalant on the crowded subway.

Every chance I had, I would take her for a drive in our tired old Ford. One day we visited Amy's Aunt Christina Tracy who lived just north of Dyckman Street in the borough of The Bronx. I had always thought of anything north of Central Park as a mass of run-down buildings like those I had seen in *Life* magazine's picture essays of Harlem, or the ones I could see from the train window on the ride to Tarrytown. The elevated tracks pass so close to the tenement apartments that one can easily observe the unhappy expressions on the faces of those depressed looking tenants sitting on their fire escapes, staring at the train as it thunders passed their third floor windows. How the laundry, hanging from the railings could ever be clean, I often wondered, as the train kicked up a black dust as it whizzed by. I remember so well wanting to hold in my arms those unfortunate souls and give them strength and anything material that I could spare. I felt the same way about my street friends in Hell's Kitchen. Of course I didn't know it at the time, but in a few years I would be devoting a good part of my life at CBS embracing the struggles of people living on the edge.

But where Aunt Christina lived was not far from the Cloisters, a preserved medieval monastery museum, located in a lovely park overlooking the Hudson River. It was a revelation to me, and, like the part of Queens where we lived, I found this section of the city to have something other than ugliness and despair. It was, in fact, a real neighborhood.

Looking somewhat like a grown up Little Orphan Annie, Aunt Christina, a piano teacher, was soft and round with bright curly red hair. She lived in a small, cluttered walk-up apartment, dominated by her piano. We had tea and cakes, and sang Broadway show tunes. Her favorite was *Finian's Rainbow*, and its hit song, "How Are Things In Glocca Mora." She was so full of good cheer that Amy was able to forget, for a while, about those uncomfortable moments she was experiencing during a difficult pregnancy. And I was happy that she was happy, and that our lives were about to take on a whole new dimension.

CHAPTER THIRTY-TWO

Way out on the west coast Hollywood, the film capital of the world, was beginning to open its collective eyes to the fact that television was here to stay and some of the major movie talent—actors, directors, writers, and cameramen—were slowly finding there way, with some misgivings, into this new medium. New York had its own, and quite different, talent pool. Here were producers, directors, writers, and actors who may have had limited experience in television, but who had learned and developed their craft at such prestigious places as The Actors' Studio, The Neighborhood Playhouse and The American Academy Of Dramatic Arts. The actors had performed live in front of an audience in the theater or even on many radio series, and young, still unknown names like Paul Newman, Grace Kelly, Marlon Brando, Joanne Woodward and James Dean were all doing live television in such stellar network dramatic shows as *Studio One* and *Philco Playhouse*, and thrillers like *Suspense, Danger, The Web,* and *Crime Syndicated*. But the very thought of that moment when the director, his voice echoing over a loud speaker system calmly counting down...ten...nine...eight...then picked up by the stage manager in the studio...three...two...one, his finger cueing the first action, was a terrifying, and almost mystifying experience for most actors in Hollywood. They were less trained and less than familiar with "live" acting and they depended on "take" after "take" to achieve what a director wanted, sometimes working several days to get it right.

It was during this extraordinary decade of the 1950s that the half-hour "movie" series was born. They were situation comedies which soon became known as "sitcoms," with as many as thirty-nine new episodes turned out each year starring those actors strong and brave enough to weather the rigorous production schedule. Leading the pack was the wondrously funny *I Love Lucy*, but there were many others including *Our Miss Brooks, Burns and Allen*, and *The Jack Benny Show* (all of which were former radio stalwarts). Then there were the dramatic anthologies hosted by the likes of Alfred Hitchcock and Ronald Reagan. Also, about this time, old Hollywood produced movies began to appear on TV. These had to be carefully screened, and edited, for content and to find exactly the right place for commercial breaks, all of which was done in New York by our department. The standards for acceptance of any questionable material were rigidly enforced, with long periods of decision making as to what could stay and what should be cut occupying hours of supervised editing.

Our little department was used to coping with one or two half-hour film programs, and preparing *The Gene Autry Show* and *Sergeant Preston Of The Yukon* for broadcast had been a part of our regular routine almost from the beginning. They were syndicated shows, which meant a TV station, such as WBBM in Chicago, could insert commercials for local products and services, as compared to the network programs with commercials geared to a national audience. The local stations could play these syndicated shows at any time they chose and it became a new path of independence for them. For the most part their daily programming consisted almost entirely of the poor quality kinescopes, or the syndicated programs that were made cheaply, shot on inexpensive 16mm film, with lots of outdoor action and very little dialogue. The insertion of commercials and opening and closing billboards was a relatively easy process.

Now the sudden influx of programs from Hollywood, shot on better quality 35mm film, with giant reels and cases, was something we were not prepared to handle. It meant purchasing new technical equipment as well as arranging for proper storage facilities and, considering that there was a new episode every week, we were up to our proverbial behinds in hundreds of bulky cases of film. Often they were shot and shipped from the west coast so close to air time that we regularly had to send special messengers to the airport, and receive priority handling, in order to make our deadlines. The commercials to be inserted also had to be 35mm, and the advertising agencies who were providing them often insisted the completed show, with commercials, be screened prior to being aired so that the client could be assured all was well. After all, with many millions of people watching, advertisers were getting unprecedented exposure for their products, and one mistake could cause the loss of thousands, even millions, of dollars in revenue. Our efforts were often rewarded with more three martini lunches, which I always enjoyed. But if my agency friends could have somehow created just a few extra hours, with a few extra hands, and a few extra phones, it would have been more productive.

There always seemed to be new developments of some sort, not the least of which was the pending birth of our new baby. Amy was getting bigger and bigger, and more and more uncomfortable, as the days went by. And I wasn't being very attentive or much of a comfort, as we became overwhelmed with this new insurgence of Hollywood made programs. Of course, there was still an ever increasing number of live shows originating in New York. There were not only the prime time dramas and variety shows but also the daily soap operas, and a new phenomenon known as the game shows. All of these were fully sponsored and one day, being curious, and even exasperated, I sat at my desk and counted twenty-six advertising agencies, servicing hundreds of products, and all of them demanding undivided attention.

But heading the list of the most important responsibilities and concerns in my life at that moment was to be ready when Amy needed me. I worried so about the old black Ford breaking down on the way to the Forest Hills Hospital a few miles away, and the thought of our baby being born in the back seat of a stalled relic on Queens

Boulevard haunted me. I worried, too, about Amy's mother arriving in time from Philadelphia to comfort her daughter, and me as well, during the whole unfamiliar, and rather terrifying experience ahead of us.

In the early evening of August 14, 1953, all my dreams came true. Our little baby was born. Mrs. Bell had arrived the night before, and early in the morning, right on schedule, Amy went into labor. We were told Dr. Silverman was on the golf course and would be paged. This was not very reassuring. We rushed to the hospital, only to wait ten hours while Amy was struggling to give birth. No one would tell us anything as to why it was taking so long, but Amy's mother, having been through the arrival of several other grandchildren, kept assuring me that everything would be fine. She was as calm and as patient as I knew Amy to be, and I had such respect for her in the way she quietly knitted, and chatted with other expectant fathers, comforting them as well as me. I walked the halls impatiently, drank tasteless coffee from a machine, and made a number of calls to the office, even though I had prepared everything I could well ahead of time. Harry and Jerry kept telling me not to worry, that the CBS Television Network would somehow carry on without me for one day.

I was almost at wit's end when the doctor suddenly appeared in the waiting room and curtly announced that we had spoiled his golf game, that mother and baby were doing fine, and that it was a boy. But his abrupt behavior was quickly forgotten when I saw Amy, looking exhausted, holding our precious little baby in her arms. And when I kissed her cheek, and touched Tony's tiny fingers, all was right with the world.

CHAPTER THIRTY-THREE

The year Tony was born one couldn't help hearing Patti Page's big hit song "How Much Is That Doggie In The Window." It wasn't one of my favorites, but it did make me think a lot about my beloved old friend, Dolph, the Doberman Pincher I had grown up with. I would tell Tony about him when, at three o'clock in the morning, he would start to cry and I would take him to the bathroom and cradle him in my arms while sitting on the closed toilet seat with the door shut so as not to disturb Amy. And Tony quieted down and would listen as I sang Burl Ives songs to him, or try to imitate Patti Page singing about her "doggie in the window." I promised him that we would get a dog to have as his friend as soon as he was old enough to hug him. Tony listened to my ramblings and would drift off to sleep. I guess he didn't understand a word I was saying but somewhere, deep down, I would like to think that he did. I guess the warmth of my body and my calm, soothing voice was all he needed. Oh how I loved him so!

Speaking of dogs, one of the most popular CBS shows at that time was *The Adventures of Lassie*. I didn't watch it very often because it made me cry, though I'm not sure why. Yet even now, I have a problem watching programs about animals, domestic or otherwise. Maybe it's because God has created such beautiful and majestic creatures that I feel they are not to be looked at, by my eyes at least, on a small screen, even though they have been beautifully photographed and under ideal conditions. I know it is educational, but I guess I would prefer being with them, a part of their environment, in open spaces, with the different sounds and smells, and, where possible, to be able to touch them and have them touch me. I don't cry at the zoo, or at a dog or cat show, or even when I see them live on television prancing around the track at the Westminster Dog Show in Madison Square Garden. I guess something is telling me, because of my experience in the television business, that a prying camera is intruding on their privacy without their permission, and it makes me sad.

I don't want anyone to think that I was overly loyal to CBS and that my viewing habits were restricted to only watching "our" programs. But one of the CBS programs that Amy and I did watch regularly was the weekly Sunday night variety show hosted by Ed Sullivan, the newspaper columnist for the *New York Daily News*. It often had animal acts that I enjoyed. I never wanted to think that they were ever treated badly by their trainers, but the jumping dogs and dancing bears always looked happy and seemed to be enjoying what they were doing.

But enjoying the dancing animals, or acrobats and jugglers, was not only what kept us loyal viewers. We kind of liked the novel, and somewhat awkward host, Ed Sullivan, and as it turned out, I think he liked me. One Christmas he sent me a bottle of Scotch in gratitude for helping him select and edit a piece of film which was shown on what is probably his most famous program next to the one, of course, with the Beatles making their United States debut.

It seemed there was a rising young star who had a very sexy voice, with hips that gyrated in a most provocative way, when he sang. His name was Elvis Presley, and I believe Sullivan was the first to give him nighttime television exposure, squeezed in among the animal acts and jugglers. Thinking I was a film expert, just because I was responsible for the preparation of the Lincoln Mercury commercials used in his show, he asked me to go with him to the Pathe Laboratories at 110th Street and help him choose a scene from a movie Presley had just finished. I picked out the clip in which he sang "Love Me Tender", and on the way back to the Production Center, (feeling a bit like a star myself having a drink served from the bar in the back of Sullivan's limousine), I told him I had suggested that song because so many of the audience would recognize the melody as "Auralee," a Scottish folk tune that I, and I was sure many others, had sung in their high school chorus or glee club. The rest is history, and Presley's erotic performance, complete with film clip, is a classic moment in the archival records of television. I doubt if any of the animal acts have been so honored.

One person who loved animals as much as I did was Amy's Aunt Tibby. Her expression of love and concern was a very special one. She always had a pick and shovel in the trunk of her car so that if she saw a dead animal on the road she would stop, pick it up, and dig a grave, giving it a proper burial in as dignified a spot as she could find without trespassing on someone's personal property. She and her husband Mahlon Hutchinson, a clerk for the eminent Judge Harold Medina, lived in Princeton, New Jersey and we often went down to visit them. We would take the express train from Pennsylvania Station to New Brunswick, the stop before Princeton, and they would meet us and then drive us around to see the area in hopes that we might move there some day. Our lease on the apartment in Rego Park would soon be up and we were thinking about a move, and considered Princeton as a good possibility as it was about half-way between New York and Philadelphia…between work and family.

We missed our families and friends so much and, even though my commute would be an hour and a half each way, I felt I could manage it, considering all the advantages. And of course, most important, we wanted to show off our son Tony, and have his grandparents get to know the dear little fellow. Mother and Dad did come to see their first grandchild shortly after he was born, but the thought of the subway or a long taxi ride to Queens was something they weren't prepared to cope with. So, we had to rev up the faithful Ford and take

Tony and all the necessary paraphernalia into the city and show him off during cocktails and dinner, served in their suite at the St. Regis hotel.

It was a scant three years after starting in the shipping room at CBS that Amy and I were able to afford to say goodbye to our little nest in Rego Park and move, with our new son, to a home in the country. It all sounded so perfect, but there were some very rough days ahead, days that it is hard to believe could ever happen to a confident, rising young executive like me.

CHAPTER THIRTY-FOUR

New developments, with many improvements, seemed to be happening almost daily in the television industry in the mid fifties, and for the consumer more and better programs, more affordable TV sets, bigger screens, and an abundance of talent, familiar and new, entering their living rooms, all made for many hours of enjoyable viewing. The initial excitement and curiosity wasn't wearing off. In fact, experts were predicting that more time would be spent watching television than listening to the radio, going to the movies, or even reading. This new media giant wasn't all fluff, and with new and innovative mobile equipment taking to the field, television was on hand to cover important news and sporting events as they happened. With cries from educators and clergy, informative programs like *You Are There* and *Camera Three* joined the CBS Sunday daytime schedule, which already was presenting the religious series, with the peculiarly catchy title, *Lamp Unto My Feet*. The Sunday "ghetto", as Jack Gould of the *New York Times* called it, had its own brand of viewer; those who already were tired of, and even bored with, a constant stream of light entertainment, and wanted programs with a little more substance and meaning.

I particularly liked the segments on the 90 minute *Omnibus* program, with the distinguished English author and commentator, Allistair Cooke, introducing us to everything from Gilbert & Sullivan's *The Mikado,* to an original play written by Maxwell Anderson, starring Rex Harrison and Lili Palmer, to A Haitian dance group performing to a throbbing drumbeat. Some fifteen years later this kind of television grew to become Public Broadcasting— entertainment programs that educated. I am still a loyal viewer as well as a regular supporter.

With much excitement and anticipation, experimental attempts at color transmission had begun, with CBS coming up with a most cumbersome concept; a color "wheel," which fortunately died an early death. I went to a demonstration of it at the CBS headquarters on Madison Avenue and even the technical people operating it seemed to have difficulty making it work. A much more sophisticated system, developed by the engineers at RCA, the parent company of NBC, was represented by the proud peacock's magnificent plumage, and it became the standard of the industry. Longer telephone lines were being utilized to extend the networks' range of transmission of the New York originated network programs. We, in the Film Department, found it necessary to open a West Coast branch office that would handle some of the heavy volume of 16mm print distribution of the film programs being made by the newly created television departments at MGM, Warner Brothers, and 20th Century Fox.

But there were still the many live shows being produced in New York, each with a variety of sponsors and a myriad of commercials. The new concept of half-hour soap operas was in full swing, along with daytime game shows geared to the homebound housewife. With a more liberal time allotment for daytime advertising, these shows could contain as many as eight or ten different commercials, and advertising an equal number of products, with a different set each day. I wouldn't have believed that there were so many over-the-counter headache remedies and laxatives, or soap products that cleaned everything from your finger nails, to your oven, to your car windows.

Keeping them all straight and scheduled properly, as well as giving directives to our people in Los Angeles by phone, or sometimes two, was more than I thought I could possibly handle on some days. On one occasion when I felt particularly desperate, I slipped away to the nearby rehearsal hall and to a sound I thought was the most unusual and captivating singing voice I had ever heard. I had never dared to go in and watch a rehearsal and the only time I had seen anyone perform, firsthand, at CBS was that brief visit to the *Perry Como Show* a few years earlier. But the strains of "Matilda" were mesmerizing, and I couldn't resist slipping through the door and sitting on the floor in a darkened corner.

It was a rehearsal for *The Ed Sullivan Show*, and the young, extraordinarily handsome man singing was the newly discovered, but not well known, Harry Belafonte. I think at that moment I first felt the magic of being in the presence of stardom, and I just knew that someday, somehow, I would be involved in the creative process and the production of a television program. When he finished, everyone applauded, including me, which I was sure was unusual for a rehearsal. Nobody seemed to notice that I was there, and I sat for a few more minutes and listened intently as the scenic designer, complete with sketches, explained the setting to be used for the performance. I was only away from my desk for about fifteen minutes, but it was quite possibly the single most defining moment so far in my budding career with CBS. The seed had been planted, but it would be several years before it would start to grow.

I couldn't wait to get home that night to tell Amy about my experience, but as seemingly interested and fascinated as she was, I knew that she was distracted and concerned about a major problem that faced us once again. Where were we going to live when our lease in Rego Park ran out the following month? Amy's Uncle Mahlon had died suddenly, and Aunt Tibby had asked us to come and live with her in her little ranch type house in the country until we found a place of our own. Amy had some reservations, as the house was not really suited to the invasion of a family of three. But we didn't have much choice and we thought a short stay with her might help her in her grieving. We placed our little bit of furniture in storage, piled our bare necessities into the old Ford, and rumbled down to Princeton, New Jersey, a charming and vibrant college town, and a place which would become a focal point of all of our lives in the years ahead.

Aunt Tibby

Aunt Tibby was very much alone, with no children. She was strangely appealing but very set in her ways, and rather bitter. Not the easiest person to be with, let alone to live with. As a matter of fact, she was really quite scary. Very tall and thin, with a beak like nose, she nervously walked around, wheezing constantly from severe asthma, occasionally cackling at one of her own smutty jokes. Her breasts, encased in drab halters, hung almost to her waist, and she showed as much of them as the law allowed. She was witch like, and terrified little Tony the minute we entered the house. Our quarters were in a corner of the dining room, partly hidden by a tall screen, and from the beginning we knew this wasn't going to work. She complained constantly and said Tony's crying made her cats nervous, and that her asthma had gotten much worse since we arrived. Poor Amy had to deal with it all day and prayed we would find a place we could afford as quickly as possible.

And we did, after a few disastrous weeks with Aunt Tibby. She was delighted when we left, complaining to the end that we had caused her nervous cats to develop mange, and that she was on the verge of a breakdown. But our next move was almost worse, with another neurotic woman involved in our housing dilemma. Had our move to Princeton been a bit premature? Had we really made the right choice? It certainly didn't seem so at the time.

The houses on Mercer Street near the center of Princeton, and in the surrounding area, more nearly resembled those in the Germantown section of Philadelphia near where Amy's family lived than those I was familiar with on the Main Line. They were closer together, without much land, and gave one the feeling they had been there for many years. I'm sure a goodly number were built originally as residences for people connected to the University as faculty members or visiting scholars. And among these rather substantial homes was a group of four little attached houses just a few doors from the home occupied by Albert Einstein and next to the elderly Schirmer sisters, famous for music publishing. They were owned by an eccentric woman with wild red hair named Anne Freemantle, a recognized writer who specialized in reporting on the liberal theology of some members of the Catholic clergy, and their opposition to the Vatican's traditional stance on most contentious issues.

In the basement of one of the two center houses in the group was an apartment for rent for $100 a month. It was an outrageous amount, at least for that time, for a single room with a bed, a table and one chair, and a hot plate for cooking. The refrigerator was upstairs, and shared with Mrs. Freemantle and her transient household of teenaged children, estranged husband, writers and painters and an odd assortment of religious gurus who came and went at all hours of the day and night. There was one window, almost too high to reach which gave us very little air, and hardly any natural light. Two light bulbs hung from dangerously exposed wires. The bathroom housed a washer and dryer, a makeshift shower, and a utility basin for dish washing, shaving, and bathing Tony.

All in all, it was ghastly, but we took it because nothing else that we could possibly afford was available. I had not, up until this time, asked my father for any assistance and I wasn't going to start now, even though I was feeling quite desperate, and my comfortable childhood seemed in the far distant past. But surely this dreary basement would be better than living in a corner of Aunt Tibby's dining room, surrounded with the ever present threat of complete chaos. At least here it was almost our own little place, and there was a sidewalk outside for strolling with Tony, and a park nearby with swings and a sand pit. But what really made all this bearable was that, within a few weeks, one of the two end houses would be available, and we were told it would be ours if we would just be patient. I think Anne Freemantle liked us, and I know she was impressed with my employment at CBS. Besides, she found Amy easy to talk with about almost anything, for Amy was a good listener, asked intelligent questions, and never tried to out-do her with a story of her own.

So we moved in to this damp little hole. The car stayed in Princeton as I was able to walk to the railroad station and take the "dinky" to Princeton Junction, where the main Philadelphia to New York trains stopped. The "dinky" was like a little trolley, with two cars, and was scheduled to meet every train arriving from both directions. It was kind of charming and I often took Tony for the three mile ride on Saturday or Sunday, something we both enjoyed doing together. But the daily trip to New York added to the commuter costs, which were eating up much of my salary. In addition, the trip, door-to-door, an hour and a half each way, was long and tiring, and if there were problems in the office, I sometimes didn't get home until very late in the evening.

Right in the middle of this helter-skelter summer, adjusting to new places to live, a long commute, and trying to be as good a new father as I could, I was asked to co-head a new CBS softball team that would play in New York's Central Park, in a league against representatives from similar companies. Being such a baseball enthusiast, I guess I was a logical choice, and I had to recruit players from the Production Center. It sounded so easy and it should have been fun, but the time spent organizing, scheduling, and playing the games after work interfered with my delicate living situation at home in Princeton. It wasn't fair to Amy, but I was selfish, and did it anyway and hoped she would understand. I needed the male bonding that is always there when playing on an athletic team, working together and striving to be a winner, "sharing the thrills of victory or the agony of defeat." Perhaps this was a harbinger of some troubling times that were facing us in the not too distant future.

CHAPTER THIRTY-FIVE

During these remarkable days at CBS it was hard to keep abreast of what was going on, but thank goodness for *Variety*, which I still devoured from cover to cover so as not to miss a thing. I had lots of time during my train rides to read, but often on the way home I was so tired that I slept for about half an hour of the trip, miraculously waking up just in time to get off the train at Princeton Junction. No doubt those martinis at lunch had something to do with my need for sleep, and the lunches were becoming a more and more regular occurrence. If they weren't with the advertising people, they were with my boss, Gordon Chadwick, who seemed to have a bottomless pit for his ice-cold-extra-dry-martini-with-a-twist-straight-up.

Years later I came across a Dorothy Parker rhyme:

I'd love to have a martini,

two at the very most.

With three I'm under the table,

with four I'm under the host.

It did remind me of those lunches with Gordon, for I sensed, after three or four cocktails and his inhibitions had been relaxed, that he might have wanted to "come on" to me. But I didn't find him physically attractive nor was I the least bit interested in having an affair with him. He was rather elegant, well educated, very amusing and we had a lot in common. He had grown up and lived in San Francisco in a social environment similar to mine, and we enjoyed each other's company very much. But that was as far as I wanted our relationship to go.

I had struggled with what I looked upon as my abnormal passions for a long time while I was growing up and I didn't want the yearnings for male intimacies to return to haunt me ever again. And they hadn't, for a while, after Amy and I were married. But not too long after, they kept recurring from time to time, and I thought, until the move to New York and my new job at CBS, that they would always be with me no matter how hard I tried to sweep them away into a dark closet. Now, with a child that I had helped create, and our hopes for a second one as soon as we got more permanently settled, I was certain the demons of the past were gone forever, or at least in a permanently dormant state.

Among the "wine buyers" who extended their gratitude to me for serving their rather special needs were the producers from independent packaging companies who created many of the very popular game shows. Occasionally they would ask me to "lift" a little sequence from the "kinne" of a show already aired, for insertion into a new episode for the purpose of continuity. It didn't happen very often, but they thought it was a big deal and a very important part of their production, and I loved being involved in that creative process. These entrepreneurs were quite different from the advertising people in that they talked show "production," rather than show sponsorship, and money was less of a focal point than creativity.

The game shows had proliferated to the point where there was at least one on every night of the week. My favorites were *What's My Line?* and *Name That Tune*, both of which had bright and amusing hosts and panel members, and dealt with subjects that appealed to me. There was another, a former popular radio show, called *Information Please*, hosted by author and editor Clifton Fadiman. It was quite scholarly and a bit more demanding which is probably why it was short lived. Most of the television audience wanted to be entertained and not overly challenged.

The real winners in public acceptance were the shows that gave away large sums of money to contestants who, in return, had to answer difficult questions about such obscure subjects as the genealogy of rare fish or the number of single Oriental women in the western hemisphere in 1902. The amount of prize money kept increasing to the point where a winner on one of the shows could receive as much as $64,000, a very large sum in those days, and at my then current salary, would take me more than ten years to reach.

It was a real shock to the millions of viewers, and to me personally, when it was discovered that there was some behind-the-scenes maneuvering, and that this big money game had been "fixed." The CBS programming chiefs were no doubt aware of what the packager of the show was doing, but turned their collective backs and closed their eyes to what was happening with the hope of assuring high ratings, and beating the other networks in viewership. So to show their concern, a widely publicized edict was immediately issued that no more gifts could be accepted by CBS employees, and lunches, cocktails, dinners and who knows what else, had to be strictly business oriented.

It was during this gloomy time at CBS that Amy, Tony and I moved into our house on Mercer Street. It had a lot of charm, but was very small, with three bedrooms and one bath. The living room had a bay window and there was a front porch that looked out on beautiful old trees and grass across the street. We were more than happy to be there after our last two housing fiascos, and even though it was a bit run-down and needed fresh paint and some repairs, we set about to make it our home for the foreseeable future. To us it was a palace compared to Aunt Tibby's dining room "suite," and the dark and dingy basement next door.

It was a kind of communal experience living in one these attached houses with a back porch that extended to connect all four of them. But it was sort of fun, at least at first. Anne Freemantle regularly included us in her little dinner parties on the porch and her guests were always interesting, with such distinguished people as Bud Shulberg, the author, and Dorothy Day, the servant of the poor and editor of the *Catholic Worker*. The conversations at dinner were way over my head, but I enjoyed it nonetheless, and between mouthfuls of Anne's tasteless overcooked food, Amy and I managed to offer enough insightful comments to warrant another invitation.

And how many people could say that they saw Albert Einstein, in person, walk past their house every morning at about 8:15 on his way to the Institute For Advanced Study? He occasionally mumbled a "Good morning" or waved his hand when he felt like it. But even when he did nothing, it didn't matter. It was Albert Einstein...and that was enough.

In spite of the unfortunate quiz show scandal and a temporary setback in public opinion, CBS Television remained at the top among the highly competitive broadcast networks and usually had the most top rated programs for the week. It had gained an enviable reputation and came to be known as the "Tiffany Network," a phrase coined appropriately by someone who chose to compare New York's finest jewelry emporium with a company specializing in the world of make believe. It was generally recognized by anyone with any knowledge of the entertainment business that the CBS family had a special quality about it, one that NBC and ABC couldn't seem to equal.

There was an indefinable spirit among its employees with a loyalty and dedication to the company that was unquestionably the motivating factor that drove it to such a high plane.

I'm sure nobody would argue the fact that this prevailing sense of family came about as a result of the quiet leadership of the president, Dr. Frank Stanton. He ran the company with much dignity and grace, qualities not often associated with such an emotionally charged business. On the other hand, Mr. Paley, the founder and Chairman of the Board, was the flamboyant figurehead with a keen insight into what the viewer wanted and an extraordinary ability to round up the talent to make it all happen.

In addition to television and radio programming, there was the CBS Records Division, long a leader in its field, and the Stations Division, with outlets in almost every city in the country. But perhaps the most respected entity that made the company so distinguished was its News Division. Since the days of World War II, CBS News radio reporters had become household names, and such outstanding correspondents as Charles Collingwood, Howard K. Smith, and Richard C. Hotelett were now hosting TV news programs, and the latest vehicle for doing in-depth reporting, the documentary.

There were many others that I admired, but there are two names that, in my opinion, will always be synonymous with journalistic excellence, and I was proud to be their fellow employee. One was Walter Cronkite, who became the most recognizable figure in the American culture. This was the result of his anchoring, with much appeal and authority, the evening news as well as various on location live events, such as convention and election coverage and, in recent years, man's journey into outer space. And who could ever forget the picture of Walter taking a deep breath, removing his glasses and announcing in a choked up voice that President Kennedy was dead.

The other was Edward R. Murrow, who was the master of investigative and informative journalism, with his weekly program *See It Now* and his probing documentaries like *Harvest of Shame*, which explored and developed awareness of the plight of the migrant worker.

I can remember so distinctly the time when we, as an audience on the east coast, first saw, live, the sunrise above the majestic Golden Gate Bridge in San Francisco. It didn't need much description from Ed Murrow, but he was as excited as the rest of us, reporting on the first pictures transmitted live, across the nation, on an intercontinental two-way telephone line. It had been developed to bring us west coast produced programs and news events as they were happening, and visa versa. This was a major step in providing the audience with a whole new means of immediate entertainment originating in Hollywood, always known for its relatively relaxed pace in the production of film.

With this remarkable technology, Mr. Murrow didn't waste any time in developing a new half hour interview type program entitled *Person To Person*. Mobile units, with remote cameras and sound, visited the homes of dignitaries in various parts of the country, and Hollywood celebrities like Humphrey Bogart and Lauren Bacall, or the beautiful Sophia Loren, in their palatial mansions. And while we saw him sitting in a CBS studio setting in New York, chatting with his guests while looking at a TV monitor, we all shared with him a personal tour of their mansions, complete with descriptions by the residents of their intimate daily lives and prized personal possessions. Even Dwight and Mamie Eisenhower, on a weekend retreat from the White House, took us on a tour of their lovely farm in Gettysburg, Pennsylvania. I had the great good fortune to work with Ed Murrow on several of these TV visits, supervising the editing and supplying film used to promote a guest's latest movie or book, cleverly integrated into the program so that it would not look like a promotional announcement. On the first Christmas eve we were in our little house in Princeton, a chauffeur driven station wagon with Connecticut license plates arrived bearing two plump pheasants, freshly killed that morning, and presented to us with best holiday wishes from Edward R. Murrow. There were instructions tied to the leg of one of the birds saying they should be hung, head down, in a tree overnight, and would be ready for roasting on Christmas day.

Amy was flabbergasted with the whole idea, and since we already had plans to go to Philadelphia, she took the advice of Aunt Tibby, borrowed her shovel, and gave them a dignified burial in Anne Fremantle's flower garden. I, of course, never told Mr. Murrow what we had done with his thoughtful gift, and I wrote in my thank you note a small lie about how delicious they were.

"What's the tune they like the best,

when the jive becomes deluxe?

What's the number one request,

720 In The Books."

The great Bon Bon singing with the Jan Savitt orchestra; a classic of the big band era and certainly a collector's item. One of the things I looked forward to most about living in a place with a little extra room, was to finally unpack my large record collection which I had started when I was about twelve or thirteen. I loved the sound of the big bands, and on many of the days and nights when I was a teenager and needed to escape to the privacy of my room, I would pretend to be a disk jockey, playing the great recordings of Goodman, Miller, the Dorseys, and Shaw. With the windows wide open, I chain-smoked Old Golds and was in a heavenly haze as I listened to the voices of Helen O'Connell and Bob Eberle sing the songs that are now considered classics. The theme song for my "show" was "Smoke Dreams" by Tommy Reynolds, a clone of Artie Shaw. I can't recall the melody but I do remember, to my complete surprise and utmost delight, suddenly hearing it live at a debutante party right near our house in Haverford. I was too young to be invited, but I did get a glimpse of the band through the flaps of the elaborate tent erected for the affair.

Late at night while lying in bed I would listen to the bands on the radio coming from road houses like the Glen Island Casino and the Meadowbrook and the ballrooms in the New York hotels. And then there were the soulful sounds of the black performers at the Apollo Theater in Harlem which lulled me off to sleep well after midnight.

So it was a devastating blow the night a severe winter rain storm hit Princeton flooding our basement and destroying the entire collection of hundreds of records, still in their boxes. I was more upset with that than the fact that the furnace fizzled out and the three of us nearly froze to death as the pile of newly delivered coal was under water. But, as they say it's always darkest before the dawn, and shortly thereafter this seeming disaster Amy announced, for the second time, that she was pregnant. How remarkable are the vicissitudes of life, and the marvels that God and man can create. To our little family would come another, and every bit as precious as the first.

CHAPTER THIRTY-SIX

During the hot summer of 1955 while awaiting the birth of our second child, we would often load up our new second-hand Ford station wagon and drive down to Beach Haven to see Grandma. Our old black heap had been through a lot and was faithful to the end but, sadly, had to be retired to the junk yard. Aunt Tibby also had a new car and she was thrilled with it. It was the latest Nash, with a reclining seat, and she would park it in front of our house on Mercer Street and lay herself out like a dead person, moaning and gasping for breath, hoping to be invited in for iced tea.

Amy and I both loved my grandmother and I'll never quite get over Amy calling Grandma Cousin Lucie. I often wondered if our children should call her Cousin Lucie as well? I suppose it would be correct, but wouldn't it sound funny if I called her Grandma and my children called her Cousin Lucie? A small dilemma to be faced in the future.

Four generations
Grandma, Mother, Tony and me

On some weekends, like Aunt Tibby, we took the hour-long drive down to the New Jersey shore to visit Amy's parents. Her mother, Tibby's sister, owned one of the original three houses in Manteloking, New Jersey, a small but very exclusive seaside town with many huge rambling summer cottages nestled in the sand dunes by the ocean's edge. The Bell family house was comparatively small and rather rundown, and unfortunately right on the main highway that connected the towns along the coastline. But they loved it, and I did too, and when the traffic noise was overpowering, we just moved into the kitchen, in the back of the house.

Life at the Bell's was much simpler than in Beach Haven, with Amy's mother presiding over a more relaxed and carefree household. The crabs and lobsters scurried around on the kitchen floor waiting for the water to boil for their final bath, and the red-winged black birds picked at the bayberry bushes outside the kitchen window. The only life really being affected by the air pollution, created by the traffic, were the Yucca plants out front majestically holding their own as the cars raced by. Even Aunt Tibby stopped complaining when she was here, and would laugh and joke as she breathed in the sea air, easing her nagging asthma attacks. But the person who seemed to enjoy it the most was Amy's father, who was constantly busying himself with the endless repairs needed by the old place. Just patching the holes in the screens was a full time job, and trying to cover the shabbiness with paint seemed to be a losing battle. And in his quiet and gentle way, he was an inspiration to me, and I respected him greatly; so much in fact that we decided to name our new baby, if a boy, Henry Bell Dale.

The daily tension and frantic pace experienced at CBS was left behind when I was at the beach on those summer weekends, and especially while on my two-week vacation. It was a pure delight strolling through the rolling waves, holding hands with my little Tony and watching the sandpipers running back and forth on the sand, never getting their feet wet. I counted my blessings that we were now settled in a nice little house, with a growing family, and I had a good job with a company that I loved. We even had a reliable car to go and visit with our old friends in Philadelphia. As good as things seemed to be, they could only get better in the coming years, and I thanked God for helping to steer me in the right direction, and for giving meaning to a life that had been filled with so much turmoil and unhappiness. But could it last? Were those ugly demons that haunted me, and that I knew so well, really gone forever? Would all those confusing thoughts disappear and become a thing of the past? I wondered and worried about it, but knew that only time would tell and that there was absolutely nothing I could do about it.

Harry Hess, Jerry McNally and I worked very well together as commercial coordinators and they were among my closest friends at CBS. But one day they both decided to leave the company and to move on to better paying jobs at advertising agencies. I wasn't that surprised as I too had been approached but, after consulting with several people I trusted who had been with the company for a while, I decided to stay. Even after such a short time—only four years—I felt a tremendous loyalty to CBS and though the salary would have been much higher somewhere else, I was moving ahead pretty rapidly, with commensurate pay increases coming at least once every year. Anyway, the offer didn't really appeal to me, especially when I learned that I would be assigned to help sell products like Geritol, a tonic for the aging, and Pepto Bismol, a stomach acid reducer. In addition, the agency representative who approached me appeared to

204

be another of those who might have wanted to become a little too friendly, a little too intimate.

Instead of replacing Harry and Jerry with two new people with similar responsibilities, I was assigned a secretary and an assistant, something I had hardly thought about as happening to me so soon. I didn't do the hiring, and I don't think I would have chosen the people selected for me. But as it turned out, Gordon Chadwick, our boss, knew best, and the two weren't nearly as bad as I had thought they would be. My assistant was a young, officious, and rather prissy young man named Sherwin, who turned out to be so efficient, and completely reliable that I had to overlook his total lack of personality or humor...and the fact that he wore excessively tight pants. He took on twice as much work than was expected of him which left me to handle the more prestigious accounts, those that were less demanding and more secure with their clients.

And, Margie, the new secretary, only had eyes for Hollywood and was sure that this was a stepping stone to her career goal of being a producer of programs with glamorous movie stars, shot in exotic locations. But she had the required skills, did her job efficiently, and was pleasant on the telephone, which probably accounted for her early departure for, what *Variety* called, Tinsel Town. She got her wish after a while and was hired by a branch office of the advertising agency that handled the Pond's cosmetics account, with all its gorgeous models. When she left, she promised to show me around the magic city if by chance, "you should ever find your way west of New Jersey."

With all this help, I had a little more time to spend at home with Amy and Tony, as we prepared for our new arrival. This time Amy's pregnancy was much easier to bear than it had been in Rego Park, with a friendlier obstetrician and hardly any unpleasant side effects. In addition to Anne Freemantle's coterie of assorted intelligentsia, we had made some nice friends who were connected with the nearby Institute For Advanced Study, a think tank and research center. With the likes of Albert Einstein and the acknowledged creator of the atomic bomb, J. Robert Oppenheimer, the Institute was a workplace for a whole different galaxy of stars than I was used to at CBS. I managed to squeeze in a little tennis with some of them on the courts of the Princeton Graduate School directly behind our house. I was becoming a part of our new-found community, raising money for a new YMCA building and joining a neighborhood acting group, appearing as a young lover in an obscure murder mystery, the name of which I can't remember. My performance was adequate at best, and was thankfully ignored in the review appearing in *Town Topics*, the Princeton weekly newspaper.

Amy's mother was unable to be with Amy during this birth, so we asked my mother to come for a few days and stay with Tony while I was at work. We were much more organized and experienced as everything was ready when another boy, Henry Bell Dale, nicknamed Harry after his grandfather, was born in Princeton Hospital on

September 7th, 1955, the same day as my brother Ted's birthday. It was a much easier time for Amy, and she only went through a couple of hours of labor. She almost looked refreshed holding what I'm sure was the most beautiful baby I had ever seen. Not that Tony wasn't beautiful. He was, but Harry looked like all the pictures you see on the Gerber's baby food jars, or the infants peeking out from under an ultra-soft blanket. He had blonde hair and a rosy complexion, and lying there next to his lovely mother, they were enchanting to behold and a sight I shall never forget.

But my mother had a more difficult time in that she had never changed diapers or prepared food in a kitchen or even pushed a stroller along a sidewalk. She had employed nurses and housemaids to do that sort of thing, and when she saw her own three sons when they were babies, they were always bathed and fed and dressed in blue, smelling of fresh talcum powder. I sometimes wonder how much time I spent being snuggled in her arms, or those of my father, when I needed their attention. Not very much I suspect, as outward displays of affection and love were not considered appropriate, at least not in my family.

So, when I got home from work, she was badly in need of my help, and I had a lot to do. She didn't complain, but I'm certain her three days alone with Tony had definitely been a difficult learning experience, and one that surely caused her to appreciate motherhood in a whole different way. I'm not at all sure she would offer her services again.

There are so many differences between generations, and it gave me a lot of satisfaction in being able show my mother, usually a lady of leisure, that people's lives are not so simple when one is not only struggling to make ends meet, but trying to help out with the chores at home. I had learned from Amy that one's values have little to do with what money can buy, and that there is nothing more fulfilling than sharing the difficult moments, as well as the good, with your own child. Perhaps my childhood would have been a happier one, and I would have been better adjusted and more prepared for the days ahead if there had been a little more physical expression of tenderness and love and a more hands-on approach to the daily trials of growing up. To this day, I sometimes have trouble expressing myself physically even though I may love someone very much. I became increasingly aware that parenting must be a first priority, and I vowed that I would never allow anything that I had control over to interfere with the care and devotion of my children.

CHAPTER THIRTY-SEVEN

There are always differences, likes and dislikes, in every marriage and ours was no exception. One thing I hadn't considered when I married Amy was the fact that she really wasn't very interested in competitive sports, in spite of the fact that her father was a loyal fan of all the Philadelphia teams. She thought it was downright silly, and rather juvenile to take winning so seriously. I didn't mention it very often, but I couldn't wait for the boys to be old enough to enjoy playing catch with me, and to get them prepared for the days ahead, an assortment of balls could usually be found in their cribs. Amy was increasingly annoyed with the amount of time I was giving to the CBS softball team, and for a short while a basketball league. But I just loved the activity and camaraderie that playing team sports could bring, and I quietly hoped that Tony and Harry would love them too, whether they were competitive in nature or not—as a player or a fan.

Now, six years after my coaching days and involvement in the athletic program at Montgomery Country Day School, I was a part of, although peripherally, a different kind of team. CBS was venturing into a new game, the television coverage of sporting events, a development that endeared me even more to this remarkably diversified corporation. I was thrilled when they announced that they would be televising the last three holes of the prestigious Masters Golf Tournament from Augusta, Georgia, and I couldn't wait to tell Mother the news. Finally there would be something on television that she could truly relate to; the soap operas and sit-coms not exactly being her "cup of tea." The new sports department had been covering some football and basketball, primarily of local teams, but the decision to expand into two-day coverage of an event requiring multiple camera set-ups, and miles away from the home base in New York was a real breakthrough. What a daunting task it was, with failure predicted by the pessimistic sports writers who were convinced it would never succeed. But succeed it did, and with the advent of color, and coverage of all eighteen holes, it became one of the premier sports attractions on television and one of the longest running annual series on any single network.

In the fall of 1956, another sports first occurred...but not at CBS. It was on a mild, sunny October day at Yankee Stadium where I saw, in person, the historic perfect no hit game pitched in the baseball World Series by Yankee pitcher Don Larson. I guess people at CBS had detected by now my enthusiasm for sports, particularly baseball. So when Larry Racies, a CBS film cameraman who was assigned to cover the game for CBS News, asked me if I would like to assist him and stand with him in the little camera platform that hung out over the field from the second deck, I was honestly dumbfounded. It was a busy work day but I managed to convince Gordon Chadwick, who disliked baseball, that it was important for me to learn a little about what was involved in shooting film. He reluctantly agreed, and off I went to one of the most memorable afternoons of my life. I stood behind Larry and his camera for nine exciting innings and watched, from the best vantage point in the stadium, as the Yankees beat the Dodgers in game five of the World Series. The incredible way in which it was done is a milestone in the annals of baseball. A once in a lifetime happening and I was there.

I don't recall if that was the day that I found Amy waiting at the front door with the news that the ceiling had collapsed in one of the bedrooms in our house on Mercer Street and very nearly landed in Harry's crib. If it was, it was the day that I was certain, in my euphoric state, that we should look for a house to buy. I was tired of paying rent for this crumbling, old structure when I was sure we could afford something of our own. In spite of floods and cave-ins, we had many very happy days there, and loved the location and proximity to the center of town. But now it was time to make a move and invest in some place that would be our home for years to come. Hopefully it would be in a neighborhood where the boys could have close friends, just as I did in Haverford when I was growing up, and we could settle into a less transient life. We had lived in six different places in our eight years of marriage, and it was time to put down some roots. However, if I somehow had known that there was going to be so many difficult and unhappy days ahead, I'm not at all sure I would have wanted to make such an important investment in our future.

Although most of the half-hour situation comedies were produced and filmed in California, there were a few that were shot on the east coast in New York. Some producers and directors were more comfortable working in a place where they could call on a stable of experienced actors, or comedians, many of whom were in plays or musicals on and off Broadway. A good example of this was the hilarious *The Phil Silvers Show*, starring the great vaudevillian and a Tony award winner for the long running theatrical production of *Top Banana*. For the half-hour television show the producer, Eddie Montagne, and writer Nat Hiken, along with Silvers, surrounded themselves with an inspired ensemble cast playing privates in the army under Silvers' Sergeant Bilko, an outrageous character who abused and protected his troops with equal intensity. It was filmed in front of a live audience, which added to the spontaneity of each episode, and was just as popular, for a while at least, as CBS's long-time ratings leader, *I Love Lucy*.

Without any experience, our Film Department was given the responsibility for overseeing all of the technical and service personnel and equipment of some of the "below-the-line" aspects of the production (studio, editing, etc.). A few of the Camel cigarette commercials were integrated into the show, with Silvers as the spokesman, and it was the first time I had been so close to a TV production from the opening billboard to the end credits—a revelation and a dream come true. Even though the studio was in another

212

building, I really started to learn about the tremendous amount of time and effort and dedication that went into the making of just one half-hour program, and what many of us viewers just took for granted while we were being entertained in our living rooms.

And I was no exception. But while most people were watching TV to put aside, for a few moments, the problems of every day life, I was running away, once again, from those disturbing thoughts that had returned to haunt me on a regular basis. I hoped, when we moved to a new house, that they would again disappear as they had when we relocated to New York from Philadelphia. But this time I was tormented continually, even as we were preparing to move. Yet I never stopped hoping that these persistent fantasies would disappear, as they had before, into their secret chamber. There surely was that possibility if I continued to be totally absorbed in my work and, in addition, the many challenges of a new property owner. It was my responsibility to provide for my wife and children the best way I could and if my libido was, once again, not in sync with Amy's, then I had to struggle my hardest to make the best of it. But there wasn't anything much I could do to satisfy her physical desires on a regular basis so I naively decided that she would be more accepting of my failure to please her if I showered more of my attention and expressions of love on the children.

We found our new home with the help of Peggy Mott, a friend of Aunt Tibby's but far less eccentric. She lived in Lawrenceville, a small town a few miles down the road from Princeton, and had watched as a new house was being built across the street from her. Mrs. Mott was a widow with two grown sons, lived alone, and worried about who her new neighbors were going to be. With her gentle persuasion, it didn't take long for us to decide that it was a perfect place for us. I finally got up the courage to ask my father for a little financial help to make a down payment, and after he made a thorough inspection, he decided it was a good investment, and a fine place for "my grandsons to grow up." He gave me a long- term loan of $5,000. With a very large mortgage, we were able to buy our four bedroom, two bath house for $26,500.

It was what was commonly known as a split level, with a fireplace, a playroom, and a one car garage. Situated on a quarter of an acre of terraced land, there were some nice big old trees and newly planted shrubbery around the house. Mrs. Mott, in addition to giving us two mimosa saplings as a house warming gift, was very helpful in welcoming us into this friendly little neighborhood, made up of a nice mixture of older, established families and younger couples, with children.

So, with the move to Lawrenceville in 1956 (which I hoped would be the last one for a long, long time), a new chapter in life's adventure began. My commute was longer, my expenses were greater, and my head was spinning. But we were happy to be in a home of our own, and it seemed that our lives together, with our babies as our primary concern, would at least be tolerable, if not even somewhat complete.

CHAPTER THIRTY-EIGHT

Beatrice Lillie was a well known English musical comedy star and a clever comedienne who came to this country to perform in several productions in New York. She married an English Lord and was known thereafter in both social and theatrical circles as Lady Peel, although her autobiography was entitled, *Every Other Inch a Lady*...which perfectly described her. My mother found her very amusing and took me to see her when her shows premiered in Philadelphia. Because she played on Broadway quite often, she kept an apartment on the east side of New York, and I was invited there for cocktails one evening after work by her nephew, Grant Tyler. He lived there, and I was delighted with the idea of meeting her and reporting to Mother on every detail of my visit. I had worked with Grant for some time as one of my many advertising agency contacts, but never knew of his relationship to the celebrated Lady Peel. But, either by circumstance or by plan, she was away for the evening, and even though I would be able to describe her beautifully decorated home, it was a big disappointment, and I felt a little uncomfortable having cocktails with Grant alone.

I did call Mother the next day, but didn't tell her that, after numerous martinis, I had been seduced by Lady Peel's very handsome and charming nephew in Lady Peel's queen sized bed, and was feeling considerable shame for my behavior. Of course, I couldn't tell Amy, or anyone, about this scandalous affair, and my memory of it was rather dim. But what really disturbed me and worried me the most was that I enjoyed it immensely. I couldn't get it out of my mind, and it was like a tiny ray of light that had entered my dark, cloudy and troubled thoughts. Was this moment of sublime sexual satisfaction some sort of a beacon to guide me into a distant world, a world which was only vaguely familiar to me, and yet seemingly close at hand? Were my adolescent experiences in years past not just child's play and mere fantasy, but a signpost to the path that I should be following? What kind of a life would that be? Would I be living a perverse existence in a society that would find me completely unacceptable? I struggled with these questions and many others, as daily life continued, and I held my secret deep in my heart.

Bob Miller, one of my new neighbors in Lawrenceville, who owned the largest and most impressive home in our little enclave of about twenty houses, also commuted to New York, and, as a good neighbor, offered me a daily ride with him to the Princeton Junction railroad station each day. One morning, as we were hurrying to make the morning train, and shortly after my salacious affair, his Volkswagen "beetle" was hit a glancing blow from behind by another car. We rolled over twice into a corn field, ended right side up, and somehow opened the doors and got out as if nothing had happened. The other car disappeared. The veterinarian across the street, being used to the symptoms of shock, took us in and advised us to lie down on the blankets that he had reserved for dogs and wait for an ambulance to take us to the hospital.

After being checked out in the emergency room and told to go home and rest, we both, being ridiculously conscientious, took a taxi to the station and made the next train to New York. Amy and Marge Miller, on the other hand, saw the totally wrecked "beetle" being towed through Lawrenceville and thought we both must be dead.

I often recall this incident, not because of the frightening accident, but only to review in my mind how much Amy cared for me as she cried with joy when she learned I was alive and unhurt. How hateful I was to be jeopardizing my marriage to someone who loved me so much, and who was again having to struggle with the reality that I was not physically attracted to her. She even tried, without much success to make herself more sexually appealing, and I'm sure she could have easily seduced most any suitor. But the fact was that my one taste, since our marriage, of a homosexual encounter with an adult opened the door to many others, and our relationship began to deteriorate completely. It became more and more difficult to even sleep in the same bed with her. I was filled with guilt and shame and painfully confused.

It is too unpleasant to recall this period of leading a completely double life, of hasty affairs in New York during the lunch hour and clandestine meetings in the evenings before making the last train. It almost seemed as though a number of my acquaintances, both at CBS and in the advertising world, had been patiently waiting for the door to open, somehow knowing that someday I would let them into my quiet room and share my passions with them.

With so much on my mind, it was really quite amazing that I was able to perform my job with the same efficiency and continue to feel reasonably comfortable around my home and my children. Thanks to Amy, she kept her frustrations to herself, and as far as I can remember, Tony and Harry were never privy to the late night quarrels we had, or the coolness that we were both feeling for each other.

With all the complications at home, perhaps it was a good thing that there were so many new things happening at CBS to think about. In our department I received another promotion and became a supervisor, specifically assigned to the integration of television's newest innovation, video tape. It was first used for the making of commercials and involved utilizing television cameras (instead of film) which electronically transmitted pictures and sound to giant recording machines using two-inch tape, and then immediately playing them back through a television set. There were no delays for film processing and printing, and the advertisers could present their messages as fast as it took to select the best "take", and edit whatever was necessary. The quality had an almost live look to it if recorded under ideal lighting conditions and, except for the purists, of which there were many, they made as good a presentation as any film commercial which had taken weeks to shoot, develop and print.

For us it became a dual operation. It meant setting up a whole new library for the video tape commercials adjacent to the recording and playback machines themselves, which, for transmission purposes, were located next to the film projectors in good old Telecine, high above Grand Central Station. In effect, we had two similar operations going, and it led to considerable confusion and masterful organizing, deciding what was to be aired on film and what on tape. Again, it must be remembered that we're talking about hundreds of different commercials everyday, seven days a week, twenty-four hours a day, representing millions of dollars of advertising revenue. The responsibilities were enormous, to say the least, and keeping everyone happy, from advertising executives and their clients to CBS management, was a daunting task.

And into this turbulent time of trouble at home and new challenges at CBS, a needed breath of fresh air came into my life. His name was Arnold Walton, and he, like so many others, had a problem with some commercials, which my ever efficient assistant, Sherwin, couldn't seem to resolve. Arnie, waving his arms and complaining in a loud voice all the way, was ushered into my office, our eyes met, and my life started anew. His arms fell to his side, his voiced lowered, and his problem became secondary. We arranged to meet that evening, for what was the beginning of a happy and loving relationship that has lasted to this very day in the year 2000, forty-two years later.

CHAPTER THIRTY-NINE

It was a steamy summer night in 1958 when Arnie Walton and I were having drinks, talking business (and touching knees under the table) in the piano bar of the Drake Hotel. We did talk about the service he was, or wasn't, getting from our department, but we also talked about other things. I told him about my grandmother and grandfather Lord, and how they rented the whole top floor of the Drake one winter when some of their children wanted to spend the holidays, and time away from school and colleges, in New York City. The apartment belonged to Enrico Caruso, the renowned opera singer, who was on a concert tour, and who wouldn't be using it during the winter months. It had plenty of room for all nine children, plus assorted servants, and Grandma and Grandpa could spend evenings going to the theater and concerts. It was something they loved to do but unfortunately were unable to very often, living thirty miles away in Tarrytown.

The winters, following the end of World War I, were much more severe in those days and it was very difficult for separated friends and lovers to get together. For my mother, Janet, at age nineteen, to rendezvous with her fiancee, my soldier father, Edwin, who had just returned from overseas, was often a frustrating and failed adventure.

Mother had been in love with him since she was sixteen when he had made his first visit to Tarrytown with his Hill School roommate and Mother's brother, Ed, and she had waited patiently for his return from that terrible war, the one that we were all told was "the war to end all wars." And so being in New York City at Christmas time with him would be a magical experience, one that could only be matched by their wedding day several years hence.

Arnie seemed to love hearing about my family and all the many tales there were to tell about them. He wanted to know everything and was fascinated by the social milieu from which they came. He seldom interrupted except to remind me that his background was quite different from mine, that he was only a second generation American. My family history on my mother's side dated back to the days of the arrival of the 110 pilgrims, with direct descendants aboard the Mayflower. He suggested he had never known anyone with such an ancestry.

In more recent times, in 1893, when she was eighteen years old, Lucie Taylor Weart, my grandmother, had traveled by stagecoach from Independence, Iowa to Philadelphia to visit some members of her family. She never returned home, having met and married Charles Edwin Lord, my grandfather, and the widower of her cousin. With her new husband, she became mother to a nine-year old child, Mary, and then had eight more children of her own. Grandpa was a successful textile merchant, and with his partner, William T. Galey, founded a cotton spinning mill in Chester, Pennsylvania and developed the Galey & Lord line of fine cotton fabrics, known throughout the fashion industry for their distinctive style.

I told Arnie about how, with his considerable success and his need to be closer to New York City, the textile capital of the world, he built a magnificent home high above the Hudson River in Tarrytown, New York and named it "Broadreach." It was a short distance from the Rockefeller estate and adjacent to Marymount College, where the dutiful nuns could easily be engaged to give the children their private catechism instruction and preparation for confirmation into the Catholic Church.

It was Arnie's never-ending inquisitiveness that helped me remember so many things that I'd almost forgotten. I told him about my father, and how he had spent the first eleven years of his life living in Brooklyn, not far from where Arnie's childhood home was located. My father's family name had been Hobbs, but he and his mother had been deserted by Mr. Hobbs, always a family mystery that was never discussed as I was growing up. Sadie Peters Hobbs, his mother, ultimately married Major Chalmers Dale, United States Army, and my father, Edwin, was legally adopted and took his stepfather's name. They lived in Cold Spring, New York, across the Hudson River from the United States Military Academy at West Point.

I told him about my father's visit to "Broadreach" and how he was smitten by sixteen year old Janet and captivated by the entire Lord clan. The four younger brothers went to The Hotchkiss School in

Lakeville, Connecticut, a rival of the Hill School and a more exclusive preparatory institution for the Ivy League colleges like Yale…which they all ultimately attended.

With this brief bit of my heritage swirling around in his head, Arnie invited me back to his little one room garden apartment near the United Nations for a late supper. I made the last train home that night, which would become a fairly regular occurrence in the months ahead. Later on that summer of 1958 I told Arnie I would be away for a week vacationing with my family at a beach house in Bay Head, New Jersey, which Mother and Dad had rented. He continued to woo me by suddenly appearing at the house with the excuse that he just happened to be at the shore visiting some other friends.

That night after he left, lying in bed next to Amy, I sobbed as I told her, for the first time, of my sexual desires, and though I deeply loved her and always would, I could do nothing about my need for male intimacy. I said how very hard I had tried to bury what I considered those hateful demons that nagged me constantly, but that I had lost the battle and had finally given in to their powers. I doubt if this came as much of a surprise, but to hear me say it as I lay in the bed right beside her, I'm sure was a shock and certainly a great disappointment. She said nothing, rolled over on her side with her back to me and gave me something I had experienced many times before when she was upset and frustrated. Silence!

The next day, while Amy was on the beach with the children, I sat for a long time in a wicker rocking chair with my feet up on a the

225

porch railing, staring at the horizon, debating my situation and wondering what the next step should be. I'm sure Amy was doing the same, as she watched Tony and Harry playing by the water's edge. When we returned home to Lawrenceville, barely communicating, I think we both had made up our minds that changes had to be made.

CHAPTER FORTY

The 1950's were known as the golden age of television and I was a part of it. I was there almost from the very beginning, not necessarily as a creative force, but as part of the whole spectrum; part of an industry that shaped the views of the world, that broadened visions, that made people laugh, and cry, and think. If many of the shows might have been considered light entertainment, they still had a considerable impact on our daily lives, whether we knew it or not. Practically everyone watched at least one of the TV family programs, like *Leave It To Beaver*, *Ozzie and Harriet*, or CBS's *Father Knows Best*, where no one raised their voices, everyone ate everything on their plate, and problems were equitably solved in less than half an hour.

Then there were the variety shows, from *The Jackie Gleason Show* which included sketches of the hilarious Honeymooners, to Sid Caesar's *Show Of Shows* with a staff of brilliant comedy writers that included Neil Simon, Mel Brooks, Larry Gelbart and Woody Allen. CBS presented *The Red Skelton Show*, along with *Arthur Godfrey's Talent Scouts*, where the likes of Rosemary Clooney, Tony Bennett, and Patsy Cline gained national prominence and stardom. With *Gunsmoke, Rawhide* and *Wanted Dead Or Alive*, CBS offered its share of westerns, with young gunslinger heroes who would become household names, like Burt Reynolds, Clint Eastwood, and Steve McQueen. If nothing else, people usually watched and shared their enjoyment with someone else, and often the shows were the subject of discussion at the office, or in the market, the next morning. "Did you see…?" were the operative words when the phones started to ring.

It was pretty much of a ritual on Saturday mornings in our house to be with my boys watching the amiable *Captain Kangaroo*, and his good friend Mr. Greenjeans. While we were all in our pajamas, I would cuddle them in my arms and try to explain a little bit about how the Captain did the things he did. And when a piece of film came on the show, I told them that I had helped pick it out, and it was my little contribution to all the funny and interesting things that happened. They were unimpressed, but just liked being with me. I didn't tell them that the one time I had met the Captain I found him rather disagreeable and that the wild animals that Mr. Greenjeans told us about would invariably leave an awful mess in the freight elevator. We had a good laugh when I imitated all my friends scratching themselves when the fleas in the visiting flea circus escaped from their container. They knew about fleas because we had a new Dachshund, named Maggie, who used to scratch the fleas in her ears until we gave her a bath.

Harry, Tony and Maggie

I looked forward to my weekends in our cozy little home in Lawrenceville, to cutting the grass and washing the car, and visiting with all the new friends that we had made. I'm sure everyone thought we were just like them, or the TV families, with common, ordinary problems...and easy solutions. What they didn't know, and would never see on television, until many years later, was a husband and father who needed another man to make his life complete. And there was Arnie waiting for him in New York City, wondering about what decisions would be made in determining the future.

There were so many things that I began to remember as I rode the train back and forth to work everyday. My eyes were closed, but now I wasn't napping. It was the only time I could be alone with my thoughts, and I kept recalling certain incidents that might have offered a clue as to what was to come. I remembered when I was eleven years old a teacher had asked me to sit on his lap and fondle him, and I had a vivid recollection of the time when I was thirteen when I was almost raped in my bunk by a counselor at summer camp, and how I fought to escape when I realized what he was doing to me. Why me? What was it about me that made them think I might be approachable?

And then, shortly thereafter, there were the seemingly serious, and emotionally charged, romances with several boys through the school years that overshadowed any love interest I had with girls…and were much more memorable. I thought about the times when I was sure that I was the only person who was inclined this way, the only person who craved an intimate male relationship. I even made feeble attempts at committing suicide. Burying my head with my pillow, or drinking Peroxide, were not very effective. Fortunately, I never thought to use my father's World War I loaded pistol, which I had discovered he kept in the bottom drawer of his bureau.

Now I knew I was not alone, and that there were many people like me, some struggling with their guarded sexuality while others accepting it as their way of life. This was comforting and gave me the courage to follow my inclinations, even though I was sure it would be at the expense of my family. But I couldn't bear the thought of being separated from Amy and the children, and just hoped and prayed, as ridiculous as it may sound, that I could go on living this double life. Were there any fellow CBS employees and young married friends floundering in the same dark waters? Did I dare discuss my inclinations with anyone?

I had talked to our family doctor one time early in our marriage and he didn't seem to know what I was talking about. At Amy's insistence I went to see a psychiatrist right after our return home from Bay Head where I had divulged my secret to her. He gave me about five minutes of his time and abruptly ended the appointment after a few questions without the slightest bit of encouragement or suggestion that I continue with therapy. I often wonder why he acted with such disregard, but it was probably because he realized that I had accepted my fate and didn't want to fight any longer.

So I was shocked, but not totally surprised, when I found a note from Amy lying on the kitchen table when I came home from work one Friday evening in September of 1958. It was not an angry letter, but simply stated that she had taken the children to her mother and father's in Chestnut Hill and that I was to be out of our house by Monday morning, when she would return. She wrote that I would be hearing from her lawyer as soon as she could arrange it. I buried my head in my hands and sobbed convulsively, then picked up the phone and called my companion, Arnie Walton, to come and get me.

CHALMERS DALE

PART THREE

CBS, ARNIE AND ME

CHALMERS DALE

CHAPTER FORTY-ONE

I left Lawrenceville in such a hurry and with such confused and mixed emotions that fateful September night in 1958 that I don't recall packing any of my belongings. As a matter of fact, after sobbing and gasping for breath with my head down on the kitchen table and feeling my whole world had turned upside down, I don't think I ate any supper or even had a strong drink. I do remember, with bleary eyes, looking for Maggie, our little Dachshund, in that empty house but she wasn't there, either. Everything living was gone. All that was left was a note that said to get out, and right away. To leave the house and family life that I loved so much. To cut what ever bonds that once held us together. Amy had made it very clear. Get out!

It didn't take Arnie very long to drive down to Lawrenceville. He had borrowed his mother's car and seemed to appear almost immediately. But actually I suppose it took him about two hours and much of that time I was dazed and confused. It felt as if my life had come to an end. I wandered around from room to room feeling hopeless until that moment when he walked in. And it was not until then that I realized that I was starting a new life and a new journey had begun. I made no attempt to urge Amy to come back and bring our boys home again. I didn't pick up the phone and call her mother's house to ask her to reconsider—that somehow we would be able to work things out. I didn't do that because, deep down, I really didn't want to. The powers of a different love and passion had prevailed. I wanted to be with a man and now, at last, I would be. I was free...just like that. No more double life. No more secrets. And Amy had taken the initiative to make it happen. My troubles were over...but were they really?

At CBS, the TV western, *Gunsmoke*, was in its third season of a record twenty year run for nighttime programming. *Marty, The Days Of Wine and Roses, The Miracle Worker*, and *Twelve Angry Men* were just some of the great original television plays that were so good that they were reworked and became classic Hollywood movies, a trend that has continued through the years. Arnold Palmer won the first of four Masters' Championships, seen by millions on CBS. The golden age of television was reaching its zenith, and "my company" was in the forefront. Some of the TV series had been so popular the first time around that stations were asking for them again, and thus started the seemingly never-ending cycle of reruns. Our Film and Video Tape Department, as it was now called, handled the syndication of these reruns, and an ever growing new responsibility was upon us.

Assistant manager

And amidst all the turmoil in my life, I had become the assistant manager of the department under Gordon Chadwick. This meant many more administrative duties to handle, like film laboratory contracts and liaison, and department budgeting and payroll responsibilities. I didn't like it nearly as well as being on the "front lines," where I had been in daily contact with rather sophisticated and interesting advertising people instead of boring businessmen who only cared about dollars and cents, contracts and deals. But I figured it was all part of a learning experience, and I was grateful to Gordon for the opportunity. I could sense, however, that amidst all the meetings and negotiations and personnel problems that there was something amiss. Gordon Chadwick was a bachelor, and as I look back I think he was disappointed and unhappy that I didn't turn to him in my time of need, possibly even to share his spacious east side apartment with him.

With the increased use of video tape it was inevitable that there would be a major restructuring affecting our department. And when I heard rumors, not long after I had settled into my new job, that there was a very good chance it was going to be done away with for budgetary reasons, I was certain Gordon had something to do with it...and not only for business purposes. For now, though, I had other things to worry about, not the least of which was to get on the cross town bus and go home to Arnie's—and now mine—one room apartment on East 47th St. and feed and walk the dog, Tiffy.

I had settled in to this little love nest, but not without considerable stress. The tears came easily, but Arnie was patient and understanding and I slowly got rid of all my hostility and adjusted to a whole new set of priorities, not the least of which was to try and make him happy and not be selfish and focus only on my own problems. After all, I was invading his space, and even though it was by invitation, it takes two to make a relationship work. And work at it we did from the very first day.

CHAPTER FORTY-TWO

He had been a radio actor in his early teens and, like so many others, had made the natural transition into television. He had never been considered a star, but sometimes it was better, he explained, to just be a good working actor and have a steady income playing all different kinds of parts. Radio shows like *Let's Pretend* and *Rainbow House* when he was young and, after a stint in the Navy at the end of World War II and a degree in Theater at the University of Wisconsin, along with study at the Neighborhood Playhouse in New York City, he had prepared for his acting career. Many directors of TV dramas found him a good type for various roles, and he was seldom out of work during the heyday of the live mystery and crime shows that were so popular. CBS alone had four or five weekly series, and the actor, Arnold Walton, received a credit in all of them, at one time or another.

Arnie, TV actor

Arnie on Broadway

Arnie probably often rehearsed for those shows right next to our offices and I didn't even know it. He seemed to be particularly well suited for parts requiring skinny juvenile kids, drug addicts, or moody malcontents. He was not a leading man, except to me, and I never got tired of hearing about his acting days and the stars he worked closely with, many of whom were his close friends. But I think he took pride in his theatrical achievements more than anything. *South Pacific*, *Wish You Were Here*, and a summer tour with the remarkable legend Zero Mostel in *Three Men On A Horse* were his favorites, and to this day the legitimate theater, including ballet, is his passion.

But with so many of the TV programs moving to the west coast, and with his close association with his mentor and best friend, director and writer Burt Shevelove in New York, he began to work with Burt as his assistant and Production Manager on industrial shows for large corporations like Milliken and Chrysler. This ultimately led him to the world of advertising, and to me at CBS. What was it about a Chalmers Dale, with the funny nickname, Chum, that he found so appealing that summer day in 1958? He had experienced many "loving" relationships with his friends and acquaintances in the theatrical world, and I used to call his past list of one night stands "the famous 40." But these seemed unimportant to him now, and anyway I was much more interested in the star names not on the "famous 40" list, and his working experiences with people like Paul Newman, James Dean, Gena Rowlands, Robert Wagner, and Joanne Woodward.

Maybe it was because I was not from the world of show business, or at least not the creative part of it, that he found refreshing. Or maybe it was that mystique that surrounds someone who is considered a blue blood, which I guess I am. Perhaps what attracted him was the fact that I was just a plain, rather unsophisticated, white Anglo-Saxon Protestant, a WASP from the Philadelphia Main Line, with his eyes wide open, in desperate need of physical love.

Arnie was Jewish and I was a Christian, and the differences in our religions were of interest to both of us. I was much less familiar with Judaism than he was with Christianity, which was understandable, considering that I had never really been close to anyone who was Jewish, or at least that I knew was Jewish. And I had been preached to by the Catholic church that the Jews were the hated killers of Jesus Christ, suggesting that it was better to avoid them at all costs. Of course I had long since dismissed such hateful rhetoric, and, for what ever reason, he seemed delighted that I would have chosen him to be my companion.

He told me long afterwards that his old friends used to say, "What does Chum Dale see in you, a skinny Jewish kid from Brooklyn? How did you ever catch him?" And what did I see? Well, he had many of the same qualities that I had found so appealing in Amy, many years earlier. Sound values, integrity, loyalty, and an attractive personality, full of good humor. It was pretty hard for me to stay depressed for very long with this kind of pixie looking, demonstrative, and very affectionate person near me, one who was used to doing things and going places whenever there was an idle moment. His aggressive nature was just exactly what I needed and our long association got off to a running start.

Arnie and me

Unlike with Amy, the physical attraction was intense, and even a reserved "fish" like me was absorbed in a romance that was everything I had fantasized about for so many years. The windows had been opened, and the fresh air had come rushing in and blown away all the frustrations and worrisome thoughts that my inclinations were either an abomination or an illness. Now I knew this was not the case. You might say the nasty demons had won the battle for my psyche, but to me they had been defeated and been swept away, but not without considerable heartache.

I was certain that living my life without lies, without deception, could only lead to my being a more complete person and hopefully be even a better father to my dear little ones. After all, I was what I was, from early childhood until now, and I was sure there wasn't anything that had happened in my marriage that had been any body's fault, least of all my precious boys. I was determined that nothing would ever separate them from me. Nothing.

CHAPTER FORTY-THREE

Tiffy was a nice little fellow, and tried so hard to be a good friend. But he was very nervous and yappy like many terriers, and might have had a difficult life with his previous owner. He was a full bred miniature Schnauzer and had been left to Arnie by an old friend, Selma Lynch (rumored to be the girlfriend of stripper Gypsy Rose Lee's mother, Rose) who suddenly died of cancer. I wasn't very happy about dogs being left in apartments all day while people were away at their jobs, and I still wonder, with such loneliness, how many of them live long and happy lives under those conditions. There was one consoling fact. Ed Balin, who lived in the apartment next door to us, was a Broadway show dancer and was home a good part of the day. His Standard Poodle was a good friend of Tiffy's and they romped together in the garden we shared with Ed.

But with my move into Tiffy's domain, and commanding most of Arnie's attention, poor Tiffy was in limbo and more yappy and excitable than ever. I love animals so much, too much I guess, and seeing Tiffy unhappy made me unhappy. But when one takes on a new partner and a new living situation, one has to make adjustments, and there were plenty that both Arnie and I needed to make, not the least of which were decisions regarding animals.

However, at the moment there was a much more pressing problem. I hadn't anticipated the sudden change in my status at CBS so soon after the relocation to a new life in New York City. I had planned to give even more time to the job, if necessary, because I no longer had the long commute nor train schedules to meet. But the rumors were true and the job had been done away with.

The use of two-inch video tape was growing rapidly, and with the addition of editing, for both commercials and shows, more and more of the huge record and playback machines were put into use and were being booked around the clock. This necessitated several people to do nothing but the scheduling of manpower and machinery, and I was offered one of those jobs in a newly revised Technical Operations Department. Although the salary was to be the same, becoming a glorified scheduling clerk didn't appeal to me at all, and I honestly felt it was a come down from what I had been doing as the Assistant Manager of a department. Whether Gordon Chadwick, for whatever reason, had anything to do with this change or not I didn't know, or really care. Instead of showing some concern for my marital breakup and wishing me well for the future, he had become rather cool towards me and didn't seem to be very upset that his faithful assistant and long time employee would be going elsewhere. Arnie was certain that he was just plain jealous, and mad that I hadn't chosen him to share my life with. The more I thought about it, the more I was sure Arnie was right.

I refused the assignment and was immediately given two weeks notice to leave the company. Gordon's boss was the one who told me, and I was in shock, dismayed that there didn't even seem to be room for discussion of other possibilities. This just wasn't a good time to be at loose ends, with Amy about to sue for divorce and child support, and Arnie expecting me to carry my share of the financial load in our apartment on East 47th Street. I felt sure I would be able to get another job, perhaps with an advertising agency or a show packager, but the thought of having to go through all the letter writing and interviews, something I had never had to do, was almost overwhelming. Something had to be done and fast, because Amy was, of necessity, in control of our small joint bank account in Lawrenceville and I had practically nothing except my weekly pay check.

So I took a chance and wrote a letter to Ed Saxe, the Vice President of Operations for the CBS Television Network. I told him of my sincere respect and love for the company and said that if my steady advancement during the seven years of employment was any indication of my abilities to do more than just schedule men and machines, then perhaps he would consider an alternate solution to my dilemma. On that final day, the day I was to receive my severance check and say the many tearful goodbyes, I received a phone call from Mr. Saxe asking me abruptly, "What would you like to do?" My answer, without a second of hesitation, was, "production."

247

So, in a matter of thirty seconds the hopes and dreams that I had experienced the day when I was sitting on the floor in the corner of the rehearsal hall watching Harry Belafonte were about to come true. I would be leaving my neat little office in the Production Center—where the most important thing I did was to make sure someone's creative work got on the air—to becoming a part of the exciting and wondrous world of creating that program. It only took a letter and a phone call to make it all happen. I'll always wonder if some outside pressure had been brought to bear, or whether Ed Saxe had simply realized, as a result of my record, that he was about to lose a loyal, dedicated employee and a real member of the CBS family. I hope it was the latter, but whatever it was, I will always be eternally grateful to him.

What new experiences were in store only time would tell, but in a matter of months my world had changed completely. A new home, a new lifestyle, and now a new job. I felt very confident that with a clearer head, and a commitment to Arnie who was like-minded in so many ways, the path ahead was going to be a bed of roses. But there were so many things to be resolved first, the most important being the need to visit my children. I missed them so, and longed to see them, and just knew that Amy wouldn't be harsh with me. I hoped and prayed that she would try to understand why this all had happened and that my love for our boys hadn't changed at all. I knew she was a forgiving person, and even though I had, without malice, hurt her terribly, I hoped she wouldn't hate me for it. I still loved her, no matter what, and I felt sure she still loved me, and knew I would always be a good father. With good feelings about each other, I was sure the boys would turn out just fine. And, so, I waited for her decisions.

CHAPTER FORTY-FOUR

Grover Dale (who was not related) and Larry Kert lived together, and right around the corner from us in a spacious flat in a nice old apartment building. They each had a dog: Grover with a dear, friendly old mutt named Skidder, and Larry with a sleek, high strung Italian greyhound named Subbie, short for Subito. The dogs were an extension of both of their personalities, and were as fond of each other as their owners. Grover and Larry had been soul mates for some time, and were both performing in the original Broadway production of *West Side Story*, for me a most extraordinary, moving piece of American theater. Larry was the leading man, and thrilled standing room only audiences with his singing of the haunting Leonard Bernstein-Stephen Sondheim score. Grover was primarily a dancer, and was magical as he performed, with such grace, the intricate Jerome Robbins' choreography.

They were two of Arnie's closest friends, and I was delighted when they became mine as well. In fact, they welcomed me into their lives and Arnie and I spent many of our weekend evenings with them, back stage at the theater, partying afterwards, and enjoying a late breakfast, a Sunday morning ritual, in a friendly little neighborhood coffee shop catering to late sleepers like us. Even though my opinion may be somewhat biased as a result of knowing Larry and Grover so well, I think the dramatic musical presentation of *West Side Story* was the finest theater ever presented, and nothing that I have seen through the years has caused me to change my mind. The story and music had such meaning to me that I saw it seven times, and cried at each performance, as I stood in the back of the Wintergarden Theater listening to Larry sing, "There's a place for us, a time and place for us...somewhere." Between that show, Grover and Larry, and their animal family, I didn't need much more to make my early days of living in the big city with Arnie as happy a time as possible, considering that I had lost my own little family, at least for the time being.

In the late 1950s homosexuality and homosexual relationships were something that were whispered about among most so-called normal people, and if somebody showed signs of being "queer," they were considered mentally unstable and in desperate need of counseling. Fortunately, Arnie and I were both in businesses that took a much more open and enlightened approach to this style of living, and we never felt uncomfortable with any of our work associates, most of whom who knew that we lived together. Yet I'm sure there were some who wondered if we slept together in the same bed, or were just roommates, but I think they really found it rather unimportant, and not worth dwelling on. They liked us individually, or as a couple. It didn't really matter.

Because of the stigma attached to unconventional sexual relationships and desires, we were a not too visible minority, and like millions of others in New York City and around the world, we tended to stick together in support of each other. I was absolutely wide-eyed when Arnie took me to my first all male bar, where there were hundreds of men of all ages and types drinking and dancing together. I couldn't help but think of the days when I thought I was the only one with these strange, and what I had perceived as deviant, thoughts spinning around in my head. Arnie was a wonderful dancer, and allowed me to take the lead, as we jitterbugged the night away. I was in heaven at that club—The Grapevine on East 20th Street—and truly able to be me. I was in the company of like-minded people for the first time in my life, people who thought and acted and loved the way I did.

It sounds as though I didn't like associating with women, which is certainly not the case. I love girls, then and now, and almost everything about them; in many instances, I am more comfortable in their company than I am with men. Some are very beautiful, and are even attractive sexually to me, and I love to hug and kiss them, but that's as far as my libido will allow me to go. Dancing and making love to my old girl friend, Libby, will always linger in my mind as being something very special and, of course, I will never love anyone in quite the same way as my wife, Amy. Even today they are my special "ladies," and are among my very best, and most respected friends…and Arnie's, too.

But in 1958, at the Grapevine, women were the furthest thing from my mind, as I discovered that men can be quite stunning also. Dressed in the latest fashions, many of these handsome creatures might have stepped right out of Esquire, GQ or even the Board Room at IBM. Arnie told me that I fitted in perfectly, and was being "cruised" by the many singles that were clustered at the bar. He joked that we should call on our friend Flossie Klotz, the Broadway costume designer, to spruce up my wardrobe, but I guess I measured up in the "looks" department. My tall, angular body and "bedroom" eyes were just what they liked, and I enjoyed being wanted. But I was not available, then or at any other time. I had made my commitment to a skinny young man named Arnie, and that was that.

I had done my share of the cooking when I was married and I kind of enjoyed it, although it would hardly be called gourmet fare. My dining experiences while growing up at my father's table were seldom, if ever, enjoyable and I guess this followed me through the years, so much so that eating had become just a necessity. But I was now living with someone who really cared about food, who loved to cook, and who was currently producing commercials for the Ronzoni pasta company. This required showing how those wonderful pasta dishes were prepared, and Arnie was honing his cooking skills in the

Ronzoni kitchens under the guidance of a home economist. When he came home he managed to turn out delicious meals in our little Pullman kitchen. We often ate out, much of the time at places catering to "our" crowd, or at Chinese restaurants where I had to develop, with some difficulty, a whole new set of taste buds. But when we were at home, he relished making us special dinners which we would eat at the long coffee table by candlelight. Fancy dining in a not too fancy setting, hardly the Four Seasons, but the food was just as good. And we both loved music, and took pride in discovering new and somewhat obscure recording artists like Ethel Ennis and Jacques Brel.

So in these first few months of separation from my children, and still not sure when I would be able to see them, I slowly adapted to my new way of life. With new friends and new interests, I was able to cope with the recurring moments of unhappiness. Perhaps most important, I was discovering how pleasurable the physical expression of love could be. I guess you could say I was making up for a lot of lost time, and with Arnie beside me, this new feeling of sexual freedom helped me get through a period where I was completely separated from my family and old friends. I hadn't seen, nor had I spoken to any of them, and even though this was a time full of pleasure and happiness, in many ways it was one of the darkest periods of my life.

CHAPTER FORTY-FIVE

I hadn't been inside a television studio in a very long time, not since "Snooks" O'Brien invited me to watch *The Perry Como Show* way back in my early days at CBS. That was in a studio with a theater stage…and an audience. A lot had happened to me since then, and now here I was in a very different kind of studio, one with lots of sets and no audience. I was at work, assigned to the soap opera *Love Of Life*, as the Production Supervisor.

The lofty job title was more impressive than the work I actually had to do, but still it was pretty exciting for someone who knew practically nothing about live TV production. But I was one of the very lucky young people, growing up in a new business, who was doing what he had hoped for. On that eventful day when I was sure I would be leaving CBS, the company that meant so much to me, I had told Ed Saxe I would like to work in production. But I didn't realize that I would be thrown to the proverbial lions on my very first day in this very different world. The work entailed scheduling and keeping track of the hours and costs of all of "below the line" show elements—the studio and stagehands, scenery, props and lighting, make-up, hairdressers and wardrobe, and all camera and sound personnel; in other words, aside from the production and acting talent, just about everything that was required for a show and that could be provided by the company.

Arnie's close friend, and now mine, Burt Shevelove, had directed, a few years before, *The Red Buttons Show*, a situation comedy in which Arnie had a recurring role. Between the two of them I was given a crash course in the workings of a studio production, from being able to read a studio floor plan, to finding and assigning dressing rooms for the actors, to the arranging for coffee and danish for the entire production unit. I was at the disposal of the producer and director and Burt gave me one special bit of advice. He told me to just get them what they wanted, without argument, and on time, and I would do just fine. Larry Auerbach, the veteran director of *Love Of Life*, was a patient and understanding soul, and was kind enough to take me under his wing and let me observe for a day or two.

When the first episode that I had been directly involved with went on the air I was standing behind Larry in the control room, and chills of nervous excitement went up and down my whole body. My knees were wobbly as I leaned against the back wall for support and watched as he followed his carefully marked script, prepared earlier when he rehearsed the actors. And with controlled hysteria, he gave instructions to the stage manager, directed the camera and sound personnel, and the music and sound effects, and cued in the commercials, presenting a half-hour of intensely dramatic action and a wonderfully creative piece of work. Often the butt of jokes, I knew it was only a daytime soap opera, but to think that all of those necessary components had come together to make the finished program, and that I had been a part of the team to help to make that happen! To me, it was better than any of the celebrated prime time dramas. When the credits appeared at the end, and the name Chalmers Dale flashed by, I had to sit down. Larry winked knowingly at me, and breathed a sigh of relief. And we did this five days a week. Wow!!

Early in Arnie's radio acting career it had been suggested that he change his name from Waldman to Walton because Waldman didn't sound "American" enough for the producer, an advertising agency, that had employed him. It was before World War II, when anti-Semitism was an ongoing hideous fact of life and Jews were, at best, considered by most people to be foreign and not "one of us," even though many of them were our most influential, prosperous, and respected members of society, in all walks of life. I had only heard a continuous stream of derogatory remarks from my father, and had never really known anyone very well, who I knew was Jewish, before Arnie.

Since my separation from Amy, I had not spoken to any members of my family. They didn't know where I was, and I wanted to leave it that way until I was ready to confront them, even though I was certain they must be worrying. I guess I was ashamed of what had happened, and was sure that they wouldn't even begin to understand all of the ramifications. So Arnie's family, the Waldman's, meant a great deal to me during that difficult time, and they welcomed me into their lives with open arms.

Arnie was the oldest of three children. His sister Ann was married with two sons the same age as my Tony and Harry. His much younger brother, Bobby, still lived at home and was going to Brown University. His mother and father had recently moved from their house in Brooklyn to an apartment in Forest Hills, Queens, not far from where Amy and I had lived in Rego Park.

My first visit there was for dinner to celebrate the Jewish holiday of Rosh Hoshanah, and we had the traditional pot roast, with potato latkes. Although they were not a particularly observant family, it was a Friday, and I joined them in the age-old tradition of the Friday evening beginning of the Jewish Sabbath, with the lighting of candles and the ceremonial prayers, said in Hebrew, before dinner. I wasn't uncomfortable, but I felt a little strange being among people with a whole different culture and whose heritage was so different from mine. I was joining a new family and had a lot to learn and adjust to.

Arnie's mother

But they made me feel welcome, and I think they sensed that a bond had been established between Arnie and me and that I meant more to him than just one of his many friends. In fact, I became so close to Arnie's mother that she would often call me on the phone when she knew Arnie wasn't home, to inquire after her "darling son." Arnie laughingly said she was a typically possessive Jewish mother who felt her son was keeping things from her. I didn't mind a bit gossiping with her about him, and found her delightful in every way. She was a good friend. From that time on, I have seldom missed celebrating a Jewish holiday with members of Arnie's family, and I have learned that those gatherings seem to be even more important to people of the Jewish faith than the observed holidays in my own religious tradition are to me. With such hatred and persecution by those of us who call ourselves Christian, it's no wonder Jewish celebrations are so meaningful. I'm sure they are thanking God they're still alive.

But my Christmas was just around the corner and aside from the deep religious significance, it is a time when families come together. So it was with mine, and I wondered just where I would be spending my Christmas. I didn't understand why I hadn't heard anything from Amy, or her lawyer, and I was becoming more and more anxious. Thank goodness for my exciting recent job assignment, along with the support from Arnie, his family, and my new friends. But nothing could take away the longing to see Tony and Harry, and particularly at this joyous time of the year when I would miss them the most. I don't pray often, but I know I did then as I silently asked God to help me find a way through these difficult days.

It was Christmas eve and a matinee day when Larry and Grover asked me to come backstage, between shows, at the Wintergarten Theater to wish me a Merry Christmas. It couldn't have been a more inconvenient time. Because of having to perform, they weren't going anywhere for Christmas, but I had made plans to travel to

Philadelphia and spend a few days with my mother and father. Grandma Lord would be there, and when I had finally broken the silence and called Mother, she pleaded with me to come. I had decided that if I couldn't be with my boys on Christmas day, then at least I would face my parents and hope that the joyousness of the season would ease a lot of the pain. Some of the legal papers had begun to arrive from Amy's lawyer, and it appeared that, until the divorce was final, I wouldn't have any visiting rights with Tony and Harry.

So on this Christmas eve of 1958, I had only a few minutes to visit with Larry and Grover before my train was due to depart. Arnie had come to see me off and wish me well, and I longed to have him go down to Philadelphia with me. But I knew my family would be much less receptive to our relationship than his family had been, so I was going to my old home in Haverford to face the music alone. Chita Rivera and Carol Lawrence, Larry's co-stars in *West Side Story* were there, along with Grover, in Larry's dressing room to wish me good cheer and to present me with a little Christmas gift. The card said that a new friend was here to try and bring me some joy, and to help bolster my spirits. And then an absolutely captivating Siamese kitten jumped into my arms. What a beauty, and what a present! And what a lovely surprise. With hugs and kisses and tears streaming down my cheeks I thanked them, wished them all a happy holiday, and was on my way.

Arnie had never owned a cat, and unfortunately was going to be left with our new addition and have to cope with poor Tiffy's adjustment in our one room apartment. I told him to close the kitten in the bathroom, and during the night the two animals would get to know each other by peeking and smelling in the space under the bathroom door. To Arnie's utmost relief it worked, and they became good friends, with Tiffy becoming much less hyper from that time on. Since then, Arnie and I have had a number of Siamese and Tolkenese cats through our many years together, but none will ever be quite as special as that first one, named Lily; that beautiful little girl who helped me through some not so beautiful days.

Christmas dinner at my Aunt Polly and Uncle Bill Galey's had been the climax to my favorite day of the year when I was growing up. Somehow all of the hostility and family squabbles between my brother Ted and me, and my father and me, seemed to vanish on this wondrous day. On the train ride to Philadelphia where my father planned to meet me, I thought a lot about the holiday season and all those delightful Christmas days at my home in Haverford. I fondly remembered the visits from Santa Claus bringing many of the gifts on my wish list, and I always looked forward to getting all dressed up in my very best clothes and going to the Galey's stately home for a final family celebration. To me, their house was spectacular, with a fifteen foot Christmas tree in the huge entrance hall surrounded by brightly covered tables displaying all of the Galey's, and visiting family members' gifts, that they had given to each other earlier in the day. As I remember it, I imagined myself in the middle of a combination of the Christmas store windows of Tiffany, Bergdorf Goodman, Abercrombie and Fitch, and F.A.O. Schwartz. There was always a standard-guage electric train, or two, circling the tree. It was magical. As I sipped my Shirley Temple cocktail, I would find a place on the big couch in the living room next to Grandma and Grandpa and listen, along with my aunts and uncles and cousins, all dressed in their finest formal attire, to the Christmas concert played on the double grand pianos by two of my Galey cousins, Jan and young Polly.

There were usually twenty or twenty-five guests for dinner, and I was so proud of my father as I watched him carve the turkey on the sideboard, while Uncle Bill tended to the roast pig, which always had a red apple in its mouth. The table glittered with beautiful silver and sparkling crystal, and in the center was a winter snow scene with a two foot high drunken figure, right out Dickens, hanging onto a lamppost...with a real light in it.

From underneath this mounting, which looked like a huge pie, bright red streamers extended to each place setting. When dinner was finished and the servants, in their crisply starched maroon uniforms, had cleared away the dessert plates, we each, in ascending order according to age, pulled our streamer to find, tied to the other end, a final Christmas gift. These were always known as the "pie" presents, and were usually something small like a belt buckle, cuff links, or a wallet. But whatever they happened to be, to me they were just about the best present of all, and I will always cherish the memories of how my Aunt Polly and Uncle Bill Galey brought so much joy to my life on the happiest day of the year.

Mother and Dad seemed barely able to speak from the time of my arrival late Christmas eve until I left Christmas night. I had planned to stay a little longer, but the whole scene was so unbearable that I left as quickly as I could. Amy had told them everything about how our relationship had deteriorated, and the reasons why, and that I had really left her, even though she was the one who had set in motion the separation. But all my mother and father seemed to want to talk about was their willingness to help me with the expense of getting psychiatric treatment. There wasn't a second of compassion for what I might be going through. I yelled a lot—something I had seldom done before—and I cried often as I told them that my life had changed, that I was a different person, and a better one, and didn't feel I needed any advice, or counseling. I insisted they listen to the recording of *West Side Story*, which I had brought with me, and hoped the story line, as told through the lyrics, would best explain my frame of mind. The song "Somewhere" said so much to me, and I hoped it would to them, but they didn't seem to get it at all. Grandma was becoming a little deaf, but I know she heard and understood everything I was trying to say, and in her silence, she was telling me that she would stand with me always. And she did to her dying day.

But there was one very important person who seemed to grasp the meaning of all that was going on. My brother Ted, who had caused me so much grief as a child, and a few moments of happiness during the war years, wrote me an extraordinary letter. He said, in a sense, to "hang in there," that I was not a terrible person, that he had some close friends from Yale and from his secret society, Scull and Bones, who were homosexuals, that it was not an abomination, and that he was sure I would emerge from all of my seemingly insurmountable domestic problems as a fine and productive human being. And, most important, he said he would support me all the way. I was deeply moved when I received that letter. It seemed almost impossible that a person so driven, so often cold and destructive, could be so understanding and comforting. He had a soul down deep beneath that callous exterior, and it manifested itself in true brotherly love. It was Ted who gave me the confidence to handle whatever might come along, and my life took a positive turn towards a much brighter future.

CHAPTER FORTY-SIX

If 1958 was a most eventful year in my own life, about the most exciting news in the world, or in fact the universe, was the sending of a tiny monkey in a rocket to the fringes of space, 300 miles above the earth. But unfortunately it was not a good year end for the monkey or our explorations in space as, due to a technical mishap, the nose cone disappeared into the ocean after scientists had already received thirteen minutes of good data on the monkey's vital signs. There were several times during the course of the year that I would gladly have traded places with that poor monkey, and I'm not sure my vital signs would have been as good as his. But now, as I celebrated the beginning of a new year with Arnie, things were beginning to look up, and it appeared as though 1959 might hold greater promise for a less turbulent existence.

At a New Year's Eve party, when I was standing between Farley Granger, the handsome young actor, and the delightfully amusing English character actress Hermione Gingold, our "Mrs. Thin Man," Myrna Loy, whispered to me at the stroke of midnight, "If you don't know which one to kiss, just duck." And that's what I did, rushing to Arnie for protection and an affectionate New Year's embrace. This was a new life for me…in every sense of the word. Being at such celebrity parties wasn't unusual, as we were often invited to join some of Arnie's friends from the world of show business. I loved it, and wasn't too overwhelmed by the glamour of it all. We attended theater openings and concerts and joined the "in" crowd at Sardi's Restaurant, waiting anxiously for the all important newspaper reviews. I often thought back to my first day at CBS when I lowered my head and pretended not to see Marlene Dietrich and Yul Brynner as they passed by me on the way to a screening.

But no less exciting than mingling with celebrities was my new assignment as the Production Supervisor in the Public Affairs Department of CBS News. It was quite a change from the soap opera *Love Of Life* and offered many new challenges. This freewheeling collection of unrelated programs was a catch-all for such far-reaching series as the *CBS Reports* documentaries, made famous by Edward R. Murrow; an intellectual pursuit named *Accent*, hosted by the poet John Ciardi; a magazine type show with Harry Reasoner, which was a precursor to the highly respected and long running *60 Minutes* program; and the religious public service programs *Lamp Unto My Feet* and *Look Up And Live*. Then there were the holiday celebrations like the *Macy's Thanksgiving Day Parade*, a Christmas Eve and Easter church service, and anything else that came along, of a significant nature, that didn't fit into the regular stream of daily or weekly programming. The offices for this department were located on East 55th Street and quite a departure from the hustle and bustle of the Production Center, on the edge of Hell's Kitchen, my "home" for many years. Juggling all these "balls" in the air was the personable, but business like department head, Jack Kiermaier, who, in his quiet yet enthusiastic way, managed to keep all of his gifted, but capricious, producers under control and on budget. He expected me to keep a tight rein on any extravagances on the part of the production crew; not an easy job considering that I tended to be a bit indulgent myself.

My first assignment in the department was a one hour ballet for the Jewish Holiday of Passover. The director was Roger Englander, whose estimable talents had brought to the younger generation (and us "older folks" as well) the *Young People's Concerts* direct from Lincoln Center with the wonderfully gifted Leonard Bernstein and the New York Philharmonic Orchestra. But this was to be a studio production and Roger told me that he would only be using the "cyc," with no standing scenery and just a few platforms. I pretended to know what the "cyc" was, but when I got home and called my production guru, Burt Shevelove, I pronounced it "sic", and he couldn't understand, even after consulting his vast theatrical reference library, what in the world I was talking about. When I spelled it, having seen it written on the studio floor plan, he realized it was the cyclorama, a floor to ceiling type of curtain that encircled the periphery of the studio. With creative lighting effects playing on it, different artistic patterns could be made, and the spaciousness needed for this ballet could be realized, and considerable money could be saved.

Call it what you will, this was a watershed experience for me. I had so much to do and I learned so much from working on that show. In addition to all the elements I had been dealing with on the soap opera, there were the additional requirements of the conductor, Maestro Alfredo Antonini, and the CBS Symphony Orchestra, special painting for the studio floor, and trying to coordinate the scheduling of the dancers and orchestra with that of the technical staff. Overseeing all of this chaos, and working within a minimal budget, was a rather grand, redheaded English woman named Pamela Ilott, who calmly smoothed, with a box of cookies, all the ruffled feathers of the eccentric talent she had assembled. It was my first encounter with this extraordinarily talented producer, who was also in charge of all religious programming. In fact, she was to be just about the most influential person in my future at CBS, in an affectionate, dutiful, and sometimes tempestuous relationship that lasted for twenty-five years.

"The day that the rains came down
buds were born, love was born,
as the young buds will grow, so our
young love will grow,
love, sweet love, rain sweet rain."

One rainy Sunday evening, listening to "our" song being sung by Jane Morgan on the radio, we drove back to New York City in

Arnie's mother's car, having visited a CBS friend who had a home on Lake Hopatcong, in New Jersey. On the spur of the moment, we decided we needed to do something to spruce up our little garden on 47th Street and make it a pretty English patio suitable for entertaining. We flagged down a truck carrying piles of one foot square pieces of sod, destined for the covering of graves at a nearby cemetery. The driver thought we were two "crazies," but pulled over and sold us some pieces, which we loaded into the back seat and trunk of the car. That night, by flashlight, we laid them out, hoped that it would keep raining, and went to bed. It was my first experience in trying to bring the country to the city, and was not completely successful, as some of the grass had already started to turn brown by morning.

But it made me realize how much I missed a green lawn and trees and flowers and all the daily chores that make country living a difficult delight. Perhaps it was the confinement of two people living in such a small apartment, but we did begin to think about finding larger quarters, and, in the meantime, we needed to get away from the city more often. That summer held a bounty of experiences that I never would have believed.

CHAPTER FORTY-SEVEN

Norma and Howard Rodman, two longtime friends of Arnie's, lived in one of the grand old apartment buildings on Central Park West, and they loved to entertain at small dinner parties. Howard, a successful writer in television and the movies, was rather intimidating and had a rabbinical air about him. He seemed to be fascinated with me and my Philadelphia Main Line background and would announce things like, "If Chum Dale eats soup with a fork, then that's the way it should be done!" He was so pleased when I would comment on the orderliness of his office, with his scripts in progress, typed on watermarked bonded paper, neatly piled on a highly polished oak table.

Before she married Howard, Norma was Norma Connelly, a successful actress who had worked often with Arnie. If we believe that opposites attract, then this marriage was the purest example. She was the antithesis of her husband, being from "down home" Maine, and full of friendly chatter and fireside warmth, while Howard was from the bowels of Brooklyn's Jewish community. Norma, along with Nancy Franklin, Delores Sutton, Muriel Berkson, and Freddie Sadoff, were Arnie's oldest friends and acting buddies, and next to Grover and Larry, and of course Burt, were the people we spent the most time with. It was with their help and advice, at one of those get-togethers, that I was introduced to a lawyer who would, with a minimum of expense, help me to deal with the legal agreements involving my boys. Actually the details weren't that complicated, but everyone advised me, and wisely so, that legal minds should deal with legal minds, and that I should not communicate with Amy directly.

My father had taken over the mortgage of the house in Lawrenceville, not to ease my burden necessarily, but to make sure his grandchildren had a comfortable and secure home in which to grow up. I think he wanted to compensate Amy for the distress, and even more, the shame he felt resulting from his son's ugly transgressions, actions that were beyond his comprehension and which he found so distasteful.

These new and dear friends were like family to me now, and even though they talked a great deal about life in the theater, about the latest movie or play, and who was doing what, and where, and with whom, and who was talented and who wasn't, they always made every attempt to involve me, and I entered into the conversations as best I could. They seemed to appreciate that, even though I wasn't one of that special breed called "actor," with a language that only they could understand, I was still connected enough to the business to make me at least an associate member of their closely knit fraternity. But the thing that was most gratifying to me was that, even by those who were married in the conventional sense, Arnie and I were accepted as a couple, as two people who had chosen each other and who were bound together by love and respect, just like them. There was never any question in their minds that their dear friend had found his mate, and they were delighted with his choice.

One of the nice things about being in the CBS Public Affairs Department family was that there was great diversity, both among the people and the shows' subject matter. One minute I was working, as the Production Supervisor, with a studio production which might be a drama, dance or discussion type show, and the next I would have the opportunity to travel with the *Accent* show to different parts of the country. This program attempted to bring into the living room some of the interesting people and places, with an eye towards social and historical significance, which have made a difference in our country's heritage. I made some important trips to small town America—in Salk Center, Minnesota, the home of the author Sinclair Lewis, and the Pueblo Indian Reservation in the mountain village of Taos, New Mexico—places I never would have imagined I would visit.

It was there, in Taos, that I was asked by Don Kellerman, the producer, to attend a tribal meeting while the Chiefs deliberated over whether they would allow us to tell the honest story of how tourists were polluting their sacred mountain lake, which was also their source of water. They feared exploitation, something Hollywood feature films had so often done in the past. The meeting took place in a completely closed structure, lasting for almost three hours, and the smoke from their peyote filled pipes, and the mesquite burning fire, nearly caused me to become ill and pass out. While we all sat cross-legged on the ground, their penetrating eyes stared at me and they spoke in a language I couldn't understand. As the time dragged on, I'm sure they were testing my stamina and dedication to both their traditions as well as to their unfortunate situation. Finally I, along with our production team, succeeded in gaining their confidence, and we filmed a most important document, one which will stay with me always. It could only have been beneficial to these dignified, and much maligned people, and I was proud to be a part of it.

On two other occasions with the *Accent* program, we visited the Remington Museum in Fort Worth Texas, and filmed the colorful exhibit of the Cowboy and Indian conflicts and life in the old west. Man's inhumanity to man was the theme, as well, in the show we did in Pennsylvania Dutch Country where developers were trying to uproot the peaceful existence and quaint lifestyle of the devoutly religious Amish community. These, and many other significant experiences, were opening new vistas for me, and leading me to a much deeper understanding and appreciation of the world around me. And I was enjoying it immensely.

I didn't realize it, but I was one of the few, if not the only one of the twenty or so Production Supervisors who was traveling out of New York City with a program. Most all of the shows were studio based and I, a junior member of the group, was assigned to a department that did many things, in many different ways, some of which involved travel. The fact that I had endeared myself to the many producers didn't sit very well with my peers, and Jack Kiermaier, the department head, was asked to put me on his payroll if I was going to be so closely attached to his various productions. I'm not quite sure how he worked it out, but it set an example for other areas, such as the daily hard news programs, to have their own Production Supervisor as a full-time employee and not just a temporary assignment. I wonder if Ed Saxe, who saved my job and made it possible for me to get into production in the first place, knew what was happening. I hope he felt he had made the right decision.

Pamela Ilott, the executive producer of religious programs, seemed to sense that I had a deep feeling for spiritually oriented subjects and, much to my surprise and delight, offered me the opportunity to travel overseas, as the Production Supervisor, to Rome and Denmark, and to work on programs for the upcoming 1960's television season. I didn't realize it then, but I think that perhaps she was evaluating my talents as a future producer of one of the religious programs. For now, my first trip to Europe was ahead of me, and I was extremely anxious and a bit apprehensive as to how, and if I would be able to successfully manage such a formidable assignment. I wanted so badly for Arnie to be with me, to share in this important experience. We were determined to figure out a way, come hell or high water.

CHAPTER FORTY-EIGHT

I could not believe my eyes when I saw a Nazi flag flying from the small flagpole in front of Max's house. Arnie was ready to turn around and take the next ferry home, and it took some doing to convince him that Max Sisk, an old friend of mine from the Film Department at CBS, was just trying to be funny and provocative, although I had occasionally detected some Fascist like comments towards those working with him on the editing of the late movies. One weekend during the spring of 1959, we had been invited to his house at Cherry Grove, one of a number of small towns on Fire Island, a 32 mile long sandbar off the southern coast of Long Island.

It was about a two-hour trip from Manhattan, with a long train ride, a taxi to the dock, and then a short ferry ride to the island; an island without any automobiles or public transportation. In fact, there were no roads—just boardwalks—and everybody walked everywhere, often pulling their little red wagons behind them for transporting luggage, groceries, and the large quantities of liquor that was consumed each weekend. The outward appearance was one of tranquillity and order, with the immaculate little summer cottages, half hidden by dwarfed pines and holly bushes, snuggled together and decorated with geraniums and petunias dangling from the flower boxes under the front window.

I thought how charming, as we walked through the bayberry bushes bordering the walkway to Max's house, but soon I discovered that inside these little bungalows were many of the most flamboyant of New York's homosexual community, here for their weekend of debauchery and high living. Max's rather tasteless display of a Nazi flag was tame compared to some of the outrageous behavior we experienced that weekend, and I never would have guessed such an enclave existed, free of harassment and abuse. But there it was, and I can only speculate that the powers that be thought it better to have this sexually charged group of men in one place, and not wandering the streets and parks of New York City on those hot summer nights, looking for conquests. They were, after all, five miles out at sea, so what could they do except make passes at each other?

At that time, Cherry Grove was the only "queer haven" among all the towns along this short strip of land called Fire Island, the others being occupied by successful New Yorkers with substantial summer homes for their burgeoning families and weekend guests. When I tried to walk on the beach to the next town, Point O'Woods, just to look at the homes from the water's edge, there was a fence that extended into the ocean to keep me, and all the other "queers," at bay. (I learned later that this included Jews and Blacks as well). But I really didn't care about that blatant exercise in discrimination. After all, I was with hundreds of fellow revelers having a wonderful weekend laughing, drinking and dancing, and "cruising" the almost nude chiseled bodies strutting like peacocks up and down the boardwalks and the beach.

And we joined the crowd at the outdoor pavilion at night and sang along with the loudspeakers belting out the songs from the Broadway show, *Gypsy*, with Ethel Merman telling us that "Everything's coming up roses for you and for me." They were for me, and hopefully they were for the many who were searching for the same kind of stability that was beginning to blossom in my own life. I watched them disappear in pairs into the dunes, hoping they had at last found "Mr. Right."

Arnie and I returned there for many summer sojourns, often with friends, during our early years together, never failing to have loads of fun and a complete escape from reality. But on one of those "getaway" weekends, I had quite a different, and infinitely more important mission. The divorce papers had come through, and I finally had my reunion with my sons, Tony and Harry. I took the train from New York to Philadelphia, and during the brief stop at the Trenton, New Jersey railroad station, Amy placed the boys in my waiting arms. As quickly as that, we were on our way to Philadelphia where my father was waiting to take us to Haverford for a weekend visit. I held back my tears of joy as I hugged and kissed them both, and told them how very much I had missed them. They returned my love, but seemed to react to my expressions of affection as if it was just like another day of coming home from the office. Children, I think, are a little like animals in that they are not fully aware of the passage of time. Their lives are so busy discovering new things that what happened the day before is even hard to remember. And how resilient they are. Amy had prepared them well and my mother and father welcomed the three of us with open arms.

The three of us

Mother and Dad
and the boys

From that time on, in spite of what the divorce decree stipulated, I saw my boys, with Amy's consent, as often as we could arrange it. She seemed to recognize that I was not a hateful person, that I loved my children as much as ever, and that if the two of us could be civil towards each other, it could only benefit the boys as they were growing up. She wasn't quite ready for them to come and stay with me and Arnie overnight in New York, but that day was not too far off, and in the meantime, we had fun together on all day excursions to the many New York City attractions. Arnie still talks about the long climb to the very top of the Statue of Liberty, and little Harry's insistence that he accompany him up into the top of the torch. He is still recovering.

It occurs to me now that they never outwardly questioned who Arnie was or what relationship he had to me. But, of course, I had no idea what was going on in their little heads except that I know they liked him. How could they help it—he was so much fun to be with. And I will always be grateful to Amy for putting the children's needs first, and for at least trying to understand the irreconcilable differences between the two of us. I guess I wouldn't have expected anything less from her. The mother of my children is a very special person.

CHAPTER FORTY-NINE

Todd Hastings was a delightfully charming aristocratic English young lady who came to this country to attend The Ethel Walker School. She lived with her aunt and uncle, the Fred Cranes, in Dalton, Massachusetts, the home of the Crane paper company. (My father would often remind us that her family were the paper Cranes, not the plumbing Cranes.) Her cousin, Fred junior, was my brother Ted's roommate at Yale, and as things happen, Ted met Todd and they fell in love and married in 1950, in a little English chapel on the Hastings family estate in northern England. At the time of their marriage, Ted was a promising young newspaper reporter with the Worcester, Massachusetts *Times-Gazette*, his first job after having been editor of the *Yale News*. But now, after a short stint with the *New York Herald Tribune*, he was a distinguished financial correspondent with the *New York Times*, stationed in Paris to cover the emergence of the European Common Market.

Ted and Todd

Arnie and I planned a ten-day vacation following my assignment in Rome and before my going to Denmark, and these plans ended with a visit with Ted and Todd in Paris. I had been unable to attend their wedding and had seen very little of them during recent years. Arnie and I adored Todd, and marveled at how she was able to deal with my brother's explosive personality. And, along with Ted, she seemed to completely understand and accept our relationship, unlike my mother and father. Arnie was never mentioned in front of my parents and, much to his and my disappointment and regret, it was many years before he was invited to their home, and never when my father was alive.

Fortunately, Arnie had been able to convince the Ronzoni people he should travel to Rome, using the ploy that, for a short time, they could do without his services filming commercials in their elaborate kitchens while he did first-hand research to discover the latest pasta dishes that would make Ronzoni even more famous. So, we would be going to Europe together, and the summer of 1959 would become one which will be remembered always.

I'm not sure why I was so nervous about going to Rome alone. It wasn't the flying, as I had been traveling a lot lately with the *Accent* show. And I was fairly confident about doing the things that Production Supervisors do, even though I would be doing it overseas, in a strange place, and working with a foreign production company. I think maybe what troubled me the most was the language question. I had studied French in school for five years and hated every minute of it, and knew that adapting to foreign tongues just wasn't one of my strong points. The thought of trying to communicate with Italians in their language, with their arms and hands waving in all directions, was pretty intimidating.

I was particularly apprehensive about having to do some research on some still pictures in the archives of the Rome Public Library. I had found one of my greatest attributes, since becoming a part of a production team, was to communicate clearly exactly what I needed for a particular show, and to anticipate problems before they occurred. But in a foreign language? I was worried and really quite fearful. If only Arnie could have traveled with me, but unfortunately he wouldn't be joining me for a few days. And so, holding back a tear, I said goodbye to him, and to his mother and father who had offered to drive me to Kennedy airport. They had a lot more confidence in me than I had in myself!

The program in Rome was to be a video taping of the first Oratorio ever written and in the church, the Chiasa Nova, in which it was originally performed. To help illustrate it the director felt the need for some historic paintings and etchings and some pictures of the original score, as well as shots of the historic church, with its centuries old ornate sanctuary, with some little known Ruebens frescos. There were graceful arches, majestic statuary, and intricately inlaid stained glass windows. Pamela Ilott, the producer, sent me on ahead to plan the taping of these visuals, and arrange for the technical coverage of this most unusual special event.

The Grand Hotel on the Via Del Corso was indeed grand, and aside from some short walks around the city in the evening, I stayed pretty close to the hotel bar where the bartender spoke some English and who tried, without much success, to explain the currency to the bewildered foreigner sitting on the stool across from him. I was afraid to go to restaurants outside the hotel for fear of making a fool of myself trying to order my favorite veal parmesan or even a simple plate of pasta. Back home, Arnie either cooked it or did the ordering in Italian restaurants, and I was relieved when he arrived two days later—when I had an extra dry martini waiting for him at the bar. He immediately fit right in with the Italians, picking up their language and dialects as if he had traveled there every year, and he was an invaluable help in the preparations for the taping of the program.

In our free moments we had a marvelous time discovering the beauty and mysteries of Rome and exploring the narrow cobblestone streets and alleys and piazzas, sitting by the fountains, or on the famous Spanish Steps, and dining in little trattorias off the beaten path. People watching was an education in itself, as the proud and stylish Romans strolled the Via Veneto.

When Miss Ilott arrived and took charge, all the necessary production elements seemed to fall into place. With Maestro Antonini and television director Roger Englander by her side, she assembled a concert orchestra and the prestigious Santa Cecilia choir, that truly did justice to this extraordinary piece of music, composed in the 16th century. After twelve hours of rehearsing and taping, we finally finished in the wee hours of the morning.

I don't think Pope John XXXIII really knew, or cared, that we had finished the taping only a few hours before. When the phone rang at eight I was sound asleep, but I do remember telling his emissary that I was sorry but I didn't think we could join the Pope at Castel Gondolfo, his summer residence, in one hour for coffee and a private audience. I rolled over and went back to sleep. It may have been one of the worst decisions I ever made, and often I have nightmares about how I had the opportunity to spend some precious quality time with one of the great figures of the 20th Century, and perhaps of all time.

The Pope had received word of our project and apparently took a great interest in it, particularly the fact that we were of assorted religious backgrounds, and anxious to bring this deeply spiritual piece of work to the attention of the American public, not just Catholics. Pamela, of course, rose to the occasion of the early morning private Papal audience, and was astounded that we had passed up the invitation, no matter how tired we were. She had become fond of Arnie, even to the point of authorizing payment of his expenses for the trip, and couldn't understand how he, of all people, wouldn't have recognized the importance, being of the Jewish faith, of having an audience with the Pope—even, if necessary, without me.

We were often reminded, as time passed, that Pope John XXXIII was the force that shepherded ecumenism into the 20th century and with his quiet guidance the Ecumenical Movement was born...and the world changed. It brought the varied religious communities to a point where they began, slowly and cautiously to be sure, to communicate with each other. The modernization of the Catholic liturgy and teachings took place during his tenure, as the Vatican "windows were opened wide" and a breath of blessed fresh air was allowed to enter the dark and ominous world of Catholicism that I remembered so well as a child.

It was with our heads full of regret for missing a chance to visit with this remarkable man that we moved on to a hastily arranged

287

second show. I learned early on that, for budgetary reasons, Miss Ilott hoped, and even expected, her staff to "pick up a little footage," if not a whole additional show, when traveling overseas or even to remote regions in the United States. This one was with Jan Pearce, the renowned opera and concert performer who she "ran into" vacationing in her hotel and, with her amazing ability to cajole artists into performing for practically nothing, and on a moment's notice, she prepared a shooting script for production the very next day.

Roger, Jan, Pamela, Me

He was to sing, and take us on a tour of the ancient Roman synagogue and the catacombs below, a reminder that this centuries old place of worship was the center of a thriving Jewish population. Located on the shores of the Tiber River, in a neighborhood of beautifully restored palazzos and charming cobblestone courtyards, it was known, and still is, as the ghetto, or gated city, an Italian word that has become synonymous with Jewish life in so many countries throughout the world. Unfortunately, too often it has symbolized segregation and discrimination in recent years.

It was here, while attending a cocktail party, we discovered that Arnie's oil painting of "Boys In Boxes," which I had grown to love, and that dominated one wall of our little apartment in New York, was worth considerably more than we ever had imagined. But that's another story, to be told at a later time. For now, we were starting our short vacation and leaving the magical city of Rome where I had learned so much. My experiences had given me many more things to talk about at dinner parties with our friends back home than an opening night party at Sardi's ever did.

CHAPTER FIFTY

As soon as we arrived in Florence and settled into a small hotel overlooking the Arno River, we called to find out if the man on the motor bike had survived. The accident hadn't been our fault, but still we kept thinking that the right thing to do was to have waited to see how serious the injuries were. When the Chief of Police answered the phone, he told us the man had died. What a way to start a three-day visit to one of the most fascinating and rewarding cities in all of Europe, the mecca of Renaissance art and culture. At least we felt that way, as we tried to put the unfortunate collision behind us.

It all happened as we were driving in our rented car through the little town of Arezzo, the birthplace of Michaelangelo. A man came racing down a hill on a motor bike and into the main square, which we had just entered. I don't know if his brakes failed, or what, but he hit our car broadside, shot up in the air, landed on the roof, bounced off the hood, and then fell down to the road beside us. Immediately, all the stores in the square were shuttered, and crowds of people came rushing to the scene of the accident, like vultures, as the man lay bleeding in the street.

I had been working on my Italian for several weeks, practicing how to purchase a pack of cigarettes in the tobacco shop across the street from the Grand Hotel in Rome, but when I had finally made a halting attempt, the saleswoman had laughingly asked me, in perfect English, "Why do you Americans try to speak Italian when you don't know how?" I was so discouraged by that experience that when the police and the ambulance arrived at the accident in Arezzo, I thought it best for me to meld into the crowd of onlookers and leave Arnie to handle the details.

The end result was that the man was considered to be the "village idiot," and everyone was surprised that something like this hadn't happened long before. This didn't make me feel any better about the whole thing, and when I saw several of the authorities discussing the situation with considerable animation, and tracing his unconscious form on the street where he had fallen, I was sure we were headed for some serious interrogation, or even jail. But Arnie finally realized they were trying to determine the amount of an obligatory fine of either 4000 or 6000 lira, depending on the seriousness of the incident.

After an hour at the police station, they arrived at the lesser amount, the equivalent of about two dollars (today's value). The police politely apologized for the dents in our car, and sent us on our way, waving goodbye as they returned to the scene of the accident. I wish I had more vivid remembrances of the wonders of Florence, but the tragic fate of the poor soul from Arezzo usually clouds the images I try to recall.

If this wasn't enough to boggle the mind on our first vacation together, we had another confrontation with the police, this time in

Paris. My brother Ted, and his wife Todd, took us to the restaurant in the Eiffel Tower, and after a sumptuous dinner Ted decided to take the bus home, and leave the three of us to have some farewell brandies and giggle and laugh together at things that Ted, with his dislike for small talk and chatter, wouldn't find amusing. On the other hand, Todd was such a wonderful free spirit and was delighted to be with, for a change, people who didn't take everything so seriously and who appreciated her dry English wit and rather liberal approach to politics, and society at large. We "closed" the place, missing the last elevator, and had to walk down the fire escape among the open steel girders, holding on for dear life and laughing all the way to the street, ten floors below.

And to make this wonderful and uproarious evening complete, we decided to take a short motor tour of Paris, with me at the wheel. I managed to drive Todd's Citroen the wrong way down a one-way street, and right into the middle of the changing of the guard in front of the main Paris Police Station. With all the grace she could muster, Todd, in her fractured French, explained to the exasperated Chief of Police that she had given her distinguished and world famous brother-in-law, Chalmers Dale, the wrong directions, that we were a bit lost, and begged forgiveness for such a foolish mistake. Well, we were not only pardoned, but because we didn't understand their rapidly delivered instructions on how to get home, they threw up their hands in disgust and gave us a police escort, complete with screaming sirens, all the way to the apartment. I'm sure the officers in charge felt that the wisest thing to do was to get these lunatics off the streets of Paris and to their home as quickly as possible.

Even with the excitable personalities of Arnie and Ted heatedly disagreeing on almost everything we talked about, and Todd and I trying to be a calming influence on both, we still had a delightful few days in Paris, and then on to London for an all too short stay before I had to go back to work, this time in Denmark. Arnie returned to New York, but not before we went to London's West End where we saw the original production of the splendid musical, *Oliver*. London theater seemed so civilized, with an air of elegance about it compared to New York, and I was so glad we saw this Dickens classic in the city where the story takes place, and about people who had lived not far from where we were sitting. Somehow, it gave it authenticity.

At that time, in the late '50s, two men traveling together in Europe was somehow a more liberating experience than it was in the United States, where same sex couples were sometimes regarded as suspiciously peculiar. London, in particular, gave us a feeling of security, a feeling that our feet were on solid ground, and with it's old world charm and it's pleasant civility, it was hard for us to say our tearful goodbyes and leave this place where we felt so comfortable. We vowed to return as soon as we possibly could, but it still remains a promise yet to be fulfilled; still among our many travel plans for the future.

The documentary that was produced in Denmark for the Jewish High Holy Days turned out to be one of the most interesting and important projects that I had ever been involved in. It was a long production schedule and during the three weeks of shooting I learned many things about the making of a documentary. I realized very quickly the many different problems and peculiar situations a production team faces when working in a foreign country. Not only did we have to cope with the language problem, but just as Rome and its people are so different from the Danes in Copenhagen, so each day's filming presented unique challenges peculiar to that country, not the least of which was the pace at which people lived and worked. I tucked all of this away in the back of my head with the hope that it would be useful in the days to come. And it certainly was.

The first thing Arnie did when he got home was to insure the "Boys In Boxes" oil painting. It had been given to him years before by the artist Larry Cabanas, who told him it had no value because he had painted, authenticated as the original, and sold a smaller version to the tobacco heiress, Doris Duke. The larger version was to be painted over when Arnie saw it lying in the hall one night at a party at Cabanas' loft apartment in Greenwich Village. After admiring its bold, yet tender composition, he was given it as a gift, with the stipulation that he would love and care for it but never try to sell it.

When we were in Rome, at the cocktail party in the now fashionable ghetto, he spotted a small painting he thought might have been done by the same artist and learned that, in fact, Cabanas lived nearby and had been invited to this gathering, but was pressed for time on a commission to paint some oils for the American Embassy. I was anxious to meet this person whose painting had become such a dominant factor in my new surroundings. We arranged to meet him in his 4th Floor walk-up studio apartment overlooking the Fontana de Trevi…of *Three Coins In The Fountain* fame. If we had wanted we could have thrown a coin and made a wish right from his window. He was tall and gaunt and rather shy and delighted that we chose to visit him. He told us, as we had tea together, that Doris Duke's version of the painting had been lost in a fire at her home, and now our large painting hanging in the little apartment on East 47th Street was the original, and probably worth about ten thousand dollars. That was a considerable amount of money in 1959, and certainly warranted insurance coverage. Arnie always thought it was a story for the New Yorker magazine, but it is appearing in print right here for the first time.

Benni Korzen became a dear and valued friend almost from the first day I met him in Copenhagen and has remained that way for more than forty years. I had hired him to be our liaison with the Danish production company and also as our interpreter during the filming of the documentary. The program was a testament to the Danish people's gallant resistance to the German occupation of their country during World War II, and focused on how they succeeded in hiding hundreds of their Jewish neighbors in their basements and attics, even in holes in the ground, and ultimately ferried them to safety, in the darkness of night, across the Danish Straits to Sweden. Benni, at age five, had been one of the many children who had been separated from their families and sent to a safe haven during this Nazi occupation. He appeared on the program, along with many others, telling the story of hardship and the heroic feats of so many of the Danish people.

Most of us have read and heard about the lives that were affected by the horrors and tragedy imposed on many millions of people during WWII by the Nazis. But not very many have known someone who was a victim of the Holocaust as well as I have known Benni Korzen. In recent years, we haven't seen each other very often, but I will always take the greatest pleasure in having been able to offer him an opportunity, following several other documentaries we worked on together, to find employment, and ultimately to marry and raise a family in the United States.

Our producer, Dick Seimanowski, was a large, red-faced man with a devilish wit, who enjoyed his cocktails morning, noon, and night. They never seemed to affect him very much and he did his best work researching and working with writer Harold Flender very late at night. He "encouraged" his entourage of production people, which he considered family, to be with him at all times. We loved and respected him and his enormous talent, but found the working conditions somewhat difficult. However, Benni and I, working with director Johnny Desmond and production assistant Lee Hayes, would prepare everything according to his desires and then call him when the filming was about to take place. He usually could be found at a cafe table in the Tivoli Gardens, deep in conversation with a Danish man of letters, absorbing all the information he could, along with the steady flow of extra dry vodka martinis.

The end result of the filming was so well received by Jack Kiermaier and Pamela Ilott that CBS decided to make it into two episodes, to be shown on consecutive Sundays on the religious program *Look Up And Live*. This was my first contact with this series, which, along with the long running program, *Lamp Unto My Feet*, made up an hour of network religious television on Sunday mornings, and was seen each week by an estimated five million people. They were not "churchy" type programs, but leaned more towards the presentation of a spiritual message as interpreted by great modern writers like Camus and Albee, or newly commissioned dramas, musical compositions or ballets. In the documentary form, the subjects focused on the human condition, and the social ills and struggle for resolutions in a world filled with poverty, suffering, and persecution. In the eyes of the various religious organizations who served as consultants, the shows were, in their words, "a window on the world," and they were able to deliver, through the CBS productions, a devotional message to a considerably wider audience than could be reached by their clergy from their respective pulpits.

I loved working on these informative and inspirational programs, and when I returned to New York I was assigned full time, at Miss Ilott's request, to the religious unit of the Public Affairs department and was given the opportunity to get back into the studio, at least part of the time, and serve as the production supervisor on these weekly presentations. Many of them were dramatic in nature, and because the series' were a public service of CBS, without sponsorship, the budget was necessarily low. The half hour plays were a great showcase for actors who were willing, and even anxious, to work for the lowest union scale in order to gain experience and exposure, and our programs were the starting point for such well known names as Gene Hackman, James Earl Jones and Joanne Woodward, to name just a few.

Dick Siemonowski and I worked well together, and drank well together, though I could hardly keep up with him. One night very late, while having a few nightcaps after we had put one more episode of *Look Up and Live* to bed, he confided in me that he was planning to leave the show to develop hour-long documentaries for nighttime viewing. He said he was recommending to Miss Ilott that I replace him as a producer of the show. I was stunned, but managed a feeble thank you, but could say nothing more. The thought of even coming close to attaining the level of such an intellectually gifted man weighed on me, and I wondered, should the time come, just how I would ever do justice to programs which required such a depth of knowledge and insight. I spent many sleepless nights and unbeknownst to Arnie, said a few prayers to the God who was so actively involved in my life, both during the day while working on the religious programs, and at night as I searched for guidance. As the saying goes," Only God knows," and I waited.

CHAPTER FIFTY-ONE

Grandma Lord and my father had the same birthday, March 11, but I don't remember them ever celebrating it together. However, on this day, 1960, she was eighty-five years old, and my father and mother came to New York for her party. It was given by my Aunt Mary and Uncle Oz (mother's brother Oswald), the fourth of Grandma's nine children. They lived in a spacious Park Avenue apartment, perfect for entertaining, and a necessity for Mary, having been appointed by President Eisenhower to succeed Eleanor Roosevelt as United States delegate to the United Nations and U.S. Representative to the U.N. Human Rights Commission.

Mary was a member of the Pillsbury family and gave much of her time in the service of her country, traveling throughout the world as an unofficial ambassador of good will, often with Oz. The title of his book, *Exit Backward, Bowing*, said it all. She was involved in so many things, from being on the Board of Directors of the 1964 World's Fair Corporation, to serving as a judge in the annual Pillsbury Bake-off contest...although I doubt if she had ever baked a cake in her life.

As a friendly gesture, in order for visiting dignitaries from the U.N. to meet people from outside their sphere of acquaintances, she often entertained at cocktail parties, inviting an assortment of her personal friends to meet and socialize with her fellow U.N. members. Several times Arnie and I were included and made sure we displayed our best social graces and cocktail chatter, but always being careful, at Mary's suggestion, never to talk to each other. On one occasion I was cornered with Krishna Menon, the delegate from India, and couldn't think of a thing to say. When I asked him if he liked America's pastime, baseball, I was politely ignored, and with a quizzical look he excused himself and quickly walked away. Maybe I should have tried big band music, my other favorite conversation piece. Her son and my cousin, Winston Lord, has followed in her footsteps, having served as Ambassador to China, and Assistant Secretary of State for East Asian and Pacific Affairs. Thank goodness he loves to talk baseball!

Aunt Mary loved giving parties and was an organized, precise and most gracious hostess, particularly when it was a family birthday party for Grandma Lord. All the great grandchildren over five years old were invited, along with the many aunts and uncles, cousins, and in-laws that made up Grandma's large and loving family. And this birthday party was particularly memorable and important to me for it included Tony, who was seven but, disappointedly, not Harry, who was only five. For the first time, one of my children spent the night with us in our apartment, after Tony and I attended the party together. I considered that a very special time, even though Arnie hadn't been invited to the family gathering. He and Grandma had become good friends, and together we visited her several times in both Tarrytown and Beach Haven. But in those days Arnie, although considered a significant other, was not yet accepted as a member of the Lord family, at least not at birthday parties.

Grandma's birthday

Tony, Tiffy and Skidder

Grandma didn't live much longer after that festive occasion, but as my own little present to her, I invited her to join me at a matinee performance of the Broadway hit musical, Rodgers and Hammerstein's *The Sound Of Music*. And what an enjoyable afternoon it was! Arnie and I had seen it on opening night and we just knew that, with such a dramatic and beautiful story and such heavenly music, she would just love it, particularly considering she was such a devout member of the Catholic church. Nothing being too good for my Grandma, Arnie was able to get Oscar Hammerstein's house seats, and we sat in the fourth row center. It was one of my happiest moments, and I was so proud to have her by my side.

While we were having luncheon in the Edwardian Room at the Plaza Hotel before going to the theater, I told her about the time that Mary Martin, the star of *The Sound Of Music*, and her fellow cast members, following an evening performance, had arrived, with a sumptuous full course down-home picnic supper in hand, at the brownstone apartment of our good friend Joe Layton. He had staged all the musical numbers in the show and they were getting even with him by "stopping by," a suggestion he regularly offered to most everyone in the cast without ever setting a specific date. They even brought wine, table cloths and napkins, dishes and silverware, and the soap and dish towels to clean up afterwards. God forbid he should have to raise a finger!

We had been asked by Kurt Kazner, a cast member, knowing we were going to be there for the evening, to keep Joe and his wife, Evie, from going to bed until they all arrived. As the taxis drove up outside their first floor apartment and Joe heard a lot of excitement, he complained that they would be having another sleepless night with partying going on upstairs. What a surprise as his performers, led by Mary Martin, burst through the front door with their shopping bags in hand and went about their business arranging the dinner party-picnic. They even brought place cards. What a party it was, and Grandma had a good laugh and enjoyed hearing a little backstage trivia about the people she was about to see on stage.

At the end of the performance we attended, I will never forget, as the final curtain came down and I was helping her with her coat, she asked me to wait a moment while she turned to an unescorted and much younger woman who was sitting on the other side of her, and helped her with her coat. That was my considerate and lovely grandmother always being gracious and unselfish to the end. Arnie and I both think of her often, and remember her as someone who was way ahead of her time, and who accepted us as a couple without question.

Arnie often tells the little anecdote of how she always greeted us on our visits to Tarrytown. So as not to be late for dinner, we were usually a little early, and Grandma, not being fully dressed for the evening, would lean over the upstairs hallway bannister and call down with a welcoming voice, "Chummy, is that you?" And with a giggle from Arnie our delightful evening would begin. She knew of our homosexual relationship because of having been at my mother and father's home in Haverford that eventful Christmas eve when they had confronted me two years earlier. What a grand lady!

Burt Shevelove was in the middle of writing, along with Larry Gelbart and Stephen Sondheim, the musical comedy *A Funny Thing Happened On The Way To The Forum.* But he found time to welcome us to Greenwich Village and our new apartment, which he helped us find, at 26 West 9th Street, directly across the street from him. This quiet, tree-lined block was the home of Metropolitan opera diva Joan Southerland whose vocalizing and rehearsing could be heard drifting out of her windows. Also living there was the distinguished poet Marianne Moore, with her tri-cornered hat, who served as our "block leader" and led us whenever there was a political protest demonstration.

Besides having a real kitchen, a living room and a spacious bedroom, our fourth floor apartment had a fireplace, and this indeed seemed like a palace compared to our tight little quarters uptown. Only cats were allowed in our new building, so Tiffy could not make the move but, happily for us, was adopted by a friend who was moving to California and would provide lots of space for him to run and play at will. We immediately purchased a companion for Lily, another Siamese cat, bought some firewood, and settled in for a long stay.

Burt Shevelove

Burt, a true Renaissance man, was a most unusual and interesting person and Arnie was devoted to him, even though, when they had worked together on industrial shows, Burt had occasionally stabbed him in the hand with sharpened lead pencils when something wasn't going just right. His apartment was constantly in a state of alteration and repair, with his large library of every conceivable kind of book piled neatly in all the available corners. Larry Gelbart jokingly prepared his epitaph to read:

"Here lies Burt Shevelove, finished before his apartment."

But he was alive and well and having him living so close was a joy, and I loved getting to know him and his circle of friends, who ranged from theatrical bigwigs, to successful lawyers and bankers, to chorus boys and bicycle messengers. Most of them were single men, like him, and although he was not particularly attractive looking, or had much sex appeal, it seemed as though he had a very active social life, both intellectually and romantically, as admirers could be found in his apartment day and night. He was such a thoughtful and generous man. At Christmas time he would buy expensive and unusual gifts for the children of his friends, and that year, 1960, he gave Tony and Harry, whom he had never met but had heard so much about from me, a model of Shakespeare's Globe theater complete with actors and scenery. It was like a gift from Santa Claus and they loved it.

Greenwich Village was an entirely different place than what I was used to. It reminded me a little bit of London and of Rome, and was a real revelation for me to see men holding hands or walking with their arms around each other during late night strolls through the narrow and winding streets. I had thought this open display of affection was peculiar only to Fire Island, five miles at sea, but I found that even in New York city, people were very slowly beginning to at least acknowledge that there were some who, if they chose, were entitled to live their own, and different, style of life. I felt quite comfortable in this somewhat bohemian, old world atmosphere, with charming little restaurants and shops, and off Broadway theater and movies that sometimes bordered on the bizarre. But the village bred creativity in many forms, from progressive jazz and traditional folk music, to comedy and supper clubs, to avant-garde art and dance, and I was thrilled to be a part of this vibrant scene. I looked forward to Amy allowing the boys to come and spend the night, sleeping on our new pullout couch. And it wasn't long before we had many enjoyable visits together.

It was shortly after our move to the Village that the executive producer of religious programming at CBS, Pamela Ilott, asked me if I would like to try my hand at producing one show for the *Lamp Unto My Feet* series. Were my prayers about to be answered? I guessed that this would be the final test of my abilities to determine if I could be a producer and create and oversee the production of my own show. But what in the world would it be? What original and artistic expression could I come up with? I turned to Arnie's family, and they were quick to come to my rescue.

CHAPTER FIFTY-TWO

One thing I was quickly learning about show business was that everyone connected with it, whether it be performers or writers or directors, seemed to have a high degree of likes and dislikes for fellow artists and co-workers, and Arnie is no exception. I guess this happens in all businesses, but in the theater or films, and even television, they tend to gossip a lot about each other, and with their fertile imaginations, they are bound to create rumors and falsehoods that are either inaccurate or just plain hearsay, and sometimes can be painful to the person who is being dissed. In those days, back in the 60's when we were so close to theater people, there were a few who, for one reason or another, didn't seem to care for Arnie, and the feelings were often mutual.

Of course he wasn't performing in the theater anymore, but still lingering sentiments could sometimes be deftly expressed and such was the case in the musical *Gypsy*, the story of the bumpy road to fame of the burlesque stripper Gypsy Rose Lee. It was written by Arthur Laurents and directed by Jerome Robbins, two talented and very successful Broadway giants who, for whatever reasons, didn't care much for Arnie. So, in *Gypsy*, as the show opens, a young boy is trying out for a vaudeville company playing a scratchy and discordant

309

tune on the violin. From the back of the theater the audience hears the director yell out in a disgusted voice, "Thank you very much, but you'll never make it in this business, Arnold." It was obvious to Arnie that Sunday afternoon we saw the final run through, before the show left for it's out-of-town tryout, that the name Arnold was used with disdain for a purpose and the two creators had gotten in an intentional dig at my unsuspecting partner. I was sitting next to the wonderfully witty and erstwhile fiddle player, Jack Benny, and he thought it was hilarious. I didn't tell him the butt of the joke was sitting on the other side of me.

But "smart-assed" or mean spirited reprisals were not a part of the theater we knew and enjoyed. Most of the shows we saw either were directed, written by, or starred friends of ours, and we wouldn't have missed their productions for the world. If the 1950s were the golden age of television, then surely the period from the late 40s to the early 70s should be considered the musical theater's finest days, and as far as I'm concerned, very few productions since then have equaled the ones in those glorious years. We saw classics like *The King and I*, *Fiddler On The Roof*, *Hello Dolly*, and *Camelot*, along with *The Sound of Music*, *West Side Story*, and *Gypsy*. And there were also plays like *Who's Afraid of Virginia Wolff* and *Two For The Seesaw* which we enjoyed just as much. It seemed as though we went to the theater at least once a week, and then, when it was a musical, bought the cast recording and lived with the musical score all the rest of the time. These were joyous and happy years for us, and we were living life to the fullest.

To top it all off, Arnie, in spite of the admonition in *Gypsy*, did make it, and got a new job as a producer at the advertising agency that handled the production of the Clairol commercials; telling the women of the world how exciting it was to be a blonde, or to cover the gray, or just enhancing the health and luster of their hair. He was in his glory, surrounded by beautiful models in high budget productions. It was a long cry from the Ronzoni Kitchens to the beaches at Malibu and San Juan, and the ski slopes of Aspen. He traveled a lot, stayed in the best hotels, and wore stylish clothes—loving every minute of it—and because our relationship was so secure and well grounded, being apart was never a problem. We thought then (as we do now) that one needs space, and, as the saying goes, absence really does make the heart grow fonder. Arnie was now bringing home a substantial salary and we didn't have to count quite as many pennies as we had in the early months of our relationship when the financial support for Amy and the children ate up a good part of our household income. "Do blondes have more fun?" and "Does she, or doesn't she?" may have been the catch phases for the Clairol Company, but ours was more like "Onward and upward."

Bobby Waldman, Arnie's younger brother, was a promising composer, having just graduated from Brown University, along with his lyricist partner Alfred Uhry (the multi award winner in later years for *Driving Miss Daisy*). Through Burt Shevelove and Arnie, they met people who could be of help and guidance and they began to mingle in circles of aspiring talent in all of the theatrical fields, looking for their first breakthrough.

In one of my regular early morning conversations with Arnie's mother, she, with motherly advice, suggested that I approach Bobby and Alfred with the problem I was facing in the immediate future. I had to come up with a creative idea for my first television production in which I was to be in complete charge as the producer. I wanted so to impress Pamela Ilott, hoping that, when Dick Siamanowski moved on, she would consider me for the upcoming job in her department. I knew how much she loved the dance, so when Bobby told me he had met a choreographer and dancer at the renowned Juilliard School who interpreted religiously inspired stained glass windows, with colorful costumes and lighting, it sounded like the perfect solution to my dilemma. Her name was Debra Zall, and she, and her dancers, gave a most creative and beautiful performance, followed by a brief commentary by the eminent historian, Robert Rambush, on the creation and significance of stained glass through the centuries.

This was the very first show that was my own doing and I guess it would be considered a success because I got the coveted job of *Look Up And Live*'s new producer. And so, with my head full of dreams, and my heart beating a whole new tune, I took my first giant step towards what was to be a thirty year career of producing over three hundred programs for the CBS News Religion and Cultural Affairs Department. I think of these many programs as teaching, not preaching, and it almost seemed as though I had completed a full circle and come back to my early love, guiding young students in a school environment. Except that now I was reaching millions of people of all ages, not just the handful, one-on-one, that had been the case in my sixth grade classroom at Montgomery Country Day School.

I was thirty-five years old and ready to start on a new career that would take me to many corners of this country, and indeed the world. I certainly would never be considered a scholar or an experienced traveler. I had no religious training or even a commitment to any particular church. I had never done any writing or directing. And I had produced only one program in my life. But I just knew, deep down, that I would be able to fulfill this enormous responsibility. After all, I was doing God's work, an extension of His teachings, and I felt quite comfortable with it. I was spiritually motivated. He had guided me through all the many obstacles in arriving safely and securely to this point in my life, and now it was my turn to do something for Him. "Break a leg! On with the show!"

CHALMERS DALE

PART FOUR

RUMINATIONS
AND
ASIDES

CHALMERS DALE

CHAPTER FIFTY-THREE

Mother was absolutely speechless when I called and told her that on my trip back from Los Angeles I sat right next to Greta Garbo. Nobody ever sits next to the great Garbo, let alone talks to her like I did. But it happened one morning on my TWA flight, when I had been moved to first class because of over booking. CBS carried a little weight with the airlines in those days, and maybe they gave me that particular seat because I looked like someone who wouldn't bother a celebrity, particularly one who doesn't like to talk very much. And we didn't, except that I did say good morning. And she replied good morning, and that was the extent of our conversation.

When the flight attendant asked me if I would prefer moving a few seats back so I could see the movie, I had to make a quick decision. Garbo, or the movie. I chose the movie in deference to the "silent one", knowing that even I, the young and "delightfully charming" new producer of *Look Up And Live* wouldn't be able to coax a conversation out of someone who only spoke dialogue, written for her in her movies, to her screen lotharios like Ronald Colman or Charles Boyer. But she was so beautiful, and so simple, and so grand. Mother agreed that I had made the right decision.

This was my first trip to California and I was there at Immaculate Heart College for Girls to shoot a documentary called Mary's Day for the *Look Up And Live* series. It was expertly filmed by one of CBS' top documentary cameramen, Wade Bingham, who went all out in capturing the festive celebration honoring the Blessed Virgin. He knew I was somewhat inexperienced, and used all his expertise to give me the most creative presentation he could. And he did just that with masterful artistry, even photographing the intricate serigraphs and designs done by the renowned artist and teacher, Sister Corita Kent. Wade had hired an unusually large crew to cover all aspects of the observance, and I was sure we had gone over budget. But I hoped that the end result would be so good that Pamela Ilott, my new boss, and the Executive Producer of the program, would forgive me, as she would so often do in the years that followed.

It was 1962, my first full year of producing programs for the CBS News Religion and Cultural Affairs Department, and this trip was the first time when I was in charge of a program outside of the studios in New York. I had already produced a couple of adaptations, which I had commissioned, of works by Ibsen and Kierkeguard, and several discussion type shows, all of which had been well received. Now I was beginning to spread my wings, so to speak, and start taking "to the road."

It was about this time that Mother asked me to come over to Haverford from New York for the weekend to look at some houses with her and Dad. They had decided it was time to move to a smaller place after thirty-five mostly happy and very eventful years in our house on Rose Lane, and I was delighted they wanted me to offer my suggestions on where they should live.

"Hillandale" held many memories for me, some of my best, and many I would rather forget. But I did love that beautiful, rambling house on top of the hill, and I hated to see it no longer be our family home. How could I ever forget the happy times with Lil and the Connetts and Dolph, and my make believe disk jockey days, and Christmas? Now it was time to put aside the many less than happy moments, those difficult times with Ted and my father, and the struggles with my sexual confusion.

My younger brother Jack was no longer living at home, having married for the second time, and the house was just too big to cope with, what with household help being at a premium. Mother had always had Polish or Irish servants, but now they were finding more desirable work that afforded them the time to live at home and raise a family in a house that was their own. It had even reached the desperate stage when Mother hired a black woman who was an active member in the Father Devine Evangelical Movement. Her name was Love Heart but didn't mind being called just Heart, much to my father's relief. Mother said she had never dared hire a black person before, because she knew that word would get around among the domestics, and if she ever engaged white servants again she would have to buy new mattresses for them.

But Heart turned out to be the perfect housekeeper, and a rock of support in the immediate years ahead when Dad became ill. But for now he had moved his Textile Sales Representative office to a small complex in nearby Bryn Mawr, just one Paoli Local stop from Haverford. Jack, after some rocky school and college experiences not unlike mine, had gone to the Philadelphia Textile Institute, and now had joined Dad as his associate in the new offices.

Jack really should have made it as a professional baseball player. He had such quiet intensity and skill, and was good enough to have been signed by the Philadelphia Phillies. He abruptly left Williams College to pursue a career in sports, but unfortunately he was hit in the head by a wicked fastball while batting for the Phillies minor league team in Seaford, Delaware and decided to learn the family business instead. I'm sure in his own mind he had always thought of himself as the "second banana" to Ted and me, particularly in his early teens when we were off fighting in a war, and he was at home...the baby of the family. So becoming a star baseball player would have been a boost to his rather brittle ego. But it wasn't to be. I'm sure Dad was secretly disappointed and would have loved to have had a professional baseball playing son. After all, he had almost been one himself.

I was amazed at how my mother and father had so completely closed off any talk about my homosexuality and all the problems surrounding my relationship with Amy and the boys, and indeed it was never mentioned by them again after that unhappy Christmas visit a few years earlier. To them, I'm sure I was considered diseased and even possibly unsound of mind, but as long as I behaved in a reasonably normal fashion they wouldn't have to be reminded of it. Maybe Ted, and his wife Todd, had intervened with some wise counseling, and just about anything they might have said would be acceptable to my parents.

I think Mother, and even Dad were quite impressed with how I was doing at my new work assignment, and maybe even respectful of my moving on at CBS to become a producer of a rather prestigious program. They actually watched a few of my shows, although they could hardly be considered regular Sunday morning viewers. Someone suggested in one of the newspaper reviews that our audience was made up of non-church going intellectuals and shut-ins. They didn't really fit into either category.

At my cousin Charlie Lord's wedding to Gay Patterson in Dayton, Ohio, I was talking with a very nice older woman whom I'd never met before, and telling her about the work I did at CBS. "Oh, I've just been talking to your brother Ted about his being a correspondent at the New York Times," she said. "Your mother and father must be so proud to have two children in the communications business." I'd never really thought of us being in the same business before, but it was true, and I think my mother and father were very proud. It's a little incident I enjoy remembering.

We didn't find the right house for them that first day of looking, but the joy of experiencing a closer relationship with them made my trip eminently worthwhile. Not long afterwards they bought a handsome Georgian style home in Rosemont, the next stop up the line from Bryn Mawr. It had a bedroom designed in a circus motif, perfect for Tony and Harry when we visited. I truly believe that they wanted me to come to them, without Arnie, but with the boys, as often as I could. And what could be a more inviting attraction to kids than to sleep in a "make believe" room filled with fanciful murals on all the walls, their father being their favorite clown.

The circus room

Mother and Dad

CHAPTER FIFTY-FOUR

It was a most important day for me. I was sitting in the office of Don Hamilton, Director of Business Affairs for CBS News, negotiating my very first contract as a producer. But what I remember most about the meeting was not the discussion of my future earnings, but something that I saw! I noticed a thin green stalk struggling to emerge from the heating duct on the floor near Don's feet. I guess he saw me staring at the strange growth and told me it was from a plant that was growing in the office directly below him, and would I please tell Pamela Ilott to tend to her vines a bit more carefully.

I probably nodded sheepishly, hoping he would think I would tell her, but of course nobody dared to tell Miss Ilott how to care for her growing things or, for that matter, anything else in her unbelievably cluttered office. She had practically created a Rain Forest in her corner sanctuary at the Production Center where Jack Kiermaier's Public Affairs Department, with all it's different programs and producers, had recently been moved. The varying sized plants occupied every inch of windowsill space and were mainly of an exotic variety, trailing their leaves over the furniture and up the book shelves and eventually, looking for more space to grow, into the heating ducts and up to the floor above.

Practically all of the other surfaces in the office were completely hidden by mountains of every conceivable kind of paper: books, files, press releases, letters and memos, scripts, and newspapers dating back to her arrival at CBS in the mid fifties. On one occasion, when the maintenance staff recommended the office be fumigated, they found a dead mouse nestled in a copy of the *New York Times* and it was determined that it had died of old age. Every inch of wall space was occupied by an assortment of religious art and artifacts collected from all over the world, and what didn't fit on the walls was in the bookcases, with literally hundreds of smaller dust collectors squeezed in among the books. Her desk had so many piles of paper on it that one could barely see her and her carefully coifed deep red hair, often topped with an outrageous hat, behind the mass of supposed works in progress…hiding as though she expected to be attacked.

A very reliable source told me that when she was a tiny baby in England, she had been left by her Gypsy parents on the estate of wealthy Welsh landowners. She had been adopted and raised by them and ultimately went to Oxford, majoring in Religious History. But she had a yen to be in the theater and despite her family's wishes, she was hired to be in a play. It soon traveled to New York, and Broadway, but it didn't run for very long and she was stranded there. It wasn't long before she gained employment at CBS as a script editor, and when it was decided to create a full-fledged department devoted to religion and cultural television, with a new director, she was the perfect choice. Judging by her unusual demeanor and wealth of knowledge, this story of her past could easily be true, and the mysterious private life she led would give credence to her supposed Gypsy heritage. Miss Ilott, without question, was a most memorable character, as anyone who ever came in contact with her would attest. She was my boss and guiding spirit through most of my producing career at CBS and I was with her longer than any of the other producers who ever worked for her. Her eccentricities were legend in the business of religious broadcasting, but her brilliant mind and extraordinary ability to oversee the many hours of exceptional programming made CBS the leader in this very specialized field. She was an executive producer, a writer, and a bottomless source of information about all the religions known to man, and the first woman to become a vice-president at CBS. She claimed she had a reason for every saved piece of paper on her desk, and that she could put her carefully manicured fingers on an important bit of information in a moment's notice. I'm not sure I believed her, particularly considering that many of her notes were written in a minute hand, and very faintly, using peculiar letter formations, usually written on the backs of old envelopes or discarded bits of note paper. When she would send one to me it almost seemed as if she didn't want me to read it. It wasn't easy.

But without a doubt she was a masterful buffer between CBS and the many different religious communities who worked with us on a consulting basis. With her very proper English accent and extraordinary wealth of information she was always respected and in command, and managed to keep them all happy and away from the CBS top management whose major concerns were more monetary than spiritual. In recognizing the various priorities of the many different groups, she devised a formula that allotted time in accordance with the number of worshippers in their flock nationwide. The B'hai denomination, as an example, might be involved in only one program a year, while the Catholic church would warrant fifteen or twenty. Between the weekly half-hour programs of *Lamp Unto My Feet* and *Look Up And Live*, plus the holiday specials, Pamela skillfully touched all the bases.

It was a CBS policy not to receive any financial assistance from these faith groups and the company, as a public service, supplied all of the resources and presented the shows free of commercial sponsorship. Miss Ilott had the final say as to what appeared on the air and with very few exceptions, CBS management was behind her all the way.

There were four of us serving as producers of the two programs, and specials, and Pamela, in handing out the assignments, had the uncanny knack of knowing each of our particular interests and expertise. We were paid considerably less than the producers of commercially sponsored programs, but we were working with material that had substance and meaning and, guided by the religious consultants, we were often on the cutting edge of what was happening domestically and throughout the world. Once we were given our task, we were pretty much left alone to produce, direct, write, conduct the interviews when needed and supervise the editing. When a show went on the air after Pamela's final approval, I for one felt very proud knowing the finished product was all mine, and no one had tampered with it as was so often the case with the high budget prime time productions. Pamela seldom had any criticisms of my shows, and when she did she made them almost apologetically, knowing how hard I had tried.

I learned early on that, being a single man, she would have liked me to be her escort at various social functions and business luncheons, but I just knew this might only lead to trouble and, in spite of her considerable charm, I certainly was not interested in her in a romantic way. So I begged off, and tried to keep my private and business life completely separate. She may have resented this, and it might have been at least part of the reason for our on-again, off-again, sometimes strained relationship, but I think she respected me, as I certainly did her.

We managed to work side by side through those eventful years when our shows, and television in general, were a most important messenger, bringing the sights and sounds, the troubles, and often turbulent times of the second half of the 20th century to help the American people to better understand the world around them. And, thanks to Pamela, I was often there experiencing many of the extraordinary moments during this period, moments that helped everyone, and certainly me, to learn more about where we had been and where we were going.

In the pages ahead I will try to recapture, with no particular time line, some of the memorable times that I experienced during my thirty years as a producer, along with recollections of some life experiences with friends and family. With Arnie Walton by my side, it has been, as they say, "one hell of a ride."

CHAPTER FIFTY-FIVE

It was during my early years, when I was having so many emotional problems, that mealtime with the family was very difficult for me. I couldn't eat because of the constant tension instigated by my father after his third or fourth cocktail. It was then that I would get a scolding, reinforced by a geo-econmic lesson. He would bark at me that people were starving in Armenia, or that there were millions of wretched souls in India who would grovel at my feet for the food I was wasting each night at dinner. This didn't help my problems at all, and often I ran to my room in tears knowing that I could sneak down the back stairs into the kitchen whenever I wanted and there I would always find something to nibble on. I was so preoccupied with my own mixed-up world that I didn't realize that in fact there were many hungry people, not only in distant lands, but right in my own country, practically under my nose, people who had no back stairs, who had nothing to nibble on when their stomachs ached from emptiness.

The solution I was told lay in the money in the collection basket at Catholic Mass on certain Sundays. It was supposed to buy food for these unfortunate people, and probably did, but I think parishioners who gave really didn't care, at least in the church I attended. They probably felt they had done their duty for the good Lord when they reluctantly gave fifty cents, or a dollar. At least, that's the way I felt.

But many years later, I found myself face to face with the reality of poverty and hunger and saw, first hand, the pockets of desperate people throughout the United States and around the world. One thing I learned very quickly was that the money filling the baskets each Sunday donated by church-going Americans, and that I had dismissed as irrelevant, were actually providing food and services to millions of hungry people. I found the work of Catholic Relief Services and the Protestant Church World Service were often, along with many others, in the forefront in trying to bring food and shelter and comfort to the neediest.

One of the places where my work brought me close to those in need was in Peru. A terrible drought in the Andes Mountains' highlands, near Lake Titicaca, had driven whole villages of people from their homes, and in telling our story about the work and dedication of the 7th Day Adventists, I saw many of the helpless and infirm collapsing along the dusty mountain roads leading to the capitol city of Lima, where they hoped to find food and water. Although my heart bled for those desperate nomads, there was something about their precious animals staggering and falling by the roadside that had an even greater impact on me. Seeing the dogs and farm animals dragging themselves along trying to keep up with their protectors, but falling from exhaustion and hunger only to be devoured, was a sad and loathsome sight, an unforgettable sign of utter desperation and despair.

Those who finally made it to the city had no place to live, and so small communities of makeshift housing suddenly sprang up in the surrounding hillsides. The structures were nothing more than cardboard boxes, with no sanitation facilities, running water, or power. One heavy rain would surely wash them all away. It was human suffering at its worst and our pictures and sound recording were never quite able to fully capture the deprivation that enveloped these impoverished people; images that are still fixed in my mind. The religious organizations did the very best they could trying to keep the people alive, but it seemed to be a loosing battle as more and more of the rural population arrived every day.

But in complete contrast, north of Lima, when we traveled in makeshift boats down the Amazon River, we discovered many small villages, previously decimated by raging flood waters, that were actually thriving. Their little houses, schools, and churches had been rebuilt with the help and guidance of the 7th Day Adventists. If the church was proselytizing and giving lessons from the Bible while it helped rebuild the homes and hopes of the community, so be it. The once destroyed hamlets were now flourishing, and the people were thanking God and His "living" disciples for everything they had. Even a church sponsored literacy program had started, so that those who couldn't read or write could begin to broaden their horizons and perhaps learn how to become better prepared for future calamities.

Yes, those little offerings in the local churches back home were at work. There was no question about it and I felt badly that I had been so critical through my early years.

On the Amazon River

Joe Leiper at Machu Picchu

Before leaving Peru we made a little side trip up the face of the Andes to Machu Picchu, near the town of Cuzco, where the spectacular ruins of an ancient Inca civilization still stand. It is an awesome site and helped ease the pain and heartache of what we had experienced. Joe Leiper, a good friend and unpaid assistant on this trip, put it so well when he noted that if Peruvians from centuries ago could survive in this remote mountain fortress, then their descendants could "make it anywhere." And with the help of God and His dedicated servants, they were trying to do just that, with all the energy and with all the hope they could muster.

I produced several other documentaries focusing on the work of the church among the hungry and the homeless. In Nicaragua and Guatemala nature's wrath had caused devastating earthquakes and tidal waves, but with amazing fortitude and strong and trusting hearts, the people of those small and depressed countries were winning the struggle to not only survive, but eventually to better their lot through more progressive forms of government. In far away Alaska, a large number of Eskimos, Indians, and Aleuts were about to be uprooted from their ancestral homes, along with their hunting grounds and fishing resources, by a newly planned pipe line to bring more oil to the lower forty-eight. Here, again, we were there to tell a story, to document the church taking a leadership role, with some success, in fighting the bureaucracy and lending support to these disadvantaged and powerless people.

I had grown up always believing that all those clichés about this being "the land of plenty" with "a chicken in every pot" was what this country was all about. Never did I imagine that here, in our own United States, there could be so much hunger and hopelessness in so many families. I was asked by Pamela to look into an organization called Second Harvest, which used church and synagogue facilities with the support of their congregations to distribute food to thousands of hungry people across America. We all knew a lot about food stamps and how they aided the poor in the purchase of grocery and dairy items, but I had no idea that there were so many large families who just couldn't make it to the end of the month, depending only on that government subsidy.

So, Second Harvest, funded by grants from a number of philanthropic institutions, with headquarters in Baltimore, Maryland, set up a group of what they called food banks throughout the country. These warehouses stored and distributed food to inner city churches, synagogues and mosques which, in turn, served the needs of the hungry in their community. Much of this food was donated in bulk by large businesses like Nabisco, Kraft and General Mills, and would have been discarded had it not been for Second Harvest's requests for these surpluses.

During the taping of the show I was able to observe, up close, the large assortment of dignified people, often families with their small children in tow, holding their heads high as they came asking for help. It was not easy for them, but judging from their sallow complexions and stringy, lifeless hair it was obvious that they were in desperate need. And I saw before me, for real, something I had experienced and that I would never forget. I had produced an earlier show of Walker Evans' startlingly graphic photographs in James Agee's *Let Us Now Praise Famous Men*, narrated by the gifted actor Pat Hingle, in which the naked emotions of white southern sharecroppers are so dramatically revealed. And here in prosperous and thriving cities, I was reliving a tragedy of our times.

In Cincinnati, after taping was completed at a food bank there, we stopped at a Dunkin' Donuts for a bite to eat, and Walter Dombrow, our ebullient cameraman, asked the clerk what they did with the leftover donuts each day. The young man proudly told him that they were thrown out and that the store took pride in selling only fresh baked goods. With a stern look and his quiet intensity, he urged the startled store manager to immediately institute a policy that would have the day old donuts delivered to the Second Harvest food bank nearby. I don't know if they ever followed Walter's suggestion, but I was so pleased that even my normally cynical camera crew was caught up in this humanitarian effort.

Then there was San Jose, California, an entirely different setting, where some of the poorest and neediest people we saw were receiving food right in the shadow of the modern offices and research complexes of Silicon Valley. It absolutely astounded me that there would be so many hungry people in one of the most productive and wealthiest communities in the world. At the Bellermine School, a Catholic college preparatory school for boys, I talked with students and faculty about this extraordinary situation and suggested they give of there free time working at the food bank.

Interview at Bellermine

I thought a lot about these experiences, and one night I sat and talked with some homeless people while they carefully, almost stoically, arranged their makeshift bedding, getting ready to spend the night in the warmth of the choir loft of New York City's historic Trinity Church. It became increasingly evident to me that the narrowness of my life was being considerably broadened through the work I was doing. What I was learning from these humbling experiences was that there are people everywhere who need someone to help them cope with the vagaries of society and nature, and if I was able to bring a message to the vast television audience, and perhaps cause some small change in the way we think about our fellow man, then I was doing my job effectively. What was even more important to me personally was that I was not just covering an assignment that was handed to me, but that I truly cared about the people's lives that I was documenting, and I would do anything in my power to ease their pain and hardship. Many of my business associates and friends have often said, sometimes with some disdain, that I was, at times, too sensitive a person. They probably were criticizing me, but I consider it a compliment.

CHAPTER FIFTY-SIX

The car I had rented from Hertz broke down on the New Jersey Turnpike and we had to wait an hour for a replacement. Every minute was so precious when my boys, Tony and Harry, were with me, and on this day they were coming to my apartment in Greenwich Village to spend the night. We had lots of plans for this crisp, sunny November day, but sadly a terrible dark shadow had fallen over me and, it seemed, over everyone else. In fact, as we waited on the side of the road for our replacement car, there appeared to be a mysterious emptiness all around, and hardly any traffic on this usually busy highway. It was as if time were about to stand still.

President John F. Kennedy had been assassinated.

It was early afternoon as I was arriving in Lawrenceville to pick up the boys when I heard on the radio that the President had been shot. I shuddered for a moment and thought the worst, but quickly closed my mind to the fact that he might die, for I wanted this day to be a happy one. When we finally got the new car and started moving again, I didn't want to play the radio, even though my good friend Reid Collins was doing the commentary on CBS. This was going to be a happy time, with a trip to Coney Island and the Aquarium on the agenda, and I didn't want the boys to see me upset.

But I couldn't contain myself when we arrived at the apartment and I turned on the television for a few moments, and sat there stunned by the terrible news being relayed to us by Walter Cronkite. With tears in my eyes, I remember hugging my boys very tight, and trying to explain the significance of such a tragedy. They didn't really like seeing their father crying, and were understandably anxious to get on with the day's activities. But even though they were only ten and eight years old, I'm sure they will never forget that eventful day. Arnie was in California shooting a Clairol commercial, and how I wished he were with me. He obviously was as distressed as I was because he made an urgent telephone call to us before we left on our afternoon excursion.

That turned out to be a sad, and unforgettable day, even though the boys and I loved being with each other, and we tried to make the best of it. But I made up for it by having some delightful times with them during those busy, and eventful days in the 60's. I took them to the Baseball Hall Of Fame in Cooperstown, New York where we looked at the Yankee pinstripe uniforms of Babe Ruth and Lou Gerhig and, of course, searched for some Philadelphia Phillies history and memorabilia. There wasn't much, just one small display: the year 1950, when they won the National League pennant. I wanted them to know all about my Phillies and love them as much as I did, but I'm not sure they got the message. From there we went on to Niagara Falls, where we sailed, along with the other tourists, in the little boat, The Maid of the Mist, right under the cascading water. It was such

341

fun staying in motels with them, and they loved being able, when they got up in the morning, to run out the front door and jump into a swimming pool. How fortunate I was to be the father of those two precious little fellas!

But the time I remember best when they were young is when they appeared on one of my television shows. In the early 60's, our department was beginning to present a number of programs dealing with the many important changes taking place in black America, and the beginning of the Civil Rights Movement. A very talented young black Chicagoan, a performing artist named Oscar Brown, Jr., came to my attention through our consultant and my close friend, Al Cox, of the National Council of Churches. He had seen him at a club in Chicago's southside, and persuaded him to come to New York and perform on *Look Up And Live*.

This suggestion was quite typical of Al as reflected in Pamela Ilott's eloquent words many years later after his untimely death, "Al was a vital link between religious faith, social consciousness, and the creation of public awareness about the truth of racism, and he represented the very best of the younger church in civil rights and reconciliation. He became an important ally to me, and our whole department."

Oscar Brown, Jr. was a writer with a deep sensitivity for vibrantly moral, funny, and tragic songs, and he performed them with great style and grace, along with a narrative that punctuated his keen sense of identity as a black American. He gave an exciting and moving performance in front of our studio television cameras, as he skillfully glided among a small group of black and white children sitting all around him on different shaped colored boxes, at different heights, enthralled as they watched his every move. Two of those children were Tony and Harry, and as I stood in the control room eyeing the monitors and whispering suggestions to director Joe Chomyn, I was captivated, watching them respond to Oscar's rendition of "Bid 'Em In," the patter of a slave auctioneer, and "40 Acres and a Mule", the plea of a poor black southern farmer. After the taping, Tony said his foot had fallen asleep while appearing to be casually sitting on it, but he was afraid to move. I'm sure if Oscar had known, he would have found a way to comfort the little fellow without missing a beat as he captured their hearts and minds with his delightful recital. This probably was my sons' first real exposure to the suffering, and struggle of black America, and I was glad that it was presented, through song and story, in such a significant, yet entertaining way.

It was shortly after this time that we presented a dramatic piece, in the same studio, in which David Greene, the son of an old friend of mine from the Mercer Street days in Princeton, sang on network television (I believe for the very first time) Bob Dylan's poignant lyric:

Oscar Brown, Jr.

"How many times can a man turn his head,

pretending he just doesn't see?

The answer, my friend, is blowin' in the wind,

the answer is blowin' in the wind."

And that song, along with many others, including "We Shall Overcome," was part of an extraordinary evening Al Cox and I spent, later that year, in Atlanta, as the guests of the Reverend Andrew Young, filming an "underground" gathering of civil rights leaders and their families.

We had just finished televising the Easter Service from Martin Luther King Jr.'s church, Ebenizer Baptist, with Martin's father, "Daddy" King, delivering a powerful sermon, and telling the country, in a most dramatic way, along with the passion of a resounding choir, that "Jesus had risen." I had been thrilled when I was much younger with such preaching and gospel singing as I listened to the radio late at night, lying in my bed with my dog Dolph right next to me. But to be in its presence was something I never dreamed would happen. After the service, Martin suggested we might like to go to the home of one of his associates, Randolph Blackwell, where there was to be a party that evening.

What a party it was! Hosted by Andy Young, leaders in the civil rights movement like Bernard Lafayette, Dorothy Cotton, and Hosea Williams, along with spouses and little ones, sang songs and told stories, some humorous and some sad, of their non-violent attempts to rid the country of racial injustice and their on going resolve to achieve dignity and brotherhood. Even though Martin was called away at the last minute (perhaps for his safety), we kept the cameras rolling for about three hours, covering this spontaneous expression of solidarity. When we finished I felt certain, with such important footage, that the program should have a one hour prime time exposure. Who else from CBS had been so privileged to be witnessing the birthing pains of such an historic movement in our a nation's history, to be in the midst of a group of people who were ready to proclaim, "We Shall Overcome."

But despite judicious editing, eliminating anything I thought might offend or disturb the sensitivities of the "higher-ups" and the television audience in general, I was rebuffed rather abruptly by the CBS News brass. I was told it was too controversial for a night-time audience to accept and understand and that it would be much more appropriate in a half-hour version, shown to "that" audience who watched public service television on Sunday mornings. I couldn't fight them, but was very disappointed that they didn't have the courage or foresight to present something that might not sit too well with certain segments of the viewing public, but an event that was so prophetic. It gave witness to the changing winds that Bob Dylan referred to. But through all of this, Miss Ilott reminded me that we still had a precious document, one that would be of historical value in the years ahead. And it has been, thanks to the infinite wisdom of the CBS archivists, as a number of documentaries have been made chronicling and celebrating the history of the civil rights movement, often using selected clips from my special evening in Atlanta.

CHAPTER FIFTY-SEVEN

For some unexplainable reason, Pamela Ilott wore a western miniskirt ensemble, with fringe, to a reception which she had helped plan. It was to honor the three foremost educational and spiritual leaders of American Judaism. They held the most important positions in the Orthodox, Conservative, and Reform branches of the Jewish faith, and they had never been in the same room together, or even spoken to each other, as far as anyone could remember. This was an historic meeting of sorts, hosted by the President of CBS News, Richard Salant, and took place in the little executive dining room adjacent to the cafeteria in the CBS Production Center on West 57th Street. Even though she had fairly nice legs for a middle aged woman, Pamela looked ridiculous and, to me, rather undignified, and at that moment I felt a little ashamed to call her my boss. I had never seen her in this outfit before, and haven't since, but she said that she thought, when she got dressed that morning, that this would be a dreary affair, and it would need a little spark, a little something to lighten it up. It was so unlike her. With her proper English upbringing, she usually knew exactly the correct thing to do, but this time she showed less than good taste, and I told her so.

(LtoR) Richard Salant, me, Pamela, Alex Kendrick

The three guests of honor—Rabbis Belkin, Finkelstein, and Glick—had participated in a series hosted by the veteran CBS News correspondent Alexander Kendrick dealing with the role of Judaism in the modern world. The dour, but kindly Rabbi Fred Hollander of the New York Board of Rabbis, the consulting group I worked closely with on shows containing Jewish themes, had helped me put this series of three shows together, and he too was startled by Pamela's outrageous attire in the presence of his distinguished contemporaries. The shows were important, not only to me personally, but I thought our audience would be interested in knowing, from three different perspectives, more about Jewish culture and religion and how the two come together in today's society to make up what may be the most complex, and fascinating minority God ever created.

I speak with some authority, my partner being Jewish, but I will never know completely the answer to "What Is A Jew?," a title I used for an earlier show. There is the secular, cultural Jew and the religious, observant Jew. How and why are they so different and yet equally Jewish, their lifestyles having intertwined throughout history? I've produced several programs written and debated by Judaic scholars, and have searched and researched the subject, trying hard to find answers, but I still don't know, and probably never will. Arnie and I, particularly in the early years, spent a lot of time talking about our differences, even to the point of arguing over whether I was anti-Semitic or not. We would lie in bed after a tough day, and a few nightcaps, and shout at each other, often bringing tears to our eyes, but always regretting, the next morning, any hurt that we might have inflicted. It was soul searching at its best…and worst.

I have always felt, and do now, that he sometimes feels that everybody who isn't Jewish is slightly anti-Semitic, whether they know it or not. And that includes me. I would always tell him that he was being defensive, that I didn't know anyone who was Jewish when I was growing up, so how could I be anti-Semitic? And I surely wasn't born with prejudices. There might have been the "token Jew" in the schools I attended, but in those days I really wasn't interested in my friends' religious beliefs, nor was I tuned in to so called "Jewish looks," or distinguishing traits, qualities that are often snidely commented on by narrow-minded people, whom I abhor. Of course, my father's dislike and disdain for Jews, and for what he perceived as their deceitful business practices, was normal dinner conversation when I was young, but I told Arnie that made me even more sensitive to the struggle of the Jewish people who had to try so much harder in order to be recognized and accepted equally in society. If I am what he says, then the question is what made me that way? What makes anyone anti-Semitic? The question still haunts me.

We would talk of our cultural differences more than the religious ones, because neither of us was very active in any affiliation with a religious institution. We recognized each other's different religious holidays and customs and respected each other's conflicting beliefs in God's presence in our lives and in the universe. He was more familiar with the Bible's Old Testament, as I was the New. But these were givens, unlike our cultural disparities which were more difficult to rationalize. We were born into different worlds and grew up in different societies, mine commonly thought of as "the establishment," perhaps more desirable by some and a symbol of success.

But there were so many more social and political, and even moral and ethical values of immeasurable worth in his makeup, values that have stood the test of time as Jews have struggled to survive. What was it about my comparatively frivolous background that made it so appealing? Maybe it was because it was largely unattainable, at least until recent years, with restrictive covenants in housing, and private schools and country clubs, where Jews were told they weren't welcomed. I'm still not quite sure why, except that "my people" may have thought that "the chosen people of God" were smarter and more resourceful, and feared they might be challenged, with their livelihood put in jeopardy.

Following the broadcast of the conversation between Alex Kendrick and Rabbi Belkin, the Chief Justice of the United States Supreme Court, Warren Berger, wrote and thanked me for such an important series, and specifically praised Dr. Belkin's new interpretation of the Jewish Talmudic dictum, "Justice, justice, thou shalt pursue." The rabbi had suggested on the program that the ancient Hebrew words would have greater relevance if they were translated as "Justice, *justly*, thou shalt pursue." And the Chief Justice thought them most appropriate for our times. This was the kind of response and recognition that made my job so meaningful.

And with Pamela's blessings and an appreciation of my relationship with my special Jewish companion, I was given the opportunity to produce, in addition to the conversation series with the three rabbis, many dramatic and musical productions, and a number of documentaries in Israel and other countries focusing on the religious and cultural heritage of the Jewish people. My strongest passions went into each of those programs and I am thankful that at least I can say that if my body of work dealing with Jewish themes is any indication of whether I am an anti-Semite or not, they surely spoke for me. Arnie agreed, but there was always a next time when he detected a note of anti-Semitism. Then our discussions started all over again, before I headed off on my next project. And here in the year 2000 nothing has changed.

CHAPTER FIFTY-EIGHT

How many times have people asked, jokingly or really being seriously inquisitive, "If there was one thing you could change in your life, what would it be?" For me the answer is simple and I've said it so many times. I would wish for a different given name, and no longer be Chalmers, with that ridiculous nickname, Chummy, or Chum. It's a little late now for any miracles, and I will have to spend the rest of my life hoping that the computer that turns out my death certificate will not call me Dale Chalmers, as most computer generated documents do now. It seems that when both Chalmers and Dale are fed into these incredibly sophisticated machines, the machines like Dale as a first name better than Chalmers. I do, too, but unfortunately that's not what is on my birth certificate. So, if I'm to be Dale Chalmers when I die, then my meager estate will be in limbo, and probably confiscated by the long arm of the federal government. All the wishing in the world will never change that!

But through the years, whenever I do my wishful thinking of improbable things that might somehow occur, the next thing on the list always relates to music, and the longing to express my inner-most feelings through joyful, or at times melancholy, melodies and lyrics created and performed by me. I've always loved listening to and

353

singing along with other people's compositions, but it's not quite the same as delivering one's own creation, as well as interpretation.

When I was about ten, my cousin Jan Galey tried to teach me how to play the piano, but I had too many more important things to do, or so I thought, and I never practiced my scales or even learned how to read music. Then, my parents paid for expensive guitar lessons, without much success. Even my father tried hard to help me master his mandolin, which he had learned to strum quite expertly, often playing along with the popular radio show, *Your Hit Parade*. If I had just persevered with any of these, I think that maybe I would have been quite accomplished, because I know the "feelings" for music certainly are there. In the back of my mind I secretly blame my failure to develop my musical talents on one major fact. I'm left-handed. Everybody knows that people who are left-handed are a little bit "off the wall," and complain that everything is designed for "normal" right-handed people. Not a very good excuse when it comes to musical instruments, I guess.

Still music seems to somehow interject itself into so much of my life. One day, shortly after moving to New York and meeting many of Arnie's theatrical friends, one of them, the newly divorced Mary Rodgers, daughter of the composer Richard Rodgers, suggested over lunch at the Fontana de Trevi restaurant, that we get married. She said she had three children and I had two and we could form a great big happy family with music as our everlasting passion. Whether she was being facetious or not, the idea was tempting, and I would have been a part of Mary's theatrical world, as she became a fine composer in her own right. But this was not to be. No coins were thrown in the fountain that day. I had made my commitment. I'm constantly reminded of this little incident as there is hardly a day that I don't hear a glorious melody written by Mr. Rodgers and even now and then one by his daughter Mary. What might have been!

Some of those "feelings" were satisfied when I was able to buy a piano for my boys, with Harry having made good use of it, composing his own musical creations. I'm envious, but very proud of him, that he is able to bring such joy to others, as well as to himself. Tony is content singing in the shower, a bit off key, and that's fine, too. And I gain much pleasure being close to Arnie's brother, Bobby, and experiencing the flow of his creativity, and the anxious moments when he has to meet deadlines for the likes of *The Robber Bridegroom* and other Broadway openings. And I particularly enjoyed working with him when he composed the music for several of my own shows.

Whenever Pamela Ilott was developing a program that included music, I implored her to allow me to be the producer. It wouldn't be my own music, but I'd be close to it, and its presentation to the millions of viewers would be the result of my creative input to whatever the theme of the program might be. I just loved attending rehearsals of the CBS Symphony, watching and listening as Maestro Antonini meticulously coaxed the musical message out of his gifted musicians. He never settled for anything less than perfection, and when we went on the air, the excitement of all those carefully arranged parts coming together and blending into a passionate expression of beautiful harmonies was a thrilling experience for me, and I actually had chills of excitement.

(LtoR) Judy Collins, Chad Mitchell, me, Jimmy Bayer (gofer)

When I worked with Judy Collins and Chad Mitchell on a Christmas special, taped in a little chapel cut into the magnificent red rock cliffs of Sedona, Arizona, I was totally captured by the angelic purity of their voices singing simple holiday folk melodies so beautifully. And in the studio there was the soprano, Roberta Peters, dressed in a stunning gown (which she had insisted I select from her extensive wardrobe), singing Antonio Vivaldi's lilting baroque compositions. There was the powerful voice of Odetta, capturing my heart in song as she walked on the beach in Carmel, California hand in hand with a young boy and girl. This special holiday program included an interpretation of the Easter message written by the author and poet Langston Hughes, and read by William Shatner.

Once, under the elevated train tracks in Chicago's loop, I taped a pick-up jazz ensemble made up of some kids from the South Side who knew more about musical expression than they did their three R's. They entertained the passing crowds on the street, and asked me if I would make them stars. To me, they were stars already, and I was amazed at their creative improvising on Count Basie's "One O'clock Jump." How I envied them in their ability to make their soulful sounds reflect their camaraderie and their desperation.

There were many other musical productions through the years, and I must truthfully admit that when the first and most important credit at the end of each of those programs gave the name, Chalmers Dale, as the producer, I would gladly have traded that honor to have in my possession the special gifts that any of those musical virtuosos offered so beautifully.

There are two significant musical programs that I consider among the most memorable I ever produced, and because of their important themes they hold a special place in my memory. It so happened that during World War II, in the Theresienstadt Concentration Camp in

Czechoslovakia, many Jewish performing and visual artists were imprisoned, but were allowed to work at their craft under the watchful eye of their Nazi captors. The camp was used as a showcase by the Nazis, a camp that they would tell the world, "See how we cultivate Jewish artists and their work." When the International Red Cross came to visit, they were treated to concerts and exhibits and were deceived into believing that the Germans were caring for the detainees in a humane, and even hospitable fashion. It became known as "the gateway to hell" and was a front for the horrors the world has become so familiar with. Many of the artists themselves died in the gas chambers during the Holocaust.

Eli Wallach, narrator
"I Never Saw Another Butterfly"

One year, after considerable research, we at CBS had the good fortune to be able to document, for the Jewish High Holidays, a compilation of the music and art that had been created and presented in Theresienstadt thirty years earlier. We had presented on an earlier *Look Up And Live* program the poignant children's art and poetry from "I Never Saw Another Butterfly," a best-selling collection of material found at the camp. We called the one hour special *There Shall Be Heard Again*, and we even found a survivor in Prague and brought him to New York. With his rich baritone voice he joined other musical artists, including the brilliant young pianist Andre-Michel Shub (long before he won the coveted Van Cliburn International Piano Competition), a children's chorus from the Hartford Conservatory performing selections from a children's opera, and the CBS Symphony. Directed by Portman Paget, they presented a powerful one hour program of music that had been composed during those bleak days in Theresienstadt, music that had never before been heard outside of the camp. Academy Award winning actress Ida Kaminska was the narrator, reading the poignant narrative, illustrated by the imaginative drawings of the interned artists, both adults and children, depicting their suffering and starvation. It was all compiled by advertising executive turned writer, Arnold Walton. Yes, Arnie is a man of many talents, and together we presented this remarkable tale of a creative spirit rising above the ashes of a nearly decimated society.

My other special favorite occurred in 1968, following the assassination of Martin Luther King, Jr. Our department was asked to prepare a one hour tribute to this great and noble man who's vision and leadership changed our nation. We only had four days to put the program together, and Pamela asked me to round up the talent and make all the technical arrangements while she prepared a narration, and chose the musical selections. I must say, we never worked more closely, or better, than we did on that project, and the end result was as fine a testimonial as we could possibly create, considering the severe time restrictions.

Along with the CBS Symphony Orchestra there was the pure and passionate voice of Judy Collins, the gifted gospel singer Marion Williams, actor Robert Hooks, and the Camarata Singers, all meshed together with the gentleness and warmth of Henry Fonda, serving as the host and moderator, making a rare television appearance. This was a live presentation and at one point, because we seemed to be running a little long, I rushed from the control room to the studio to give Fonda some cuts in his script, while the singers were performing in another setting. He was the consummate professional, calmly taking the changes in stride as if he did it every day. But our cuts were not quite enough, as we were taken off the air by the pre-set computers—who favored a toothpaste commercial—three seconds from the final solemn notes of the requiem. The only comment from Bill Leonard, the CBS News Vice President, immediately following this important telecast, was a terse inquiry as to why we couldn't get off the air on time. Fortunately, a glowing review in the *New York Times* the next day calmed our distress and disappointment, and made the whole experience, in spite of Mr. Leonard's apparent lack of soul, completely worthwhile.

Speaking of reviews, it is time to admit that when we lived in Greenwich Village I used to stand out on the corner of 8th Street and 6th Avenue on Sunday nights, at midnight, and wait anxiously for the reviews in the early edition of Monday's *New York Times*. I usually had an inkling that one might appear when the television critics from the various dailies would call me for pertinent information on that week's program. And I must say, perhaps in deference to their knowledge of our limited budget and sensitive subject matter, the reviewers were generally kind, and even oftentimes praiseworthy, particularly when the program was devoted to music. Occasionally, the president of CBS, Dr. Frank Stanton, would send me a one line inter-office memo of congratulations. I wonder if he knew how much that meant to me.

It is hard to evaluate the importance of those newspaper reviews, but I'm certain that they were read carefully and perhaps influenced the top brass who were the ones determining whether our little low budget public service programs should be renewed each year. But time has shown that we kept right on quietly doing our thing. Being a part of it all gave me considerable satisfaction and much enjoyment throughout my producing career at CBS. I take great pride in having been a member of a team that has brought, along with the dramas and documentaries, great and inspiring music into millions of homes. I know I was never meant to be a composer or a musician, but instead merely a messenger, delivering one of God's greatest gifts. I feel very much on the side of the angels.

CHAPTER FIFTY-NINE

I can't imagine any other decade in the modern history of the United States having as many social and technological changes as we were witness to in the 1960s. It was an exciting, revolutionary, and turbulent time and we in our rather small but very busy department of CBS News, with our two weekly half hour shows, were often in the forefront, on the cutting edge, presenting significant programs reflecting these new and sometimes controversial ideas from a spiritual perspective.

We mourned four assassinations—the Kennedy brothers, Dr. King, and Malcolm X—and rejoiced as we listened to a man talk to us while he walked on the moon. We praised the peaceful demonstrators in the Civil Rights Movement, and were troubled and fearful of a controversial and divisive conflict in Vietnam. And if that wasn't enough, we experienced flower power, peace marches, drug usage, the beginnings of gay and women's liberation, Woodstock, and sexual freedom. The religious community, with whom we worked closely, was involved in one way or another in all aspects of our constantly evolving society, and the clergy were hard pressed to keep up with the rapidly changing times.

At Glide Memorial United Methodist Church in the Tenderloin district of San Francisco, the Sunday service took on the form of a true celebration of life, with the pastor, The Reverend Cicil Williams, preaching with passion and fervor a message that championed the rights of all people. And those who filled his church to the rafters were a microcosm of our world. He brought together and nurtured human beings who were unconditionally accepted for who they were, no matter what their race, age, ethnic background, religious belief, sexual orientation, or gender. To the beat of music in the modern idiom, this extended family celebrated their diversity, and he urged them, through spirituality, to gain the power to move forward and bring about equality and empowerment for all people.

I have learned, been moved, and excited by many of the "ministries" I've had the privilege to work with through the years, but have seldom been so inspired by such a congregation, one that fought so hard against dehumanizing forces and made loving one another its basic imperative, its mission. Glide Methodist was far removed from my doctrinaire, over structured Catholic upbringing, and I think that if something like it had existed back in the thirties and forties on the provincial Philadelphia Main Line, I would have been a willing and active church goer. The whole uplifting experience would have made quite a difference in my confused little head and I surely would have been a lot more aware of what was going on in the world around me.

The title for this episode of *Look Up An Live*, suggested by Miss Ilott and taken from the Bible, was "Many Mansions," and how appropriate it was. In addition to the upbeat worship service, we covered a number of church conducted programs touching on many different activities, from serving free meals, free health clinics, and shelter for the hungry and homeless, to workshops and instructional classes dealing with domestic violence, gay and lesbian orientation, and the struggles of young people seeking to determine just who they really were. With Pastor Williams' flair for the unusual and dramatic, everything that happened at Glide took on a life of its own, and the good word spread throughout the city and to nearby communities. It was a remarkable experience, and through the years Pamela chose to repeat the program three times.

In December of 1965, in my own little "mansion" back home, Arnie had a 40th birthday party for me. Though the party itself was a complete surprise, the guests were even a bigger one. My brother Ted and his wife Todd came up to New York from Washington, now his base of operations with the *New York Times*, and brother Jack and his wife Ray came over from Philadelphia. But the best present and biggest surprise was to see Amy and the boys there to celebrate with me. I was so thrilled to have them by my side that when the party was over, I arranged for them to be delivered safely home to Lawrenceville in a chauffeur driven limousine. I heard afterwards that Amy invited the chauffeur into the house for a cup of coffee before his long drive back to the city. Tony was dismayed, and told his mother that she shouldn't do that. I'm sure Amy thought it a kind gesture, but somehow Tony considered it quite improper.

I never really could stop loving Amy, and had mixed emotions when I learned she had remarried a few years after our divorce. With her new husband, Bob Gatchell, she became a mother again with a dear little girl named Lucy. Tony and Harry were thrilled to have a baby sister, and I was just delighted for all of them. Bob was somewhat older than Amy, but was a kind and loving spouse, and an attentive and compassionate stepfather to my boys. I knew they were happy with him as their everyday mentor and friend. He was from Baltimore, but a longtime Princetonian, having attended college there, and stayed on afterwards, working in the well known Cousin's Wine and Spirits shop in the town's charming shopping plaza, Palmer Square. (My father always preferred to tell people that Amy's new husband was "a dealer in fine wines.") Bob had a son, Tyler, by a previous marriage, who was working his way up in production management in the theater in New York. He and his companion, with whom we had a lot in common, became good and lasting friends through the years.

Arnie and I drove down to Lawrenceville to see the whole family on several occasions, and as time went by, Amy began to accept Arnie, and our lifestyle together; there was no animosity that could be found anywhere. We were a big, extended family, and everybody seemed to like everybody else. How fortunate it all worked out that way, and Amy deserves most of the credit!

When a number of our New York friends arrived at the birthday party that wonderful evening, Amy was a bit surprised when she realized this was not to be just a family affair. She whispered in Arnie's ear that she had often read John O'Hara novels, filled with marital intrigue, but never imagined that she would be "living" one of them. But it seems, that's the way the times were in the 60's, where life was considered too short to have a lot of worries and complications. As Bob Dylan sang, "The times they are a changin'." And they were!

Things were also changing down on the Philadelphia Main Line, but not happily, as shortly after Mother and Dad's move to the new house with the colorful circus room, Dad's health started to decline. It was all as a result of his heavy drinking through the years, with all those extra "nips" while he was preparing his beloved Old Fashions in the pantry before dinner and regaling the servants with his latest jokes. He developed liver cancer and, in spite of Mother's, and the kindly Love Heart's tender care, he finally died in a nursing home in 1967.

Though I felt it was my duty as a son to visit him there quite often, it was difficult, for a father-son relationship just didn't exist. There were too many scars that had never healed, and even to his dying day I don't think he really liked me very much. Sometimes I think that maybe he saw something about me that reminded him of his own father, Mr. Hobbs, who had suddenly deserted him and his mother when he was eleven years old. I will always wonder if perhaps the mysterious Mr. Hobbs was a homosexual, and ran off with a lover. If one believes that homosexuality is an inherited state, which I do, perhaps he was my genetic source. People have often reminded me of the fact that there are some very desirable traits that I gained from my father, like an enjoyment and interest in people, attractive looks and personality, and a strong stomach. I don't miss him, and I wish I did. He worked very hard, trying to "keep up with the Jones," providing for his children, and giving Mother all the luxuries she had always known. In many ways he succeeded, but unfortunately not for me.

CHAPTER SIXTY

One of the things I love and admire about Arnie is his ability to tell a story. I think it is his favorite pastime and the stories are most often funny, sad, or informative. Some include "name dropping" and are true, and some are about himself, his family and old friends, and some just good old dirty jokes. When he has a new audience he rolls them out like cookies in an assembly line. If the person he is talking to has a story of his or her own, he generally has one to top it, and it's usually better. The late, great Borscht Belt raconteur and a regular on the old *Ed Sullivan Show*, Myron Cohen, had nothing on Arnie, particularly if the story was embellished by a little Jewish dialect. In the past, a lot of Arnie's stories were about me and my experiences producing shows for CBS, and in many cases he knew them first-hand, having left the advertising business in the early 70's, to become a freelance writer. With Pamela Ilott's considerate approval, I was often able to hire him to help me with all the many facets of my job and, of course, we had the added good fortune to be able to see the world together and be paid at the same time.

Understandably, the best audience for his stories was my dear friend and confidant, Arnie's mother. I think she was very fond of me, and was so pleased that I made such a nice and orderly home for

369

her multi-talented, but scatterbrained son. Any stories about me, and my doings, she found doubly enjoyable. She is gone now, having died suddenly during those volatile days in the 60's. But the stories she delighted in hearing from her "dear Arnie" linger on, and a few of them are worth sharing.

Chum and Arnie
another story

Someone who Arnie and I liked very much was Rabbi Fred Hollander, our consultant from the New York Board of Rabbis, who once was aptly described as always looking as though he was either going to a funeral or coming from one. One day he nervously called his wife at home from my office while we were waiting for an important guest to arrive. He said, "Hello, Yetta, it's me, your husband, Rabbi Hollander. Listen to me! If Golda Mier calls, don't hang up. It's her." I almost wet in my pants.

*****

During the Eucharistic Congress in Philadelphia in 1976, the overall theme was "Jesus, The Bread Of Life." On one of the afternoons of this week-long event, thousands of nuns gathered in the Convention Hall to hear a number of speakers, including Princess Grace of Monaco and her family, and Mother Theresa of Calcutta. Arnie was with me on this trip, and we were positioned next to our camera and sound men at the edge of the stage covering this important event. As Mother Theresa completed her talk on the significance of the convention's theme, many loaves of bread were wheeled out and placed next to her so that she could share this "bread of life" with the adoring audience. The hysterical nuns pushed their way nearer to the stage to receive their piece from this saintly woman's own hand, but when she broke off the first fragment, she walked directly to Arnie, and gave it to him, the only non Christian in the hall! We all looked at each other, smiled, and agreed that this was ecumenism at its finest.

*****

371

While we were both in Israel, working on a program dealing with Jewish Family Services, I was helping Rabbi Hollander to arrange the positions of the speakers in preparation for an audience participation forum. I had no idea that Miss Ilott had come to Israel, let alone was there at the conference, when suddenly she burst into the auditorium and started to rant about CBS policy in regard to coverage of a news event, that staging for television was forbidden. Her diatribe was ridiculous, unnecessary and extremely embarrassing to me. Still angry at dinner that night, and after a few martinis, I picked up a whole fish from my plate, hurled it at her, and stalked out of the restaurant. Arnie told me later, after he had helped her get cleaned up, that she had simply said that I was probably a little over tired, and everything would be fine in the morning. It was, and not a word was ever uttered again about this unfortunate incident.

*****

During those hedonistic days of the 60's and 70's, we taped a discussion between the noted Harvard theologian and author, Harvey Cox, and the publisher of Playboy Magazine, Hugh Hefner. It was part of a *Look Up And Live* series of shows entitled "The Playboy And The Christian." It took place on the lawn at the Playboy mansion in Los Angeles, amidst the nude sun bathing bunnies, and exotic animals and birds roaming the property. For obvious reasons, it seemed to take the crew an interminable amount of time, with many trips to the van, to carry and set up the equipment, as they threaded their way back and forth through the lovely ladies lying on the grass. Hefner delayed us even further, wandering around in his dressing gown trying to make a decision as to what he should wear. I told him anything would do just fine and to please hurry up.

If that wasn't enough aggravation, during the course of the conversation, with the camera rolling, a large green parrot slowly climbed up the arm of the chair that Harvey Cox was sitting in and settled on his shoulder. I thought it seemed to add a touch of the bizarre to the whole proceedings, and I didn't ask the cameraman to stop rolling. Harvey was being a good sport and continued his dialogue with Hefner, when suddenly he let out a piercing scream. The parrot had bitten him on the ear lobe, and blood came gushing forth. Hefner ordered the bunnies, who were watching the proceedings, to run to the mansion and bring out the first aid equipment. When they arrived, they carried a stretcher and an oxygen tank and more bandages than are used by the Red Cross in a serious emergency. Harvey lived, but he politely asked me to please cut the sequence out of the edited program. Of course I did, but I wish I could put my hands on those precious out takes.

To top off this most eventful decade, in March of 1969 Arnie and I bought a converted carriage house on River Road in the tiny village of Grandview-on-Hudson, New York. This charming little home, dating back nearly 150 years, is right on the shore of the Hudson River about twenty-five miles north of New York city. With a small addition, we are still living there.

Our house-1969

Our house-2000

We had spent a one month vacation in a beautiful rented house in Bridgehampton, on Long Island, and I came to the conclusion that ten years of living in the city was quite enough. As exciting and stimulating as the many experiences had been, I found that the city life was closing in on me, and I needed space away from the tall buildings and the traffic, the crowds, and the noise. I longed for some grass and trees and birds and squirrels and, even more, a place that we could call our own. Arnie had spent his life in the city, but after some hesitation, and sensing my enthusiasm, he agreed it was a good investment and a wise move. To be so lucky as to find, almost immediately, a little place that we could afford, overlooking the river, and nestled into a mountainside with its majestic pines, was an absolute miracle. Thirty-one years later we are still counting our blessings.

With our move to this hamlet of about three hundred people, Arnie had a whole new audience for his assortment of stories and in our first year in our new home he was able to add one more to his repertoire. He had always had a fervent interest in politics and serving the public, and when a vacancy occurred on the Grandview village board shortly after we had settled in, he jumped at the opportunity, obtained the required signatures, and placed himself on the voting ballot. No one else seemed to want the position, so his election seemed a forgone conclusion. We may never know why, whether it was because he was Jewish, or a suspected homosexual, or the combination of both, but it is very possible that he is the only person in history who ran for public office unopposed, and lost! An overnight write-in campaign had been organized, and he suffered a heartbreaking, and dehumanizing defeat.

This story, and his tale of being replaced by a dog in the National Company of the Broadway musical *Wish You Were Here* when he was an actor, will always be two of his favorites, although somewhat self-deprecating. Even as the years grow short, there is always room for one more. And in spite of his annoyance and even hatred of so much that goes on around him in the world, he will keep me young laughing at his sometimes delightful way of looking at life, with all of its idiosyncrasies, in a thoughtful and humorous way. And this can't help but be appreciated, and even admired, not only by me but by the most discriminating of his assorted friends, and even his adversaries. After all, with just the slightest excuse, they all might end up in his big bag of anecdotes.

CHAPTER SIXTY-ONE

Being strip searched on the tarmac wasn't exactly the way I had envisioned my very first time in the Holy Land. But that's what was happening at Lud Airport on the outskirts of Tel Aviv. Our welcoming committee was army personnel, all of whom couldn't have been ruder or less hospitable, with arrogance oozing from their unsmiling faces. True, there had been several bomb threats recently and a shooting at the airport, as well as the previous incidents of terrorism at the Olympics in Munich and the hostage taking in Entebbe. History has shown that the birthing pains of this new nation have been extremely painful. With so many acts of aggression against Israel and the Jewish people, in retrospect, I can understand that tight security is certainly warranted at this country's major airport, probably more than just about any place I can think of in the world. But did those "protectors" have to be so impolite? I suppose that when you are uncertain about your life from one day to the next, you're entitled to be a little overcautious, and even abrupt.

Arnie and I had been looking forward to visiting Israel for a long time and for rather different reasons, and a little airport inconvenience wasn't going to dampen our spirits and our thrill at just being there. Of course Arnie wasn't an Israeli citizen, but he felt very close to this

Jewish homeland, and he and his family had supported its creation and development through Jewish Philanthropies in the United States, since the early 40's. They often memorialized the passing of friends and relatives by dedicating a tree to be planted there. So, to be in this dynamic new country where he was surrounded by people of his own religious faith and culture was a profoundly moving experience that was hard for him to describe, even to me.

I, on the other hand, being a romantic, looked forward to seeing and feeling the mysteries of the city "touched by God," Jerusalem, with Jews, Christians and Muslims, the believers and the secular, all living and working side by side. My religious education as a Christian was certainly limited, but only a fool would not be curious about the many historic places in this holiest of lands, places that are described in the Bible and that are such a part of the life of Jesus Christ and his followers. During the time we were there, I could hardly believe that, not far from Jerusalem, I crossed the River Jordan to the hillside overlooking the Sea of Galilee where Jesus stood when he delivered the Sermon On The Mount. Even the trips through the desert land, with the wandering Bedouin tribes herding their goats and camels along the winding road to Nazareth in one direction, and Bethlehem in another, left me almost without words to describe the wonder of it. With its high concentration of salt, I quietly floated without making a ripple, in the therapeutic waters of the Dead Sea, looking up at the famous and controversial Golan Heights off in the distance.

It was indeed inspiring, just to drive through the barren lands and then to curve around a mountain only to find a remarkable transformation of the brown of a parched desert into a thriving and vibrant green countryside with beautifully irrigated farm lands, carefully tended by those modern day pioneers who chose to live on a kibbutz, or in a moshav commune. On the Jewish holiday of Passover, and being a gentile, I had the great honor of being adopted, for that one special evening, by a family at their kibbutz, and ate at the traditional Seder table with a thousand Jewish "relatives" all around me. They were amazed at how many of the readings from the Hagadah, or Seder prayer book, that I seemed to be familiar with, and I still have my place card with Chalmers Dale written in Hebrew.

I wanted very much to fit in and so like most everyone else in Israel, I wore a pair of sandals, newly purchased for the occasion. Arnie said they were ugly and hardly showed my feet to their best advantage and added that my dusty toes were ugly, too, and begged me not to wear them the next day when we were to meet with the Israeli president. I ignored him, and while in the President's office, I directed Arnie's eyes to the very same sandals with ugly toes peeking out from under the desk of our esteemed host. What did he know!

Arnie and I made several trips to Israel, and on one of them we covered the Greek Orthodox Easter Sunday service from the Church of The Holy Sepulcher, where Jesus Christ is believed to be entombed. It was unusual, but in that particular year Passover, and Christian and Orthodox Easter fell on the same weekend, and

379

Jerusalem was a madhouse. Trying to transport and set up our equipment in the midst of the crowds and up on the rooftops in the Old City with narrow, winding streets and passageways was a feat in itself. But we had conquered most of the problems and difficulties set before us until a most disturbing thing happened. We were doing our final set-up when for some unknown reason, on the Saturday afternoon before Easter Sunday, all the doors of the Church were bolted closed…with all of us locked inside! It was rather frightening, to say the least, being alone in this sacred shrine, echoing unfamiliar sounds, until we were finally rescued, an hour or so later, by a kindly old caretaker who led us through the Franciscan custodian's private quarters to freedom. We were gently scolded, and I was sure the many religious faiths connected with this holy place were conspiring against us for invading its premises with television cameras.

The service was a one hour live telecast relayed back to the United States, with English commentary, but all did not go well. With fifteen minutes left, two of our cameras broke down and we finished covering the climactic moments of the service with one camera trying to do the work of three. I'll always be curious as to whether the audience really noticed, or was this first ever televised event from Jesus' tomb so uplifting that no one really cared? Al Thaler, our very experienced director, and I, cared a lot, and worried throughout the hour that we might lose our presentation all together. Abraham, Jesus, and Muhammed, or a multitude of special deities must have been watching over us that day, for what we heard from the executives watching in New York were huzzahs and blessings upon us for having been able to pull off such an extraordinary accomplishment.

If I didn't learn anything else from these trips to Israel, I found the Israelis, from the aging Zionists to the new young generation of settlers, to be incredibly courageous and persevering. With the everlasting memory of the Nazi holocaust always present in their minds, and the threats of something similar happening again, their spirit can only be greatly admired. As a result of several other trips, I became even more aware of some of the horrors that occurred during World War II.

When I visited, with Arnie, the death camp at Aushwitz, in Poland, we were stunned, not only by the mountains of personal possessions confiscated from the Jewish prisoners, but by row upon row of dismal barracks, now covered with ugly weeds, that stood as grotesque reminders of life, and death, under Nazi tyranny. Cows were grazing in the very meadow where thousands of the detainees had been murdered, their bodies then thrown en masse into huge pits, dug into the ground by the prisoners themselves. We were there to create a show commemorating the 40th anniversary of the Warsaw Ghetto Uprising, where thousands of Jews rose up to defend their homes and lives against the Nazi's oppressive power. From all over the world people, many of whom had lost loved ones during those dark days of the Nazi dictatorship, came to pay their respects...and to never forget.

In Czechoslovakia we filmed *For They Are Ever With Me*, a special program focusing on a young Jewish man's search for his roots in a country he knew very little about; and hopefully, through the discovery of family members, both alive and dead, he would find a fuller meaning to his life. During the filming, near the city of Bratislava, we were taken to a secret passageway that led to a Jewish graveyard which had been covered over by an eight lane autobahn built by the Nazis. As the cars roared overhead, we saw, with our battery powered lights, what looked like a tiny village, with little crypts shaped like houses in amongst the steel pillars holding up the roadbed. There were burned out candles standing beside them, and the whole eerie picture was a little like something Edgar Allen Poe or Mary Shelley might have created.

But I think the memory that will stay with me the longest, of all my experiences dealing with the horrors of Nazi belief and behavior, was the time we returned one evening to our charming little hotel, hidden in the mountains of Guatemala, after shooting a segment of a documentary on agrarian reform. We found, alone in the dining room, forty or so middle-aged former German soldiers, and their wives, celebrating a reunion. They were on their yearly vacation together, and following the meal and their loud, drunken conversation, they rose and sang the Nazi anthem, Deutchland Uber Alis, followed by the familiar "Heil Hitler" salute to their beloved leader, Adolph Hitler—arm raised, chanting, "Seig Heil, Seig Heil, Seig Heil!" It made me feel quite sick, and my Jewish assistant, Joan Dolgen ran hysterically weeping to her room. I've often wondered if Arnie's reaction would have been the same had he witnessed this obscenity, this blatant worship of someone who had been responsible for nearly eliminating an entire race of people. (Knowing Arnie, he might have started World War III right there and then.) I read once that when someone who is Jewish dies, every Jew feels the pain. Well, I came about as close as I could get to feeling it that night in Guatemala.

I had the good fortune to be able to produce a number of religious and cultural programs in many other countries, including Greece, Holland, France, and England, and it's hard to choose a favorite place, or program. And working closely with the various religious, and specialized secular groups often opened doors through which most people have never been privileged to enter. I know one thing for certain. CBS gave me the opportunity to see and feel the joys and the anguish of people in many parts of the world, and with that awareness I became, in a way, a teacher again. But unlike in a classroom setting, where results can be measured immediately, I can only hope that the distant and impersonal audience viewing my programs felt the same excitement, and gained some of the same knowledge and fulfillment, that I did during these extraordinary times.

CHAPTER SIXTY-TWO

Only once can I remember Mother trying to prepare food in a kitchen and that was when she came to our little house on Mercer Street in Princeton to take care of Tony while Amy was giving birth to Harry. She did her best, and fixing a little lunch of a peanut butter and jelly sandwich and a glass of milk for Tony and herself wasn't all that difficult. She had always had servants doing all the things that make a house a home, with cooking being high on the list. So mother never seemed to find any reason, or the need, to learn how to do it herself. Frying an egg would have been a real production for her, and the only time she ever entered the kitchen was to plan, with the cook, the menu for the day and prepare a grocery list. One of the things Dad loved most in life was a few bourbon Old Fashions, with a maraschino cherry, or a couple of extra dry Martinis, always straight up, with an olive and a twist of lemon rind, followed by a home cooked meal that had been prepared just the way he liked it by a real cook. He never would have allowed the woman he loved to slave away in a hot kitchen. I think he would have given up just about anything before losing our cook, who often made him special things like popovers with his roast beef and a fluffy cheese soufflé for Saturday lunch before his golf game.

But Dad was gone now, and Mother decided to give up the house in Rosemont, move to a condominium in Haverford, and try to fend for herself. Love Heart, who was the last of her servants except for cleaning women, helped her with the move, got her established in her new home, and even spent a few nights in the guest room, so that she could teach her some of the basics in the kitchen. Quite surprisingly, Mother did very well, broiling fish and chicken and relying on a few frozen things, like Stouffer's Turkey Tetrazzini, that didn't require much work other than setting the proper oven temperature and following the instructions on the package. But her habits never changed. She still took her bath before dinner and put on her velvet lounging robe. With precision timing, she was able to watch the evening news on television with her one pre-dinner cocktail and have her food ready just as Dan Rather said goodnight and right before the stomach gas and athlete's foot commercials came on, which she detested. And she finished her dinner just in time for he favorite show, *Jeopardy*. She followed this same routine pretty regularly for the twenty-three years she was alone, until she died peacefully at age ninety...thankfully, not of malnutrition.

She never had any serious ailments during her later years, working as a volunteer three days a week on an American Red Cross blood mobile that took her to schools and factories all over the Philadelphia metropolitan area. She came in contact with people quite different from her and her way of life, and made the comment one day that meeting so many different kinds of people made her reading so much more meaningful. And she was a prodigious reader and very well informed. I think she really began to accept the fact that there was more to life than the Philadelphia Main Line, dinner parties and country clubs, although she belonged to the Merion Golf Club to the very end, and loved taking guests there for dinner. I loved her very much and talked to her every Sunday morning on the telephone. I know she recognized the difficulties I had in my earlier years and I think she was happy that I was happy in my work and in my life with Arnie, even though she never could fully accept him.

Ray and Jack

(LtoR) Lucy, Mother, Gwyn and Peggy

My brother Jack and his wife Ray lived just a few miles away from Mother with their two daughters, Peggy and Gwyn, whom Mother adored. She had always been surrounded by lots of men in her life. She had grown up in Tarrytown with five brothers nearest in age to her, and then had a husband and three boys of her own, then two grandsons, Tony and Harry. So, having some little girls to fuss over gave her hours of pleasure; making them clothes, buying them dolls, and talking girl talk. I visited her as often as I could, and Pamela Ilott, knowing how much I cared for her, gave me many shows to produce that were in the Philadelphia area. I particularly tried to be with her on holidays, but it was not always possible as I had to produce my share of the Christmas Eve and Easter Sunday live church services and specials.

387

One Christmas I did a show in Philadelphia at a church in a black neighborhood in the northeast section of the city. It featured the dynamic gospel singer, Marion Williams, a very large woman with even a bigger voice than the more famous Mahalia Jackson. Shortly before going on the air she emerged from behind the alter to model for us the bright red dress she had made herself for the occasion. It was a magnificent piece of work, but sewn over every inch of it were thousands of twinkling sequins and shiny bugle beads. When the video man, seated at his console in our television mobile unit parked outside the church, saw this huge mass of flashing lights on the television screen, he threw up his hands and loudly proclaimed that home television sets would be unable to handle such an explosion of sparkling brilliance.

After trying to make adjustments, it was decided she would have to wear something a little more subdued. What to do, with just a few minutes before air time? I saw in the congregation that was assembling, an equally large woman coming down the aisle to her seat and asked her, with considerable reservation, if she wouldn't mind exchanging her lovely royal blue dress, with a minimum of spangles, with Marion's equally beautiful red dress. With thirty seconds left before going on the air, Marion dried her tears and made the exchange, and our unsuspecting television audience never knew. They were thrilled beyond measure as she sang with great feeling and emotion, "God Bless the Child." And she looked just splendid. Oh, what a television producer has to go through!

This was certainly not the first difficult situation, nor was it the last. While we were televising an Easter Sunday service from a Methodist church in Chicago, and the pastor was delivering his sermon, the phone rang in the mobile unit. It was Pamela Ilott calling from New York to tell me that there appeared to be an Easter Lily growing out of the minister's head and would I please do something about it. I looked more closely at the screen and, sure enough, she was right. The camera angle was such that it seemed exactly as she had described. But there was a problem! That particular camera was stationary, and so was the minister standing in the pulpit. I knew I would be seen if I crawled in behind him and tried to move the glorious Easter Lily plant. The only solution was to cover the rest of the sermon from a camera in the balcony, and I hoped his powerful delivery and inspirational words would compensate for the poor pictorial coverage. I learned, once again, that doing a live show was a most nerve racking experience, but that there was something about it that was incredibly exciting, except, of course, for times like these.

Finally, just one more memorable holiday moment. In order to try and give equal time to everyone, it was decided one year to televise live the Christmas Eve Service from a Chinese Lutheran church in New York City's colorful Chinatown. As the service progressed, it seemed to be moving along at a much faster clip than we had planned, in spite of the fact that we had carefully gone over the approximate segment timings with the minister. When we got near the forty-five minute mark of the one hour program, the minister was giving his benediction and the people were beginning to put aside their hymnals, collect their children and their coats, getting ready to file out.

With the ghastly vision of an empty church with nothing for the millions of viewers to see or hear, I ran up to the choir loft, lay on the floor at the feet of the startled choir members and their conductor, and, out of sight of the camera, handed out additional music for them to sing for the remaining fifteen minutes. With one camera focused on the choir and another on the immense Christmas tree in the sanctuary, with its vast assortment of oriental ornaments, we were able to present a little ethnic concert to close the program, and no one was any the wiser. I'll never be certain if the music that I had hastily snatched from a shelf, written in the Chinese language, was appropriate for Christmas Eve, but nobody seemed to complain and the Chinese community was thrilled that we had given them such an honor as to present their service to the entire nation.

Following the program I drove to Mother's apartment in Haverford and arrived on Christmas morning at five A.M., still shaken by the experience. I had a long day ahead, what with helping her prepare for a big luncheon (to include Jack's family), and then the drive to New Jersey and a second Christmas party in Lawrenceville with my boys and Amy, Bob, Tyler and Lucy.

Gatchells and Dales

When I finally got home that night and had a little bit of Christmas cheer with Arnie, I was completely exhausted, and had enough to think about for a whole year. But I'm surely not complaining. What could be more gratifying than to bring an inspiring religious expression to my television "family," the millions of people across our land, and then share the Christmas festivities and celebrations, in a more personal way, with all the people I loved, the family that God so graciously had given to me. And all of this within twenty-four hours!

CHAPTER SIXTY-THREE

I'm not sure just when I first heard the word "gay," as referring to homosexuals, but I do think it has a little nicer ring to it than the words "queer" or "fag," or even "sissy," "pansy," or "fairy." My mother used to talk about gay parties, and people being gay when they were having a good time, and I'm sure when they named the wonderful Fred Astaire film, *The Gay Divorcee*, they weren't referring to him as being a homosexual, but rather a friendly bon vivant who was very attractive to the ladies and who found them appealing as well. Cole Porter's lyrics often contained the word, and now that I look at them, many seem to have a double entendre. But the sophisticated Cole Porter was always ahead of his time.

When we moved to our little house in Grandview-on-Hudson, and the villagers there saw two men who lived together being their new neighbors, I wondered just how they referred to us. Were we "gay" like the suave and debonair Fred Astaire, or were we, as some right-wing religious fanatics would have it, "gay" like those depraved deviants who were destroying the morals of our children and were a disease to all of mankind? Were the phones in the village ringing off the hook with calls back and forth, trying to figure out if we were acceptable or not? As I tended my garden, and took out the trash, I didn't know what they thought, as they walked along beside the river and passed our house. Nor did I really care very much, or at least that's what I kept telling myself.

We moved to our delightful new home in March of 1969 feeling secure in our beliefs and behavior. We thought of ourselves as ordinary, fine upstanding citizens who paid taxes and experienced the same daily trials that life brings to anyone else. Our only difference was that we chose a same sex partner to live with, to love, and to share those everyday experiences with. We had a resounding clue as to the thinking of at least some of the Grandview residents when Arnie was so soundly defeated when he ran for office soon after our arrival.

One family apparently had no trouble deciding however; our next door neighbors, Jack and Barbara Keil and their three children, Peter, Nick, and Betsy. Our house was, at one time, the carriage house for their large and comfortable Hudson River Gothic home, and stood in close proximity to their property. But if the two structures were near to each other, we and the Keil family became even closer as friends, and have remained that way for thirty-one years. They not only embraced us with outstretched arms, but introduced us to all of their many friends as if we were just a plain old conventional married couple waiting for the Welcome Wagon. We became part of the social circle, which was rather active for such a small village, and nobody seemed to care very much that we lived an alternate life style. I'm sure there were questions in people's minds, but I think when they got to know us that they just plain liked us for who we were, not what we were.

Since living here in Grandview, I have seldom been reminded that I was "different," and a member of a minority group, which I am. It's probably because the approximately 10% of our country's population who are gay are slowly becoming more and more visible and in the mainstream of society at large. Yet gays are still condemned, despised, and blatantly discriminated against by many narrow minded, ultra-conservative bigots, with hate crimes occurring on a regular basis throughout the country.

Sometimes I even feel a little uncomfortable among my oldest friends, those Haverford School classmates and their wives, with whom Amy and I shared so many happy times. Many have chosen to remain, like lovely, contented cows, in their small, conservative, fenced in world on the Philadelphia Main Line. (Amy and Arnie, let it forever be known that "there but for you go I.") I don't mind admitting that I do love to visit and be with them whenever possible, and talk about old times and our children and grandchildren, and I try to ignore, as they do, any dissimilarities that might exist. They will always be very special to me. I hope and pray the feeling is mutual.

Through the years, most of our friends here in Rockland County have been heterosexual couples, with our gay associations being somewhat limited. This is not necessarily by choice, but it just happens to work out that way in the community in which we live. When we have wanted to be with people who live an alternate lifestyle, there is always a gay party to go to, or a dance bar nearby, filled with what we laughingly call "the hairdressers from New Jersey." But neither of us have needed that association as a constant thing, having had our fill when we lived those fun and frivolous days in Greenwich Village, where being gay almost seemed to be the norm.

I have heard it said that Arnie and I have become icons in the changing world of sexual freedom and equality and because of the respect we have received in the community and at CBS I think it is very possible that we have been something of an inspiration and an example to many others. We have never made this our mission, our goal. We have just been who we are. I like to think that perhaps we have given some young people the confidence to lead their lives in a dignified way and without fear of reprisal. I sincerely hope this is true and that gay people, having known us, will have greater courage and feel more comfortable in whatever situation they choose to live and work.

Arnie, having made the choice to be a free lance writer and doing his work at home, has had time to become quite involved in the local scene. He became a Democratic Committeeman, County Youth Board member, and a valuable volunteer, and rather vocal advocate, in several public school programs and projects. He is very civic minded and deeply concerned with the many divisive issues in the county where we live, as well as in the nation, and spends a great deal of time trying to make our world a better place, not only for gays, but for all people. But, with so much volunteerism in his desire to improve everyone's way of life, and freelance writing assignments coming on an irregular basis, it has not always been easy for us to maintain the lifestyle we had grown accustomed to when we lived in Greenwich Village.

With our income cut almost in half from Arnie's halcyon days of producing Clairol commercials, I felt sometimes that I couldn't make ends meet all by myself. We found that country living, and owning a house in such a desirable location, was a lot more financially challenging than we had expected, but it has all been well worth the effort. As happens in all relationships, those few times when I wondered if my choice of life partner had been the right one, I was always reminded, along with an abiding fondness, that my success as a producer of programs dealing with important issues involving the human condition might not have been nearly as effective had it not been for Arnie's considerable knowledge, moral support and encouragement, and an abiding passion to make this a better world. And, of course, a delicious home cooked dinner and a good laugh never hurt either.

So we were the Fred Astaires of Grandview-on-Hudson, with problems like everybody else, but dancing our way through life along River Road. Our gay, happy existence continued to be full of surprises, as Arnie waltzed off to an important county meeting, and I tapped my way through airports on my way to another CBS production.

CHAPTER SIXTY-FOUR

It was at the USO's 40th Anniversary party weekend, being held in Washington, DC that I met Bob Hope. He was being honored, and my interview with him lasted only about thirty seconds, but at least I can say that I talked to very possibly the most recognizable show business performer ever to live on the face of this planet...or any other planet, for that matter. He did it all, and everywhere! From Broadway to Hollywood, on radio and television, he was a shining star. On battlefields and battleships in several wars he made our fighting men and women forget their fighting, and for a few memorable moments, just laugh and cheer. And if anyone deserved to wear the title, "Mr. Show Biz," it was surely Bob Hope.

It can't be that I have had too many martinis because I don't drink them anymore, but for the life of me I am unable to recall why I was there, producing a show about the USO. But I remember him well, and his good looking light blue silk summer suit with a yellow tie, and his being very affable as he saw me push through the crowds with a microphone and a cameraman right behind me. He held up his award and said he was thrilled and honored and I told him I was, too, just to be meeting him. He laughed and said, "You guys talk to presidents and kings. I'm just an old broken down hoofer." I laughed and thanked him for his time, and that was about it.

I did do an interview with then Vice President George Bush, but never any kings (except Martin Luther), and most of my interviews were with significant but everyday people who were kind enough to share their thoughts, experiences, and passion for things that mattered—to a small group, a community, and, in many instances, to the world. I found interviewing about the most satisfying part of my job, more so than directing or writing, or supervising the production and editing. I felt completely comfortable doing it and I think I did a good job, always being well prepared, never using any distracting notes, and always considering the interview as a conversation rather than a series of questions and answers. And I was never in a hurry.

With so many shows, and segments of shows, in various stages of production, it was sometimes hard to keep all the different pieces in their proper order, and many times I would be up at five in the morning in my hotel room frantically reviewing background information; preparing for my dialogue with particular upcoming show guests like the dynamic Reverend Jesse Jackson, the flamboyant Congresswoman Bella Abzug, or the shy and introspective poet W.H. Auden. And often there were five or six interviews per day, and I did a lot of "boning up" while the lights and camera were being set in place. Because of some late night unwinding at the hotel bar, or just plain fatigue, I tried wherever possible to make sure I was not seen on camera, with those telltale bags under my weary blue eyes.

Once I interviewed a serial killer at the Florida State Prison in Starke. The show I was doing was about capital punishment, and the faith community's mixed feelings regarding the death penalty. We were not in the prisoner's cell, but in a large recreation room, with an armed guard, accompanying Arnie, about fifty feet away.

We talked about the Roxboro section of Philadelphia where he had lived and committed his heinous crimes, and I was just as happy he had never heard of Haverford, my home town. We got along just fine, and he told me in a gentle voice that the prison chaplain was kind and helpful to him while he awaited execution. But afterwards, Arnie, with a relieved look on his face, told me that the guard had whispered to him that this seemingly quite man had a fierce temper and that, if by chance I had asked him something that irritated or upset him, he would have lunged at me and tried to strangle me, even though his wrists and ankles were shackled. It apparently had happened before, but the authorities neglected to tell us about it. I think I was better off not knowing.

Another time, in the northern California grape country, when I was interviewing Caesar Chavez, the dynamic labor leader and powerful force behind the United Farm Workers Union, there was a giant and rather vicious looking German Shepherd sitting right beside him, glaring at me with an evil eye through the whole session. It was a little unsettling, particularly considering that we were in Chavez's secret compound, La Paz, with his bodyguards all around, watching our every move.

But I admired Caesar so much, as he led his workers in peaceful protest against intolerable working and living conditions throughout the Salinas Valley, and mounted a national boycott, urging the nation to refrain from the purchase of grapes and lettuce. And all of this with the blessing and support of most of the religious community. When I finished talking with Caesar, we went out to film some of the laborers, with their children, in the fields, and to document their miserable little unsanitary shacks that were provided as shelter by the growers.

No sooner had we arrived at a suitable location when gunshots were fired over our heads. But this obvious warning from the growers only made us more determined to expose the terribly humiliating injustice that prevailed, not just in California, but wherever migrant labor was to be found throughout the country. Being there to see, and feel, first hand, the human tragedy that was happening in our own backyard led me to better understand the meaning and the indignation in the life of people like Caesar Chavez, people who truly lived in the image of Jesus Christ.

In a whole different vein: I had trouble holding back the tears as I interviewed several men dying of AIDS. It was the 1980's and AIDS was no longer just an isolated illness; it was an epidemic. And with love and compassion a Catholic Church in Atlanta sponsored a candlelight dinner in their church basement. As Gladys Knight's recording of "That's What Friends Are For" played in the background, hundreds of suffering and slowly dying men, many of whom were gay, along with their care givers, were served by the church elders and their children at beautifully set tables, complete with linen tablecloths, napkins and a bouquet of flowers. It was a sincere and moving testament to this Catholic Church's solidarity with the gay and AIDS inflicted community; all too often ostracized by society, but embraced by this parish every Thursday evening.

It was here that an older guest, and a very wise man, told me a little of his fascinating life story; of his troubled childhood, of his business successes and failures, of sixty years of sadness and joy. He didn't have long to live but his attitude was friendly and upbeat as he held my hand, looked into my eyes, and said, "I hope when you are in your golden years you can say, as I do, that it has been *a life full of days*." I knew exactly what he meant.

Other than the casualties I was witness to during my service in the Navy in WWII, I had not experienced any deaths, other than my father, among family members or friends. But as I grow older, I do recognize that we are not immortal as we sometimes thought when we were young. And when I think of people who were dealing with death and the loss of a loved one for whatever reason, I am reminded of the time we covered some seminars in a Fort Worth, Texas 7th Day Adventist church, aimed at making the period of mourning a little less traumatic for family members and friends. I certainly didn't look forward to the time that I would lose someone close to me in the years ahead, but I knew I was much better prepared to deal with it as a result of those informative gatherings, and the emotion packed interviews that I conducted; conversations that almost seemed like an extension of the therapy they had been receiving.

While filming a program that hit awfully close to home, I talked with a southern textile worker who was suffering from Brown Lung disease. By a strange coincidence, he had worked all of his adult life in a spinning mill that my father represented, and I recalled how irritated Dad was when a union was formed to help protect the mill workers from breathing the polluted air. I'm sure he didn't wish them harm, but the health and welfare of mill workers was of little concern to him. He said unionization was slowing production, was much too costly, and it was ultimately affecting his sales and commissions. I hope he was watching and listening from his resting place as the man coughed and gasped for breath trying to answer my questions.

But the demands of the textile union, which we carefully reported, have greatly improved conditions in the mills and there have been far fewer incidents of Brown Lung in recent years. But the young man I interviewed was disabled for life due, I'm afraid, to the greed and lack of concern on the part of people not unlike my father. I felt ashamed, and was reluctant to reveal my connection to the industry, but knew that my program would help serve as a reminder to people how destructive selfish motives can be.

There is one interview that I enjoy recalling which was much less significant, but extremely emotional, and it took place at the time of Catholic University's 45th anniversary celebration of it's prestigious drama department, and its founder, Father Gilbert Hardke. Honored

402

at the event was the grand lady of the American Theater, Helen Hayes, who also happened to be a neighbor of mine in nearby Nyack, NY. As interesting as the conversation with Miss Hayes was, I had the surprise of my life when I was ushered into the office of the department head. There, seated behind his large desk, waiting patiently for his interview to begin, was Bill Graham, my old Navy buddy from the battleship New Mexico. I don't know when I've hugged anybody with more enthusiasm than I did Bill, and we both had difficulty holding back the tears. We never really realized how close we were during those lonely days forty years ago when those horrific Kamikaze planes were threatening our lives. A precious memory.

Things didn't always go smoothly, however. One interview that I was never able to complete was with the Mayor of New Orleans, Moon Landrieu. Right in the middle of our discussion on low income housing, Bobby Clemens and his camera crew were called away by their supervisor in New York to stake out a remote lake in Florida. It seems that the estimable Don Hewitt, Executive Producer of the top rated *60 Minutes* program, had received a hot tip that the body of the missing powerful and controversial leader of the Teamster's Union, Jimmy Hoffa, was lying at the bottom of the lake. My documentary crew were the closest to the scene and could get there the fastest, and I was left hanging as they raced to a hastily arranged charter flight. I certainly understood that Don's show should take precedence, but it would have been thoughtful if he had at least offered a hint of an apology, particularly considering that no body was ever found.

I received the ultimate compliment one day when a veteran cameraman, Keith Kulin (now the producer of my old friend Andy Rooney's segment on *60 Minutes*) told me I was the best interviewer he had ever worked with. Kind words, but I don't know that I could ever compete with Mike Wallace or Bill Moyers, or even Barbara Walters. But after several hundred very intense conversations through the years I have learned more than any school book could ever teach me, and I feel I'm quite ready to talk to a president or a king, or even have a much longer chat with Bob Hope.

CHAPTER SIXTY-FIVE

There is absolutely no question that one of the greatest pleasures in life was watching my children growing up, from adorable little babies to their bubbling, rascally, pre-teen years, and then awkward adolescence and teenage angst to glorious manhood. Perhaps, not being with them everyday, I could see and marvel at the changes more clearly than someone who is so busy keeping up with the daily adjustments that their children are grown before they know it. And I could savor the times during their early years when they made me very happy to be their father. How proud I was that summer day when I learned that Tony and Harry each had received Best Camper Award in their respective age groups at the Keewaydin Camp for Boys; a first for brothers to be recognized and so honored at one the oldest, and most prestigious summer camps in the nation!

On the other hand, when I was with the boys, which was often, it usually was only for a few hours at a time, and I sometimes felt I didn't really know them, and often wondered how well they knew me. We seldom sat down and just talked about any old thing, because we were usually pressed for time; on the move seeing or doing something, or there were a lot of people around and not much of a chance to be alone together. They had very little idea of what I did those many times when I was away on a trip.

So, when the boys were about fifteen and Pamela Ilott suggested that I take Tony first, and then Harry, on a production assignment with me to serve as my "assistant," I was ecstatic. Of course there would be no salary, but all expenses would come out of our budget, and somehow she would bury them in her jumble of confused figures that nobody, including the accounting department, could ever understand. It was the nicest, kindest thing she ever did and I will always remember her for that special "gift," and not for the occasional disagreement or disturbing situation which I have buried in a dark corner of my mind. In those twenty-five years of producing shows with her as the executive in charge, the pluses always outweighed the minuses, and this considerate act, a chance for me to bond with my children, certainly went a long way in tipping the scales.

The three of us

In July of 1968 Tony and I flew off together to Alaska on an exciting three-week trip to film four half-hour shows for *Look Up And Live* on the effects the construction of an extensive new oil pipeline would have upon the native Alaskan people; how their ancient culture and life style would be disturbed and even uprooted by it. Long trips on airplanes, sleeping and eating side-by-side in motels and lodges, and just being close to each other twenty-four hours a day in this magnificent country was as much an inspiration as it was an education. And we were sharing a totally different experience together for the very first time.

There were some particularly enduring moments for us that I will always cherish. Shortly after our arrival in Anchorage, we flew by seaplane to a distant and very small island where the Eskimo families were sitting on the rocks by the shore looking frightened to death by this huge "bird" that was invading their private domain. Apparently it had been many years since they had such a visitor, and some of the children had never even seen a plane up close, nor strange people climbing on to their land with cases and cases of ominous looking technical equipment.

I thought we might have a serious problem gaining their confidence when all of a sudden Tony, spotting an old basketball hoop nailed to a tree, picked up a ball and made a perfect shot. Slowly, little smiles began to appear on the faces of the children and they seemed to recognize that he was not so scary after all, and they gathered around him, urging him to play a game with them. The ice was broken. Tony had earned his keep, and we had a very productive day of filming, with lots of fond farewells as they waved from the rocks as we left. A remote and serenely beautiful little enclave, and a very happy day.

And then there was a time, a rather frightening time, in another small village. While we were setting up the equipment and waiting for the person I was to interview, I suggested that Tony, who was about to apply for his driver's license, do some practicing on the one road in town. There were no other cars, and so he was told to drive the mile down the road to the dead end, turn around, and come right back. He was gone for almost an hour before he finally returned to his worried father. He explained he hadn't been able to turn the car around because there was a puddle of water at the dead end, and a large brown bear was drinking from it. He just had to wait until the bear was finished, and I'm glad he did. Tony is very charming and delightful, but I don't know that the bear would have been captivated by his friendly personality.

But the time I remember best was the day we were flying in two small bush planes, side by side amongst the towering mountain peaks in northern Alaska. The one that had Tony and the equipment suddenly swooped down into a valley and disappeared. I was sure there had been trouble, and when we lost radio contact I thought I had lost my son forever. We landed at our destination, a remote village with only a dirt road as a runway, and as we debated what to do, Tony's plane came in for a gentle, safe landing right behind us. He explained that he had spotted a herd of moose down in the valley and mentioned to the pilot that he would love to see them up close. And he did, as the pilot gave him a tour that he, and the rest of us, will never forget. That little plane had a very valuable cargo, and I thanked God for Tony's safekeeping. I'm sure Wade Bingham, the cameraman, was saying a few prayers of thanks himself for sparing the $100,000 worth of technical equipment.

It was two years later, on a trip through the southwest part of the United States, that I took Harry as my "assistant." It was quite a different experience, as different as the boys are from each other. We were doing a series of shows on the difficult living and working conditions some American Indian tribes were subjected to on their barren, and non-productive reservations. I don't recall any particular incidents that were memorable, but just being with Harry was enjoyable enough. He was a most thoughtful, inquisitive, and perceptive companion and seemed to be absorbed in all that was going on around him. He made very few observations, and at times almost seemed antisocial.

But I know the trip meant a great deal to him, as we visited the Pueblos in Taos, New Mexico and the Navajos on their 26,000 square mile reservation where four state corners come together: Utah, Arizona, New Mexico, and Colorado. We drove many miles through this magnificent countryside, past the famous Chimney Rock, and visited the Native Americans in their hogans, built of logs and mud, with the door traditionally facing east. I have a picture in my mind of Harry walking slowly up a lonely dirt road following an old Indian man leading a donkey, as the howling wind whistled and the dust blew, making an almost surreal picture. He seemed to be one of them, and in his mind, I think he was.

We traveled on to Los Angeles and at one point, while we were staying at the Holiday Inn on Hollywood Boulevard, just a block from the infamous corner of Hollywood and Vine, Harry, always curious, decided to take a walk and have a look at Grauman's Chinese Theater and the movie stars' hand and footprints imbedded in the sidewalk. I suddenly realized, while looking out of the hotel window, that a naive, blond, good looking fifteen year old on that particular boulevard was a ripe target for just about any pick-up artist. I ran to save him from the evil world of perversion and vice, which I had learned a little something about while living in New York City.

If there was only one lasting impression from those two trips with the boys, it was that they were very much a part of me, mirroring the many sides of my own complex personality, as seen and told to me by others. There was Tony, the charmer; a likable, entrepreneurial, fun loving, socially motivated young man, with his personality on his sleeve and the world his oyster. Then there was Harry, the individualist; introverted, mysterious, intellectually curious, and a peace loving little brother, with the world and all its creatures still to be understood and changed for the better, if at all possible. How proud I was to have them both as my sons. They were so very different, and yet so much alike in their affection for me. There could be no greater gift.

CHAPTER SIXTY-SIX

"It's such an ancient pitch,

but one I wouldn't switch,

'cause there's no nicer witch than you."

The closing words of Frank Sinatra's recording of "Witchcraft," which I sang, along with Seymour and Chet, as an evening ritual before heading for my home in Grandview-on-Hudson through the tangled traffic along New York City's dreaded Westside Highway. And my home away from home, my favorite haunt, where we did our raucous off key singing, leaning over the jukebox, was the Slate. It was a little dive—I guess you could call it a hangout—with a long mahogany bar. It took up two floors in an old Hell's Kitchen tenement on Tenth Avenue and West 56th Street, around the corner from the CBS Production Center, and it had witch like powers over me and a couple of dozen others who were as crazy and as wonderful a bunch of characters as I have ever known, or probably ever will.

There were executives and impresarios, producers and actors, truck drivers and clerks; some of them from CBS, and some not; and we all shared our work problems and our personal problems. But mostly we just laughed at each other and with each other. It was not a place for the faint of heart, and everybody was subject to abuse. No egos were allowed. But nobody got too serious, and we bonded together as we drank, played games and cared more for each other than for anyone, except maybe our immediate families and loved ones. (I'm afraid even they took a back seat sometimes to the camaraderie that existed among us.)

There was Milt, the chauffeur from the funeral home nearby, who used to park his hearse illegally in front of the Slate, run in for one beer, and sadly listen to Bunny Berrigan sing "I Can't Get Started With You," while moaning over his heavy work load. Once the hearse was towed away with a body in it as he went screaming into the street, chasing it up the avenue. He didn't even get his quarter's worth of Berrigan's final trumpet solo.

And there was George, the gifted producer and engineer from CBS, who must have surpassed Winston Churchill's daily liquor consumption, but functioned just as brilliantly, except when he umpired our late afternoon softball games. He spent so much time going over the ground rules that we barely were able to complete a few innings before darkness set in. He stalked off the field in a rage, saying he couldn't make judgment calls under such terrible conditions. But we played anyway.

I'll always wonder how the drivers of the huge *New York Times* trucks, after many, many drinks at the Slate, drove hundreds of miles in the dead of night, sometimes under the worst of weather conditions, to places like Syracuse and Schenectady so that the subscribers would have their morning paper right on time. To this day, when I drive at night on a highway, I think of them, and hope they are safe.

I'm not sure what brought all of us together, aside from bartender John's, or Bobby's ample "dab of the brush," as owner Seymour used to call it. We saw little of each other outside the Slate, but inside we were a most varied and astounding cast of characters. There was the bespectacled little man known only as the Inspector, formally of Scotland Yard and, along with Professor David Goddard, taught at The John Jay College of Criminal Justice up the street from the Slate; and there was Marie, affectionately known as the bag lady, of *Cosmopolitan* magazine, who spread her little samples of beauty products on the bar for the boys to chose from and take home to their long-suffering wives. There was Bill Kearns, a Roosevelt Hospital fund raiser, who walked a half a mile, past three or four bars, to get to the Slate for his many martinis before lunch. Howard was the organizer; Phil, the friendly arbiter and statistical maven; "Pee", the larger than life entrepreneur; and delightful little Dennis who, deformed from birth, played softball and golf better than most of us, and constantly reviled us with his acid tongue.

But the one who, in my opinion, stood out above all the others was the extraordinarily complex and utterly fascinating Chet Merola. He was like a precious, uncut diamond who had everything going for him…except self-confidence. He wrote a long letter to me from Vietnam, expressing his hope that he would someday succeed at CBS when he returned from the war. And he did, to a point, but probably

414

would have gone a lot farther had he been more aggressive. His sharp mind, his wit, and his totally disarming personality made this very charismatic, yet mysterious, character a joy to be with. He was a treasured friend.

The drinks were tall, the food hearty and the price was right, but very possibly the catalyst that brought us all together was the "Beanbag," a brilliantly conceived baseball pool that Chet and I created. Each day, for one dollar (known as a "bean"), a player could pick three major league batters, and the participant whose chosen players had the highest total number of hits that day won the "beanbag." There were anywhere from ten to twenty-five players each day and I, having been anointed Lord Bean, was in charge.

It was a lot of work, checking the newspaper box scores, trying to tally the hits from the late west coast games, and being constantly needled for not being more efficient. I was accused only once of making a mistake, the charge being that I confused the ball playing Cruz brothers, Hector and Jose, one of whom had a number of hits that day. I was right, and continued to administer the game for the many years we were all together. As a token of their gratitude, the gang at the Slate gave me a gold pocket watch inscribed to Lord Bean, the Keeper of the Bean Bag. And Arnie gave me a beautiful Springer Spaniel puppy who we named Beans to remind me of those good times.

But, like everything else, all good things come to and end, and that included Beans, who was run over by a car in front of our house

415

on River Road. I have never quite gotten over it. Perhaps it was an indication of what was to come, as ominous looking people with black hats and big cars started appearing late at night at the Slate, and apparently there were some dirty doings going on in the upstairs dining room. I don't really know what happened, but the Slate changed hands and ultimately closed, and we all became almost invisible once again, barely ever seeing each other.

But what a wonderful ride it was, and even though I was traveling quite a bit, and when in New York extremely busy, my day seemed incomplete if I didn't spend some time with my Slate buddies, those lovable beings I considered to be my extended family. One day Bill Leonard, vice president of CBS News, snidely remarked to Pamela Ilott, "Every time I go to the Slate, I see Chum Dale there." Her crisp, but polite reply was, "Isn't that funny, he said the same about you." I guess I was a fixture there, sitting at the end of the bar by the window with my specially concocted drink, a "Chum-rum," in front of me. But my work didn't suffer and, as a matter of fact, I think I can honestly say that the types that drifted in and out were great food for research. After all, the vagaries of the human condition were my focus and at the Slate the examples were plentiful.

Chum and "Chum-rum"

Did they know I was gay? They knew I had lived with Arnie for many years, and they liked him a lot. I don't think they gave it very much thought, except when a golf weekend was planned at Hilton Head, North Carolina. Because they were sharing rooms with each other and, I presume, nobody wanted to room with me, I was odd man out, and wasn't invited. I understood, but felt the pain. They will never know how much. But I know they cared for me. I was given a box of oil paints and a set of outdoor dishes as house warming presents when I moved to the country, and champagne was poured on my head, as the winning pitcher and manager, when the team from the Slate was the victor in the softball championship.

Along with the many shows I produced, and all the people associated with them, these memorable moments, kept in a special compartment labeled Fun and Games, will be with me forever.

Maybe, with a little luck, we will all meet someday at the big Slate in the sky, spend a "bean" or two, and sing out to each other, "there's no nicer witch than you."

CHAPTER SIXTY-SEVEN

I know we had a very limited budget and our shows were produced for the proverbial "$1.98," but this was carrying penuriousness a bit too far. Eight shows, in eight cities, in eight days. I don't know why I ever agreed to do it, and it almost did me in. How the big bands, or the comedians, or in today's world, the rock groups and pop singers do one night stands for months at a time I'll never know. It was a series that was proposed by our consultant at the National Council of Churches, Al Cox, and the idea was certainly a good one. We called it "We Will Speak, Who Will Answer?," and the plan was to have a member of the clergy and distinguished lay people in each city talk about current national issues, like civil rights and the Vietnam War, and how their faith, their lives and their community was affected.

The discussion programs were taped in the studios of the local CBS affiliated stations in Cleveland; Kansas City, Missouri; Portland, Oregon; Fresno; Tulsa; Baton Rouge; Charlotte; and Hartford, in that order. It gave people in medium sized cities a chance to be heard nationally, and the programs were hosted by the local station's top news anchorman, thrilled that they were afforded network exposure. But the logistical nightmare of getting from one city to another each day, making all the arrangements with the local stations for studio and video taping facilities, technical crew, set, director, etc. over the telephone, and then hoping it would turn out even close to the way I planned, was almost more than I could handle.

Fortunately, Al Cox was a day or two ahead of me in each city, arranging for the most important entity, those who would participate in the discussion. But still it was considered a remarkable achievement, a most informative and well produced feat, and the eight programs were aired on eight consecutive Sundays on the *Look Up And Live* series. After some time, and a great deal of positive response, the eight half-hour shows were edited into a one hour special, using the highlights of the discussions from each of the cities. It almost became a dialogue, with the people of each city seeming to talk to one another and share each other's views.

My son, Tony, was with me on the first leg of the trip, Cleveland, and we couldn't resist going to a baseball game before I had to start work the next day. It turned out to be quite an evening as we were welcomed as important visitors from CBS by the Public Address announcer in Cleveland's Municipal Stadium as we watched the Cleveland Indians beat the Washington Senators. Together, we rose and waved to the sparse stadium crowd. But the highlight of the game was an unassisted triple play made by Washington's second baseman, Ron Hanson. Only baseball purists will recognize the rarity of such a play, and what a thrill it was to be there and see it happening in person. (I wonder if I'm the only baseball fan, living or dead, who has seen, in person, both a perfect no-hit game and an unassisted triple play.) And that first night of leisure was to be the last for eight days. There wasn't a minute to spare, and as Tony returned home following the first show, I silently wished he could have been with me in the days ahead. What a help he would have been making this crazy schedule work!

The actual production of each of the shows has become kind of a blur, but I met lots of interesting people in each of the cities we visited, people who I remember very well. But there was one who will always remain as an all time favorite. He was Father Dan Allen, a Catholic priest who founded an organization called Neighbors In Need, in Tulsa, Oklahoma. With my deep seeded disdain for the Catholic clergy always lingering in the back of my mind, my eyes were jarred open by this rough, dirty talking, hard drinking, yet saintly man with a heart as big as the oil refineries that rose out of the dusty soil that surrounded his little parish. He was an aggravation to his Bishop, but a godsend to hundreds of transient migrants.

Al Cox, Fr. Dan Allen and me

His creative ministry was in his compassionate care for those people known as "Okies." They were a marginal group (brought to our attention in John Stienbeck's *The Grapes Of Wrath*), and as they passed through Tulsa in their tired old cars and broken down pick-up trucks, Father Dan was there, always ready to embrace the large, sickly families, half starved to death and in desperate need of nourishment, medical care, a hot bath, and a place to rest their heads. He was a neighbor indeed, as he established a small clinic with volunteer doctors and nurses. And he fed the needy with food donated by his parishioners, and temporarily housed them in refurbished pre-fabs, made livable by his own hands, on a lonely, dead-end road near his church.

It was here that I recognized how innovative he could be when I saw, on a Sunday afternoon, a number of expensive looking cars

422

jammed into this short narrow road, unable to turn around. Suddenly the caravan was surrounded by a bunch of tired and scrawny little children offering lemonade, at 5c a glass, to the wealthy occupants, while their parents waved to them from their rickety porches nearby. There was Tulsa's high society, dressed in their Sunday best, sitting in their polished cars, trapped, and gazing in wonder at the weary hosts in their overalls and tattered dresses. It seemed that Father Dan, in hopes of raising some money for his mission of mercy, had learned of a Beautiful Homes Tour for the prosperous residents on the other side of town. In the dead of night, he rearranged the posted arrows, changing the direction of the route so that the last stop on the grand tour were the tidy, but not such "beautiful homes" in his bedraggled little village of disadvantaged people. He walked among his captive audience, cajoling them through their half-closed car windows, passing his church's collection basket, and gathering hundreds of dollars for Neighbors In Need from the exasperated "tourists," before he unsnarled the traffic, wished them well, and invited them to come back real soon.

On the next leg of the trip, while passing through New Orleans on the way to Baton Rouge, I came across an idea that developed into one of our most important programs. Our unit was preparing a future six part series for *Look Up And Live*, with the overall title "Games Of

God." The series would be an examination of the interaction and interplay of religion and plays written for the stage.

The Free Southern Theater was a professional company of black actors who brought quality theater productions with themes that spoke to and for the people in the depressed communities of the city. It seemed to be just what we were looking for, and I returned later to tape a program with them in Desire, a poverty ridden ghetto of New Orleans. The "theater" was an old boarded-up warehouse with no windows, and in the intense heat and dilapidated setting, the play seemed to take on an added dimension as it was performed for a hundred or so African- Americans, who were sitting on hard wooden benches experiencing something completely new to most of them—a live theatrical performance.

Our taping of this unusual event was almost canceled when it was discovered that the local camera crew had come prepared for trouble, and some of them were carrying guns and knives for self-protection. The performers refused to go on until they were assured that all the weapons were removed from the premises and that I had talked to the production company management to make sure that the arms were disposed of. I said I would assume full responsibility for any disturbance, and I'm not sure to this day what I would have done had trouble erupted. Although tensions were high, fortunately it didn't, and we captured on tape not only a dynamic and moving presentation by the actors, but a spirit and excitement in the audience that was as powerful as the drama itself.

The setting, the performances, and the audience seemed to awaken the consciousness of God in man, and that love, not hatred, must enter the human spirit. And I, too, felt it deep in my soul as I stood in this repository of every social ill imaginable, a place of total despair and degradation. It was an experience that will stay with me always, and my hope has been that our television audience heard the message and felt and remembered it the same way I had.

That title, We Will Speak, Who Will Answer?, could have been given to so many programs that I was involved with through the years, and certainly this very special event in a ghetto named Desire is one that I would put near the top of the list. We are all familiar with the well-known *Face The Nation* and *Meet The Press* (My brother, Ted, was often on the panel), Sunday morning talk shows, but an hour or two earlier, the discussions on our programs were sometimes just as informative on issues dealing with the human condition. Perhaps not headline news, but of continuing significance.

425

CHAPTER SIXTY-EIGHT

It was a large package that arrived at my office one summer day in 1984, and I examined it just like I usually do, turning it, shaking it, trying to figure out what was inside without opening it. But this time I was pretty sure I knew what it was. I had received an urgent phone call from Los Angeles telling me that I had won television's most important accolade, an Emmy, presented by the Television Academy of Arts and Sciences for exceptional achievement in special daytime programming. Because of our limited budget I, as a nominee, had been unable to fly to the West Coast for the awards dinner and, frankly, I had put it out of my mind, never expecting to win.

I had never cared much about awards and always kind of poked fun at the Emmy's because of the large number of categories, and it seemed as if just about everybody was at least nominated for one. But when you consider the number of hours, day and night, that are filled with such a large selection of different types of programs, and the huge number of talented and creative people involved in them, I guess winning an Emmy is a pretty special honor after all. So, when I opened the package and saw the statue up close, with my name on it, I felt really quite proud. This considering my little production about a special school in Texas had been selected over the spectacular *Rose*

Bowl Parade and the very popular *American Bandstand*, both of which, oddly enough, were in the same category. And what surprised and delighted me, almost as much as the award itself, was the fact that it was inscribed Chalmers Dale, and not Dale Chalmers, as could easily have happened (and did on several citations I had received through the years).

In 1974, *Look Up and Live* had been awarded an Emmy for the best religious series, and I had received an Emmy then, along with several of my colleagues, as we shared in the various productions. This one, to complete my pair of bookends, was somewhat more important to me because it was for a single show in the new religion and cultural affairs series, *For Our Times*. In 1978, with a change in CBS top management, and a lot of budget tightening, the thirty year old programs, *Lamp Unto My Feet* and *Look Up And Live*, had evolved into a single half-hour program with the new and, in my opinion, much more provocative title, *For Our Times*.

The new show's permanent host and narrator was Douglas Edwards, the longtime television and radio news correspondent who had been such and important part of Amy's and my television viewing back in our early days of marriage. What a pleasure it was to be working directly with him on my own program! He was the consummate professional and added, not only dignity and stature to the new series, but a sense of understanding and compassion.

It was hard for all of us to swallow this cutback in programming, and was particularly upsetting to Pamela Ilott, the executive producer, who had shepherded most of us through the many years those two very prestigious programs had been such an important part of CBS' Sunday schedule. Despite the belt tightening, she somehow managed to hold on to most of our jobs and salaries, even though our workload was somewhat decreased with only one program to produce each week.

It ended up that instead of doing twelve to fifteen shows a year I produced only about seven or eight, plus a few holiday specials. But it was enough to keep me busy, as I began thinking that perhaps the time had come to retire in the not too distant future. I had, at this point, produced over two hundred and fifty shows, many of which had been shot away from home, away from the people I love, and I was longing to be able to spend some leisurely days with friends and family in my little carriage house by the river in Grandview-on-Hudson.

And so, during that summer of 1984, one of my assignments for *For Our Times* was to develop a program about the very unusual alternative school, The Wilhelm Schole in Houston, Texas. It was a unique place which stressed the importance of community over the individual and reminded me so much, with its sense of family, of Montgomery Country Day School where I had been so happy teaching almost forty years earlier. But the two schools were really very different. Here they had children from age two to fifteen, from more than twenty different nations and almost as many different religions. They were grouped according to ability, not age, and the inter-disciplinary, inter-cultural, inter-lingual approach brought the arts, sciences, and humanities together into a global vision, always anchored to traditional values. We called our television program "To See A World," and I think the school's unusual curriculum and teaching methods were well ahead of their time. I like to think that the judges saw that, and the way we captured the contagious feeling and excitement of both teacher and pupil was why the Academy awarded us the Emmy.

We not only spent time in the small school building taping the dynamic founder and educator extraordinaire, Mrs. Marilyn Wilhelm, with her teachers and diverse assortment of students, but we traveled with them to art and cultural centers in Houston, to the state capitol in Austin, and to a meeting with the Governor. And we spent a most delightful and informative evening sailing through the maze of canals in the historic and picturesque city of San Antonio, with a Mariachi band accompanying our tour.

Our hostess there, and someone who became a very dear friend, was one of the most extraordinary women I'll ever have the pleasure of knowing. Her name is Amy Freeman Lee. In addition to being a member of the Board Of Directors of The Wilhelm Schole, she is an artist, lecturer, educator, author, civic leader, humanist, humorist, conservationist, and a spirited and spiritual human being. And she has deep feelings for animals the way I do, and holds a top position

429

with the Humane Society. I loved her the minute I met her, so much so that I returned the following year to do a show specifically about her and her passion for just about everything that has any meaning in life. That program also was nominated for an Emmy, but that year we did lose to the *Rose Bowl Parade.* In my opinion, Amy Freeman Lee should have been the parade's Grand Marshal. She gave me one of her delicate watercolor paintings, which means a great deal to me, much more than another Emmy would, and always refreshes the memories of my times with her that another gold-plated statue could never do.

Amy Freeman Lee with
Keith Kulin's crew and me

By the time 1986 had rolled around, I and many of the people I had worked with for so long at CBS felt as though we had been hit by a terrible plague...total disillusionment! People were being let go, or urged to take early retirement for no apparent reason other than to reduce the workforce and satisfy the stockholders and their greed for more money. Loyal employees who had given a good part of their lives to the company were no longer the backbone of what had been a big, extraordinarily creative and productive family, whose members were proud to be a part of the "Tiffany Network," CBS. Mr. Paley was gone. Dr. Stanton was gone. Accountants and computers had taken over, and the morale was as low as it could possibly get. Everyone talked of nothing but how afraid they were of losing their jobs, and how they had lost faith in a company they considered their second home. And I, along with many others, couldn't wait to leave, whether forced to, or not. I think these must have been the darkest days in the history of a once proud and magnificent communications and entertainment empire, and the public responded by changing its viewing habits, sending CBS to a last place finish in the ratings race, and earning a reputation for having sold its soul...to the stockholders.

Our small Religious and Cultural Affairs Department, not being a money maker, was quickly done away with and I, with the advice of people like Dan Rather, took my pension, sold my stock, picked up my Emmys and literally ran for the hills, half in tears, and half in joy and relief. I was sixty years old and had been with the company thirty-five years, and there was no sense continuing to try to be productive in such a dreary and debilitating climate. I didn't seem to be wanted, anyway. With the demise of our department, Pamela Ilott, after scratching and clawing for as long as she could, finally had to be evicted. It took months to clear out her enormous collection of paper, plants, and memorabilia from her corner office. Deep down, I'm glad she made it as difficult for them as possible. Nobody seemed to care about what she and her staff had accomplished through the years, and how they had added so much dignity and prestige to a business known for its crass commercialism. With her departure, only a few of CBS's legendary figures remained, to try and pick up the pieces and save the badly bloodshot CBS eye from closing all together.

Thank goodness for my Texas ladies, Marilyn Wilhelm and Amy Freeman Lee, who made my life worth living during those final years leading up to the early retirement. I'm sure they weren't aware of it, but my heart was breaking to see my CBS, my company, my world around me crumbling before my eyes. I had arrived quietly one rainy morning in May of 1951, and left just as quietly in the late afternoon of a sultry September day in 1986. There was an attempt at a farewell party for a group of us, and by coincidence, it was held in the same studio where I had produced my first show. I received a CBS engraved Tiffany glass candy jar (without candy) and an ID card that allowed me to enter the building to use the men's room if I had the urge. And that was it. I didn't fill the jar with candy, or use the men's room. At least not for twenty-four hours.

And what happened after twenty-four hours? Why, nothing much—except that the phone rang in my living room and I was asked to come right back to CBS on a freelance, part time basis, and produce four religious and cultural specials a year. And to work primarily from my home, and with a paid associate, who was right beside me, Arnie Walton. Is that making the best of a bad situation, or what? Having one's cake and eating it, too. The best of all possible worlds. No need for anymore clichés. And I had barely taken my jacket off and put my Emmys away!

CHAPTER SIXTY-NINE

Eliazer Lord was my great, great uncle. He had lived in a magnificent castle high up on Clausland Mountain in Rockland County, very nearly behind my little red carriage house down by the river. He might have, one day, even been in my house for all I know, as he was a most prominent citizen of the area in the mid 1800's and surely he had known the family that lived next door in the big house now occupied by my dear friends, the Keils. He was a former ordained preacher and the founder and President of the New York and Erie Railroad which terminated in Piermont, the little village one mile south of Grandview-on-Hudson. Piermont was the beginning or the end of the line, depending on how you looked at it, but when it was the end of the long run from Dunkirk, New York on Lake Erie, the freight would be rolled out on to the long pier he had built with landfill, and it would be loaded on to ships and sent down river to New York City.

I was an instant celebrity when I moved to Grandview, as Uncle Eliazer was known throughout Rockland County as a famous and prosperous railroad tycoon and landowner. As he did in life, looking from high up in his castle over his little railroad town and people, so in death did he watch over them: he was buried at the top of the hill, overlooking their graves, in the Rockland Cemetery, next to General John Charles Fremont, a Civil War hero.

I, frankly, had barely heard of him before Isabel Savell, the County Historian and a Grandview neighbor, knocked on my door back in 1969 to welcome me and to inform me of my instant status in the community. She had done her homework, relating me to Eliazer, and knew all about the Lord family and my grandparents' big estate, "Broadreach," across the river in Tarrytown where my mother had grown up. Mother told me, when she made her only visit to my home in Grandview before she died, that when she was a small child she had looked down and across the river from her bedroom and could see my little red house on the opposite shore.

She said she used to wonder what was on the western side of the Hudson, which in those days could only be reached by boat. The Italian gardeners who tended "Broadreach" used to come over by ferry everyday from Nyack, the village just north of Grandview, and Mother told me how she used to hear them talking about farm lands and orchards and wide open spaces on the other side of those palisades and mountains that bordered the shore. But it all changed in 1953 with the building of the three mile long Tappan Zee Bridge from Tarrytown to Nyack, and the once rural Rockland County is now a thriving suburban enclave with almost 300,000 residents and boasting one of the ten largest malls in the United States.

But with constant vigilance, and regard for the environment and ecology of the river and fragile shoreline, where the striped bass come up-river to spawn, Grandview-on-Hudson has nearly succeeded in remaining an oasis of beauty and tranquillity. This, in spite of only being a short distance from New York City, and in the shadow of the massive bridge. The one mile long road is a little more traveled now, and many of the one hundred or so houses are a bit fancier. But fortunately the people who have lived in this tiny incorporated village through the years have desperately tried to keep development to an absolute minimum with the strict enforcement of zoning laws, laws that Arnie likes to call the village's "constitution." They have managed to preserve one of the few remaining areas along the shore where no high rise condominiums and commercial ventures can be found. Grandview may have lost some of its "funkiness," but it is still a little gem amidst the urban sprawl.

Writers Henry and Madeline Misrock, from whom we bought our house, loved it so much that they asked permission to have their ashes, when they died, sent to us from their new home in California to be spread under the two huge tulip poplar trees that look down on us from part way up Clausland Mountain. Arnie and I have asked for the same, hoping that with all that fertilizer there will be enough growth, along with the poplars serving as sentries, to prevent any erosion and destruction of our precious dwelling down below.

And so it was here, with roots firmly planted, where I had planned to sit back, kick off my shoes, and stay awhile—and then that phone call came from CBS asking me to return to work on a freelance basis. The offer from Jack Blessington, the part-time executive who replaced Pamela Ilott, was too good to refuse. With Arnie thrown into the mix as writer and production associate, we had a happy and productive five years of working together, along with the religious community, on some interesting and worthwhile projects. We were each paid for twenty weeks of work per year, plus expenses, but actually with research, travel, shooting, and editing, we spent many more days than that in the production of the four shows each year. It didn't matter though, because we were working at home a lot of the time, on our own schedule, and in lovely surroundings. And, except for the editing, we were away from the gloom of the CBS Production Center with all its unhappy and restless employees.

I was delighted to have someone doing the research and writing, a time consuming, but important part of every documentary production. Because of budget constraints, in recent years I had missed occasionally being able to hire, in addition to Arnie, talented freelance writers such as Stephan Chodorov, Jean Claude Van Itallie, Craig Gilbert, Jonathan Donald, and Lee Hays. Their skills had added so much more to each of the shows they worked on than I could have brought, and now Arnie was carrying on in that tradition.

One show I know he was particularly pleased to be working on was shot in Madison, Wisconsin, where he had gone to college and where he and actress Gena Rowlands had performed together. It was here that we explored the involvement of the religious communities' leaders, along with their flock, and together with the Madison Police, in bringing the new concept of Community Policing to the city. This entailed a closer relationship between the policemen on their beat and the inter-city citizens in an attempt to prevent the seeds of criminal activity from ever taking root. It was a very successful pilot project, and our show has served as a teaching tool throughout the country.

On another occasion we traveled to Nashville, Tennessee where the focus was on adult literacy programs developed by various church organizations. At a gathering of many of the old time civil rights leaders who were now involved in voter registration and networking with literacy programs throughout the rural south, I had the great pleasure of introducing Arnie to the venerable Rosa Parks, the woman who's courage changed a nation in December of 1955. The wheels of the civil rights movement began turning when she took a stand for equality by refusing to give up her seat to a white man and move to the back of a Birmingham, Alabama bus.

The decision by CBS to restore, on a limited basis, religious programming had come about, not because of CBS feeling it was important or necessary, but rather as a result of the various faith groups voicing their very strong feelings to CBS management, the FCC, and even the United States Congress. They said, in no uncertain terms, that in fact a door was being slammed in their faces, and that the company was silencing their platform in the electronic media for expressing their concerns in bringing God's message to a wide audience. Jack Blessington, once a seminarian and educator and former member of CBS management, admitted knowing very little about television production, and he chose to leave us almost completely alone to do our job, while he expertly managed to smooth the ruffled feathers of both CBS and church hierarchy, keeping our programs as low profile as possible. I think we were the only entity at CBS that was not income producing, and in the financial climate that existed it was best that we be almost invisible, at least to the accountants, not to make any waves, and still keep the faith groups (which now included the Southern Baptists), satisfied. It seemed to work, and our small operating budget was renewed year after year.

When a contentious issue surfaced in a news or entertainment program involving questions of morality or ethics, CBS management could always point to us and remind the protagonist of the fact that the company was well aware of its responsibilities; that they made inspirational programming available to a network audience, and were indeed mindful of the discriminating tastes of even the most conservative of the television viewers.

But in 1991, after adding to my long list of provocative programs and meaningful associations, I was just plain tired out, and decided to call it quits and leave the company for the second, and last, time. It was a hard decision to make, as things had worked out so well, and the company that I loved had been so good to me. But something deep inside said it was time to really "go home." Someone I hardly knew, but a regular viewer, wrote to me, "Chum, you've made a difference." That was good enough for me. I didn't need to hear any more.

Arnie continues to work at CBS assisting another producer. I watch silently over his shoulder, content and happy with my memories of life there. However, it's surprising how often I'm called on for information and advice, and I have managed to retain thirty years of assorted bits of information, useful as a free archive for inquiring researchers. But I seem to spend most of my time in harmony with nature, worrying if the water is clean enough for the majestic swans and cygnets as they go gliding by in the Hudson River in front of my house. And I will constantly work towards keeping Uncle Eliazer's mile long pier a charming and inviting walking path with adjacent marshland serving as a sanctuary for wild creatures and rare birds. I keep hoping that the beautiful and graceful deer will survive in their hideaways up the mountain near Uncle Eliazer's castle behind me (in spite of trying to keep them from feasting on my tasty roses and marigolds).

Uncle Eliazer

At one with nature

CHAPTER SEVENTY

One day, in the elevator at CBS, the country's most recognizable gentleman, Walter Cronkite, remarked, "Chum, one of the best feelings in life is when you have your first grandchild." And as I looked over at him I said to myself, "And that's the way it is." I think he had just had his, and I was looking forward to mine. When Kai was born to my son Harry, and his wife Elisa, I knew just what Walter meant. I was beside myself with joy and excitement. I guess it has to do with continuity. With a newborn grandchild you come to a realization that this new life is an extension of what you have been from your birthday to the present, with your own offspring being a kind of conduit, guiding him along the sometimes bumpy road to maturity.

I often sit on my terrace admiring the gulls standing proudly on the rocks close to the river bank and, as they seem to be planning their next move, I ponder what lies ahead for Kai and his two younger brothers, George and Julian, and I think about son Tony and Kit's young son, Ted and his dear little sister, Kelly. I wonder about their future in this crazy, mixed-up world much more than I ever did with Tony and Harry when they were small.

442

I guess when I was a young father I just assumed my children would have a happier and less difficult childhood than my own, which I think they did, thanks to Amy and their stepfather Bob, with me close beside them in my thoughts, and physically never very far away. Having divorced parents certainly wasn't easy for them, but Amy and I were never contentious as they were growing up, and as she was always their mother, I was always their father...and very proud to be that!

But now, being further removed in years, and having experienced so much, I tend to observe my grandchildren's development as it relates to my own life more so than I did my childrens', perhaps because I have more time to dwell on it. Maybe that's why grandparents sometimes have a closer relationship with their grandchildren than they do their own children, because there's no rush, no preoccupation. Of course, the nicest part of it all is that you can love them and have fun with them and then when you're tired out you can hug and kiss them goodbye and not have the day-to-day worries and responsibilities that go with parenting. You can delight in pleasant memories and store up your energy for the next encounter.

I love it when the families come for a visit to Grandview, or I go to see them. Tony lives in Baltimore, where he is an upwardly mobile, successful businessman. Harry, in Princeton, is a public school teacher and man of many talents. The little ones always seem so excited to be with me, whether I'm bearing gifts, or not. And when they are at my house they love my special basket of toys and assorted doodads, that seem like something new each time they come. Then there is always the river, and an endless supply of rocks to throw. They always refer to the Hudson as "Grandpa's river," and it is...and theirs, too.

Tony's family

Harry's family

My love for them is so strong that I just want to be with them forever, or at least until it's time to say farewell. I'm more patient than their parents when I see them doing all the same annoying things I used to do: being picky about their food, spreading their toys everywhere, and nagging and irritating each other. In Kai's case (he is now fifteen), I watched him quietly sulking through the early teens, and then beginning to open like a beautiful flower, becoming a charming, delightful, and very handsome young man.

Oh, how I hope none of them have any worrisome demons eating away at them as I did, and that they will always be accepted and loved by everyone for who they are, no matter what. I will always be there for them when they need me, because I like to think that I probably would understand whatever problems or worries they might have maybe even better than their own parents. Only because I had so many. I especially don't want them to go through my years of silent misery, not understanding those confusing feelings—a force that dominated and affected every facet of my life. But there is no reason why that should happen. Or is there? What elusive genes might be lurking in their little bodies? Only God knows for sure, and He's not telling.

On the subject of family, I have neglected, except for old Eliazer, and of course my grandparents, to talk very much about that great big Lord clan who, as a result of Grandma and Grandpa's wondrous summer "hotel" in Beach Haven, have been close to each other through the years, if not in body then certainly in mind. And there is always someone to take on the task of keeping the family up to date on marriages, travels, illnesses and celebrations, and, of course, the passing of the old and the arrival of the new. More than twenty members of the family attended The Hotchkiss School, and there have been periodic reunion weekends there in Lakeville, Connecticut. As many as eighty members have assembled to celebrate, always winding up the festivities in the school chapel, with a prayer at the alter railing, which is dedicated to Grandma and Grandpa.

Reunion-1997

At the most recent reunion, in 1997, Arnie was invited, for the first time, to be a part of a Lord family gathering; not just as a guest, but as a true member. How pleased we both were! My, how times have changed, and how much kinder and more accepting is the world my grandchildren will find when they are older and wiser, and can appreciate such things for themselves.

My brother Ted, being his irrepressible self, made it to this gathering before he died of cancer last year. The family's lasting memory of him will be a typical Ted gesture, throwing his tennis racket in disgust in a losing cause in the finals of the family round robin tennis tournament. (My son Tony was on the opposing team.) I don't think he heard Arnie call out from the sidelines, "Warning!" as if he were the referee at the U.S. Open, much to the amusement of the gathered relatives. At his memorial service at the Washington Cathedral, when I stood to read a passage from the Bible, the words wouldn't come out, as I gasped for breath and held back the tears. Little did I know, as I was growing up, that he would mean so much to me through the years. Mother always told me that he had some gentle, caring qualities underneath his vibrant exterior, and she was right. I'm so happy that I slowly began to recognized them.

Family gatherings of the Lord clan were a significant part of our lives. Aside from birthday parties and get-togethers in Tarrytown and Beach Haven, there was a smaller reunion of about forty, this time on a seven day cruise to Bermuda as guests of my Uncle Oz and Aunt Mary. What a time, and what an extraordinarily generous display of affection for the family! It was a year or so after my father's death, and I proudly escorted my mother aboard the Queen of Bermuda.

Grandma and Grandpa would have loved it, and I'm sure were watching every move and listening to every bit of family chatter from their cabin in the sky. Thanks to my cousin Bill Lord and his wife Joan and their cottage by the sea, we all had the good fortune to be able to make our headquarters and have lunch there during our stay on the island. There was always so much catching up to do; I don't think any of us stopped talking, except to eat and drink, the whole time we were together for this special occasion. And never let it be said that a Lord family member didn't enjoy a cocktail or two!

Now a new generation, my generation, has taken over. Mary and Oz's son Charlie, his wife Gay, and their three delightful children have taken on the responsibility of keeping the family abreast of each other, now that the last one of Grandma and Grandpa's children, Uncle Squidge, died recently at age ninety-five. His whimsical sense of humor was always a breath of fresh air as he served as a fountain of information, and the Lord family's own personal internet. His daughter, my cousin Betsy, much to my delight, has said that my personality is very much like his. A great compliment, and I hope I live just as long.

As for Chalmers Dale, or Dale Chalmers if you prefer, having spent the first seventy-five years of my existence in the last seventy-five years of the 20th Century, there is life after CBS. As I glide (I hope gracefully) into the 21st century, there's my precious 150 year old home to look after and, with a few nails and an ample supply of gaffer's tape, to keep from falling down. And there's my computer to continually challenge my mind and my patience. Thank goodness that there is Arnie to pick up after and to share in life's constant mysteries, always with a laugh or two. I'm even considering taking a cruise to some far distant lands, and adopting a dog to keep me active in the years ahead. I will make sure my new friend sleeps in my room, like dear old Dolph used to, and hopefully protect me from the fears and anxieties that older people are prone to have.

I'm thankful for my good health, having survived a bout with bladder and prostate cancer (probably caused by excessive smoking) that very nearly did me in. After a nine hour operation, I now have what is called a Neo-bladder, made from a piece of my intestines with tiny valves at either end. I was, I believe, only the two hundred and first patient to ever have had this amazing procedure, and it eliminates the need for any unpleasant bags or tubes. Thanks to Arnie's diligent and compassionate care, I am now able to lead a perfectly normal existence, except that I must (if anyone cares), relieve myself at least every four hours. When I think of all the people who are suffering or who have died from cancer, it is a small price to pay. Most older people have to go that often anyway. I don't smoke Lucky Strikes or drink martinis or Chum-rums any more, and have probably become a tiresome old dullard at parties. Late in the evening when people, who have had one or two too many, ask me if they are boring me, I generally laugh and say yes and find my way to the front door. I hope they don't remember my rudeness in the morning.

People my age have a tendency to constantly talk about their ailments and I remember Mother telling me she stopped enjoying parties with her old friends because that's all they ever did. And here I am doing the same thing! But I love to tell the story of the old black garage attendant who looked after my car every day when I had hurriedly parked it askew, and without regard for my fellow CBS employees. He was known as the Reverend and, in addition to shuffling cars around, he was an evangelical minister and held Sunday services in a corner of the garage. When I told him that I had lost the sight of my right eye to Glaucoma, but was still able to drive a car, he intoned with a somber smile: "Mr. Dale, God gave you two eyes so that, should something happen to one of them, you would still be able to drive...badly."

So, with a little bit of luck, I just might live long enough to see, with my one good eye, the day when the Philadelphia Phillies win another World Series and the big bands of old come back to play, with my favorite jitterbugging love, Libby, leading the revival. I'll make sure my grandchildren and their parents and Amy and Arnie, and everyone else who I have loved so much, are there beside me. And I sincerely hope that my God, who has guided me along this lengthy, circuitous path, and who I have tried so hard to serve, will quietly whisper in my ear, "Nice goin' Chummy my boy."

All of us together

CHALMERS DALE

ACKNOWLEDGMENTS

During the writing of several drafts of *A Life Full Of Days* I sought out the opinions and suggestions from a number of respected friends, and tried to include their wise observations wherever possible. There are about twenty of you who will never know how much you helped me through my first effort at a full length piece of literature, stroking my ego, and urging me on into the mysterious world of publishing. I thank you all so very much.

But I must offer extra thank yous to a few who not only offered their enthusiastic critique of my memoir but made a significant contribution to it. Jack Keil, Marie Fenton-Griffing, Jay Hirsch and Terry Tally actively pursued a means of publication; Lynn Temple volunteered to use her expertise in correcting my bad grammar and punctuation; and Catherine Whitney and Paul Krafin gently advised me in general formatting.

And some special hugs and kisses to Christine Baker, who gave of her time and technical expertise in designing the cover and scanning the photographs; and to my ultimate critic, who added what he called "color" to my already colorful life, Arnie Walton.

CHALMERS DALE

ABOUT THE AUTHOR

Born in 1925, Chalmers Dale grew up in Haverford, Pennsylvania. After serving in the US Navy for two years in the Pacific Theater during World War II, he taught and coached athletics at The Montgomery Country Day School in Wynnewood, Pennsylvania from 1946 to 1950, attending the University of Pennsylvania at night. From 1951 to 1991, he was employed at CBS Television in New York City, starting in the shipping room, and becoming, ten years later, a producer/director/writer of Cultural and Religious programs in the News Division. He produced more than 300 drama, art and music, and documentary programs, world wide, exploring the state of the human condition and the role of religion in people's lives. He has received two Emmy Awards and numerous citations. He retired in 1991 and devotes much of his time to environmental concerns, particularly involving the Hudson River, on whose shores he resides.

Breinigsville, PA USA
10 February 2010
232275BV00001B/15/A

9 781410 726070